THE SAVAGE, NOBLE DEATH OF BABS DIONNE

THE SAVAGE, NOBLE DEATH OF BABS DIONNE

RON CURRIE

G. P. PUTNAM'S SONS

New York

PUTNAM
— EST. 1838 —

G. P. PUTNAM'S SONS
Publishers Since 1838
An imprint of Penguin Random House LLC
penguinrandomhouse.com

Library of Congress Cataloging-in-Publication Data

Names: Currie, Ron, Jr., author.
Title: The savage, noble death of Babs Dionne / Ron Currie.
Description: New York: G. P. Putnam's Sons, 2025.
Identifiers: LCCN 2024009274 (print) | LCCN 2024009275 (ebook) |
ISBN 9780593851661 (hardcover) | ISBN 9780593851678 (epub)
Subjects: LCGFT: Novels.
Classification: LCC PS3603.U774 S28 2025 (print) | LCC PS3603.U774
(ebook) | DDC 813/.6—dc23/eng/20240229
LC record available at https://lccn.loc.gov/2024009274
LC ebook record available at https://lccn.loc.gov/2024009275
p.   cm.

International Edition: ISBN 9798217046263

Printed in the United States of America
1st Printing

Book design by Ashley Tucker

For my grandmother Rita Talbot Currie (1930–1992)

and

for her mother, Rose Talbot (1910–1973)

and

for her mother, Apolline LaPierre Talbot (1876–19?)

and

for her mother, Celina LaPierre (1843–1900)

and

for her mother, Rose Cormier LaPierre (1815–1894)

and so on, until the very beginning.

Je vous aime, et je me souviens de vous.

THE SAVAGE, NOBLE DEATH OF BABS DIONNE

We have to live in English, it's impossible to live in French. This is the secret thought of the Canuck in America.

—JEAN-LOUIS LEBRIS DE KEROUAC,
LA VIE EST D'HOMMAGE

I am the prophecy
I did not come from nothing
And nothing came from me
I took your name in vain
I burnt your effigy

—IDLES, "CAR CRASH"

PART ONE

PRÉLUDE

1668–1968

Think of generations as a chain, one link leading to and binding the next, and all of them—even the most distant—forever connected and inseparable. Forget about ancestors the way we usually talk of them, as if they are somehow less real than we are. Those who came before are not footnotes to the Very Important Life you're living now. They are real people, and still. They breathe through you. They bleed and cry and dance, pull their rotten teeth with pliers sanitized in bootleg rye. They plow fields and pray for rain. They sing their children songs at night: *Frère Jacques, Frère Jacques, dormez-vous, dormez-vous.* They clutch their sheets in fever. They run great machines that make cloth and paper for the whole world. They fight in wars. They tell lies. They sit awake long after everyone they love has fallen asleep, a hand-rolled cigarette pinched between their fingers, waiting in desperation for first light, eternally.

Their ghosts are all around you, clamoring to be seen and heard, like Marley rattling his chains. And like Marley, they have things to teach you.

So: Think of them all as yourself. A single entity, spanning centuries. Finding its current but by no means final iteration in you.

Once, for example, you were a woman named Evangeline LeNormand: Parisian orphan, ward of the church, survivor, and cynic. You came to Nouvelle-France in 1667. Many of the girls who traveled with you believed the promises the priests had made—handsome husbands of noble birth, the riches of the New World theirs for the asking. But you knew better.

The boat smelled of shit and wet rot, rolling for months over endless waves. After the first week both passengers and crew began to get sick, clawing at rashes and grabbing their skulls in agony. You waited your turn, watching as ten of the other *filles du roi* died, their corpses wrapped in cotton cloth, given a box-check blessing, and dropped overboard. A dozen others went insane with fever. Yet you somehow remained healthy, dumb luck—though whether this luck was good or bad, considering how things would turn out, was debatable. By the time the ship docked in Quebec there were twenty-one girls left, each still somehow convinced that fortune smiled broadly as they promenaded off the ship. Then there was you, pulling up the rear and dragging your chest through the mud, trusting no one to carry it but yourself.

The other girls went fast, married and pregnant and drying beaver skins before you could say *tabarnak*. In a place where men outnumbered women eight to one and winter lasted six months of the year, it was inevitable someone would claim you. His name was Joshua Currey. He traded tools for furs with the Mi'kmaq, and because he was Scottish you did not understand him and he did not understand you. As was his right, he took your trousseau and the fifty livres and when the money was gone he left you in the fall of 1673 with two daughters, Dominique and Madeleine.

A hundred years after that you were Madeleine's great-grand-daughter Aimee, your hair an unruly black corona just like the women before you, and as with the women before you, men were drawn by that hair and the desire to tame it. You did your part to resist the British by cutting two Redcoats who thought they could take what they wanted from a *canadienne* whore without paying.

English-speaking Protestants ruled now, people who hid their prejudice and evil intent behind proper manners. The lies began anew, the same lies they'd told the Acadians before burning their farms and scattering them to the wind, lies they would tell again and again to all you wild-haired Frenchwomen still to come: You can keep your Pope. You can keep your customs and your language. We will not kill you. We will not drive you out. We will not herd you into ghettos and let diseases burn. We will treat you as equals. We will not tar and feather your priests. We will not rape you. We will not, for generation upon generation, make your lives miserable, and then harrumph at society dinners when you behave as miserable people do.

A nd so, after two hundred more years of lies, you were Barbara Levesque, the eighth-great-granddaughter of Evangeline LeNormand. Everyone called you Babs. The year was 1968, and at fourteen years old you had a head of hair as black and round and gravity-defying as Evangeline's had been centuries before. You lived in Waterville, Maine, and had never known the Quebec of your forebears, because your grandfather Leonard Levesque had traveled by train to Waterville in 1918, braving the Spanish flu and the Klan to work at the Hollingsworth & Whitney paper mill. Leonard and his ten sons, including your father, André, all worked at H&W, and between them had lost four fingers, a right hand at the wrist, and most of a right foot to the mill's pitiless, grinding machinery. That accounting did not include your father's youngest brother, Paul, who was crushed from the knees down when a picker pulled the wrong stick from a pile of spruce logs in the H&W lumberyard and the whole thing came rolling down in an avalanche of timber. Paul had been paid two thousand dollars apiece for his legs, and used the money to open Levesque's Variety on the corner of Water and King Streets in the heart of Little Canada, the low-lying neighborhood that always flooded first when the river jumped its banks in spring, the neighborhood where French was spoken on every street corner, the neighborhood you called home.

That February your brother Jean had traveled home from Da Nang in a flag-draped casket, the first of your family buried in Waterville's Saint Francis cemetery, which was not its own cemetery at all but just a back lot in the larger Protestant graveyard. The Catholics were granted half a dozen acres of crabgrass at the edge of a hill where people dumped their trash, and from Jean's grave that summer, you could see one rusty corner of a discarded washing machine poking up over the crest of the hill. That April, Martin Luther King had been shot in the head, like your brother, and now it was June, and Bobby Kennedy had just been shot in the head, too, and though the country heaved and burned, you were preoccupied only with your new summer job, that of minding the register at Levesque's Variety from eight in the morning until two in the afternoon each weekday.

A reality of life for Franco business owners like your uncle was that the Waterville police took whatever they wanted, whenever they wanted, a plain, long-standing fact about which no one complained if they were smart. Beat cops carried the keys to every store, hotel, and car dealership in town, ostensibly to do inspections and investigate reports of break-ins—except more often than not, they were the ones breaking in. Their larceny ran the gamut from petty to profound. Sandwiches from LaCroix's Hamburger Haven, mary janes for their daughters from LaVerdiere's Clothing. The past two years a rumor had circulated that a shift sergeant had opened the gate at Boucher Marine and driven off with a brand-new Carver runabout, 225-horse inboard with sleeper cabin, a gossip-bold heist even for the cretins of the Waterville PD. And gossip people did. Waterville was corrupt as shit and oddly proud of the fact; being known as a hub of scandal and intrigue in a landscape of homogeneous little mill towns carried, after all, a certain cachet.

Two pairs of cops patrolled Little Canada through the week, and both came regularly into Levesque's while you worked the counter. Mondays and Thursdays brought Jimmy Hamlin, thin and ashen with a nose like an eagle's beak, and Kevin Smyth, whose belly muffled the jangling of his utility belt. On Mondays they each took a carton of Pall Malls, and on Thursdays Jimmy took another carton for the weekend, while Kevin helped himself to Banana Flip cakes and Pop-Tarts, which he ate straight from the box as he considered other items he might steal, littering your uncle's floor with crumbs.

"*Souriez simplement*," your uncle Paul told you. He knew your soul, and he didn't want any trouble. "Smile like they're doing you a favor. Pop-Tarts don't cost anything."

But you couldn't even muster a smile for your uncle, let alone the men who stole from him. All you could think of was a line from

Romeo and Juliet that had burned itself into your brain the previous semester: "O calm, dishonorable, vile submission." You hadn't understood, at the time, why the line stood out to you as though lit in neon, but now you realized that Mercutio could have been talking about your uncle, your whole family, the entirety of Little Canada, where people anglicized their names and played by the rules of a rigged game and accepted broad-daylight theft as simply the cost of doing business. You'd been watching them submit your whole life, and "dishonorable" and "vile" barely covered it. These men stole from a cripple. Their fathers sat on the draft board that had sent your brother to his death. And now you were supposed to smile at them? *Mais non!* You would sooner slit your own throat. Or one of theirs.

To that end, by July you were keeping your brother's paratrooper knife under the counter, being sure to scoop it up each day at five minutes to two, just before your uncle limped in on his wooden legs and took over the register.

Tuesdays, Wednesdays, and Fridays brought the worse pair, the pretend-to-be-sick-so-you-didn't-have-to-work pair: Roy Davies and Scott Markee. Davies was fine. An imbecile, to be sure, a Protestant and a thief—but fine. The problem was Scott Markee, who had been born neither Scott nor Markee, but Sacha Marquette. Scott Markee had changed his name precisely so he could be a cop. He was a traitor and a fraud, eager to be absorbed and erased by a culture that loathed him. Scott knew French but refused to speak it. He'd been baptized and confirmed at Notre Dame but could be found every Sunday in the pews at First Baptist. He'd moved to the north end of town and married a woman named Matilda—Matilda, *pour l'amour de dieu*! And every Tuesday, Wednesday, and Friday he clanged the door open at Levesque's Variety, scuffed the floors black with the soles of his boots, and filled a shopping basket with things for which he never paid a dime.

Whenever Scott came in that July you eyed him as he moved up and down the store's aisles, tallying in your mind the price of what he took and entering the total in the spiral notebook that served as your uncle's credit ledger. Hershey bar, six-pack of Schlitz, a dozen eggs, and a copy of *Time*: $2.07, including tax. Cake mix, a pound of sirloin, nail polish remover, bottle of aspirin, another sixer of Schlitz: $2.94. And so on. You had no reason for doing this, other than compounding your fury with each number entered in the ledger, because you could sooner lick your own elbow than make Scott pay for what he took.

Smile, your uncle Paul had told you, smiling himself despite his half-gone legs and the sores where his knees used to be, despite only having a dozen or so yellowed teeth left in his mouth, despite what was left of Jean's body being buried in the shit part of the cemetery where garbage sprouted like weeds.

For customers who did pay, all credit came due at the beginning of the month, and you spent most of August 1, a hot, swampy Thursday, settling accounts and sweating through your Carl Yastrzemski jersey, which like many of your clothes had once belonged to your brother. You took cash and made change and erased lines in the notebook until only a few remained, and in between you fanned yourself to little avail with the local section of that morning's newspaper, feeling sweat trickle through the downy hairs on the small of your back.

One of the last customers to settle up was Bernadette Roy, an old widow who came in once a week for cigarettes and cat food. Barely five feet tall on a good day, Bernadette had lost a couple inches to a slipped disc that spring, and the globe of her bob haircut only just cleared the counter as she hobbled up and stacked tins of Friskies, one by one, in a little tower on the checkout counter.

For a few moments the only sound was the clatter of the register as you punched numbers. Then Bernadette piped up. "I should apologize to you, *p'tite* Barbara," she said.

"What for?" you asked, ignoring the diminutive, counting up the tins of cat food by twos.

"Your brother. Jean. I haven't talked to you when I come in because I didn't want to have to mention him."

You snapped open a paper bag, turned toward the cigarette rack, and grabbed a carton of Bernadette's brand, Winston Menthol 100's. "You don't need to apologize, Mrs. Roy. He's dead. There's not much to say."

"They should leave our boys alone," she said, helping bag the cat food. "Let them fight their own *maudite* war."

And that was when it hit you: Markee instead of Marquette. First Baptist instead of Notre Dame. Police blues—instead of army olive. You froze, the last can of cat food hovering in your hand over the mouth of the bag.

"How much do I owe for last month?" Bernadette asked. "We can just add this to it."

You didn't answer.

"Dear," Bernadette said.

You heard her, but dimly, as though you were underwater and she were talking to you from above the surface, her kind face rippling and unreal.

"Barbara." Bernadette put her hand, no bigger than a kindergartner's, over your own. "Are you okay?"

Her touch brought you back to yourself, slowly. You blinked and dropped the cat food into the bag. "Fine," you said, looking up at the register display. "Nineteen dollars and forty-eight cents."

"Did the Winstons go up?"

"I . . . I don't know, Mrs. Roy. Let me check."

You turned away from her and made a show of examining the prices on the cigarette rack, trying to gather yourself. The price of Winstons had not, in fact, gone up, but you wondered if Bernadette had asked because she was cash-poor. There were all kinds of reasons someone in Little Canada might be broke, even when their check had just come in.

"Yep, you're right," you lied, turning back to her. "I overcharged you ten cents a pack, somehow. So your total's only eighteen forty-eight."

She handed you a twenty, and with the tips of your fingers you dug two quarters and two pennies out of the drawer, handing them over along with a dollar bill. Bernadette placed the bag and her purse on the top of her walker, asked God's forgiveness for your brother in a whisper, and left.

By the time Scott sauntered in later that afternoon, thumbs hooked through his utility belt, .38 special clacking against his hip with each step, the late sun had killed any semblance of a breeze and turned the store into a brick furnace. You hadn't seen a customer in nearly an hour, and out on the street nothing moved; even the birds had gone silent in the heat. But here was Scott, picking through the snack aisle, careless and carefree and not even *sweating*, the son of a bitch; was his life was so charmed that not even a jungle-hot day like this could get to him?

On the radio behind the counter, a DJ told you the Pope had

affirmed that both he and God disapproved of birth control. Big fucking surprise, you thought as you followed Scott with your gaze. Keep having twice as many kids as you can afford. Work like mules but stay poor as shit. Drink and smoke to blunt the misery. Grow old before your time and die without complaint, forever and ever, world without end, amen. Thanks a million, Pope Paul, you're the best.

You drilled your eyes into Scott, willing him to feel your glare and look up. But he just kept perusing and pilfering: a can of Potato Stix here, a bottle of Coke there. He jammed the bottom of the Coke cap against a shelf and popped it with his fist, releasing the cap and tearing a small chunk of wood away from the shelf. Maybe he didn't intend the vandalism, but he also didn't regret that it had happened. No acknowledgment, no apology, no attempt to make it right. He drank half the soda at a pull, then yanked a *Boston Globe* off the newsstand and moved for the door.

"Sacha," you said.

You had no idea what you meant to say or do next, but your voice had the desired effect: Scott paused, hand hovering over the doorknob, and turned his head in your direction.

"My name is Scott," he said, his eyes lit up with the quick, righteous anger of one who believes it's his birthright to walk through the world unchallenged.

"And my name is Tinker Bell," you said, still not sure what you were doing. You made a show of flipping through your uncle's ledger. "It's the first of the month, *Sacha*, which means all credit accounts are due. According to my records, your balance from July is twenty-six dollars and seventy cents."

He dropped one hand to his belt and turned to face you. "Excuse me?"

"Due and payable," you said. "Today."

Scott continued to glare, his eyes narrowed, lizard-like. Then suddenly he smiled, chuckled, moved toward the register. He set his Coke down and placed both hands on the counter.

"You're a kid, Barbara, so you don't understand how this works," he said.

"I understand just fine," you told him. "And don't talk down to me."

"I may have to discuss your smart mouth with your uncle," Scott said. "I wonder what he'd have to say about this."

"You know what he'd say. 'So sorry, Officer Markee, sir. Never happen again, Officer Markee, sir.' He's a coward, just like the rest of them."

Scott smiled again. "But not you, right? You, you're braver than everyone else."

"Brave's got nothing to do with it," you said. "I'm just fed up."

"Oh? With what?"

"People like you."

He stood back and folded his arms, feigning amusement, and in that moment you noticed a drop of sweat had gathered finally on his left temple, ready to slide down parallel to his sideburn. "People like me?" he said. "This ought to be good. What about people like me?"

"You're a coward, too. Like my uncle. Ashamed to be what God made you. So you put on a mask with your uniform. Use flash cards to learn the Queen's English. You figure if you fake it hard enough, they have to let you into Protestant Heaven."

Scott's face darkened again, and he took a deep breath. "Listen, Barbara," he said. "I'm willing to let this go, seeing how your brother died recently—"

"You make it sound like he went in his sleep," you said. "He didn't *die*. He was killed. Shot in the head. You know how I know that, Sacha? They didn't tell us. The casket was closed, but I opened it. I wanted to see for myself."

"Terrible war," Scott said, not sounding particularly vexed by either the war or its terribleness.

"Yes, terrible war, such a shame. But you're not going to find out anytime soon, are you? Because I realized something today. Police are exempt from the draft, aren't they?"

Scott shrugged and smiled, like: *You got me.*

"My brother's dead, while you walk around this neighborhood safe as Sister Mary Margaret's virginity. You should be in that casket, not him."

"And what about your virginity, Barbara? Are you still as pure as Sister Mary Margaret?"

"Sorry to disappoint, but you're too late to claim that prize."

This was a lie.

"Eh," Scott said, "virgins are overrated."

"Then what are you waiting for?" You glanced at the clock. "My uncle won't be here for another hour. It's not like anyone else is coming in today."

Scott peered at you, suddenly uncertain, while you kept your face expressionless as a stone.

"Going once," you said. "Going twice . . ."

He swallowed hard.

"No sale," you said. "What a surprise. You've got no problem taking whatever you want, but when someone offers it freely, you turn out to be just another limp dick."

Something seized the front of your Yaz shirt, and after a moment you realized it was Scott's hand, curled into a fist, lifting you off your feet. His knuckles, bone-white, jammed against the base of your nose; you could smell the tar from Chesterfields lingering on his fingers. And then, something thick and red on his hand, running like a trickle of melted ice cream on this summer day: blood, from your nose. Scott was strong, stronger than you would have imagined. He jerked you toward him, pulling you halfway over the counter, and you heard threads in the collar of your shirt tear and pop. You grasped under the counter for your brother's knife, but it was so far out of reach it might as well have been in your dresser at home. You looked up from Scott's fist into his eyes, and what you saw there made you realize you had miscalculated, and badly: he was going to kill you. Whatever was human in him had departed, leaving a simian rage in its place, his pupils broad and black like puddles of ink, lips peeled back from his teeth. He lifted his left hand in a fist behind his head, and you stopped searching for the knife and raised your own hands, not to ward off the blow but stretching toward him, trying to get at his eyes. But he held you fast at arm's length, and your fingernails found nothing but air. His left fist rose higher, cocked like a claw hammer, about to come down on your head— when the bell over the door rang and Bernadette shuffled in, her walker clattering over the lip of the doorway ahead of her.

At the bell's high chime Scott's transformation was instantaneous. His lips closed back over his teeth, and his eyes filled again with the warmth of human consciousness. He let go of your shirt as if it were hot to the touch, straightening his jacket and offering a one-hundred-watt Officer Friendly smile as Bernadette made her way to the counter beside him.

"Mrs. Roy," he said, tipping his cap with one hand while he wiped your blood off the other on the seat of his trousers. "Beautiful day."

She looked at him. "It's hot as shit," she said evenly. Turning to you, she said, "Barbara, I went home and did some math and realized you undercharged me for my Winstons."

Scott kept smiling. He gathered his Coke, Potato Stix, and newspaper and headed for the door as though he'd just remembered he had somewhere to be, and urgently.

"Sacha," you said, wiping at your nose. "There's still the matter of your unpaid balance."

Scott turned once more to face you. "I'm pretty sure," he said, "that we're even steven. And my name is Scott."

"So you told me," you said. "But maybe I should speak in a language you understand, so there's no confusion: *Paye ce que tu dois, connard.*"

His eyes narrowed—but then he smiled again. "You ladies have a nice afternoon," he said, and then, looking directly at you: "And be careful out there."

Be careful? You'd be damned if you were going to spend your days looking over your shoulder for Sacha. This was *your* home, these were *your* streets; he had given up any claim to them. And when you didn't see him again for three weeks, you made the mistake of thinking you had won, that he had been sufficiently cowed and embarrassed and perhaps even frightened by his own rage to stay away.

In all the years to come, with all the enemies you were to know, you would never again assume one was beaten until they were dead.

August 26, 1968. Who knows why Scott chose that afternoon: broad daylight, Halde Street across from the playground, where at any given moment from dawn to dusk there might be a dozen witnesses. Maybe after seething for nearly a month he'd finally lost control of his anger. Maybe he really just believed he could do anything he wanted and get away with it. And maybe he would have been correct in this assumption, had he done it to anyone but you.

You were heading home from your uncle's store with your best friend Rita, as always. You walked shoulder to shoulder on the same side of the street as the playground, a chain link fence and a narrow strip of bluegrass between you and the basketball court, where four grade-school boys took turns heaving a ball from their shoulders toward the hoop without much success. Later, you would recall this afternoon as fragmented, comprised only of discrete moments untethered in memory and stripped of context. The hollow *thwop* of the basketball on cracked pavement. Rita laughing at a joke you'd memorized from your father's not-well-hidden *Playboys*. Yellow bedsheets hanging to dry on a tenement's third-floor porch. Vulcanized rubber crunching over pebbles behind you. The sudden pain of Scott's grip on your forearm, like the Indian burns your brother used to dole out when you got on his nerves. Rita pummeling Scott with both fists, screaming *Let her go!* and being tossed aside into the grass. Then a black space, as dark and silent as not-being, before coming around to the musk of old aftershave and cigarette smoke on the cruiser's leather seats. The long, slow wail of the siren, neither approaching nor receding, forever overhead. Rough hands pushing you down a hill into the woods, toward the river. Pine needles stuck to your palms and pricking your back. The branches of an elm waving in the breeze overhead, flashes of blue and white beyond the fluttering leaves. An odd drowsy feeling, as though you'd been drugged, and the sense that, if not for Scott's dull thrusting, you could have fallen asleep there under the trees.

One thought played over and over through your mind as you lay there: you lived an hour's drive from the rocky postcard shoreline that hundreds of thousands of people visited every summer, and yet you had never seen the ocean. In that regard, you could have lived in Nebraska and it would not have been much different. The ocean that in so many people's minds was synonymous with Maine might as well not have existed for you. This is what you thought about, lying there under Scott's rough weight.

For decades after, time and again, you would hear skeptical men ask women, in courtrooms and on TV and in the newspaper, why they didn't fight. Those women always cited fear—they had felt the strength of their assailant and their own helplessness in the face of that strength, and they submitted for fear that to fight would spell their end. For you, it was different. You wanted Scott to believe he had broken you. You wanted him to go on thinking the world and everything in it was his, because while he was taking something from you, he was also giving you something important: the fury that would determine the course of your life in every moment following this one.

And so, once Scott had finished: the steel of your brother's knife in your pocket, then in your palm. The click of the blade coming open. An ancient, rust-rotted Model T nearby, abandoned in the woods for decades and sunk to the tops of its wheels in silt. Scott, spent and careless, sweat gleaming on the back of his neck, tucking his uniform shirt back into his trousers. His gasp as the blade tip pierced his back. The hitch as the knife caught on a rib. The burble of eddies in the river, nearby but unseen. The gush of blood when Scott's lung was pierced. The sight of his face as he lay on his own back now, heels kicking weakly against the dirt, looking up at you as if for help. His mouth moving soundlessly, a doomed fish in the bottom of a boat. Air whistling in and out of the hole in his back, loud and urgent, then softer, slower, easing and accepting. Finally: silence, except for that high breeze rustling branches, a single cry from a gull.

You wiped your brother's knife on Scott's shirt, then noticed his key ring, still attached to his belt by a spring-loaded cord. Scott's power, you knew, did not come from his sidearm, or from his badge and the authority it represented, but from these keys—they gave him access to, and thus ownership of, everything in Little Canada. You flipped the clasp on the key ring and lifted its weight in your hand, then turned and began climbing the steep bank away from the river, grasping trunks and saplings to pull yourself up.

At first your hands were slick and you had to be careful, but after a while most of the blood had rubbed off on tree bark, and your grip became sure. You felt no fear, either at what you had done or its consequences, and even as you climbed your breath came slow and steady. Two hundred feet up you crested the bank, emerged from the trees, and saw Scott had brought you to the end of Water Street, a part of the road largely untraveled and barren except for the new sewage treatment plant a few hundred yards farther down, where the road ended altogether.

No one around, and likely no one would happen along. This gave you time to think, but really what you needed was time to accept. You had one option. In order to stay, you had to leave. In order to claim and own the place where you were born, you had to, for a time, let it go. If killing Scott was a violent expression of your resolve to live where and how you would, first you had to give yourself over to a greater entity, one as powerful as the state that would now come for you, one that could shield you when you could not shield yourself.

So you turned right onto the road and, with Scott's blood stiffening on your shirt and bare legs, began the long walk back into town. Past the last few straggling houses on Water Street, where no one was home because they all worked first shift at the mill. Then into the more heavily populated section of Little Canada, where it was impossible to avoid being noticed. The men were gone, as they always seemed to be, swallowed up by the brick monolith of the mill during the day and the barrooms after second shift ended, but the women were there hanging laundry, and the children were there playing in puddles from the previous night's thunderstorms, and as you walked past slow and calm they stopped what they were doing and gawked, some of the kids following at a distance for a few steps. No one spoke. No one asked what had happened, whether you were okay, where you were going. The mere sight of you, the horror and mystery of it, precluded talk of any kind. Everyone recognized that, at least in those moments, you existed in a state beyond language. There was something holy about what they were witnessing—the solemnity, the sacrament of blood—and your people knew to surround the holy with a good deal of silence. In fact, those who saw you were reluctant to talk even to each other, at least until you had passed, and even then they gathered close and spoke only in whispers as they kept an eye on your receding figure.

You turned left onto Grove Street and climbed the hill, past the cemetery where *pauvre Jean* rested, your pace steady, your eyes up and on the road ahead. At the top of the hill you turned right onto Gold Street, then left onto Preston. By now switchboard operators downtown were bombarded with a rush of phone calls, and had these calls not all come at once they might have dispatched the police a few minutes sooner. But most everyone trying to report the teenage girl naked from the waist down and slathered in blood got nothing but the dull blare of a busy signal, and before the first police car made its way into Little Canada you had already passed through the doors of Notre Dame Parish and into the perpetual twilight of the nave, where no one but God could punish you for Scott's death.

You walked to the first set of pews in front of the altar, took a seat on the right, and waited. The pew was cool under your thighs, and you could feel Scott's blood binding wood and skin like glue. On the wall behind the altar, of course: Jesus, hanging limp and dead, stripped to the waist, a bloody gash between his ribs.

You'd spent hundreds of hours in this room. Five feet from where you sat you'd been baptized, at six days old, so small you fit in one of your father's big, gentle hands. More recently you'd been confirmed on the very same spot, white as January in your special dress, on display for God and the whole neighborhood. In this room you'd stood for the Gospel and knelt for Communion, exchanged handshakes with your neighbors and dropped crisp dollars from your father's billfold into wicker baskets as they passed among the faithful. But most of your time in Notre Dame had been spent ignoring homilies and mumbling through prayers while you contemplated the one thing about the entire affair that actually interested you: the Stations of the Cross.

From where you sat you could see all fourteen Stations, depicted in stained glass around the perimeter of the nave and backlit by sunlight. Over your right shoulder, Jesus was condemned by Pilate to death; over your left, his body was placed in the tomb in advance of the Resurrection. In between, on twelve windows equally spaced around the circular room, the whole of his ordeal played out in hues of red, orange, and blue. Up until today the only time you'd spent in the church that wasn't mandated were the long moments you passed contemplating these images. Your interest was hardly devotional—you were just fascinated by how macabre and obvious the whole thing was. The blood, the agony, the melodrama. The message that to suffer is to be divine, a subtext so obvious it barely qualified as subtext. Studying the Stations, you sometimes wondered what an alien would think if you told them the central religious ritual of a third of Earth's inhabitants involved simulated cannibalism. Instead of praying at the Stations as was expected, you would kneel and think about how if Jesus had been executed in America, everyone you knew would probably wear a little gold electric chair around their neck.

Now, though, you gazed around at the Stations from where you sat and thought about nothing.

"You look," said a man's voice in French, "as though you're in need of confession."

You turned and saw Father Clement Thibault, though at first you almost didn't recognize him. He appeared the same as always from the neck up—brown crew cut atop a cherubic face that made him look half as old as his thirty years—but what threw you off were the jeans and madras plaid. Since he'd arrived at Notre Dame less than a year before, you'd only ever seen Father Clement in his alb during services, or in a black shirt and pants on the front stairs of the parish after Mass. Now here he was, dressed like he should be seated next to you in civics class.

"Are you hurt?" he asked.

You shook your head.

"That's not your blood," he said, half statement, half question.

"Not most of it," you told him.

In the short time he'd been in charge of the parish, Father Clement had developed a reputation as easygoing and casual, a Vatican II priest all the way—which not everyone in the neighborhood, particularly older men who had a hard time seeing someone half their age as a proxy for God, cared for. He smoked openly, often right outside the door of his rectory across from the church, and was said to be a regular at Huard's Tavern on Gold Street, always at the bar, always alone, always with a glass of whiskey, neat. He was the first priest anyone had ever known to perform Mass in French instead of Latin. Wild rumors about his life before the priesthood abounded: he'd been a jazz trumpeter, he'd had problems with drugs, he'd been *married*.

You hoped that in one way, at least, Father Clement would behave just like the church always had—making wayward sheep, particularly young ones, disappear when they got into trouble.

He gazed at you for a long moment, then walked briskly up the aisle and locked the doors. "Did anyone see you come in here?" he called out.

"I don't know," you said.

Father Clement lingered at the entrance, peering through the glass up and down the street, then came back down the aisle and walked straight past you toward the sacristy.

"Father," you said.

"Don't say anything," he called over his shoulder. He passed through a door directly underneath where Jesus hung and was gone for several minutes.

As always, the church was kept cool, and you'd been sitting long enough that a chill had gathered in your legs and was now creeping up the small of your back. Outside, somewhere distant, a siren started up, wailing over the valley. It was joined, shortly, by another, a shrill, vengeful call-and-answer.

Father Clement returned with a hand towel and a rumpled pair of jeans. He approached and gave you the towel, careful not to let his eyes stray below your face.

"Use that to clean up best you can," he said. "These pants probably won't fit great, but they were the first thing I found in the donation pile."

This close you could hear his breath coming fast, and see the confusion in his eyes despite his efforts to remain calm and priestly. "Don't you want to know what happened?" you asked.

Father Clement held up a hand. "Obviously I have no idea what's going on," he said. "What I do know is you came to me because you need help. And I intend to help you. But we have to do this the right way."

"Okay," you said.

"Listen, and understand," Father Clement said. "If you say anything out here, we're just two people talking. Whatever you tell me I can, and maybe will have to, report to someone else. If you wait until we're in the confessional—if we do this right—I cannot and will not tell anyone a word of what you say. Because I will know your sins as God knows them, and no man can compel God to tell what He knows."

You cocked your head.

"That's Thomas Aquinas," he said. "He had thoughts on a few things."

You just stared.

"Never mind," he said. "Go to the ladies' room, clean yourself up, and come find me. *Comprenez-vous?*"

Ten minutes later, mostly free of Scott's blood, and hitching up the pair of men's size 32 jeans with one hand, you let yourself into the penitent side of the confessional and closed the door.

"Good afternoon," Father Clement said, his shape barely discernible on the other side of the latticed privacy screen.

You knelt facing the screen and crossed yourself. "Bless me, Father, for I have sinned," you said. "It's been eight days since my last confession."

"May the Lord help you to confess your sins," Father Clement said.

"Amen."

And then, for a few moments, neither of you spoke.

"I don't know how to start," you said finally.

"I think," Father Clement said, "that we can skip the missed homework assignments and unclean thoughts, and get straight to the reason you showed up at God's house covered in blood."

"I killed Scott Markee," you said.

"The cop?"

"I stabbed him."

"One would guess," Father Clement said. "*Tabarnak.* Are you sure he's dead?"

"If he wasn't when I left him," you said, "he is now."

"But *why*, Barbara?"

"The same reason I came in here with no pants on."

At this, Father Clement was silent for a moment. Then: "Pray for him with me."

"What? *Non.*"

"Barbara. Jesus agonizes over his soul, same as yours."

"You sure that's the point you want to make," you said, "when I can still feel him inside me?"

Another pause from Father Clement. Then he recited the Hail Mary alone, so hushed you could only hear the *s* sounds whistling faintly between his teeth.

"Now," he said when he'd finished praying in vain for Scott's salvation, "tell me everything."

"God already knows what happened."

"True," he said, "but I don't. And in order to help you repair a mortal sin, I have to know everything God knows."

"A mortal sin?"

"You killed a man, Barbara."

"He *raped* me."

"Please. Just tell me what happened."

"What happened was, Sacha forgot where he came from."

"Sacha?"

"That was Scott's name. Before he changed it."

"I don't understand."

"Sure you do. Uppity Frenchmen change their names. Turn their backs on their own people. Sacha was stealing from my uncle's store. I told him to stop, so he raped me. Then I killed him. The end."

"Barbara," Father Clement said, "if I'm going to help you, you have to be sorry for what you did. *Genuinely* sorry."

"But I'm not."

"I understand. But you—"

"You don't, actually. You can't."

"I'm trying," Father Clement said.

"Let me ask you a question."

"Of course."

"If Jesus died for my sins, why do I have to repent?"

Father Clement paused, and you heard him breathe deep and let it out slow. "It may surprise you to know," he said, "that this is a question I wrestle with myself. Quite often."

"So what's the answer?"

"The answer," he said, "is that there is no neat answer. Real faith, contrary to popular sentiment, is hardly blind. God's favored children are those who struggle hardest to know Him. And in return for that favor, we must do what He asks even if we don't think it makes sense. *Particularly* if we don't think it makes sense."

"That doesn't make sense."

Father Clement barked a laugh. "Fair enough," he said. "We don't have much time, Babs, so let me tell you how I see things."

"Okay."

"I have a friend with the Sisters of Saint Joseph in Vermont.

She'll take you in. You'll leave right away. You will not see anyone or say goodbye. You may not ever be able to come back. Do you understand?"

"So I have to pretend to be a nun?"

"No pretending," Father Clement said. "As far as the Sisters are concerned, you will be there as a novitiate. You'll help with their work in the school and with the poor. You will pray your ass off morning, noon, and night. You'll take classes and tend the gardens and probably get pretty good at quilting."

"And then?"

"And then, if we decide you can come back, you'll have to be ready to confess and repent. I can't emphasize that enough, Babs. It might be a year. It might be three. However long, you should think of it as the time necessary for you to find your way back to God. Focus only on that. In the meantime, I'll do what I can here."

"God's going to be disappointed," you said, "if He's waiting around for me to say what I did was wrong."

Father Clement sighed again on the other side of the screen. "Pride is the mother of all sin, Babs," he said. "That's Thomas Aquinas, too."

"I'm getting sick of him already," you said.

I n your absence the story of what you'd done to Sacha grew and transformed, whispered behind hands and retold over beers in the lumberyard and the Laundromat, living rooms and barrooms. Imagine, a girl of fourteen gutting a grown man—a cop no less—and leaving him to bleed out in the woods! And when you returned five years later everyone in Little Canada knew but did not say: This was your neighborhood, these were your streets, and it would remain thus, *pour toujours et à jamais, amen.*

CHAPTER ONE

June 30, 2016

When did a person's future become locked in? Consider: on this evening, Sis Dionne was still alive, but in twenty-four hours she would be dead, murdered, in fact. Was it possible for a different choice to be made between now and then that would forestall her departure from this life, and the violent dissolution of a family and a neighborhood that followed? Could her mother, Babs, have done something other than what she did? Her older sister, Lori? Maybe, but impossible to know. The bulk of reality remains just beyond the edges of our ability to perceive, alas. God's still not talking and the physicists haven't figured it all out quite yet, so we're left with the same speculation and superstition as always. Here's what we do know: at this point, in this life, in the story about to unfold, Sis would be killed in little more than a day's time, her body burned with utter lack of ceremony and left in a junkyard. Her end could be viewed, on a long enough time line, as the result of innumerable choices stretching back centuries, the clash of armies and ideas, the appreciative glance and fertilized ovum, every ripple and undulation of history even remotely connected to her life, a change to any one of which might have kept her from such a violent demise. But practically speaking, in our lives, we make our choices and things happen as they happen and that, as they say, is that. As such, Sis would soon be dead.

Tonight, however, she was still out there somewhere, drawing breath, and it was, instead, her sister Lori who had just died.

Lori lay on the floor of the bathroom in a bar called You Know Who's Pub in Waterville, Maine, where her mother, Babs, she of the mind like a shark's mouth, had raised her and Sis. Beside Lori on the floor sat a hypodermic needle, empty, a crust of Lori's blood drying on the tip. Her legs lay scissored and motionless one over the other, spike arm stretched out and already stiffening on the floor in front of her, the sleeve rolled up to her skinny biceps, which was mottled with gray-green bruises, and because she had only just died and because the heart dies before the brain, she was dreaming:

A convoy of military trucks rolls along Highway 1 in Wardak Province, Afghanistan. Humvees, stout MRAPs bristling with machine guns and grenade launchers, massive LVSRs like futuristic tractor trailers painted in desert tan. The landscape they move through is impossibly flat and dusty, ringed by distant mountains. The mountaintops are capped in snow, but on the ground here it's hot as Hades, the sun pounding rock and dirt. Nothing lives or moves other than the trucks, which crawl along the blacktop, diesels growling.

Lori sits in the driver's seat of the sixth vehicle in the convoy, a 10x10 LVSR loaded with cargo containers. She's dwarfed by the vehicle's massive steering wheel but at ease behind the controls, her hair pulled into a neat ponytail that peeks out beneath her helmet. On her shoulder she wears a staff sergeant's chevron: three stripes up, one down. Next to her sits Sammy Menendez, and as is usually the case—even when he sleeps— Sammy is talking.

"'Follow the Highway of Death north,'" Sammy says. "'Stop at every bridge, watering hole, horse hitch, and outhouse along the way, so Colonel Hajji can meet with his soldiers—who may or may not be plotting to blow you up. When you get to the end of the road, turn around. Head back the way you came. Try not to get killed.'"

"Orders are orders," Lori says.

"Being as my ass belongs to a supply battalion, I'll admit I'm not well-versed in tactical best practices," Sammy says. "All the same, stopping every half an hour in broad daylight in the most dangerous place on earth to babysit a fake colonel does not seem like, you know, the wisest use of personnel and equipment."

"We're not escorting Colonel Ahmadi," Lori says. "We're transporting power equipment and food supplies. That Colonel Ahmadi happens to be along for the ride is incidental to our mission."

"Right," Sammy says. "So if I get blown up while he gabs at some checkpoint, will I be incidentally dead?"

"I suppose so," Lori says.

"Great," Sammy says. "Make sure they put that on my death certificate. It'll be a huge comfort to my mother."

Lori smiles and hits the brakes as the vehicles ahead of her slow, then stop altogether.

"What now?" Sammy groans. His view of the road is blocked by the LVSR directly in front of them, but Lori's got a line of sight to what's happening up ahead.

"ANA's guarding a bridge. I imagine the colonel's going to dismount and say hello."

"Of course he is," Sammy says.

Chatter over the radio reveals the real reason they're stopped: cross talk that an IED has been discovered four kilometers up the road by a bomb dog; EOD is deploying now from Bagram via Blackhawk.

"*Better get comfortable,*" *Lori says.*

"*Outstanding,*" *Sammy says. He grabs his rifle and reaches into his ruck on the floor of the cab, pulls out a large plastic package of Twizzlers.*

They get out. Up and down the convoy line, Marines are dismounting, eyeballing the area, checking the ground for any sign it has been disturbed by men. But that's the thing about the land here: it keeps its secrets. Lori doesn't like the look of a set of hills to the right of the road, three hundred meters distant, at the foot of which sits a cluster of mudbrick buildings, but as she comes around the vehicle she says nothing, not wanting to get Sammy riled up.

But Sammy doesn't require prompting. "*Again,*" *he says,* "*I'm more or less a glorified supply clerk, but if I were a real Marine I would consider this a very, very bad place to stop.*"

"*Not a lot of cover up there,*" *Lori says.*

"*Plenty of cover in that village,*" *Sammy says.*

"*That's a Hazara settlement,*" *Lori says.* "*They hate the Taliban more than you do.*"

"*Maybe yesterday,*" *Sammy says.* "*Today, who knows?*"

"*Well, now's your chance to improve relations,*" *Lori says.* "*Here comes the welcoming committee.*"

A dozen boys, who'd been batting around a volleyball when the convoy rolled up, now make their way toward the trucks. Sammy loves these moments, which is why he's never without Twizzlers.

Three Blackhawks thump overhead, pointed north. The racket of their rotors breaks the spell, and everyone seems to remember suddenly that nobody can be trusted, not ten-year-old boys, not friendly Marines bearing gifts. The kids retreat to their makeshift volleyball court, clutching handfuls of licorice. Sammy comes back to the front of the LVSR, where

Lori's checking a hose on the tire inflation system. It's been acting up without ready explanation, and she's cranky.

"Are they really going to make us wait for the next three hours while EOD plays Operation?" Sammy asks.

"Before you get going on another rant, know that (a) I don't like it any more than you do, and (b) there's nothing to be done so I don't want to hear it."

"Wow. Aye, aye, Staff Sergeant."

"I'm serious, Sammy. If you're so worried, do your job and keep an eye on that ridgeline until word comes through that it's time to move out. And don't forget to hydrate."

Half an hour passes in silence, by far the longest Lori has ever known Sammy to stay quiet. She starts to think maybe she's been too hard on him. She plays back the words she said and how she said them and hears her mother, Babs.

Lori's stirred from her thoughts by a low whump, like God stamping His foot just beyond the horizon: the familiar sound of matter being suddenly and violently ripped into its constituent parts. Distant, but never far enough, that noise. The concussion unfurls languidly around the valley, echoing in waves off the hills until finally it fades. And then, less than a minute later, the radio gives word—the IED up ahead now cleared, the convoy can be on its way.

They mount up, Sammy still silent.

"You got any of those Twizzlers left?" she asks Sammy.

"I thought you didn't like licorice," he says.

"I don't. It's disgusting."

They smile at each other across the cab, and the convoy starts rolling. He hands her a stick.

They rumble slowly over the bridge. Lori glances out the window at

a pair of ANA sentries, and there's something about them she can't im-
mediately put her finger on. Then she realizes: They're alert, *and that's*
fucking weird, and out here anything weird, no matter how seemingly
innocuous, needs a second look. Ninety percent of the time, especially on
guard duty, ANA soldiers are listless at best, dicking around and smok-
ing, slumped like sulky teenagers. These two are upright, weapons at the
ready. They look edgy, like they're anticipating a fight. But then Lori
remembers the colonel, and assumes they're putting on a show for his
benefit.

In the very next instant, there's a tiny, brief sound in the cab of the
truck, like someone has rapped once on the driver's-side window with
something hard and sharp—a pebble, maybe. In the same instant, Lori
feels something tug at the air in front of her face. All this—the sound
and the sensation—happens simultaneously, and though her senses take
the information in, it's too fast for her brain to process what it means. So
she seeks more information. She turns her head toward where the sound
came from and sees the driver's-side window is splintered, spiderweb
cracks zigzagging out from a hole near the center of the pane. More con-
fusion. She turns to Sammy to ask if he knows what's going on. His face
is turned toward her, and he's smiling—but now there's a hole in his
cheek, just below his left eye. This hole is about the diameter of a penny,
dry and dark as though punched in plywood rather than flesh. Alarm
dogpiles on confusion in Lori's mind. Then Sammy's facial muscles slowly
go slack, and gravity pulls the corners of his mouth down. For a moment
his face is as blank as any Lori has ever seen—not just expressionless, but
untenanted. And then his jaw falls open slightly, and blood pours over
his chin as if a tap has been opened, soaking his blouse black.

Lori understands none of this—what has happened, what it means.
She doesn't understand when the Humvee two vehicles in front of her

lifts from the ground on a column of flame and comes back to earth side-
ways in the road, or when the chatter of small-arms fire starts up in the
hills to the left of the convoy, or when the M16s and .50 cals burst to life
around her in furious response. She is nothing but amygdala and hypo-
thalamus, blood ionized and mind blank, as she stumbles out of her
truck and into a shooting gallery, leaving Sammy behind.

For some reason—or no reason—she closes the driver's-side door be-
hind her as she exits, and the moment she does a round pings off the
door's armor and ricochets, whining, into the sky. Other bullets hit the
road in front of her, sending up little shards of fragmented pavement. If
she were thinking straight, or at all, she would scramble for the compar-
ative safety of the opposite side of the convoy, where most of the other
Marines—the ones who aren't already dead or unconscious or moaning
as they get acquainted with their own blood—have taken cover.

Instead, she walks off the road toward the hills.

She is unarmed and on autopilot and striding calmly downrange
into incoming fire. A bullet whings off the ground near her feet. An
RPG sizzles along a horizontal shaft of smoke fifty meters to her left,
smashing into the side of her LVSR and setting one of the cargo contain-
ers ablaze. Another bullet cuts the air near her, then others, coming faster
now as the men in the hills zero in on this target that has inexplicably
presented itself like an offering. Behind Lori, voices implore her to come
back, scream hoarsely about what in the fuck she thinks she's doing.

But Lori just keeps walking toward the hills, and as her mind comes
back she realizes why: nothing can hurt her. She's sure of it, that pecu-
liar, ironclad certainty of dreams. And the moment this revelation settles
on her, the soles of her boots leave the desert floor. She's levitating—no,
flying, leaving the broken world below. The sounds of battle fade, scoured
away by the wind in her ears, and she smiles, tentatively at first, then

broadly, and then she's laughing, twirling, weightless and free. She drops her helmet, pulls the quick-release on her armor vest, and laughs as it falls.

From this height, Afghanistan is something it has never been before: beautiful. The bladelike mountain ridges draped in mist, the rusty red of the desert highlands directly below her, and beyond that, far to the south, a patchwork of farmland, big rough rectangles in every possible shade of green, bisected by the undulating black line of a river. It's heaven. How had she not realized, until now?

In the 568 days she's spent in Afghanistan, Lori has often felt as though she might die here. She has never, until now, felt like she could die here and be happy.

But then she's braced by an odd hitch directly behind her breastbone. A sudden stillness inside her that she recognizes as wholly incompatible with life, eerie and instantly terrifying—followed by a wallop as her heart starts again, slamming against her ribs. She gasps and plummets like Icarus, end over end, limbs flailing helplessly, earth and sky trading places over and over as she drops, and she can feel but not hear herself scream as the rocky foothills rush up to meet her—

Lori shot upright from the floor of the bathroom at You Know Who's, eyes flying open, a scream still in her throat, instantly dopesick. Where was she? *When* was she? Clues: A sink. A mirror. Twin toilet stalls with shared middle divider, the grimy bases of the toilets themselves visible from her dog's-eye perspective. Plastic trash bin beside the sink, overflowing with crumpled paper towels. Her hands and ass wet with something from the floor. A second, full-length mirror on the wall opposite her, its edges graffitied crudely with black Sharpie, its center featuring a moving picture of Lori staring at herself, shoulders heaving with each breath, hair chopped short and jagged, a lifetime's worth of baggage under her eyes and the overhead fluorescents not helping one bit with that. She was twenty pounds underweight, her forearms jutting from the rolled-up sleeves of her shirt like bruised bones, and by now she knew exactly when and where she was, not Afghanistan, not Iraq, not Lejeune or COP Sayed Abad but home; she was home in Maine and that explained the state of things, and further she was not the least bit surprised to find two men in the mirror with her, crouched on either side of her legs, both wearing the dark blue uniform of fire department paramedics, and one of whom, the older one with the mustache holding the empty syringe of Narcan with which he'd saved her life, she was pretty sure she recognized from somewhere around town.

"Welcome back, asshole," this man said to her.

CHAPTER TWO

July 1, 2016

Did she *want* to die? A stupid question, as far as Lori was concerned. Still, the doctors had to ask, in that danger-to-yourself-or-others kind of way. Boxes to check, paperwork to file, after all. Laws to heed and lines to stay on the right side of. This was the irony of how the rules worked—if she had intended to kill herself, they had the legal power to take her belt and shoelaces and lock her in a room with a metal mirror and a door that opened both ways so she couldn't barricade herself inside; if, on the other hand, she'd killed herself by accident, out of neglect or disregard, she was free to leave and do it again pretty much immediately if she chose.

"I did a lot of reading when I was deployed," she said to the doctor. She lay on a bed in the ER, and he loomed over her with a clipboard in hand, making no effort to hide the fact that he wasn't listening. "One time I read this thing meant to dramatize the suicidal impulse for someone who's never gone through it. Basically the writer invited you to imagine you're high up in a burning building. There's lots of smoke, and it's getting hard to breathe. Flames are moving closer, second by second. The only way out is through the window. You see where I'm going with this."

"Uh-huh," the doctor said.

"So the point is, when the fire gets close enough and you jump out the window, you're every bit as scared of falling as you would be otherwise. You don't *want* to fall. You just have a slight preference for falling, over having your ass burned to a crisp."

"Right," the doctor said, pulling his phone out of his pocket, reading something, back in the pocket.

"But of course the people on the ground screaming at you not to jump don't understand the choice you have to make. They only see the fall. They don't feel the fire."

"Right," the doctor says.

"Like you," Lori said. "You're just some asshole on the sidewalk, telling me not to jump, when you have no idea what you're talking about."

He glanced up from his clipboard, looked directly at her for the first time.

"No," Lori said evenly, holding the doctor's gaze. "I don't want to die."

"Great," he said, marking something on the clipboard. "The nurse'll get your discharge papers ready."

Fifteen minutes later Lori walked out through the hospital emergency entrance, wearing the same jeans and chambray shirt she'd had on the night before, her truck keys, phone, and cigarettes hanging from the fingertips of one hand in a plastic bag marked PERSONAL BELONGINGS. The crepey bangle of a hospital bracelet still encircled her right wrist. Heat was already gathering again at seven in the morning, the air so humid Lori half expected a fish to swim by in front of her. And now she had to walk the three or so miles to Little Canada, where her truck still sat parked outside You Know Who's.

But first, much as she didn't want to, she needed to check her phone.

Lori reached into the bag, pulled out her phone, tapped the display. On the screen, three messages, all from Babs, none of them good:

9:38 PM: *Where are you?*

1:19 AM: *Where is your sister?*

2:04 AM: *And why is no one taking care of their goddamn business?*

Still under the concrete awning of the emergency room entrance, Lori groaned, began to type, paused, erased the half response, thought a minute. She looked out over the parking lot, as if it held some clue regarding where her sister was or what Lori could possibly say to mollify her mother. At this early hour, the lot held only a handful of vehicles, nice late-model rides in the staff section, beaters held together with chicken wire and Bondo in the section reserved for patients and visitors. Across the street from the parking lot lay a small playground and a soccer field where masses of little kids chased balls around and trampled each other on Saturday mornings. Beyond that, the river, beyond the river the green hills, and beyond the hills a whole world where Lori would never again have to worry about her mother's rage or her sister's fecklessness or the way one fed the other in an endless feedback loop.

Lori slapped the side of her head to clear it. Instead of responding to Babs, she typed a message to her sister, whose Christian name was Celeste but whom everyone had called Sis from the very beginning, for reasons now lost to time.

7:06 AM: *You picked a great night to duck Babs. Get your ass out of bed and put some coffee on.*

Y ou would've said Little Canada had seen better days, except it never really had. Different days, sure—but not better. Everyone had more trouble than money when Babs was a girl, and everyone had more trouble than money now. People worked too hard for too little when Babs was a girl, and people worked too hard for too little now. Back then, beer and rotgut liquor flowed through the gutters; these days it was heroin. And so on. Poor was poor and remained so, and the rest was just calendar dates and details.

There were, however, three chief differences between the neighborhood of Babs's youth and the one she lived in and presided over now.

First, instead of daily Mass, Notre Dame du Perpetual Secours held services only on Saturday evening and Sunday morning (not that this made a difference to Babs, who hadn't set foot in the church since she'd left for Vermont in the predawn of August 27, 1968). Monday through Friday Notre Dame's doors were closed and locked, and if you found yourself in need of a priest, you had to pick up the phone.

Second, every Praise Be and Christ Have Mercy at Notre Dame had, since Midnight Mass in 1990, been uttered in English rather than French.

Which leads to the third chief difference between Little Canada 1968 and Little Canada 2016: Fifty years earlier it would have been impossible to walk the streets and encounter someone who didn't speak French—but now it was near impossible to encounter someone who did. In fact, the majority of the people who still spoke French regularly in the neighborhood were now seated at Babs's kitchen table—all of them women, all of them friends of many years, none of them somebody you wanted to fuck with, *tabarnak*.

Babs Dionne (née Levesque) sat at the head of the table, grim and silent, cigarette smoke hanging like a storm cloud over her head. She listened to the other ladies talk and alternated between putting a coffee mug and a lipstick-stained Marlboro to her mouth. The usual rabble among the ladies was more subdued this morning, owing to the fact that everyone knew there was serious—and personal—business to discuss. But it was Babs's place alone to bring the subject up, and she hadn't yet, so it just hung in the air along with the smoke.

On the wall opposite Babs, beyond the far end of the table, hung an 8x10 of her and her husband, Rheal, taken a few years before. In the picture they were dressed up for something Babs didn't remember—a wedding, maybe, since they were dancing, side profile with their heads turned toward the camera, her hand folded into his at shoulder height. Rheal smiled, dentures gleaming, while she did not. Babs had had a lot of time to herself in the eight months since Rheal died, and she'd spent a good amount of that time sitting in this same seat, study-ing the photo, trying to remember where it'd been taken, but to this very morning she'd come up blank. One thing that had come to her, though: If she got up and moved very close to the picture, she was al-most certain she could see the slightest tinge of yellow at the edges of Rheal's eyes, a hint of the liver cancer that had killed him. Maybe this was a trick of the mind. But damned if she couldn't help seeing now what she'd failed to see then, when it might have made a difference.

Slowly, Babs realized that the talk around her had ceased. All the ladies sat in silence, pulling at their coffee mugs and doing their best not to look in her direction. Babs's eyes fell away from the picture and onto these women, her friends and partners in the business of Little Canada. She took a long last drag of her cigarette and stubbed it out in a green glass ashtray, big as a serving plate, at the center of the table.

"What?" she said, looking around.

Nothing from the ladies. Stella, who was drunk all the time, including now at nine in the morning, snorted a little, then caught herself and put a hand to her mouth. Carmeline, as self-possessed as Babs herself, flipped placidly through the morning paper's grocery circular as if she hadn't heard Babs speak. Bernette and Stella kept their eyes on the Taster's Choice in their mugs. And Rita, who comprised the personal part of the day's personal business, stared at Babs, her expression somewhere between pleading and defiant.

Babs looked around the table, sighed, noticed her right hand trembling on the table next to her pack of cigarettes. To still it, she picked up her phone and tapped out a message to her daughters.

9:01 AM: *One of you better respond to me soon, or I'm going to get really angry.*

"Look at that," Carmeline said in French, jabbing a finger at the circular. "Pickle spears are two for three dollars this week."

"What's the regular price?" Stella asked.

"One seventy-nine per jar," Carmeline said.

"Sixty cents isn't nothing," Stella said. "There any limit?"

Carmeline squinted at the fine print. "Four per customer," she said.

"See, there's always a limit," Stella said. "That's the trick. They get you excited to come in and buy discount pickles, and you end up paying full price for all kinds of stuff you don't need, just because you're at the store. Next thing you know you're walking out of there with rib eyes and caviar, all full price, along with your four measly jars of pickles."

"Speaking of pickled," Carmeline said, deadpanning at Stella.

"Would you two knock it off?" Babs said.

B ruce Coté stood at the kitchen sink in the house he shared with Sis Dionne, scrubbing a frying pan with a tattered piece of steel wool, thinking about the time in seventh grade when DJ Hawes had kicked his ass. DJ had gotten a breakaway in gym class soccer and against all odds Bruce, who'd been stuck in goal by Mr. Knight because that's where you put the worst athlete on the team, managed to stop DJ's shot. It had been a glorious moment for Bruce, who even as a kid had rarely managed to do anything successfully. This one time, he'd done everything right: he watched as DJ streaked toward him from the left, moved out of goal a bit to cut the angle and give DJ less of a target, then lay out just as DJ brought his leg back to shoot, and smothered the ball with his chest. Sometimes, like now, Bruce still thought about it, still experienced a mixture of pride and awe that he'd ever been able to manage such a feat under pressure, that he'd stayed calm and read the play and really without even thinking been able to do the job he'd been assigned, and even to do it with a little style.

Standing at the sink, really laying into the frying pan with the steel wool, Bruce tried, as always, not to think about what came next.

Because immediately after gym class, in the boys' locker room that smelled of wet socks and industrial sanitizer, DJ made public his intention to give Bruce a beating after school. Which meant Bruce had the rest of the day to feel the news spread through passed notes and whispers between desks, and to sweat what would happen when the bus dropped them both off at the bottom of Grove Street in Little Canada that afternoon. At lunch, Bruce ate his smooshed soggy

PB&J on white and worried about DJ. In Biology he sawed half-heartedly at the rubbery skin of a dead frog and worried about DJ. In U.S. History he ignored a discussion of the French and Indian Wars and worried about DJ. By the time the buses lined up in front of the junior high at the end of the school day, though, Bruce had stopped worrying and settled into the usual tense resignation that descended when he had had enough time to anticipate a thrashing. After all, as long as Bruce could remember, people had always found reason to kick his ass, and DJ was nowhere near the biggest or scariest of those people.

And so, when the bus pulled to the curb on Grove Street, instead of trying to make a break for the safety of his father's house, which sat within sight of the bus stop right around the corner, Bruce just plodded down the metal stairs and waited for DJ. He dropped his book bag to the dirt, arms loose at his sides. A handful of other boys, most of whom normally got off at other stops, descended behind Bruce and lingered in a semicircle at a distance, gleefully anticipating carnage. Finally, DJ himself emerged, grinning at Bruce's attempt at courage in facing him instead of running when he had the chance.

"Ready to get your whuppin?" DJ asked. He wore a MY CHEMI-CAL ROMANCE hoodie sweatshirt and black jeans with black leather straps all up and down the legs. A head taller than Bruce, at thirteen he already had a few downy beard hairs on the point of his chin.

"I guess so," Bruce said simply as the bus pulled away.

DJ was too cool to carry books or a backpack, so he had nothing to set aside. He spread his feet slightly, his back heel up and ready to pivot, fists cocked at his chin and cheek. Looking at him, Bruce remembered DJ was always going on about how his older brother was a Golden Gloves boxer, as if the fact that his brother was (allegedly) a badass made DJ a badass by association.

"Put your hands up," DJ told him.

Bruce closed his hands into loose fists and raised them to his chest.

"Put your hands *up*," DJ said.

All Bruce wanted was to get it over with so he could go to his room and resume painting his set of pewter Lord of the Rings figurines. After he cleaned the blood off himself, of course. And since no matter what he did he was going to catch a beating, and since the figurines were all less than an inch tall and required a precise touch to paint well, he had no intention of throwing any punches and messing up his hands.

"Just . . . go ahead and hit me," he said to DJ.

A more honorable boy in a more honorable time might have passed on the invitation. But DJ was not an honorable boy, and neither were the others who had gathered for the sole purpose of watching Bruce catch a beating. They cheered and threw their own fists in the air as DJ knocked Bruce to the ground with a jab and a right cross, jostled and shoved each other as DJ raised his waffle-soled boot, his knee almost touching his chest, and drove it straight down into Bruce's sternum, making him gasp and choke and roll over onto his side in a vain effort to turtle up and protect himself.

And you'd have thought that DJ would stop there, with Bruce bloodied and gasping, one hand wrapped protectively around the back of his head, the other clutching his chest as he struggled to breathe. The other boys certainly thought DJ would lay off at this point. They'd stopped their cheering and shoving and now stood still and awkward, some with hands in pockets, realizing in their guts that this had maybe gone too far, when DJ drew the same foot back, took aim at the back of Bruce's hand, and delivered a mighty kick.

Bones cracked, loud enough for all to hear, and Bruce howled as though gutshot. He rolled onto his back, clutching his busted hand with the good one, legs flailing weakly at the dirt as if to carry him away.

And then a man appeared, tall and scowling, his torso like a keg of beer, flattop haircut military-precise and graying at the temples. He moved with the stuttering power of a hydraulic digging machine, turning the corner and heading straight at them, shitkickers clomping the sidewalk. The other boys, including DJ, froze—they didn't know who he was, just that an adult was coming fast with obvious intent, and given what they were up to, that seemed bad indeed. This had gone well beyond playground fat lips and bloody noses. Bruce was hurt. They were in real trouble, and trouble had taken the form of this monster of a man closing the last few yards between them with strides that seemed to almost shake the ground.

The man stopped, legs spread wide, breath coming fast through his open, snarling mouth. He looked at the boys, who flinched as his eyes fell on them, and then at Bruce, who had stopped weeping and now stared up at the man with a silent terror born of long familiarity.

"You kids," the man growled, still glaring at Bruce, "clear on out of here if you know what's good for you."

Just fucking dandy as far as they were concerned, but before they had a chance to move, the man reached down and grabbed Bruce by the front of the shirt, lifting him—and *holding* him—clear off the ground with no evident effort whatsoever. Bruce's legs dangled, and he began to cry again, quietly, still clutching his broken hand against his chest as though cradling a wounded bird.

"The fuck is the matter with you?" the man demanded of Bruce.

Bruce mewled through snot and tears: "Dad, I—"

The boys, DJ included, forgot their intention to flee and instead stood there agape. This was Bruce's *father*?

"What do we do when someone hits us?" the man asked. He

cuffed Bruce across the face, quickly, almost perfunctorily, but with a hand like a bear paw the blow still snapped Bruce's head around.

"What do we do?" the man asked again.

Bruce could only manage incomprehensible blubbering in response.

Harder now, a real slap. Bruce's cheek blazed red instantly, and the boys stared.

"What do we do when someone hits us, Bruce?"

"*We hit them back!*" Bruce wailed, and this was the strangest, purest sound any of the boys had ever heard, the sound of distilled heartbreak, and even decades later some of the boys, grown men who hadn't thought consciously of Bruce in forever, would startle awake with that cry echoing off the walls of their darkened bedrooms. And they would remember.

Standing at the kitchen sink now, grown himself, still a little drunk from the night before and thinking of a quick slug from the bottle of vodka in the toilet tank once he'd finished with the dishes, Bruce turned his head toward the small table behind him, where his son, Jason, sat still and upright with his hands in his lap. Nine years old and thin as a cattail reed, a welt under his left eye bulging like an aneurysm. A glass of orange juice sat on the table in front of him, along with a plate of scrambled eggs and toast gone cold.

"How's the juice?" Bruce asked, though he could see plain as day Jason hadn't touched it.

The boy fidgeted in response.

Bruce placed the frying pan, more or less clean, in the dish drainer beside the sink. "That's fresh-squeezed, you know," he said. "I got up early and bought those oranges just for you."

Yeah, and you also smacked him and don't even remember it, you complete piece of shit. Why don't you have another drink?

He would. Just as soon as he got the kid to eat, he would go into the bathroom and close the door and lift the tank lid quietly and pull the bottle from the water and let it drip over the tank to keep from getting the floor wet and he would take one good slug, that was all he needed, just enough to still the fluttering in his chest and quiet the basketball sneakers squeaking in his head, one drink and then he would get on with it, him and Jason, the two of them moving through the world alone, the boy's mother nowhere to be seen for two days now—or was it three?—and Bruce would limit himself to that one good solid medicinal slug of vodka and no more, and then he would, today, love his son a little less imperfectly.

That was the plan. Such as it was.

He turned away from the sink, trying to smile. "Hey, you gonna eat those eggs, or what?"

Jason just looked at him, the welt gleaming ugly in sunlight from the window.

Bruce smiled again. "Well, listen, I'll eat 'em if you're not gonna."

Jason was about to mumble some kind of appeasing non-answer when he was saved by a knock at the back door. Brisk footsteps in the hallway, and a moment later Lori walked in without waiting for an answer.

"She's not here," Bruce said to her.

Ignoring this, Lori looked down at Jason, noticed the black eye, and took his chin in her hand to get a closer look.

"You okay?" she asked gently.

The boy nodded.

Lori glared up at Bruce. "Then go get in my truck," she said.

"He's finishing his fresh-squeezed orange juice," Bruce said.

Lori lifted the glass and drained it. "My truck," she said to Jason, setting the glass back down empty. "Go on."

Jason got up and left through the back door.

"Where you taking him?" Bruce asked.

"Where's Sis?" Lori asked.

"Haven't seen her for two days."

"She missed a pickup yesterday, Bruce."

"What?"

"If you know something," Lori said, "tell me now."

"I haven't seen her for two days," Bruce repeated.

There was a pause as Lori considered him. Then: "You and I are going to talk later about Jason's eye," she said, and followed the boy out.

B abs waved her cigarette in the air, tracing a loop-de-loop of smoke like a tiny skywriter. "If he wasn't your son, you'd be calling for his head same as the rest of us, Rita," she said.

"Tim's a good boy, Babs," Rita said.

The other ladies scoffed into their coffee mugs.

Carmeline, who had never in fifty-nine years let a word of English escape her lips, though she understood it perfectly well, piped up in French: "He's a junkie and a retard."

"He cleaned Larry out," Babs told Rita. "Took everything."

"Even the shit that won't get him high," Stella said.

"How do we know it was Tim?" Rita asked.

"Rita, think," Babs said. "It's a pharmacy. There are cameras."

Bernette stood and went to the coffeemaker on the counter next to the stove. "Tim should count himself lucky that Larry came to us instead of the cops," she said, pouring a fresh cup.

"Now people all over town can't get their prescriptions filled," Stella said.

"Retard took my Lipitor," Carmeline said.

Rita looked around at them, disbelieving. All eyes on her. All signs pointing to Tim suffering actual consequences, despite the fact he was kin.

"We can't let it go," Babs told her. "Not this time."

Now Rita focused her gaze on Babs. "This is your *nephew* we're talking about," she said.

But Babs just shrugged, like: *Be that as it may.* She stubbed her cigarette out and shook a fresh one from the pack. As she lit up, through the window she saw Lori's blue Chevy pull to the curb, and while she expected a flare of anger at her daughter's belated appearance, instead she felt something much more uncomfortable: relief. And not relief that her daughter was okay—Babs never doubted that—but rather that Lori was here to help, to serve as backup. Babs despised wanting help, but worse than that was feeling surprised by the need. If she were going to be so weak, it was far better to know in advance, before the weakness waylaid her.

Her right hand, trembling again on the tabletop. She clamped her left hand over it and said to the ladies, "My grandson's here."

With that, everyone switched to speaking French.

"Singling out Tim won't help with anything," Rita said. "It's not as though he's the only addict running around."

"He's the only one stealing my Lipitor," Carmeline told her.

Jason and Lori entered through the back foyer, and immediately the ladies descended on the boy with a thunderous fuss, blowing cigarette smoke and coffee breath in his face—*Look at the curls in your hair! Mon dieu, you've grown a foot—how long has it been since I saw you?* Jason made his way slowly through the gauntlet, accepting their affections with shy good humor, until he stood finally before his grandmother. Babs took him by the hands, careful not to let darkness cloud her face when she noticed his black eye.

"Hello, my favorite boy," she said in English.

"Hi, Mémère," Jason said.

Babs hugged him to her breast and looked up at Lori. "His father do this?" she asked in French.

"He didn't walk into a lamppost, Ma," Lori said.

Babs took a breath, pasted on a smile, and pulled Jason to arm's length. "Are you hungry?" she said.

"Dad made breakfast," Jason said.

"That's not what I asked."

"I don't really feel like eating," Jason told her.

"I imagine not," Babs said. "Well, listen, you want to stay at Mémère's tonight? We can play *Sneak King* on the Xbox."

"*Sneak King* is lame," Jason said.

"Fine, go play whatever you want." Babs gave him a nudge toward the living room. "You and me will get some lunch in a little while."

They all watched him leave.

"Have you heard from Sis?" Lori asked Babs.

"Your no-account sister can wait," Babs said in French. "We have a bit of business to attend to here."

She looked around the table—all eyes averted once again, except for Rita's. Babs held her gaze, and in that moment fifty years passed between them. Babs was first to look away—just above and behind Rita, at the picture of Rheal and herself. She took a last drag of her cigarette and stubbed it out.

"All in favor of moving Tim on to greener pastures," she said, raising her hand as her eyes fell on Rita once more.

Slowly, not without regret, Carmeline, Stella, and Bernette raised their own hands. Rita's hands, of course, stayed folded on the tabletop.

"Thank you, friends," Babs said. "I need to talk with my daughter now."

"Before you dismiss us," Rita said, "let's maybe talk for a second *about* your daughter. The other one."

"Aunt Rita," Lori said. "Don't make this worse."

"Not at all," Babs said. "Take as much rope as you need, Rita."

"Sis fucks up, she gets a pass," Rita said. "Tim fucks up, he gets excommunicated. What's the difference?"

"The difference?" Babs said. "The difference is she's *my* daughter."

Rita scoffed at this.

"Were you expecting a different answer?" Babs asked. "Expecting me to make a logical argument for why Tim has to go and Sis can get away with whatever? There *is* no other answer. She's my daughter. The end. You don't like it, hit the bricks."

"It's not fair," Rita said.

"Of course it's not fair!" Babs said. "Rita, come on. 'Fair' is a load of crap they sell to patriots and good citizens. The chamber of commerce crowd, the nice college kids up on the hill. Down here we know better than to believe in 'fair.' Or at least we *used* to."

Tears glossed Rita's eyes. "Goddamn you, Babs," she said.

"Besides," Babs said, "we're doing Tim a favor. Bates isn't going to let him get away with this any more than we will. Tim sticks around, he's looking at ten years in Warren. Is that what you want?"

A beat. The air vibrating. "What I want," Rita said, "is for you to finally realize that other people aren't just things for you to do with as you please."

Rita stood and stalked out, leaving her cigarette still burning in the ashtray and the front door wide open behind her.

"Rita," Babs called after her. But she was gone.

After a minute the other ladies rinsed their coffee cups in the sink one by one, bid Babs and Lori *à plus*, and departed.

"Goddammit," Babs said, lighting a fresh cigarette.

"That went well," Lori said.

Babs took a drag and blew it out forcefully, her eyes still on the door. "Do you think she knows what she just did?"

"Who? Rita?"

"Who else?"

"What did she just do?"

"Walked out of here for the last time," Babs said.

"Ma."

"I can't have her challenging me openly," Babs said. "Not even Rita can get away with that."

"So, what, you're going to waste her?"

"No," Babs said. "You are."

"Ma."

"Take a joke," Babs said. "I'll deal with Rita. You've already got Tim on your to-do list."

"I caught that, thanks."

"Why don't you pour yourself some coffee?" Babs said. "You sure as hell look like you could use it."

Lori fell into a chair and pulled Rita's half-smoked cigarette from the ashtray. "That's the last thing I need right now." She closed her eyes, let her head roll back, and brought the cigarette to her lips.

"Ah. Feeling tense?" Babs asked. "Maybe something more in the other direction?"

"Are you really going to excommunicate Tim?"

"Not me. *We.* You saw the vote yourself."

Lori sat forward again and opened her eyes. "Something's up with Sis."

Babs shot a look toward the living room. "Lower your voice," she said, "or speak French."

"*Ta fille a disparu.*"

"*Mon* argent *a disparu.*"

"Bruce said he hasn't seen her for two days."

"I'm losing patience with that husband of hers, Lore."

"It's their business."

"Their marriage is their business," Babs said. "That boy is *my* business. If your father were still alive . . ."

"Well, he isn't."

An impasse, the two of them staring at each other. After a moment Babs put a hand on Lori's forearm.

"You look sick," she said.

"You look old," Lori said.

Babs laughed and patted Lori's arm a few times. "Your sister will turn up. Until she does, Jay-Jay stays here with me," she said. "Meantime, you need to find your cousin Tim and give him the bad news."

CHAPTER THREE

July 1, 2016

Survey one hundred junkies and ask the first thing they'd do upon deciding for the umpteenth time to kick dope. Five, given health insurance and other resources (e.g., people who still actually gave a shit about them) might go to a proper rehab. Another ten or fifteen would wind up in an emergency room, to be shuttled to an underfunded detox ward on the fifth floor of an underfunded public hospital, where in the company of schizophrenics, drunks, and well-meaning but callous staff they would drool and cry and tremble for a week, after which they'd be given the address of a methadone clinic and wished all good luck. The remaining eighty would sweat their way through five or six hours of sobriety, until the real Horsemen of Withdrawal galloped onto the scene, at which point those eighty would to a person be willing to mug their own mothers for a fix, and get back on the merry-go-round of addict anguish posthaste.

None of those surveyed, it almost goes without saying, would kick off their sobriety with a good, long run. But that's just what Lori did after leaving her mother's house.

Though to call it running would have been, depending on your perspective, either charitable or hyperbolic. Already sweating clear through her MARINES T-shirt and gym shorts before she'd gotten out of her truck, now as she hobbled a two-mile loop repeatedly around Little Canada, her body streamed perspiration as though a bowl of water had been dumped over her head. Even her shoes were soaked with it.

A casual observer, glancing at Lori as she passed, would not have noted anything remarkable about her—just a thin, grim-faced woman making her dogged way through some exercise under a scalding sun. Looking more carefully, though, that same observer would note an even greater heat in her eyes, blazing and unmistakable—hatred. She hated this place that had birthed and weaned her, the tilted old houses with their stripped paint and moldy vinyl siding, the clusters of weeds that passed for lawns, the skinny dogs tied out with rope that never stopped barking. She hated the people, too, but they knew and respected her: lily-white gangsta wannabes cleared the sidewalk as she approached, and neighborhood drunks lifted their beer cans in a kind of salute.

As far as Lori was concerned, the community her mother clung to no longer existed. The language was hardly spoken anymore. The church was an oversize paperweight anchoring the neighborhood's southwest corner, more a monument to a bygone time than an actual, active place of worship. There was no organizing principle here anymore, if, as Babs insisted, there ever had been. Just a rural ghetto, which Lori had left the instant it became possible and still sometimes woke up confused when she found herself there again.

After her third lap of the neighborhood, instead of turning right onto Water Street and heading toward the playground and cemetery again, Lori turned left and went down the long hill that mimed the path of the river, past the squat brick building of the Forest J. Paré

VFW Post 1285 (where three generations of Dionnes had been members, though not Lori), past the weathered white facade of Scottie's Variety (where she'd worked making pizzas in high school), past the long-vacant Chez Paree nightclub (where one night in 1984 a man had entered with a chain saw, intent on cutting up Lori's father, Rheal, and landed in the hospital with a fractured skull and short one chain saw for his trouble). She passed the defunct Waterville Florist (an old message written in grease pencil on the inside of the empty display window: HOPE BLOOMS) and a derelict, graffiti-pocked Kentucky Fried Chicken that had served its last bucket of birds four or five years earlier, before finally coming upon the building that had been the only reason Little Canada existed in the first place: the Hollingsworth & Whitney mill. Siren for thousands of illiterate, starving Franco farmers. Papermaker to the world. Provider of livelihoods and carcinogens. Taker of digits. Destroyer of river life. Emblem of American ambition, prosperity, and vigor.

Also, now and long since, defunct.

Lori stopped and hooked her fingers through the chain-link fence surrounding the mill. It stood as it had since 1846: six windowless brick stories at one end, formerly the home of boilers and pulp digesters, and another building, half the height of the boiler house but as long as four city blocks, where giant cast-iron rollers had whirred day and night, drying wood pulp and pressing it into infinite sheets of paper. The first-floor windows had all been covered with particle board, and most of the windows on the second floor were broken. Trash and last fall's leaves gathered in corners and against stairwells. The smokestack, which had fumed angrily throughout Lori's childhood like a giant cigarette stood on its filter, was now and forever dormant.

The equipment was gone and the timber was gone and the workers were gone, but Lori knew the ghosts remained. Plenty of them.

She turned away and ran toward downtown. One more easy quarter mile, once she got up the steep but short hill where Water Street merged with Main Street, but it gave her enough time to cycle back and forth twenty times between thinking today was not the day to quit dope after all and then to resolve again that it was. Finally, she stood beside her truck, sweating and shaking. She pulled the door handle, but it was locked. Tapped her shorts pockets, found nothing. Peered in the window and saw the keys on the passenger seat, next to her phone. Fuck.

A round the same time, Jason and Babs stepped out her front door and were about to get into her station wagon when a late-model Mercedes SUV pulled to the curb and gave a curt, friendly little beep.

Babs looked over at the vehicle, one foot already in her own car. "Get in," she told Jason. "I'll be right back."

As she approached the Mercedes the driver's-side window rolled down, revealing a couple in their thirties. Great teeth, good skin. Expensive clothes, though casual.

"Man, it's a hot one today," the man said to Babs.

"Can I help you with something?" Babs asked.

"We're hoping you can," the man said, showing off his teeth again. "We got off the highway looking for lunch and got a little turned around. Not much of a phone signal down here. Do you know where we can grab some lobster rolls?"

Babs smiled darkly. "You're about a hundred miles from the nearest lighthouse, friend," she said.

The man and woman both smiled back at her, a little uncertain now.

"Here's a bit of trivia most people don't know," Babs said. "Lobster used to be prison food. It was considered cruel and unusual punishment to have to eat it more than twice a week. Then some smart marketer came along, and now nice people like you are happy to pay ten dollars an ounce for what's basically a giant prehistoric cockroach."

The man laughed. "No kidding," he said. "That's really interesting. Anyway, if you could maybe give us directions . . ."

Babs stared at him a moment. "Sure, I'll give you some directions," she said finally. "Go to the end of the street, take a right. Follow that to the four-way stop, bang a left. Eventually you'll reach I-95. Get on the highway and keep going until you're back in Massachusetts."

The couple stared at her now, their expensive smiles snuffed out.

"And don't ever come down here again."

The window rolled up, slowly, and the very nice SUV with the very nice couple pulled away, Babs watching it go with a satisfied smile.

S till dripping sweat and cursing under her breath, Lori searched the ground around her truck for something to break a window with. Her eyes down, she didn't see Shawn Paradis walk past her on the sidewalk, but he sure noticed her. He stopped and stared openly for a few moments, disbelieving.

"Lore?" he said finally.

She startled, looked up, startled again when she saw who was standing there.

He grinned. "As you were, Marine."

"I'm not a Marine anymore," Lori said.

"Once a Marine, always a Marine, right?" Shawn asked.

"Not when you're court-martialed," Lori said.

The two of them stood there quietly for a beat, tripping out on each other's presence.

"I have to admit," Shawn said, "you are the absolute last person I expected to run into."

"Same," Lori said.

"You look like roasted shit."

"Thanks. What are you doing here, Shawn?"

He pointed to his feet: cheap little sandals from the salon, freshly painted nails.

"Getting a pedicure," he said. "It helps me relax."

Lori looked at his toes, nonplussed. "And what shade is that?"

"Little Black Dress," Shawn said. "One of my go-tos."

"So what's next? A Brazilian wax?"

"No, I'm growing it out. Maybe you haven't heard up here in the hinterlands, but big '70s bushes are back."

Lori smiled in spite of herself. "What I meant is: What are you doing *back home*?"

"I could ask you the same thing."

"I live here."

Shawn did an exaggerated double take, eyebrows raised. "You don't say."

"I do say. And you?"

"My father's sick."

"I didn't think you cared one way or another about your old man," Lori said.

"I don't. I'm here for my mother."

Another pause. Feeling worse with each passing second, and all too aware of the picture she presented, Lori wanted nothing more than to beg off, get in her truck, and lay custom rubber all the way home. But her keys remained on the passenger seat, and the door remained locked. So she just stood there like an idiot, not knowing what else to say.

Shawn broke the silence for her. "So. What are you doing later?"

"Stop right there."

"What?" Shawn grinned. "I'm simply making an innocent inquiry regarding what you planned to do with the rest of your day. And/or evening."

"Do I look date-ready to you, Shawn?"

"That's for me to decide."

Lori gazed around the parking lot. "I have a few things on my plate," she said. "But I can probably make time, if you'll do me a favor."

"Name it," Shawn said.

"Know how to break into a truck?"

Shawn looked at her quizzically. "Don't *you*?"

And because she couldn't bear even a moment more of this—the shaking, the sweating, the dogs barking in her head, Sis missing and silent, Shawn appearing out of the dead-and-gone past and laboring under the mistaken belief that he still cared for her, that big hard sun beating on her head like her mother's nightstick—Lori bent at the waist, hoisted a chunk of broken curb in one hand, and turned to heave it through the driver's-side window of her truck like a shotput.

Just as she was about to let fly, though, Shawn put a hand on her shoulder.

"Might I suggest an approach with slightly more finesse?" he asked.

Lori turned to look at him, and her eyes followed his hand as he pointed at the truck cab.

"Other side's unlocked, genius," he said.

And so it was—the black plastic knob on the inside of the passenger door stood fully, cheerfully up.

"Great," Lori said, then tossed the chunk of pavement through the window anyway, just to hear something break.

The clientele of Sunset Beach in Belgrade, Maine, a twenty-minute drive due west from Waterville, consisted mostly of those who couldn't afford their own cottages on the lake: young blue-collar families, townie teens, two-bit trustees of illicit pharmacology. Unlike these other people, of course, Babs could have bought a lakefront home for cash, same as she could have owned a much nicer house in town and a car manufactured in this century. She chose to live in the house where she was born; chose to drive, and keep up at great expense, the 1978 Ford Country Squire wagon that Rheal had bought new for a wedding gift; and chose, as she had for years, to pay the three dollars per person and five-dollar parking fee to bring Jason to Sunset Beach.

The dress code at Sunset was strictly redneck casual: cutoff jorts and two-piece bathing suits strained beyond capacity. People milled about, drinking cheap domestic beer from cans and cooking burgers on charcoal grills chained to rocks so they couldn't be stolen without a blowtorch. Competing classic rock hits blasted from open hatchbacks, and garbage cans overflowed onto the lawn, disgorging potato chip bags, soda bottles, dirty diapers.

Babs and Jason, having arrived relatively early, had managed to secure the table closest to the small beach, at a distance from the rest of the crowd. The remains of a deli lunch sat on the table between them, and kids splashed and shrieked in the shallow water nearby.

"You remember when we used to come here just about every week-end?" Babs asked.

"Yeah," Jason said.

"Then you went and grew up, didn't want to spend time with your *mémère* anymore."

"That's not true."

"Oh, no?"

"Dad said I had to start doing stuff around the house. So I could come to the beach, or I could play baseball. Not both."

"Is that a fact," Babs said.

They were quiet for a moment. Babs heard a commotion behind them and turned to see a fat woman, bare arms riddled with amateur tattoos, yelling at a toddler, threatening to make him sit in the car for some transgression. Behind her at a picnic table, a man with a belly like a hairy planet mixed milk and coffee brandy in a giant plastic Dunkin' Donuts cup.

Babs turned back to Jason. "Used to be a lot nicer," she said.

"Used to have a waterslide," Jason said.

"They did, didn't they? I wonder why they got rid of it."

Jason just shrugged.

"Somebody probably sued when their kid got a wedgie hitting the water," Babs said.

The idea made Jason giggle.

"Whole world's gone soft, Jay-Jay," Babs said. "But not you. And not me."

A Jet Ski roared by too close to the beach, throwing a rooster tail of water that almost hit the kids. Babs glared as it sped away, then took a breath and leveled her gaze at Jason.

"We need to talk about your eye, kiddo," she said.

Nothing from him.

"Did your father hit you?"

"Then he made fresh-squeezed juice," Jason said.

"Is that how it goes? He hurts you, then he does something nice?"

Jason nodded once, minutely, his expression a tangle of dueling loyalties: to his father, to his *mémère*, to the self and its desire to keep uncomfortable secrets secret. Babs sighed and put her hand across the table for him to take.

"Jay-Jay," she said, "does he hit your ma, too?"

Jason shrugged.

"I'm gonna need more than that," Babs said.

"Not that I know," Jason said. "They fight a lot. Usually after I go to bed."

"But he doesn't hit her. Just you."

He shrugged again.

Babs looked out across the water, toward a tiny island near the center of the lake where, as a child, before Sacha, before Babs fully understood who and what she was, she and her siblings used to row out from this same beach and pick wild blueberries.

"Mémère. Why are you shaking?"

Babs looked down and saw Jason had released her hand, and sure enough, that treasonous hand trembled visibly on the tabletop next to the crusts of her sandwich.

"Something's wrong with Mémère," she said to Jason in French. He stared at her, uncomprehending.

"I'm afraid to find out what it is," Babs said, again in French.

"I can't understand you, Mémère," Jason said.

"I know," she said in English. "But I need you to understand, Jay-Jay. I need you to learn French."

"Why? No one speaks French anymore."

"Listen to me," she said. "If you don't know your language, then

65

you don't know who you are. And if you don't know who you are, then everything your *pépère* and me built, everything we worked for and protected—it's gone. Do you understand?"

That look on Jason's face again, as though he were wrestling with sets of loyalties at direct odds with one another. Babs gazed at him, prodding with her eyes, but after a moment she saw that the boy was just about used up, and she relented.

"All right then," she said, standing up from the picnic table. "You ready to swim?"

"You don't have a bathing suit," Jason said.

"That's because I only go in up to my shins," Babs said. "Or don't you remember?"

Jason grinned. "Your pants always get wet," he said. "And you always get mad."

"Grab your towel, smart guy."

They moved toward the water, edging over to the side of the beach opposite the kids splashing in the shallows. Babs cuffed her pant legs as Jason waded to his knees and worked up the nerve to dive in— high summer or not, Maine's lakes, particularly spring-fed ones like this, were cold.

Babs winced as she slid her feet into the water. "You know how earlier I said you should stay at Mémère's house tonight?" she asked.

Jason stood waist-deep now, hands clasped in front of his chest, goose bumps standing out on his shoulders and arms. "Yeah," he said without turning to look at her.

"Now I'm thinking you should stay longer than that," she said. "It'll be just like old times, when you used to stay with me and Pé-père for days and days. Back when they used to have a waterslide at this dump."

"I don't think Dad will let me," Jason said.

"Mémère will talk to him." Babs inched forward, ankle-deep now. "You going in, or what?"

With a whoop, Jason dove forward and disappeared. The surface rippled, then was still, and Babs felt an abrupt stab of fear in her chest. Beyond fear—a terror, sudden and absolute, the kind she had, until this moment, only ever experienced in dreams. But then Jason's head bobbed to the surface again, and he was laughing, gasping, giddy with the cold. The lake bottom had not opened up and swallowed him. He was still there, still alive. He turned to look for her, and she tried to smile and felt how grotesque she looked in the attempt, her face like wax.

And then Jason was laughing again, pointing at her, saying something she couldn't make out. She followed the invisible line from his finger and looked down, saw the cuffs of her pants dark and heavy with lake water.

"Goddammit," Babs said.

CHAPTER FOUR

July 1, 2016

At the same time Babs was lamenting her wet cuffs, The Man, neither young nor old, neither Black nor white, uncanny yet of this world, hurtled south on I-95 in a late-model Chevy Impala the color of sun-bleached bones.

As always, he had business to attend to.

The Man was elemental, amoral, impervious to reasoning or bargaining. Pleas for mercy quivered on a frequency he could not hear. He was the fifth late notice on a long-overdue bill. The eviction order, the threatening call from the collection agency, the garnishment, the lien, the *Fuck you, pay me.* He was the evaporation of the future you'd imagined. By the time he showed up on your doorstep you'd had abundant warnings, everything short of a marching band carrying a banner that read HEY ASSHOLE YOU ARE FUCKING UP, and as such he was not in the business of negotiating. His job was to make clear you were not in charge or control, nor as smart and capable as you might once have imagined. To remind you that some problems, allowed to fester long enough, ceased to have solutions. He could seem unreal, illusory, but denying The Man existed conferred no protection from him. He didn't need you to believe in order to collect what was owed.

The Man's Impala looked as though it had just been driven off the dealer lot, not that you could have noticed this, given that The Man was doing half again over the speed limit. A whitish blur, viewed from a standstill at the side of the road. Not, understand, that The Man was in any hurry. In point of fact, he never hurried, even when going extremely fast. He did not experience urgency the way normal people experienced urgency. His pulse rarely rose above sixty (forty if he was sitting still). He'd never had a need for antiperspirant. Not once in his life had he suffered the stress-induced cortisol hangover that characterized modern life for most people. Perhaps this was genetic. Whatever the reason, his autonomic nervous system remained dark and dormant in any situation when the average person's would be screaming five alarms, pulling every hormonal and cardiovascular lever to prepare the body for a mortal threat real or imagined. It just didn't register for him, and never had. He could recognize stress or peril intellectually, but his body refused to respond. Not only did this explain the fact that he was capable of only one mood—namely, cheerful impassiveness—but it also made The Man 100 percent indifferent to the fear and pain and hopes of other people.

Eyes on the road ahead, hands at ten and two, he drove.

Long ago, before he realized he'd been put on earth for the purpose of humbling people, The Man had trained as a hairdresser. Pierre's School of Cosmetology, in Toronto. He was good. Quick study. Steady hands. And Pierre's was no fly-by-night outfit where anyone could learn to do a chop job. You couldn't just say *I guess I'll cut hair for a living* and go to Pierre's. They were the Harvard Medical School of hair design. Savagely competitive. Exacting. Cattier than a ballet company. Pierre's students were not above subterfuge or sabotage, because Pierre's top graduates got near-automatic appointments to chairs in the finest salons all over the world. Charged three thousand dollars a cut, more. If there was a fad hairstyle seen everywhere from Chicago to Hong Kong, chances were a Pierre's alum created it. You had to have talent. Drive. Vision. You had to understand hair intuitively. Understand it with your *hands*, not your brain. You had to live for the ribbon curl. You had to hate split ends like they'd killed your grandmother. You had to be able to gauge porosity, tonality, hair density, and a dozen other factors, and using those observations do the calculus of what the client wanted versus what was actually possible while simultaneously having an in-depth and empathetic conversation about their mother-in-law.

Even among this best of the best, The Man had shone. A shoo-in for valedictorian, and having received that honor he could have gone anywhere he wanted. Nine Zero One in Los Angeles. Balmain in Paris. His own line of shampoos and spritzes. Riding clients' private jets to cut hair all over the world.

Except.

Except that in order to graduate, every Pierre's student had to learn the dying art of straight-razor shaving. And every Pierre's student knew, well before starting the straight-razor program in their fourth year, that completing it would be the greatest challenge of their lives. The program had a higher attrition rate than Navy SEAL training, despite the fact that passing required nothing more complicated than shaving twenty balloons. The lead instructor, a Frenchman named Arthur Pepin, was known among students as Attila, a nickname he was aware of and glad to have. He would strut imperiously among a group of hopefuls as they scraped shaving cream from the balloons, pausing in front of each one, his gaze like an auger. He never spoke, to leverage either encouragement or criticism. Every day for months he stared silently, his thoughts and impressions of each student known only to him and God. In his stern inscrutability, Pepin contributed to the difficulty of completing the program, but the plain and immutable fact was that most students, even the confident and capable, simply didn't have the temperament for straight shaving, Pepin or no Pepin. They got nervous even with the balloons. They held their breath, tensed up, and—POW! The first time this happened, Pepin would pause for emphasis while the guilty party stared in horror at the desiccated flap of their balloon, then fold his hands behind his back and walk on without a word. And no words needed to be spoken—everyone knew you got exactly one failure. When the second occurred, Pepin maintained his silence, simply indicating, with a curt sweep of one arm toward the door, that the student was to leave and never return.

Of course, The Man had no such problems. While other students dry-swallowed tranquilizers in the bathroom before class and used their free hands to still the trembling of their razor hands, he literally whistled his way through his work, no more anxious than if he were reclined on a Caribbean beach at sunset. He became the first student in Pierre's history to complete the twenty-balloon gauntlet without popping any. Pepin, between himself and God, hated The Man, because the best-kept of Pepin's many secrets was that he himself had never been able to shave twenty balloons in a row. And even if Pepin was the only one who knew the student had become the master, it was a fact he could not abide.

And so when it came time for the final test before graduating—that of straight-shaving Pepin—The Man had failed before he even set the cream brush to his instructor's cheek. At ease as always, and as certain of his future as anyone could be in a capricious universe, he reclined Pepin gently while an audience of Pierre's students settled into the amphitheater seating that ringed the shaving chair. Pepin sat still, eyes closed, barely seeming to breathe. The Man waited until the seats were full, then draped a steaming towel over Pepin's face, folding it up and around until only the instructor's nostrils could be seen. He pressed the towel gently with his fingertips so that it made contact with Pepin's cheeks and neck. Out came The Man's new razor, purchased for the occasion: obsidian harvested from Hawaii's Mauna Loa volcano after an eruption in 1984, black and gleaming under the warm yellow lights. This blade was purportedly five hundred times sharper than Japanese steel, and the sight of it sent up a murmur among the students. The Man placed the blade on a side table as he finished counting silently to ninety, then lifted the hot towel, folding it into fourths and setting it beside the blade. He lifted a small basin and badger-hair brush, frothed the shaving cream, and worked it in with the bristles, no rush, no nerves, not even what could be called patience, since patience, in order to exist and be exerted, required a counterpart that The Man was neurologically incapable of: impatience.

Finally, the moment had come. The Man lifted the obsidian blade and spread the skin of Pepin's throat under the thumb and forefinger of his free hand, then pressed the edge just below Pepin's Adam's apple at a perfect ninety-degree angle. Short, brisk strokes, like brushing bits of lint from a jacket, and the two-day growth on Pepin's neck fairly melted under the obsidian.

The Man's fellow students held their breath and felt their hearts thump against their ribs as he worked steadily across Pepin's throat. One misstep, however small, and obsidian could easily flay their instructor's neck wide open. So how could The Man be so at ease? How was it possible to be this careful and casual at once? And was he *humming* to himself, for God's sake? That couldn't be. And yet, he was! Improbably, impossibly, as if taking a stroll in the woods, The Man hummed a cheerful tune as he stroked, pausing every few seconds to wipe the blade clean—carefully—on his apron.

The other students didn't know whether to feel envy or admiration, incredulousness or childish wonder. In the next moment, however, they would all feel precisely the same thing: horror.

What happened was, someone coughed.

This was not merely bad timing, however. This student had been promised an A in the shaving course by Pepin in exchange for the simple act of coughing, once, at an inopportune moment during The Man's test, thereby giving Pepin a plausible excuse to move his head. The idea was that this would almost certainly cause a nick, maybe even a small cut, which would, of course, mean that The Man had flunked immediately and, for the sin of his perfection with the balloons, would be denied his place as valedictorian, denied a chair at Balmain, denied his own line of products, denied the entirety of the life that appeared set out in front of him like a suitcase full of cash.

The problem was that Pepin didn't know about the obsidian razor, because his eyes had been covered with the towel when The Man removed the blade from its sheath. Pepin *had* heard the murmur among the students at the sight of the razor, but hadn't thought much of it. And he noted a conspicuous lack of friction as The Man shaved his throat, but never imagined this was due to the fact that the blade on his skin was so sharp it could cut individual hair cells cleanly in half. He guessed, in fact, as he sat there with his eyes closed waiting for the cough, that the lack of friction was attributable to some technique The Man had developed that removed shaving cream with a minimum of pressure. This explained neatly how

The Man had been able to avoid popping a single balloon, but was less than ideal, Pepin thought with relish, for actually shaving stubble— as they would soon see.

And in that moment it occurred to Pepin that perhaps he should ignore the cough when it came, remain stock-still, let The Man finish—and let his humiliation be complete when those assembled saw what a poor job he'd done. Let them all know and understand that The Man's infallibility was, in fact, counterfeit, cheap sleight of hand, befitting a carnival sideshow, perhaps, but having no place in the august halls of Pierre's School of Cosmetology.

Pepin did not know, of course, that in this moment he was actually deciding whether to live or die.

In the end, there was nothing more damning, Pepin decided, than injuring a client. Besides, by now The Man had almost finished with Pepin's neck, creating plenty of evidence to demonstrate that he had no idea how to shave someone, let alone well enough to be entrusted with the imprimatur of the most demanding cosmetology school in the world.

And so, when the cough came from the upper tier of the room's seating, to a collective gasp from the rest of the students—just as The Man laid the blade against Pepin's throat for one final pass, directly over where Pepin's carotid artery pulsed with oxygen-rich blood slated for the brain—Pepin followed through on the plan, jerking his head to the left, slightly, and just enough.

In the next instant Pepin's eyes flew open, and students three rows up in the gallery recoiled at the sudden panic they saw there. A vacuum descended in the shaving theater, everyone as still as the dead, breath catching, hearts pausing. There was, at first, no obvious sign of just how badly sideways the proceedings had gone—except for those eyes, staring at something majestic and terrible just beyond this world that was visible only to Pepin.

It was the cut that caused the confusion. The blade so sharp, the incision so fine, that at first no one could see it. Not even The Man. He stood over his instructor, head cocked as he took in the curious contrast between the terror in Pepin's eyes and his utter, electric stillness. Several seconds went by. Still no sound, no movement. And then two things happened in succession: Pepin's eyes, so bright and blaring, clouded over as if suddenly filling with skim milk. And then a crimson line appeared on the left side of his throat, looking for all the world like a very long paper cut, then running and blurring, red rivulets followed by a red curtain followed by a red torrent, all the blood north of Pepin's shoulders draining as from a spigot, soaking his clothes, cascading to the floor with a sound like a hard rain on pavement.

A coed chorus of screams and strangled animal noises issued from the gallery as the pool of Pepin's blood expanded outward and seeped around The Man's shoes. Students who'd walked in as strangers clutched one another, weeping and invoking God and, here and there, vomiting. Several students ran for the exit to summon help, though one hardly needed medical training to know there was no earthly thing that could be done at this point to bring Pepin back to his mortal form.

The Man, for his part, continued to just stand and stare, blade in hand, his socks growing warm and wet, watching his future drain away but not caring because, for the first time in his life, he felt something other than nothing. The static drone of his interior, uninterrupted for twenty-two years, was suddenly alive with a strange and urgent signal. He started to shake, ever so slightly. His pupils dilated, and his breath caught in his chest. Before now he'd never had anything that could be called a feeling, and so lacked the context by which to recognize and name what he was experiencing as his fellow students began to flee the shaving theater en masse and Pepin's legs twitched as though he meant somehow to join them.

But, reader, there's only one word for what was happening inside The Man in that moment: *lust*.

A straight line could be drawn between this swoon of lust and now, as The Man sped along I-95 in central Maine, ten miles from Waterville and closing fast. Because Pepin's death had brought The Man to an entirely different line of work, work that offered regular opportunities to feel this one feeling he was capable of. After all, as a hairstylist he couldn't go around opening up people's throats whenever he had the urge. But in his current job, not only could he, but also he was obliged to do so somewhat regularly. And The Man never took vacations; unlike most visitors to Maine, he was here on business.

Behind him, though: flashing blues. Work would have to wait a few more minutes. The Man eased off the gas and pulled into the breakdown lane, a State Police cruiser on his back bumper. He put the Impala in park and left the engine running, his hands on the steering wheel where they could easily be seen, his eyes forward and motionless, his expression blank.

It was impossible to tell how old The Man was because his face bore no wrinkles, had, in fact, no texture at all. His complexion gave him the uncanny appearance of a wax figure, or a cyborg.

The Statie came up to the driver's-side door, sweating in his heavy blue uniform and looking like he was grumpy about it. "License and registration," he said, taking inventory of The Man, his hands, the interior of the Impala front and back. As a whole, the scene made the back of the Statie's brain tingle—the car so spotless, the person behind the wheel looking like a goddamn mannequin or something.

The Man moved his right hand to pop the latch on the glove box—and the Statie saw there was nothing in there *except* the registration. This just kept getting weirder, he thought as The Man handed the paperwork over without looking at him.

The Statie scanned the registration, which, like the car's plates, was from Quebec. "You're a long way from home," he said.

"My work often takes me to far-flung places," The Man told him.

"You staying around here?"

"I've been in Waterville for several days," The Man said, "but today I had business in Benton."

"Have any idea how fast you were going?" the Statie asked.

"Ninety-five," The Man said, still staring impassively through the windshield as traffic whisked by.

"On the nose. What's your hurry?"

"I thought that was the speed limit."

Now the Statie paused in examining the license and registration, leaned down toward the window, and said, "Excuse me?"

"That's what the signs say," The Man said, still staring straight ahead. "Ninety-five."

The Statie was like 90 percent sure the guy was yanking his chain, but he played along. "It's, uh, *not* the speed limit," he said. "It's the highway number."

At last, The Man turned his face toward the Statie.

Time stopped. The Statie stared into the void, and the void stared right back.

"Well, then," The Man said. "I'm glad you didn't catch me earlier on 201."

Held fast by an expression that could have turned Medusa to stone, the Statie dropped The Man's license and registration through the window with numb fingers.

"Officer," The Man said, "part of my work involves asking a few questions of people I've just met. A kind of informal survey. Would you mind if I asked those questions of you? Do you have time?"

"I . . . I . . . sure," the Statie said.

"Excellent," The Man said. "The questions are very simple. Here's the first: Do you ever have a sense of imminent doom?"

"Doom?" the Statie asked.

"You know," The Man said. "The feeling that it's all coming apart. A whiff of blood on the wind. Dread, ambient and inescapable."

"Well, sure," the Statie said. "I mean, I *worry* about stuff."

"What stuff?"

"Bills," the Statie said. "Whether I'll make sergeant. My youngest boy has a congenital defect with his legs that—"

"I don't mean petty concerns," The Man said. "Let's be honest: no one but you cares about the minutiae of your own life. I'm asking if you have worries on a proper biblical scale. If you ever dream about whole cities being swept into the ocean. If the orange glow of a sunset ever makes you think, even for a second, that maybe the whole world has caught fire."

"Well, I guess," the Statie said. "Sometimes I think about stuff like that. Who doesn't?"

"And when you do," The Man said, "when you do think about *stuff like that*, how do you comfort yourself? How do you get on with your day, having just seen a vision of the end?"

The Statie thought for a second. "I don't know," he said. "You just realize it's not real, right? Just your mind playing tricks on you."

"But what if I told you it *is* real?"

The Statie laughed nervously. "It is?"

"Oh, it most definitely is," The Man said.

"Well," the Statie said, "I guess I have more important things on my mind, most of the time."

"Of course," The Man said. "Bills and such. One last question. Do you know what Carl Sagan said when he was asked why, if there are so many solar systems in the universe, we have never seen evidence of extraterrestrial life?"

"Who's Carl Sagan?"

"He said life would almost always destroy itself before it had the capacity for interstellar travel."

The Statie stared at him a moment. "Just . . . keep it under seventy, okay?" he said, then double-timed it away without waiting for an answer.

But The Man offered one anyway, to nobody: "No problem, Officer," he said. "Have a great day."

CHAPTER FIVE

July 1, 2016

Even back in the '70s, when bowling occupied a prime Saturday broadcast spot on ABC and Babs and Rheal had been part of a league every spring, the Spare Time Bowling Center in Waterville could have most charitably been described as run-down. Forty years later, tenpin having nearly gone the way of the woolly mammoth, Spare Time looked postapocalyptic, especially in the context of the woebegone industrial park it called home. Weeds and delicate elm saplings sprouted from cracks in the otherwise empty parking lot. Broken pallets, broken bottles, and one bald, rimless car tire littered the grounds. Orange pill bottles, of course, common as pigeons. The sign over the main entrance, owing to several neon tubes that had burned out around the time Lori was in high school, read SPA TIM.

Babs came in through the main entrance, ignoring a notice on the door that prohibited the carrying of firearms. The place was deserted as usual, lanes shining and silent under the fluorescent lights. To her right, the twentysomething stoner attendant was fast asleep, his forehead pressed against the edge of the desk. Babs walked past him toward the back of the building, entering the mechanic's room through a door marked EMPLOYEES ONLY.

Ten minutes later, Daryl Bates, Waterville's chief of police, opened the emergency exit opposite the mechanic's room. Tall and stick-thin, Bates normally resembled a heron in both appearance and gait, but today his loping stride was thrown off by the walking cast on his left foot. He wore plain clothes and a Red Sox cap, his left eye covered with a black cloth patch.

Bates peered into the bowling alley with his good eye, spotted the attendant still sleeping at the desk, and crossed the area between the emergency exit and the mechanic's room as quickly and quietly as he could.

"Chief Bates, punctual as always," Babs said as he let himself in and eased the door closed behind him.

"How many times do I have to tell you," Bates said. "No names."

"Relax, Daryl, nobody's recording anything in here. What happened to your eye?"

"Scratched cornea."

Babs pointed at the cast. "What about the hoof?"

"Fell over an ottoman."

She folded her arms in appraisal, grinning. "It's not a look that inspires confidence, Chief."

"You wear an eye patch and see if you don't trip a time or six."

"Can you see this chair? That table? Wouldn't want you to take another tumble."

"We need to talk about Tim," Bates said.

"It's being taken care of as we speak."

"No," Bates said. "This is the fifth *unsolved* robbery in a month. The city council's up my ass, not to mention the newspaper. I need to law-and-order this."

"It's my pocket Tim's robbing," Babs told him. "He'll be moving on today."

"*Our* pocket," Bates said. "Speaking of?"

Babs pulled an envelope from her purse and handed it over. "This is a neighborhood matter," she said. "No blood spilled. Besides, Tim's my nephew. I can't have him land in prison."

"Well, that's too bad, because you're going to have to get used to seeing him in an orange jumpsuit."

"Fine," Babs said. "You go talk to the judge, get your paperwork squared away. We'll see who gets to Tim first. My money's on Lore."

Bates tucked the envelope into his back pocket. "Speaking of things that need taking care of," he said.

"Excuse me?"

"All the ears you have to the ground in this town," Bates said, "and you've got no idea what's going on with your own daughter?"

"Lori's not the daughter I'm worried about, at the moment."

"The Tim conversation is over," Bates said. "He's going away. And the drugs he stole better still be in his possession when we pick him up."

Babs pushed past Bates and made her way to the door. "Always a pleasure, Daryl," she said. "Don't have another accident on your way out."

Bates turned toward her departure. "Can I see you later?" he asked.

"Go to Sunnybrook and see your wife, for a change," Babs said as the door closed behind her.

W hen Lori walked into the basement barroom at You Know Who's, the place was empty except for a couple of leathery old drunks arguing in French at a table in the corner, underneath a big framed print of Bonnie and Clyde. That print had been hanging on the wall since before she'd started coming here with Rheal when she was five. Back then, Lori would shine shoes for a buck a pop and buy an endless series of glass-bottled Coca-Colas with her earnings, while Rheal played cribbage for fifty dollars a game with his buddies. Now, as Lori entered, Big Bucky Desjardins, the proprietor and daytime bartender, looked up from slicing limes. Six foot five and well north of three hundred pounds, as gregarious as he was gigantic, Bucky smiled from behind his Grizzly Adams beard and put two rocks glasses on the bar.

"The lady stirs!" Bucky said, his laughter ringing through the room. The old men in the corner paused their argument and stared.

Lori glanced toward the old-timers, who quickly went back to minding their business. "Knock it off," she said to Bucky, taking a seat at the bar.

"So sorry," Bucky said. "Of course. I absolutely, one hundred percent will knock it off—if you promise to take a break from dying in my fucking bathroom."

"I'll make you a deal," Lori said. "Fix that goddamn sign out front, and I'll stop dying in your bathroom."

"What's wrong with the sign?"

"I've told you before. The possessive form of 'who' is W-H-O-S-E. W-H-O-apostrophe-S is short for 'who is.' Which means, as of right now, your place of business is called 'You Know Who Is Pub.' Which makes you seem like a fucking idiot."

"Like anyone but you knows the difference," Bucky said.

"Just give me a drink, please." Lori rubbed at her eyes with her thumb and forefinger.

Bucky lifted a bottle of Wild Turkey from the well and poured. "No Sis today?"

"Apparently not."

He rested the whiskey bottle on top of the bar. "Shit, you two haven't missed afternoon teatime in, what, eight months? She lose a leg or something?"

"She's gone underground. Don't know why."

"Mmm. *Ce n'est pas bon.*"

"Not that out of the ordinary," Lori said. "She'll turn up."

"You trying to convince me?" Bucky asked. "Cause it sounds like you're trying to convince yourself."

"Little of both, probably," Lori said.

Bucky picked up the bottle and topped off Lori's glass, then filled the one meant for Sis. "You know I'll keep my ears open. And in the meantime," he said, raising a toast, "I'll drink witcha."

Lori nodded thanks. Bucky knocked back three fingers in a swallow, then crossed the bar and went back to slicing limes. As he worked Lori took her phone out of her pocket and typed a message to Sis.

1:32 PM: *Do you need help?*

Too plaintive? Too alarmist? Lori hit send before she could think better of it. Sis needed to understand she was starting to scare people— maybe that would cut through the fog of whatever combination of booze, drugs, and petty distraction she'd gotten into. Lori put the phone down on the bar and stared at it for long moments, willing the screen to light up with a response. Nothing. She drank more whiskey. Nothing. She watched a twenty-four-hour news channel playing silently on the TV behind the bar for a minute, then glanced down at the phone again. Still nothing.

She sighed, leaned back and stretched, looked absently around the room, and was neither surprised nor alarmed to see her dead father, Rheal, had posted up on the last stool at the bar. A pint of piss-pale lager rested on the mahogany to Rheal's left. He lifted the glass and drained it, wiped his mouth on his shirtsleeve, and made a show of suddenly noticing her. He set the glass back down, smiled his jester's smile, and waved. Lori waved half-heartedly in return, noticing as she did so that Rheal's glass was full again though Bucky hadn't poured him another beer.

"Two in the afternoon's a bit early for me."

The voice still so familiar, like a favorite T-shirt gone missing and rediscovered years later in the back of a closet. Lori half turned on her stool to look at Shawn.

"You're on vacation," she said. "Live a little."

He straddled the seat next to her. "I suppose the sun's over the yardarm somewhere in the world."

Big Bucky came over, wiping his canned-ham hands on a dish towel. "Welcome, my yuppie friend," he said to Shawn. "What're you having?"

"What makes you think I'm a yuppie?" Shawn asked.

"Aside from your entire vibe? Nothing, really."

Lori snorted, and did it feel good, not to mention novel, to enjoy even a moment's levity. When was the last time she'd laughed? She had no idea.

"Well, I'm not a yuppie," Shawn said to Bucky. "I'm from here."

"And yet the question remains," Bucky said. "What do you want to drink?"

Shawn peered at Lori's glass. "Make it two of whatever she's having. Jonestown Kool-Aid, is it?"

Lori smirked while Big Bucky poured.

"So," Shawn said to Lori. "Last time I saw you I was picking up a rented tux and under the delusion we'd be spending the rest of our lives together."

"Going to excuse myself from this particular conversation," Bucky said, heading back across the bar.

"It was prom, Shawn," Lori said. "Not a wedding."

"You do get style points for shipping off to boot camp before collecting your diploma, though."

"I could try to explain my reasons," Lori said, "but I'm not sure they make sense now."

"No need." Shawn took a drink, winced, sucked air through his teeth. "Your old man broke it down for me."

"How's that, exactly?"

"I showed up at your house the morning after prom. Like a lost puppy. He took me out for a drink. Brought me here, in fact. We sat at that table right there. He told me you were gone, and why."

Lori glanced over to where Rheal sat, and he raised his pint to her. "Not sure how he could have known any better than you did," she said.

"He said you had to get away from Babs. That you weren't made to stay in a place like Waterville. And with you gone, I realized: neither was I."

"Guess he knew me better than I thought."

"And yet, here you are," Shawn said.

Lori nodded in concession and swirled a finger in her whiskey. "So what about you?" she asked after a moment.

"Me? Senior portfolio manager at PricewaterhouseCoopers. A big, empty brownstone in Back Bay. A dog that hates me. Lots of nice shoes and watches."

"Sounds terrific."

"You should see these watches. I mean, real quality timepieces."

Lori looked up, trying to smile but not quite making it. "And yet," she said, "here *you* are."

At that moment her phone buzzed, and she practically lunged for it, convinced, because she wanted to be, that Sis had finally come to her senses and returned her message. But it was Babs.

2:07 PM: *Bates is after Tim. Forget the eviction. Just get the drugs and get out.*

Lori stood up and gunned the rest of her whiskey.

"Where are you going?" Shawn asked.

"Duty calls."

"But we just got here."

"And now I'm leaving." She pulled a rumpled twenty from her hip pocket and tossed it on the bar.

"How about tonight?" Shawn asked.

Lori stopped, planted one palm on the bar, and fixed Shawn with a gaze so piercing that he flinched.

"Listen," she said. "Whatever assumptions you're making based on how I look, I assure you the reality is far worse. You see my father sitting at the end of the bar?"

Shawn was too confused by the question to turn around and look.

"I asked," Lori said, "if you see my father sitting at the end of the bar."

Now he turned and, of course, saw nothing but an empty stool. "Uh, *no*," he said.

"Of course you don't. But I see him, plain as day."

Shawn didn't know what to say to this.

"I'm a junkie, Shawn," Lori said. "I'm trying and failing to hold my family together. Ever since I got my brain scrambled in Afghan-

istan, I see ghosts. And I can't go half a day without getting high—
I'm high right now, actually, even though I don't want to be. This
morning I promised—*promised*—myself no dope. And I meant it.
For about three hours."

"Jesus, Lore."

"I see my father. Guys I served with. I talk to them, have drinks
with them."

"Okay," Shawn said.

Something in Lori's expression shifted suddenly, frustration mor-
phing into fear. "Wait," she said. "You're alive, right?"

"Far as I know," Shawn said.

But Lori wasn't about to take his word for it. She reached out to
touch his arm, testing—and when her hand met warm flesh, relief
flooded her face.

"Go back to Boston, to your dog and your nice shoes," Lori said.
"There's nothing for you here."

She turned to leave.

"So should I call you later, then?" Shawn asked.

"Obviously," Lori said without looking back.

Metric Motors consisted of a corrugated-steel building the size of
an airplane hangar plunked down on two acres of scrub grass
and dirt at the far northern edge of Waterville's city limits. The aes-
thetic was pure speed-freak chic: jacked-up American muscle cars,
Subarus and Toyotas customized within an inch of their lives, and a
handful of BMW and Yamaha performance motorcycles waited pa-
tiently for service in neat rows out front. In the back lay the victims
of poor judgment and/or weather conditions, cars bashed and smashed
in all degree of severity, some so badly crumpled they resembled

wadded-up sheets of paper. Groundhogs and chickadees flitted among the wrecks, and the buzz of pneumatic wrenches drifted nonstop through the hangar's bay doors, opened against the heat.

Tim Talbot crouched in the shade on the east side of the building, trying to pound a dent out of a quarter panel with a body hammer and, as usual, fucking it up. He hammered and cursed, wiped sweat from his forehead, hammered some more. After more than half an hour he'd succeeded only in transforming one large dent into half a dozen smaller ones, and was just about to throw the panel to the ground and go get high when Lori walked up.

"I need a word with you, Tim," she said.

He squinted up at her. "'Bout what?"

"You know 'bout what."

Tim leaned the panel against the building and got to his feet with a groan, hammer still in hand. "Golly, it's nice to see you, too, Lore," he said. "How long you been back?"

"Better part of a year," Lori said.

"I'm guessing this ain't a social call, then, since I haven't seen you that whole time."

"My mother's the one big on family," Lori said. "Me, I can take it or leave it."

"I won't lie to you, Lore," Tim said. "That hurts my feelings."

"I don't want to be having this conversation any more than you do," Lori said. "Just show me the pills."

"What pills?"

"From the pharmacy."

"What pharmacy?"

"You're starting to piss me off, Tim."

"Well, oh no," Tim said, mock alarmed. "Look out, everyone, Lori's pissed off. What are you gonna do? Kick my ass?"

"There you go, mistaking me for my mother again," Lori said. "The drugs here? Or at home?"

Tim just glared. After a beat, Lori stepped toward the garage doors, throwing a shoulder into Tim as she passed.

"Where do you think you're going?" Tim asked.

"To your locker. And if I find what I think I'm going to find there, you're going to regret making this harder than it has to be."

"Lore."

She stopped and turned to face him again.

"Let me keep the dope, at least."

"Can't do it. I'm sure my mother will be happy to extend you credit."

"Hell she will," Tim said. "Besides, it's not for me. I need to sell it. I'm underwater with everything."

"Trust me when I say that being behind on your rent is the least of your problems."

Tim's tough-guy sneer evaporated, and a childlike worry spread across his face. "What's that supposed to mean?"

Lori almost—but not quite—felt bad for him, too dumb to understand that knocking off a pharmacy meant his life was now fucked one way or another. "Just . . . show me the drugs, Tim."

But he summoned his nonexistent courage once more, literally puffing his chest out. "Only if I get to keep the dope," he said.

"That's not going to happen."

An impasse. Tim hung his head for a moment, seeming to acquiesce—then suddenly sprang forward, windmilling his fists and making a sound somewhere between growling and moaning. Slowed by dope and whiskey, Lori reacted half a second too late, and Tim managed to land a half-assed right across her jaw. But this turned out to be more his misfortune than hers—on impact a metacarpal in his hand snapped clean, one jagged end thrusting up and popping through the skin, and suddenly Tim didn't care in the least about Lori or the drugs or really anything else in the world other than that nub of bone, perfectly cylindrical, pink with marrow at the center, staring him in the face.

Tim howled, clutching his busted hand with the good one and dancing in circles. Genuinely pissed now, Lori shook off the punch and came up behind him, swinging one open palm hard into Tim's ear, which had the dubious benefit of making him forget about his hand for a few moments. He stopped dancing and bent forward at the waist, good hand cupped over his ear, moaning now as though he were going to die, and Lori lifted one foot and planted it squarely on his ass, sending him sprawling face down in the dirt.

"Your locker," Lori said, straddling Tim's legs. She kicked him again, lightly, in the calf. *"Aweille.* Get up."

What little fight he'd had in him now fully extinguished, Tim did as he was told, but slowly and with no small amount of drama, pushing himself up with the good hand and grabbing on to Lori's pant leg to climb to his feet.

"Enough," she said, giving him a push. "Let's go."

Tim led the way through the bay doors, where half a dozen other grease monkeys were arrayed around the garage, working their magic under the hoods. Wrenches whined, lug nuts rolled loose, and a grinder threw a rooster tail of sparks into the air. No one seemed to care, or really even to have noticed, who'd hit whom or why.

"You behave yourself, maybe I'll let you keep a little something," Lori said. "You're gonna need it with that hand."

"Mighty white of you, Lore."

On the other side of a door marked TRESPASSERS WELCOME—DOG FOOD IS EXPENSIVE sat Metric Motors' employee room, a multipurpose space with a small Formica table, a cube fridge, and a love seat and lounger that looked like they'd been scooped up off the side of the road after a fire. A locker bank lined one wall, and in the back corner sat a freestanding toilet gobbed with toilet paper, no sink.

"Love what you've done with the place," Lori said.

Tim made a show of opening a combination lock with one hand. After several tries the aluminum door popped open, and he pulled out a pillowcase bulging all over with pill bottles and the sharp corners of prescription boxes.

"There ya go, you fucking jerk," Tim said, handing it over. "You got a funny way of treating family."

"Let's not forget who took a swing at whom," Lori said. She shook the pillowcase, testing its weight. "This everything?"

"Minus one thing of Dilaudid."

"Anything left of that?"

"Course not," Tim said. "But there's a couple bottles of Oxy in there."

"Not for you, there isn't."

Tim collapsed into the lounger, sending up a puff of dust. "Great," he said, holding his hand against his chest. "What am I supposed to do now?"

"At the risk of stating the obvious," Lori said, "your first priority should probably be a hospital."

"You know what I mean."

Lori gazed at him—broken, literally and figuratively—and felt a twinge of sympathy cut through her irritation. She sat in the chair opposite, hung her head for a moment, rubbing the back of her neck with her free hand.

"Tim," she said after a moment. "Real talk."

He looked at her.

Lori held up the pillowcase. "This is over," she said. "I'm talking as your cousin now."

"Okay," Tim said.

"You need to get out of here."

"What do you mean?"

"I mean *out of here*. Gone. Leave town. Do not pass go. Do not collect two hundred dollars. And do not ever come back."

"I don't understand."

"You don't need to. Just go. You're already wasting time you don't have."

Tim stared at her for a few seconds, realizing, finally, what she meant.

"What about Babs?" he asked.

"She can't protect you anymore."

"Can't?" he asked. "Or won't?"

Lori looked at him. "Does it matter?"

Real hurt on Tim's face now, like a kid who just realized he's been left behind by his parents at a highway rest stop. "It does to me," he said.

Lori sighed. "I'm leaving, Tim," she said. "If you're smart, you will, too."

"No sense in running," Tim said. "If Babs isn't covering me, I'm screwed. Might as well just sit here and take it."

"Suit yourself." Lori stood to leave.

"Will you wait with me?"

"Not with a pillowcase full of stolen drugs, Tim, no."

"Wait with me," Tim said, eyeing, with an odd calm, the little bone protruding from his hand. "It's the least you can do."

Lori sat down again, slowly. After a moment, Tim looked up from his hand.

"You remember when we were kids?" he asked.

"You're going to need to be more specific than that."

"You and Jean always called me 'Elmer,'" Tim said. "You thought I didn't know why. And I didn't, at first. After a while, though, I figured it out."

"Tim, really, you should just get out of—"

"I always tried to hang out with you guys, but you never wanted me around."

"That's not true."

"Sure it is. Elmer. He sticks to you like glue."

"Tim . . ."

"You thought I was a dumbshit and a pest. I got it. But I still looked up to you. I thought maybe if I spent more time with you, some of you would rub off on me, and maybe I wouldn't be so dumb. Maybe I'd learn how not to be such a fuckup."

Sirens in the distance. Lori stood, lifted the pillowcase, and moved toward the door.

"And I did learn something, Lore," Tim went on behind her. "Don't you want to hear what it is?"

Lori stopped, but didn't turn around.

"You're the smart one. Always have been. But there's one way I'm smarter than you, Lore. I learned not to treat family the way you treated me."

Lori stood there a moment longer, opened her mouth to say something, said nothing instead.

"Now get out of here," Tim said, "before they bust both of us."

As she walked back through the garage Lori caught sight of blue strobes dancing on the corrugated-steel walls—and now the other mechanics, no doubt worried about their own extracurriculars, finally looked up from their work. Lori slipped through the bay doors just as two cruisers and an unmarked sedan pulled in, kicking up dirt. She got into her truck cab while the cops—three unis and Detective Cloutier in his signature JCPenney suit—raced into the building. They paid her—and the pillowcase—no mind.

CHAPTER SIX

July 1, 2016

Like Babs's place, Rita's bungalow two blocks south on Paris Street, though a century old, stood out for how well-maintained it was compared to its neighbors. The gabled roof hunkered tight as a Roman phalanx, having been reshingled only a month earlier, and pristine white shutters and flower boxes framed every window. Rita had laid the brick walkway connecting the sidewalk to the front steps with her own hands, and even with the heaving of the ground as it froze and thawed repeatedly in winter, she kept this walkway so level you could place a baseball at the center and it would remain exactly where you put it.

This was the sort of attention to detail—the insistence that things be done and remain *right*—that Babs would have appreciated, had she come to Rita's on more pleasant business. As it stood, though, she marched up the walkway without noticing its abiding craftsmanship at all. She mounted the steps and leaned on the doorbell, then turned back toward the driveway as she waited for Rita to answer. In Babs's station wagon, Carmeline, Stella, and Bernette waited, their figures obscured almost entirely by a fog of cigarette smoke inside the car.

A full minute went by, Babs watching the sun edge behind the top of the white pine to the left of the driveway. She knew Rita had heard the doorbell and she would not effectively plead with her to answer by ringing it again. This, more than anything, was Babs's great strength—patience, rooted in an unshakable self-confidence. If belief in one's judgment, decisions, and abilities had been a sport, Babs would have been considered a generational talent. So there on Rita's porch, Babs did what she was better at than anyone else, and waited. One ring was enough. Rita knew Babs was there, knew that refusing to answer the door would be as futile as climbing into a cab and asking the driver to take her to the moon. And knowing this, she eventually opened up, a glass of merlot in hand, teetering almost imperceptibly as she glared at Babs.

"You're the last person I want to see right now," Rita said.

Babs nodded acknowledgment of this fact. "We've been friends over fifty years, Rita. Family almost that long."

"And that whole time, it's been Babs's way or no way at all."

"I understand why you're angry," Babs said.

"Do you? I raised that boy."

Babs's eyes flashed. "I raised a son, too," she said. "Or don't you remember?"

The mention of Jean was enough to make Rita look away, chagrined.

"And I know you brought up Tim," Babs continued. "I helped, if you recall. But we didn't get it right."

"According to you," Rita said.

"'According to me' is all that matters," Babs said.

Rita set her wineglass down on a table to the left of the doorway. "I don't think you understand what's going on here, Babs," she said. "I want to hurt you right now. I really want to hurt you."

"I wouldn't respect you if you didn't," Babs said. "But before you take a shot at the title, there's something you should know."

"And what's that?"

"I changed my mind."

Rita blinked. "What do you mean?"

"You were right," Babs said. "The rules should be different for family. I told Lore to get the drugs and let Tim be."

"So he can stay? Just like that?"

"Not exactly. There's another problem."

"Bates?"

Babs nodded.

"So tell him to stand down. We'll take care of it. *I'll* take care of it."

"His stance is we've had plenty of time to take care of it," Babs said. "Now he's feeling the heat."

Rita stared. "So tell him to stand down anyway."

"I've got no leverage here, Rita."

"No leverage? You could put Bates away for three lifetimes, with what you have on him."

"And he could return the favor," Babs said. "To all of us. He knows I'm not going to go mutually assured destruction over Tim."

"No, of course not," Rita said. "Why would you? He's just my only son."

Babs put a hand on her sister's shoulder. "Rita," she said, "you chose to have a child, which means you chose to have your heart broken, over and over, for the rest of your life. Don't pin it on me. Or even Bates."

A moment of quiet followed between them, Babs feeling Rita's fury and sadness vibrate under her hand. She looked over at the driveway, and Rita followed her gaze, saw the other ladies crammed into Babs's station wagon in the driveway.

"Where's everyone going?" Rita asked.

"To Bruce's."

"I'll get my purse."

"No."

Another quiet moment, this one decidedly less collegial, charged with angry ions.

"I should be there," Rita said.

Babs gazed at her wearily. "Jesus, Rita," she said. "I'm trying to be nice about this."

Rita narrowed her eyes. "You're not *nice*," she said. "You're never *nice*."

"Pour another glass of wine. Draw a bath. We can handle Bruce without you."

"But we always do these things together—all of us."

Now Babs's impatience materialized, as it always did, in her posture: she stiffened, drawing back her shoulders and looking down at Rita, giving her a good view of the point of her chin. "Are you going to make me spell it out for you?" she asked.

"Yes," Rita said. "I am."

"Fine." Babs dropped her hand from Rita's shoulder. "Then here it is: This isn't the first time you've made the mistake of acting like you have veto power in my house. But it *is* the last."

And though she'd had a sense of what was coming, Rita was still shocked into silence as Babs performed a curt about-face, went down the steps, crossed the perfectly level brick walkway, and turned toward her car. It was only when Babs opened the driver's-side door that Rita was able, finally, to unstick her tongue.

"You can't do this, Babs!" she cried out. "We're sisters!"

Babs paused and looked up toward the porch. For a moment something human—regret, perhaps, or maybe the pain of fractured love—flitted across her face, like the shadow of a bird passing overhead. But then it was gone so quickly that anyone watching could not have been sure they'd seen it in the first place.

"Way I remember it," Babs said, "my parents never *legally* adopted you."

And with that she was gone, the old station wagon backing quickly into the street and pulling away. No one in the car looked back, or even glanced in a mirror, as Rita stood rooted to her top step, drunk and grieving and furious, with no idea what she could or would do next.

A cross town, The Man's Impala slipped into the Lovejoy Medical Clinic parking lot, which as dusk fell was empty except for one other vehicle, a late-model Range Rover with enough luxury and tech features to satisfy a Saudi prince. The Man got out of his car, examined the Range Rover briefly but with no small amount of appreciation, then went up the stairs to the clinic entrance, finding it locked. Though he was wanted in both the United States and Canada—one RCMP detective had recently taken early retirement after growing so obsessed over a decade of hunting The Man that he'd had a nervous breakdown—he made no effort to hide himself from the clinic's security cameras.

Inside, Michael LaVerdiere, D.O., sat at the desk in his office, updating patient records and smoking a joint, tapping ash onto the floor for the overnight cleaning service to deal with. Like The Man,

LaVerdiere was a criminal. Unlike The Man, LaVerdiere assumed—incorrectly—that his extralegal activities were not known to law enforcement, and so he hid in plain sight, even presented himself as an altruist of sorts, working for substandard pay at this clinic that serviced mostly poor, rural patients. The public-facing LaVerdiere was thought of roundly as a great and generous professional, a true Hippocratic hero. This selfless healer routine, deployed over drinks, had even gotten him laid a couple of times. The truth was, though, that LaVerdiere worked at the clinic because he was a shitty doctor, and could afford to stay in that job because of his felonious side hustle, which, until The Man's arrival that night, had been low-impact and lucrative in equal measure. Unlike most of his classmates from St. George's Medical School in Grenada, LaVerdiere had long since paid off his student loans. Though single, he owned a seven-bedroom house with several acres of lakefront in the coveted (and very expensive) Belgrade Lakes region, not far from Sunset Beach. He took three trips to Las Vegas each year to lose gobs of money at high-limit blackjack and drink himself blind at the Red Rock. He owned a boat, two motorcycles, the Range Rover, a vintage MG, a condo in Myrtle Beach, and a penthouse time-share on Isla Mujeres off Mexico's Yucatán Peninsula. He always paid for expedited shipping when ordering items online. Every weekday he burned two dollars in gas to drive clear across town and order a sextuple vanilla bean mocha latte to the tune of $8.72. All this, and as far as the IRS was concerned he made $60,000 a year after taxes.

LaVerdiere slept like a dead baby because he considered himself no more accomplished in immorality or wastefulness than his neighbors. He saw the drifts of garbage tossed from windows on the highway and overheard the high-minded, righteous conversations of woke moms in yoga pants made by de facto slaves in Bangladesh. He read the same news about breached wastewater ponds and puppy mills as everyone else, but unlike everyone else he realized wringing his hands over such things was a grotesque act of hypocrisy. He understood capitalism as a zero-sum Darwinist game with a ticking doomsday clock, which afforded no space for considerations of fairness or legality. What was fair and legal was whatever one could get away with before the whole thing went tits-up, and thus far LaVerdiere had gotten away with everything he'd ventured.

Intent on what seemed to be an error in a patient file, LaVerdiere did not notice when The Man materialized, suddenly and silently, in the doorway to his office. And The Man was happy to wait there, smiling his Medusa smile, until the doctor finally felt his gaze, glanced up, and jumped in his seat as though he'd been given an electric shock.

"Jesus Christ!" LaVerdiere said.

"I'm sorry," The Man said. "I didn't mean to startle you."

LaVerdiere stared.

"Okay," The Man said, "I *did* mean to startle you."

"How did you get in here?" LaVerdiere asked.

The Man hooked a thumb toward the entrance. "Through the front door," he said.

"I told Claire to lock up."

"She did."

The blood fled from LaVerdiere's face. "Who . . . who are you?" he asked.

The Man stepped into the room and leaned against a bookcase, arms folded. "Who I am is not important at all," he said. "What I want is much more relevant to this conversation."

"Okay . . ."

"But the truly important thing is who I work for. I assume you've heard of Ogopogo?"

LaVerdiere's eyes widened. "I've—he's—"

"In the interest of saving time, let me fill in some blanks," The Man said. "There are two Ogopogos in Canada. The first is a mythical monster. Lives in a lake in British Columbia, according to legend. A serpent, fifty feet long. This isn't the Ogopogo who employs me. Perhaps that goes without saying, but I always like to clarify."

"Clarity is . . . good," LaVerdiere said, not sounding at all certain about the merits of clarity.

"The second Ogopogo is my employer—and he is no myth. Ogo *is* Canadian, however, which means he is polite, enjoys ice sculpture and hockey. But he has a cruel streak. Once, on his orders, I fed a live human being to a pair of white tigers. This person was, until the time of the tiger incident, one of Ogopogo's private drivers. And his crime was having failed to pick up Ogo's mother from a hair appointment on time."

LaVerdiere swallowed. "That seems . . . out of proportion?"

"One could make the case, yes," The Man said. "The point is this: Canadian children, raised on the story of Ogopogo, are afraid to go into lakes, convinced a serpent will swallow them. But adults—if they're smart—aren't afraid of myths. They fear men."

The Man paused, gauging the effect of his words on LaVerdiere. To all appearances, the doctor seemed to be experiencing the correct type of fear.

"And that brings us to why I'm here," The Man said. "I need to know who *you* work for."

"For the clinic," LaVerdiere said, shifting in his chair. "I'm a doctor."

The Man sighed extravagantly. "You're a doctor who has written thousands of fake opioid prescriptions in the past five years," he said. "And Ogo, as the principal distributor of heroin in the eastern United States and Canada, wants to know who is filling and selling those prescriptions."

LaVerdiere stared for a moment, then closed his eyes and threw his head back. "Oh fuck," he said.

"Indeed," said The Man.

"I can't tell you anything," LaVerdiere said. "If I say a word I'll be in deep shit."

"You're in deep shit now," The Man said. "You were in deep shit the moment you agreed to be part of a narcotics ring. The moment you were born. The moment your ancient forebears emerged from the water on clumsy finlike appendages. You were in deep shit, Doctor LaVerdiere, from the very moment five billion years ago when an amorphous cloud of gas and dust began to spin, ever so slowly at first, then gaining speed until gravity took hold and bits of matter started to stick to one another, forming first the Sun, that unremarkable star, then the planets of our solar system. Including the one we find ourselves on now, discussing the depth of the shit you're in."

"I don't have contact with anyone," LaVerdiere said, his voice trembling.

The Man took a step toward where LaVerdiere was seated, then, slowly, another. "Of course," he said, "when viewed with the same lens—that is to say, the lens of geologic time—the shit you're in doesn't even register. Is, in fact, no shit at all. If, like the most accomplished Buddhist monks, you could place your life and its relative insignificance in the larger context of all creation, you likely wouldn't care even a little about the shit you're in. As with monks self-immolating, the terrible things I will do if I don't learn what I want to know would be of no more importance to you than a housefly's death. Yet, as things stand, it feels safe to assume you're not capable of such an enlightened perspective. You're trapped, as most are, deep in the illusion of a Self, with all its frailties and petty desires. The desire to forgo suffering. To not experience pain. To avoid, at all costs, for example, having someone peel your face off and hold up a mirror to show you your own grinning skull."

LaVerdiere was still. He'd ceased to breathe. He stared unblinking into The Man's eyes and understood, surely and clearly, that this was a person who had no use for idle threats, that he would do exactly what he described with all the dispassion of a bus driver pulling to the curb to let passengers off.

The Man took another step forward, within grasping distance of LaVerdiere now. "So," he said. "Would you like to talk? Or would you like the tigers?"

"I don't have contact with anybody!" LaVerdiere said. "I mail the scripts to a PO box!"

"Surely someone pays you in return?"

"Cash. It gets dropped in a safe deposit. Randomly. Sometimes it's two weeks. Sometimes I get payments on back-to-back days, for no reason. Sometimes they send enough to cover six months in advance. I never know what I'll get, or when. Just that sooner or later I'll be paid for exactly what I deliver."

"But back when all this began," The Man said, "there must have been someone who approached you."

"It was a long time ago," LaVerdiere said.

"Nevertheless. Tell me what you remember."

"A—a woman," LaVerdiere said. "A girl, really, but she looked older than she was. Like she burned the candle at both ends."

"More."

LaVerdiere chewed his lip, thinking. "Oh!" he said suddenly. "Didn't use an actual name. Called herself 'Sis.'"

The Man nodded, smiling.

"Sis," he said.

T he only way this day could be made worse—or so Bruce thought— had come to pass, and big goddamn surprise. First his boy had been basically kidnapped. Then he'd fucked up and got wasted again, though he'd sworn this morning that was it, he was cutting back for a while, and for real this time, no joke, no dicking around. Now, insult to injury, he'd blown the last two hours of his life watching the Red Sox get clobbered by the Angels. The house was empty and quiet with Jason gone and Bruce's wife, Sis, that whore, still nowhere to be found.

Bruce reclined on the couch with a plate of fish sticks and crinkle-cut fries, mostly eaten at this point, resting on his belly. A six-pack of Busch Light, three of its plastic rings hanging limp and empty, sat on the floor near at hand. When Bruce had lain down with his sticks it'd still been light out; now the only light in the room—in the whole house, actually—came from the TV screen, on which the Red Sox continued to flail and flounder and generally behave as though they'd never played baseball before in their lives, the bums.

A knock at the front door—three raps, quick and sharp, no-nonsense. What the hell? Bruce and Sis had visitors maybe twice a year, and certainly no one ever came around after dark. The only possibilities were nothing that interested Bruce: someone wanting signatures for some political bullshit he didn't know or care about, or, worse, those horrid Latter-Day Saints, looking to come in and drink two pots of coffee and talk his ear off about Jesus. Bruce had gotten more than his fill of that Holy Roller shit as a kid, thanks very much. He didn't move from the couch.

THUMP, THUMP, THUMP. Whoever it was, they were now using their fist to pound on the door so hard it sounded like it might splinter. Fueled by booze, Bruce's frustration flashed over in an instant, and he leaped from the couch, sending the plastic plate clattering to the floor. Muttering darkly, he stomped into the foyer in his stockinged feet and yanked the door open, ready to berate whoever stood there—then fell silent when he saw Babs, flanked by Carmeline, Stella, and Bernette, who each held an empty cardboard box.

"We have a new rule," Babs said. "No Sis, no Jason."

"Okay . . . ," Bruce said, his glance flitting from one face to another.

"I'm here for his things," Babs said.

"What things?"

"He'll stay with me whenever Sis isn't around."

"Why?"

"The boy's things, Bruce."

"But I—"

"Get out of our way."

"I'm just—"

"Moving," Babs said, shouldering him aside and entering the house. "You're just moving."

Still holding their boxes, the other ladies shoved past Bruce as he stood there, mute and impotent. Babs mounted the stairs to Jason's room, still talking as she climbed.

"Only thing Jason needs here is stuff," she said. "Socks. Undies. Baseball glove. He doesn't need you at all."

The stairs creaked and snapped as all five of them climbed, Bruce

pulling up the rear. A bare bulb above the landing cast their shadows, elongated and monstrous, against the wood-paneled wall of the
stairwell.

Jason's room was, to put it mildly, spartan. A poster of David
Ortiz taking a mighty hack, his heels twisting holes in the dirt, was
the sole wall decoration. A twin bed sat beneath the room's only
window, comforter and top sheet twisted up at the foot. Little dunes
of clothes dotted the floor—a hoodie sweatshirt and inside-out dun-
garees here, a couple dirty socks poking out from under a black
T-shirt there—and the top drawer of Jason's dresser hung open, ad-
vertising little bundles of clean socks folded into each other.

Babs turned to Bruce, who stood in the doorway.

"That boy is my charge," she said, "and there will be no more
harm on him. Not so much as a hair out of place. Do you understand?"

Bruce nodded as the ladies set about picking up Jason's clothes
and putting them in the boxes.

"Where's Sis?" Babs asked Bruce.

"I don't know."

"You hit her, too?"

"No!"

"Then why'd she leave?"

"You know how she is," Bruce said. "She leaves. She comes back.
Most of the time I have no idea why she's disappeared, let alone how
long she'll be gone."

"But this time you know why."

Bruce just looked at her, tried to get away with not responding.

"I'll ask you again: You use fists on my daughter?"

"No. I swear."

Babs turned her gaze to the ladies, who had finished up with the clothes on the floor and moved on to the dresser and closet. "I find out otherwise," she said, "then Sis won't need you, either. Jason doesn't need you, and if Sis don't? Well, then, no one does."

Bruce had a strong enough idea of what this meant.

Babs looked at him again. "Tell me about the last time you saw her."

"Monday," Bruce said, rubbing his forehead with one hand, eyes closed. "May have been Tuesday."

"May have been?"

"Babs. You know I drink."

"No kidding. I could smell you from the front porch." Babs took a breath to settle herself, and then: "Tell me what you remember for sure."

"It was late. She came home loaded, and we fought. Then she ran out."

"And you did nothing to her?"

"Just yelling."

"That's it?"

"Some cursing."

"Yelling and cursing. Nothing else."

"No, ma'am."

Babs squared up to Bruce and leaned in. "You don't even remember what night it was, but you expect me to believe you?"

Finished ransacking the room, Bernette and Stella pushed past Bruce without a word, their boxes overflowing with Jason's things. Carmeline, however, held back. She looked around, spotted the Ortiz poster, and decided that needed to go, too. She ripped it off the thumbtacks that held it to the wall, rolled it into a cylinder, and placed it on the top of her box. Then she followed the others out, sparing a sneer for Bruce on her way through.

Now Babs and Bruce were alone. She stepped close to him again, and though he was fully a head taller he shrank from her, pressing his back against the doorframe. Babs noticed a red stain just below the neck of his T-shirt, formerly white, now dingy, yellow under the arms. She put a finger to it.

"That ketchup?" she asked.

"Uh-huh."

"What's for dinner?"

"Fish sticks."

Babs smiled, but the smile did not touch her eyes. "Best get some bleach on that," she said. "Once it sets, it'll never come out."

"Yes, ma'am."

"It's like blood," she said. "Permanent."

"I—I'll take care of it."

"See that you do," Babs said. She backed off a step, but didn't follow the other ladies down the stairs, just stood there beside Bruce, looking around the room. Bruce didn't understand what, if anything, he could or should do or say but, not wanting to disturb what seemed like a sudden and likely fragile detente, he just stood looking around his son's room, wondering what it was they were supposed to be paying attention to—especially now, with most everything but the bed having been whisked away in a huff.

Finally, Babs broke the silence. "There's one more thing," she said.

Eager to accommodate—and move Babs along so he could get back to drinking—Bruce perked up. "Sure," he said. "Whatever you need, Babs."

She turned toward him again. "I want to make certain you understand," she said. "I'm taking Jay-Jay to make sure you don't beat on him in the future."

"Okay," Bruce said.

"But this is for the past."

Bruce was still trying to figure out what Babs meant even as he watched her pull the black nub of an expandable nightstick from her jacket. Only when she flicked her wrist and the nightstick snapped out to its full length did his brain make the association between the object and Babs's intent. But even if he'd been able or inclined to do something to protect himself, this realization came too late.

After, when glimpses of the beating tormented him through a haze of pain, Bruce would remember one thing with more clarity and insistence than any other: affixed to the tip of the baton was a silver disc about the diameter of a nickel, which bore the calligraphic, almost florid *S&W* logo of the Smith & Wesson armaments company.

And then the side of Bruce's neck exploded in pain, and he dropped to the floor of the bedroom, wailing like a kicked dog. Babs set upon him, straddling his waist and leaning down with the nightstick raised high overhead. Three whacks, five, blood beginning to flow and splatter, Bruce crying out for mercy and Babs completely deaf to his pleas, gone animal.

CHAPTER SEVEN

July 1, 2016

A junkie in her truck after nightfall, trying to stay clean for one lousy day. On her jaw a bruise, loose and baggy, from getting socked in the face by her own cousin a couple hours prior, a cousin she then condemned to a decade in prison on her mother's orders. Fuzzy-headed from the reappearance of a long-buried love and increasingly distressed by the disappearance of her sister. Grief seeping from her pores and a literal pharmacy on the bench seat beside her.

Not a good setup, but at least Lori wasn't entirely alone. Her dead friend and fellow Marine Sammy Menendez sat on the passenger side of the cab. Instead of field cammies, he was dressed in a Santa suit, complete with beard and bowl full of jelly. The sack of drugs rested on his red velvet lap, and he pulled out one bottle of pills after another, offering each to her in turn.

"Ooh, this sounds good," Sammy said, rattling a bottle like a maraca. "Side effects may include back pain, increased urination, and necrotizing fasciitis of the perineum."

Lori made a face.

"That's flesh-eating bacteria of the taint, in layman's terms," Sammy said.

"Yeah, figured that out myself, thank you."

"Not what you're in the market for?" As he dug through the sack again, Sammy's Santa beard slipped down, revealing the dark and bloodless hole in his cheek.

"I'm not 'in the market' for anything," Lori said.

"Sure you are. Why wouldn't you be? This mortal coil is a real bitch compared to what comes next."

"Yeah, I almost found out last night."

Sammy paused and looked at her. "Really."

"Really. Got some dope cut with too much fentanyl."

"That'll do it," Sammy said. "Look, I'm just trying to be helpful here. No one begrudges you taking the edge off a little bit."

"I can't keep doing this, Sammy. I've got to figure something else out."

He held up a bottle of Valium, eyebrows raised in hopeful inquiry.

"*No*, Sammy."

"I get it, not strong enough." He kept digging. "What is it you think you're going to 'figure out,' exactly?"

"I don't know. How to live a normal life?"

"Overrated," Sammy said. "Ill-defined. Plus, for people like you and me, impossible."

"Seeing as how you're dead," Lori said.

"Yes, in my case the impediments are somewhat more obvious. But how about you? You're sitting here in your truck with a busted face and a pillowcase full of stolen pharmaceuticals, talking to your dead war buddy. I'd say you're pretty far removed from normal life, at the moment."

"Fair enough," Lori said. "So what are my alternatives?"

"Next time you decide to OD, do it somewhere nice and private where no one will find you."

"You're telling me to kill myself."

"Not exactly," Sammy said. "I'm simply inviting you to consider that in your decision-making, you have an advantage most people don't—namely, access to the perspective of dead people. And *as* a dead person, I can tell you that life doesn't seem as great or precious as we all think when we're alive. In retrospect it seems like a real pain in the balls, mostly. The struggle and the hustle, having to take a shit twice a day every day. I spend a lot of time wondering why I didn't just belly flop onto the first IED I ever saw and get it over with."

"For what it's worth," Lori said, "there were moments when I considered tossing you onto an IED myself."

"No doubt," Sammy said, pawing through the drugs again.

"What's so great about being dead?"

Sammy didn't look up from the pillowcase. "Everything that's making you want to dry-swallow a bottle of pills right now?" he said. "The sadness, the desperation, the hope, the confusion, the love, the fear, the push and pull, the yearning to understand but never, ever understanding? It's all gone."

"Gone?"

"Well, not exactly," Sammy said. "Just in perspective. You feel plenty, it's just that none of it means much in the context of the in-conceivable miracle of simply being."

"So being dead is like being high for eternity. Is what you're saying."

"Forever and ever." Sammy made a face of exaggerated excitement and pulled a bottle out of the pillowcase. "Jackpot!" he said, holding it up for Lori to see. "Oxy."

Lori stared at him, at the bottle. She nodded, and Sammy handed it over. At that moment Lori's phone rang, and she dropped the pills in Sammy's lap as if they were hot to the touch.

"I'm sitting in my room at the Hampton Inn," Shawn said on the other end, "with only a bottle of bourbon to keep me company."

"Sounds like a lousy blues song," Lori said.

"It's been one long lousy blues song ever since you shipped out."

"Uh-huh."

"Room 304," Shawn said.

Lori thought a moment. "I've got a stop to make," she said, "then I'll swing by."

She hung up. Sammy had disappeared, and the bottle of Oxy sat atop the pillowcase. Lori looked at it, then opened the glove box and threw the bottle in.

A t Sunnybrook Retirement Home, all was quiet as night came on: dinner had been served and cleaned up, evening activity time had come and gone, and as they did every night at 7 p.m., lights in the common areas had dimmed automatically to half their daytime wattage. Per facility policy, all residents were in their rooms, and the half dozen or so inclined to scream through the night had been sedated. Everything, and everyone, in its place.

In room 208, Chief Bates sat at the bedside of his wife, Melinda. She lay gaunt and pale, far gone with early-onset dementia, eyes locked on the television. Most of the time, these days, Melinda was lost entirely in the nightmare wilderness of her failing mind. But she still could readily summon every correct question in an episode of *Jeopardy!*, despite not having any idea of who or where she was. For years she'd been a reluctant parlor trick for their children, who would bring their friends around to marvel at the seemingly limitless knowledge that floated loose in their mother's brain, until Bates convinced her to actually go on the show in 1994. She'd been a five-time champion, sweeping her opponents aside like cookie crumbs and making the last round of that year's Tournament of Champions, which she lost because of a bad gamble in Final Jeopardy.

Thus had her *Jeopardy!* career ended, but even after she stopped recognizing people she'd lived with for decades and developed a habit of scooping glasses of drinking water from the toilet, even after she moved to Sunnybrook and spent most of her days bedbound and semi-catatonic, with a feeding tube the only thing tethering her to life, Melinda still could blast through an entire episode without missing one question. As she did now, with Bates at her bedside.

The show went to commercial break, and Bates, not for the first time, fantasized about kicking off his one shoe and crawling under the covers with his wife and getting the first decent night's sleep he'd had since moving her to the home more than a year prior. But this, of course, was not possible; even if regulations allowed it, which they did not, the chance was too great that Melinda would wake at some point and see not her husband but a stranger in bed beside her.

So instead Bates's thoughts turned to home, which was not without its comforts, however meager. He'd made a pretty good one-pot penne rosa, and had a bottle of Pinot Noir in the pantry to go with it. He'd recorded the first two hours of the Sox game and could, as was his habit, watch it from the beginning and catch up to the live action by skipping commercials. In the cabinet over the kitchen sink he kept a bottle of twelve-year Macallan, a healthy slug from which almost guaranteed two or three hours of sleep. The only problem was that big, empty bed. He could never fill it, or keep it warm on his own, and so most nights he slept in his clothes on the couch, a throw blanket Melinda had knitted twenty years prior pulled over him.

As the commercial break came to an end, Melinda sat up and, in a sudden panic, tried to extricate herself from the bedcovers. Bates had seen this dozens of times, and he rose calmly from his seat and rested his hands on Melinda's shoulders to get her attention. She stopped struggling and looked up at him, her eyes sparking with panic.

"What's the matter, darling?" Bates asked.

"I forgot Daryl and Missy at school! I have to pick them up!"

"Darling," Bates said, stroking Melinda's shoulder, "Daryl and Missy haven't been in school for years."

But Melinda ignored this. Her eyes darted to the clock on the nightstand. "It's almost seven thirty! I was supposed to be there five hours ago!"

"Melinda. Look at me."

"But I—"

"Look at me, darling."

She did, her mouth and chin trembling, able to contain her anxiety with only the most wrenching effort.

"The kids aren't stuck at school," Bates told her. "Daryl Jr. is in Atlanta, with Kate and the kids. Our grandchildren. Missy . . . well, who the hell knows what Missy's up to. But one thing I know for sure is she's not at school. Okay?"

He looked into his wife's eyes, hoping yet knowing better than to hope. This was their marriage now: Bates trying over and over to relieve the terror of Melinda remembering herself, always in vain. Still, for a moment it seemed as though his words were almost getting through. Melinda held his gaze, searching the contours of his face for the information that would tell her where and who she was.

But then her eyes darkened and narrowed slightly, and Bates bowed his head, knowing what came next.

"Who are you?" Melinda said. "Get your hands off me!"

Bates did as his wife ordered, releasing his grip on her shoulders and standing upright. He gazed down at her as she continued to scream, and an observer might have thought he looked sad and hopeless, but Bates hadn't felt sad or hopeless for a long time. What he felt was beyond those two things, beyond even despair. What he felt was akin to what he imagined it would be like to stare into a black hole.

"Why are you here?" Melinda demanded to know. "Who are you? Get out! Get out!"

A nurse came into the room at a trot, but Bates was already on his way out the door. "I'll just go," he said to the nurse. "This isn't going to get better if I stick around."

The nurse went to Melinda, and Bates made his way down the hall toward the exit. His phone started ringing in its holster just as he reached the door and stepped out into the humidity that lingered in the night's stillness.

"Bates."

"We've got a problem, Chief." It was Farley. "Somebody came sniffing around Doc LaVerdiere earlier tonight."

"What does that mean, exactly?" Bates asked.

"Not sure. He called us in a panic. I'm headed there now."

"This is the last fucking thing I need," Bates muttered, more to himself than Farley.

"Chief? How you want me to handle this?"

Bates snapped back to himself. "No one but you talks to the doc. I'll meet you there. And, Farley? No paperwork. No recording. Nothing."

CHAPTER EIGHT

July 1, 2016

Lori walked into Babs's house to find her mother and Jason sitting together on the floor in the living room, surrounded by the detritus of a take-out pizza dinner, box flopped open and grease-stained paper plates and bits of gnawed crust, laughing and playing *Sneak King* on the Xbox. Babs looked up as Lori came into the living room doorway, the bag of pills slung over her shoulder.

"We happy?" Babs asked in French.

"We're happy," Lori said.

"Tim?"

"Singing 'Jailhouse Rock' by now, I would imagine."

Babs nodded toward Lori's swollen face. "Looks like he took some convincing," she said.

"I broke his hand for him," Lori said in French.

"Good girl."

Lori turned toward the TV. "I see you're playing *Sneak King*."

"Jason's teaching his *mémère* a lesson," Babs said.

"Careful, Jay," Lori said. "You don't want to make her mad."

"Go put those up in the kitchen cabinet," Babs said to Lori in French.

A minute later Lori came back without the pillowcase and wedged her way in between her mother and nephew.

"Anything from Sis?" Lori asked in French.

"No," Babs said. "But I paid Bruce a visit."

"And?"

"He took a bit of convincing, too."

Lori flashed her mother a *what-the-fuck* face.

"Have some pizza," Babs said, turning her attention back to the game.

But Lori didn't take her eyes off Babs. "What about Rita?"

"Rita's not someone I'm concerned about at the moment," Babs said, mashing buttons and sticks more or less at random, with predictably dismal results. "If you want to check in on her, be my guest."

"Not tonight. I've got a thing."

Lori snagged a piece of pizza, and Babs patted her shoulder once, lightly, and plopped the controller in her lap.

"Your turn, Aunt Lore," Jason said.

Lori took a big bite of pizza and put the rest of the slice back in the box. "Now don't take this personally, Jay-Jay," she said. "I've got no choice but to beat you down."

"Big talk," Jason said, starting his turn in the game.

"I don't want to," Lori said. "I hope you know that. It's just the sooner you learn there's no mercy in this family, the better off you'll be."

Half an hour later, Babs walked Lori to her truck, despite the fact that Lori had asked her repeatedly not to. She didn't want to have any private conversation with Babs, let alone the one she knew was coming.

"Thanks for dealing with Tim," Babs said, a step behind Lori on the walkway.

Lori reached the curb and turned, one hand on the door handle of the truck. "I'd say it was my pleasure, but . . ."

Babs stopped and looked at her daughter squarely. "If I get a copy of the pharmacy's inventory list, will everything be there?" she asked.

Lori didn't flinch. "Can't say for certain," she said. "Junkies lie."

"They do," Babs said, her gaze steady. "Indeed they do."

"Ma, I'm not in the mood for beating around the bush, so why don't you just say what you have to say."

"I heard about last night," Babs told her.

"Yeah, I heard a story, too," Lori said. "About some crazy old bag who put a beating on her son-in-law."

"The family needs you."

Lori pointed to the bruise on her face. "I'm here."

"This is the last time we're going to have this discussion," Babs said. "I don't care what you have to do. Just clean it up."

Lori let her hand drop from the door handle and took a step toward her mother. "You ever have this conversation with Sis?" she asked. "About how the family needs her?"

"When your sister comes up for air, she'll get her talking-to, same as always," Babs said. "Besides, I expect her to be a fuckup. You, I have to be able to count on."

"Well, I've got news for you, Ma. I'm not here so you can *count on me*. I'm not here for *you* at all. I'm here to protect everyone else *from* you."

At this, Babs's air of cool authority slipped just a little. "What the hell does that mean?" she asked.

"In Afghanistan there are tribal feuds that go back a thousand years," Lori said. "These people have been at it since there were only sticks and rocks to kill each other with. Sometimes the conflicts are hot, and sometimes they go quiet for decades. But no one ever makes the mistake of thinking they're over."

"That's all very interesting," Babs said, "but I don't see what it has to do with this discussion."

"Three years of my life, I spent there—"

"*Against* my wishes and advice."

"Three years, Ma, and I learned exactly one thing, something you still don't understand: that violence only begets violence. Maybe not today, maybe not next month. But it always, always comes back around. Despite what Father Clement would tell you, no one ever forgives, and no one ever forgets."

"Still not seeing your point. And I have to get back inside."

"Then let me spell it out: if you beat on Bruce, you might as well be hitting Jason with your own hand."

Babs scoffed and turned away, walking back toward her front steps.

"How many people have to break themselves against you before you figure it out, Ma?" Lori called after her. "And now Sis is missing. She's ducking you. I don't know why. But she is."

Babs stopped halfway up the steps and turned, sheathed once more in a calm that bordered on indifference.

"You came back," Babs said. "So will she. Jay is safe, and that's what matters. Go do your thing, whatever it is. Tomorrow, we'll find your sister."

An hour later, Lori and Shawn lay together in his hotel room, still a touch breathless, his and hers whiskey glasses in hand and a bottle of Wild Turkey on the nightstand. They'd fallen into bed pretty much the moment Lori walked in the door, and as such had barely spoken until now.

"Was it good for you?" Shawn asked.

"Hard to say. It's been so long I've got no frame of reference."

"Should I ask what happened to your face?" Shawn said.

"No." Lori sipped her whiskey.

"I assume the other guy looks worse."

"The other guy's my cousin, and he's in County."

Shawn shook his head, scooting back against the headboard to pour another drink. "You Dionnes," he said. "Still crazy after all these years."

"You don't know the half of it," Lori said. She held her glass out for more and Shawn obliged, splashing in a couple of fingers over the ice. "How's your father doing?"

"Couple more weeks. Maybe a month. According to the hospice nurse. She said, and this is a quote, 'It's hard to know, until you know.' Whatever that means."

"You're staying here? However long it takes?"

Shawn switched his glass to his left hand and allowed his right to trace a gentle path along the length of Lori's arm. "I'm as comfortable at the Hampton Inn as I am at my own home. Which is to say, not very."

"Seems like you've built a nice little life for yourself," Lori said. "With a fine watch collection."

"Fuck you very much."

They both smiled, and for a moment they were quiet, contemplating the bottoms of their drinks.

"So what are you running from, exactly?" Lori asked.

"You're direct as ever."

"That the question is rude and presumptuous doesn't relieve your obligation to answer it."

Shawn gazed at her for a beat, amused and bemused in equal measure; Lori could see the gears turning in his head as he determined what to tell her, what percentage of his words should be the truth. Finally, he looked away across the room and took a breath.

"It's not what I'm running from," he said. "It's what I'm running *to*. My therapist tells me—"

"Your *therapist*?"

"Yeah." He glanced at her again. "What. Doesn't everyone have a therapist these days?"

Lori held her glass up. "Around here, we prefer to deal with our issues the old-fashioned way."

"And how's that working out for you?"

"Swimmingly. Isn't it obvious?"

Shawn chuckled, drank. "What happened to you over there, Lore?"

"*Non*. Nope. Negative. You're not going to think of or treat me like some sad-sack PTSD case."

"Aren't you?"

"Sure. But that's not the point."

"Is that when you started seeing ghosts?" he asked.

"I don't *see* ghosts. They're just *there*. But to answer your question, yes. The dead started appearing to me when I woke up in the hospital at Ramstein. My buddy Sammy was sitting there waiting for me to come around. He had taken a round in the face the same time I got hurt. Dead as a doornail. But there he was, wanting to chat."

"Okay," Shawn said. "But how did you know he was really there?"

"I didn't," Lori said. "I assumed I was fucking cracked. I told the doctors, and they said 'Yeah, makes sense, you've got a bruise on your occipital lobe, might clear up, might be seeing things the rest of your life.' So I left the hospital thinking I couldn't believe my lying eyes. Sammy following me around everywhere I went, insisting he was real, going on and on about how he didn't blame me."

"Fun."

"Barrel of monkeys," Lori said. "But at least I had the comfort of knowing I was nuts."

"And then . . ."

"And then it kept happening. I get up one morning and find a boot from my squad named Lincoln—"

"Boot?"

"Fresh out of boot camp. Doesn't know shit."

"Got it."

"So there's Lincoln sitting in my living room, and he's got one of his forearms, which is severed at the elbow, sitting in his lap. He's talking about how it's my fault he's dead, how if I'd been around he wouldn't have touched that teapot."

"So?"

"So last I knew, Lincoln was alive and well and still in-country. I get the call later that day that he's gotten his arm blown off clearing a house in Kandahar. Like a boot, he touched something in the kitchen that was wired. Bled out on scene."

Shawn had turned pale. "Oh."

"Then, two months later, same thing. This time my lieutenant's sitting on the front step, watching kids play in the street. Shrapnel holes all through him. When the phone rang the next day, I knew what it was."

"So if I'm following," Shawn said, "the thesis is your brain injury made it so the dead manifested to you."

"No. The brain injury made it possible for me to know they were there. But they're everywhere, all the time. You carry your dead around with you, too. And if someone clocked you in the head with a two-by-four, or if you had a stroke or got hit by lightning or whatever, you might start seeing them."

Shawn had no idea how to respond to that. So he just waited, while Lori pressed the cold of the whiskey glass against her sore jaw.

"There are whole worlds above and below and inside of us all the time, Shawn. Someone a lot smarter than me could probably explain the physics. All I know for sure is that like the man said, the past isn't dead. It's not even past."

"So if that's true," Shawn said, "then how do you live? How do you move into the future?"

"If I knew the answer to that question," Lori said, "I would not be here in purgatory with the rest of the lost souls."

Shawn sat silent for a moment, then lifted the bottle again and drank straight from the neck. This had the desired effect—Lori laughed, briefly but genuinely, as much out of frustration and loneliness as amusement.

"You understand," Shawn said, coughing and wiping his mouth with the back of one hand, "that this is extremely hard to believe. But I believe it, because you're you."

"Because I'm me?"

"Yes. If you tell me something is true, then it's true."

"That's a terrifying amount of faith to live up to."

"Sure is."

Lori put her head back and sighed, stretching her legs and arms in an effort to get the junkie tension to leave her muscles. "Still think you want to get back together?" she asked.

"I mentioned my therapist," Shawn said.

"Indeed you did."

"She says I'm the easiest patient she's ever had. Gives me the same advice every week."

"I'm sort of afraid to ask."

"Don't bother, because I'm about to tell you."

"Shawn—"

"She says that if I have recurring dreams of loss and grief featuring the same person for a decade, it's her clinical opinion that I should at least try to get that person back in my life."

Lori set her glass on the nightstand and rolled onto her side, away from him. She pulled the comforter up over her shoulder. "I can't go there right now," she said. "I need to get some sleep."

"What you need is to get away from this place," Shawn said. "Come with me to Boston."

He hadn't even finished before Lori tossed the covers and got to her feet, pulling on clothes as she found them.

"Lore," Shawn said. "Wait. Slow down. What . . . don't put your panties on over your jeans, for God's sake."

But Lori wasn't laughing. "If you want to get back at me, there are less elaborate ways of doing it," she said, scanning the carpet for a missing sock.

"What are you talking about?"

"I broke your heart," Lori said. "With reckless indifference. Guilty as charged. So if you want to settle accounts—"

"Wait a minute," Shawn said. He set his glass on the nightstand and stood to face her. "You didn't break my heart. You broke a *promise*.

You destroyed any belief I had that people could be taken at their word. So don't trivialize it by talking about broken hearts, like this is some goddamn Hallmark movie."

"And I'm sorry, Shawn. Add it to the list of things I'd change if I could. But what you're doing, it's just cruel."

"Offering you a way out? Is cruel?"

"Yes. Why are you doing it?"

"Because I'm still in love with you," Shawn said. "This is real. I knew the moment I saw you this morning. Fucked-up as you are."

Having located the rogue sock, Lori stopped dead and stared at Shawn. "I'm going to tell you something you obviously need to hear," she said. "Listen, and let it sink in: you're not in love with me."

"No?"

"No. You're in love with the memory of a person who never existed."

"That'll be news to my therapist," Shawn said.

Lori stepped into her boots and grabbed her keys from the nightstand. "If it appears I'm getting smaller," she said, "it's because I'm leaving."

"Very clever," Shawn said. "Gonna go out for a little joyride, upset and with a head full of whiskey?"

"I'm fine."

"You're fine. Well, do me a favor, if you would, and be sure to put it in park before you fix."

"Fuck you, Shawn." She moved toward the door.

"I'll say it again, Lori. You need to get out of this place."

Lori paused, her hand on the doorknob. "What I need is time to think," she said.

"The way it looks from here," Shawn told her, "you don't have much time left."

CHAPTER NINE

July 1, 2016

With Jason in bed and asleep, Babs took the pillowcase full of drugs from the cabinet and went out her front door. She hadn't locked up for forty years, and even with Jason at the house she didn't bother to throw the dead bolt now, because no one in Little Canada would be foolish enough to cross her threshold without explicit invitation. The night air hung still as death, so humid that Babs's face bore a sheen by the time she reached her car. Just as she was about to get in, Bates's Lincoln Continental glided to a stop at the end of her driveway, and the chief stepped out and limped toward her.

"I know I've said this before," Babs said as he approached, "but it bears repeating: you couldn't have picked a personal vehicle that screams 'I'm a cop' any louder than that thing."

"You're assuming I don't want people to know I'm a cop," Bates said, adjusting his eye patch.

"I thought you were going to spend time with your wife."

"I did."

"She remember who you are?"

"She remembered Alex Trebek."

"Well, in fairness, he *is* unforgettable. That mustache, my goodness."

"Listen," Bates said, "we have a problem. Someone put a scare into LaVerdiere tonight."

Babs felt something unfamiliar in her chest—a jolt of worry. "Why is that our problem, and not his?"

"The good doctor was spooked enough to call us. But by the time we arrived, he remembered he was neck-deep in a drug ring and clammed up. Claimed it was a simple B&E."

"And how do you know it wasn't?"

"No B," Bates told her. "Whoever it was waltzed right in—and didn't take a thing. Here's the weird part, though: LaVerdiere said the guy sounded Canadian."

"French, or English?" Babs asked.

"English, I assume."

Babs opened the back door of her car and tossed the pillowcase in. "Of course," she said. "But I'm still not seeing how this is our problem."

"Whoever this is, he's got LaVerdiere shitting kittens. He knows about the fake scripts. This—"

"Did LaVerdiere say that, or are you just assuming?"

Bates looked at her. "I'm *surmising*, based on thirty years of experience in investigative work."

Babs smiled. "Well, then. I defer to your superior skill in making shit up based on incomplete information."

"This person is powerful, connected. And he's not after LaVerdiere. He's after *you*."

"More surmising?"

"Yes," Bates said. "And you'd do well to listen to me."

Now Babs opened her driver's-side door. "Let's say I believe your theory, and this guy is using the doctor to find out who's behind the local pharmaceutical trade. That means he's after *us*, Chief."

"Why do you think I'm here at ten o'clock on a school night?"

"Just making sure you understand we're in this together," Babs said. "Listen, I have to go. It's not getting any earlier, and my grandson's inside sleeping."

"One more thing," Bates said. "We pinched Tim."

"I know. I let you."

"When we picked him up all the drugs were gone, except for half a bottle of Dilaudid. Isn't that curious?"

Babs stared at Bates, then got into her car, turned toward the back seat, and rummaged through the pillowcase. After a minute she reemerged and held a prescription bottle out to him.

"Now how did my eye medication end up in your possession, pray tell?" Bates asked.

"Call it Christmas in July," Babs said. "And stop asking questions. Now if you'll excuse me, I have some stolen property to return."

Bates turned and limped back toward his Lincoln. "Get your ear to the ground, Babs. We need to find this person before he finds us."

Babs said nothing, just watched Bates clamber into the driver's seat and pull away. When he turned left and his taillights disappeared, she looked around the darkened neighborhood, went back up her walkway, mounted the stairs, and checked each of the four porch windows to make sure they were locked. Then, with no small amount of fumbling, she located the key that she believed locked the front door. She slipped it into the keyhole and, after jimmying it a few times, managed to get the tumblers to dislodge from where they'd sat for four decades, and threw the dead bolt. Only then did she return to her car and set out to deliver prescriptions to Little Canada's residents.

ori drove aimlessly through Waterville's downtown, high as God
from the ninety milligrams of Oxy she'd crushed and snorted on
the dash of her truck after leaving Shawn's room. She weaved between centerline and sidewalk, even bumping the curb, as she fum-
bled with a pack of cigarettes over the steering wheel. Because of
Babs's relationship with the police, Lori could have crashed through
the front window of Stearns Clothing Store and not gotten sent up
on DUI charges, but all the same, between the whiskey and the Oxy
and the upset and the general fatigue that lingered from having died
the previous night, she knew she should probably point the truck
toward home.

Instead she pointed the truck toward the bridge over the Kennebec River, less than a football field upstream from the brick-and-
mortar corpse of the Hollingsworth & Whitney compound. This
bridge had witnessed eighty years of log drives, the transition from
trolley to automobile, hand-to-hand combat between Franco strikers
and Pinkertons, and every roll of newsprint the mill had relentlessly
produced over a century. It had also seen twenty-three suicides since
its erection in the late 1800s, including those of three members of
Lori's family—most recently her great-uncle Paul, who'd leaped into
the hydroelectric turbines after his corner store went bankrupt in
1993. Lori drove across the span of all this history, climbed the steep
incline on the opposite side of the bridge, and continued out into the
winding darkness of the hills.

eanwhile, Babs made her second stop of the evening, at Kelly
Dupont's house on Carrean Street. Kelly lived alone with her
two girls and had served breakfast at the Villager restaurant down-

town for eight years, since she'd dropped out of high school at six-teen. The younger of her kids was diabetic, type 1, bad, and that was what brought Babs to Kelly's doorstep. She knocked, waited, knocked again, and after another minute the curtain in the front door win-dow slid aside, and Babs saw an eye on the other side of the glass. The curtain snapped back into place and the locks opened one after the other and Kelly stood before her in a dingy nightgown, the youn-ger of her girls peering up at Babs from behind Kelly's leg.

"*Bonsoir, petite Émilie*," Babs said to the girl. Emily smiled but tucked herself a little more securely behind her mother.

"Am I in trouble?" Kelly asked.

"Not in the least," Babs said. She handed over two boxes of rapid-acting insulin. "I'm just here to drop these off," she said.

Kelly looked at the boxes, then back up at Babs. "Oh my god," she said. "Thank you."

"You can thank me by getting that child to bed," Babs said, walking back toward her car.

L ori sped along the cracked and rutted asphalt of the North Pond Road, every dip and bend of which she still knew by heart from high school. When her cousin Carrie lived on Pattee's Pond, the two of them would cruise the country roads for hours, ripping Camel Lights and listening to N.W.A so loud they couldn't hear for hours after. Toward the end of the North Pond Road, where it formed a T-intersection with Route 202, lay a steep, sudden rise that leveled off right before the stop sign. Immediately after Lori got her driver's license, she and Carrie had identified the rise as perfect for catching air, and they must have done so five hundred times or more. Eventu-ally just jumping the rise wasn't enough; as with drugs and money, it took ever more to get the same effect, so they started making the jump at night with the headlights off. Eighty miles an hour, pitch-black, knowing the rise was coming but not when, and that was the key to the whole thing, the inevitability of *what* crossed with the uncertainty of *when*. Eyes straining against the dark, muscles tensed, and amygdala blaring a primordial alarm, feeling your stomach drop to your feet as the front wheels hit the incline and then, an instant later, feeling gravity give way, your self still intact and alive but suddenly without mass, floating in the night like ground fog. For about two seconds.

This was the feeling Lori sped toward now, as she slingshotted through one last long turn before the straightaway that led to the rise. She almost lost it on the gravel shoulder at the outside of the turn, then yanked the truck back to the right, hit the accelerator, and clicked off the headlights about two hundred yards out. She knew well that in her current state, driving blind, she could easily drift off the road and into the ditch before ever reaching the incline, but that was a bargain she and Carrie had been comfortable with long ago, and certainly she didn't feel as though she had more to live for now than she had then.

She wasn't afraid to go into the ditch and become one with a tree trunk but she also did not *want* that to happen, so she leaned forward into the steering wheel with her hands at ten and two, straining to see the edges of the road in the minuscule light from a moon banked by thick clouds. The speedometer needle trembled around eighty-five, pretty much the top end for the old F-150 but plenty for Lori's purposes. The ground beneath her wheels stayed smooth and level. The truck was chewing up space at near 125 feet a second, and she was too close to miss at this point. Any moment now.

And then she saw something. A figure in the road, the outline of which was just barely discernible in the contrast between the black of the road and the charcoal of the sky. Though it happened so fast that, afterward, Lori would not remember seeing anything. All she would recall was her hands torquing the wheel to the right, almost of their own accord, the same way your hand jumps back from a flame well before the burning registers in your brain. The old Goodyears she never bothered to rotate screamed as the brakes locked up and the truck yawed perpendicular to the roadway. The truck sideways now on the right shoulder, its momentum continued forward, and there was nothing left for Lori to do, no movie-stuntman driving finesse that could alter one bit what happened between now and when she finally, one way or another, came to a stop. So she waited. She waited for the impact with what- or whoever she'd seen in the road. When that didn't happen, she waited for the truck to flip, as it seemed inclined to do. When that didn't happen, she waited for the sudden and catastrophic deceleration that occurs when speeding vehicle meets glacial erratic boulder. But instead the truck just plowed through grass and underbrush, trembling and shimmying and slowing gradually enough for both it and Lori to survive mostly unscathed.

She sat there in the sudden quiet, a fixed point once more on the hurtling Earth, knowing yet doubting that she was still alive. The volume had been turned up so loud on her senses that she could feel the dust from the spinout drift in through the open windows and settle on her face and arms. She listened to herself breathe for a few moments. Then she popped the glove box, dry-swallowed another Oxy, grabbed the Maglite, and followed the twirling furrows her tires had cut through the grass until she reached pavement.

Though she'd neither felt nor heard a collision, she was still afraid of what the flashlight would reveal in the road. Something had been there, of that she was certain. And whatever it was, it had been alive. She traced the flashlight beam back and forth, shoulder to shoulder—nothing, mercifully, just rocks and dirt, an iced tea bottle, a fallen tree branch. She caught her breath when the light fell on a long narrow thing, sinewy and limp—cat? *child*?—but further scrutiny revealed just an old weather-beaten flannel, tossed from someone's car a lifetime ago. As Lori scanned up the slope of the hill and found only more detritus, a flap of blown tire, a plastic grocery bag, she began to wonder if she'd imagined it after all, if the only thing that had been in the road was some phantom bit of mental projection. Certainly it wouldn't have been the first time her mind had played convincing tricks on her. But then she moved the beam to the crest of the hill and, finally, saw the fox.

She was, in every way, a typical fox. Reddish-brown fur. Upright ears tapering to sharp points. Eyes like a cat's. She sat in the road, exactly where Lori had first spotted her, a chicken hanging dead from her mouth and her long tail wrapped casually around her back legs like a feather boa. Placid as the Buddha himself. Hadn't moved at all, even when Lori's truck had come within inches of crushing her.

The fox squinted in the beam of the flashlight, but her gaze on Lori was steady. Calm. Knowing, somehow. She dropped the chicken from her jaws, seeming to forget it even before it hit the roadway. Lori felt not just seen but exposed by the animal's gaze, as if the fox were God Herself, but a different God from the one she'd learned about at Notre Dame Parish. This fox-god saw and knew all, just like the God she'd been instructed to believe in, but unlike Him the fox judged nothing. Her power and purpose was simply to observe and, in doing so, reveal Lori to herself in her entirety. All the things she knew she was—woman, daughter, addict, Marine, killer—but also the things she had forgotten or thought dead: lover. Hero. Seeker and seer. A human being who, like the song said, wanted to do right— just not right now.

All these people encased in one form called "Lori," an upright bag of meat made only to suffer, utterly alone in the dark of a country road, staring at a fox.

Lori sat cross-legged on the shoulder and clicked off the flashlight. When her eyes adjusted to the dark she found the fox again, and the two of them sat considering one another for a long time.

H aving returned all but one prescription to every person in Little Canada who needed it, Babs found herself on the evening's final doorstep. She'd come here to offer something, but also to ask for something. It was late but, she hoped, not too late.

She rang the doorbell and waited. Time passed. Eventually the porch light blazed to life overhead, and like Lori, Babs was struck with the feeling of being suddenly exposed. The door opened, and Father Clement stood before her with a rocks glass in hand, dressed casually in shorts and a T-shirt emblazoned with the logo of something called the MARIE JOSEPH SPIRITUAL CENTER. His legs, which Babs realized she'd never seen before, were hairless and pale as alabaster, almost translucent, shot through with purple spider veins.

"I don't normally take confession after two bourbons," Father Clement said.

"Go ahead and pour a third," Babs said, "because I'm not here for confession."

"God can wait forever, Babs," Father Clement said, a smile playing at the corners of his mouth. "You can't."

Instead of responding, Babs held out the last prescription bottle. Clement took it in his free hand and squinted at the label. "Thanks," he said. "I was starting to wonder how long I could expect to survive without this."

"Maybe you should have been my first stop instead of my last."

Father Clement shrugged, smiling again. Neither of them spoke for a few moments. He gazed at Babs, and though he felt old as Moses his eyes were still sharp from fifty years in the priesthood, and he saw clearly that Babs was wrestling with herself. Finally, he raised his eyebrows in inquiry: *You got something you want to tell me about?*

Babs, who otherwise kept her own counsel without fail, relented as she always did with Clement: "Sis is missing," she said.

He looked at her a moment longer, then stepped aside and swept one arm toward the interior of his home. "Let's have a drink," he said.

Only three blocks away, Lori lurched into her driveway, killed the engine, and made her way inside without turning off the truck's headlights. First things first: the one-two combo of whiskey and another Oxy. Then she would set about packing her things, or at least the things she would need to get the hell away from Waterville and her family and Shawn as quickly and seamlessly as possible, which amounted to clothes, boots and running shoes, the USMC Dopp kit she'd had since graduating from Basic, and the go-bag she'd kept for nearly as long: KA-BAR knife, cordage and tarp and other gear for camping, compass and maps, enough MREs to eat for a week, a Glock 19, wide-spectrum antibiotics and other first aid, and ten thousand dollars cash. Everything else she'd filled this house with over the last eight months she neither wanted nor needed.

Lori tossed her keys on the end table in the foyer and marched into the kitchen, so focused on washing down an Oxy with a slug of booze that she had the whiskey poured and the glass to her lips before she finally noticed Sis sitting at the kitchen table.

Lori froze. Choked. Nearly coughed up the whiskey and the pill, then fought them back down as her fright curdled almost instantly into anger.

"Where the hell have you been?" she said, wiping her mouth with a rumpled dish towel next to the sink.

Sis remained hunched and silent, her hair covering her face. Didn't move. Didn't even glance up. Which meant she was, of course, blotto. She was also a mess, her hair matted and wet, her flannel shirt stained burgundy around the shoulders and chest like some kind of Rorschach inkblot. Lori left the kitchen, returning a few minutes later with a suitcase and her go-bag, a battered Marine-issue duffel from her first deployment. She glared at Sis, who sat with her head down.

"Babs is ready to kill you," Lori said. She dropped the bags on the linoleum and poured more whiskey for herself, then sat opposite Sis at the table. "*Bonsoir?* Are you loaded?"

More silence in response.

"Listen to me," Lori said. "That husband of yours hit Jay-Jay again. So whatever's going on, you need to shake it off and get your ass home."

Not a sound. No movement. Lori couldn't even be sure her sister was breathing. And this made her angry.

"*J'ai mon voyage!*" Lori said. "Hey asshole, can you hear me? Bruce beat the shit out of Jason. Does that matter to you at all?"

Finally, Sis lifted her face, and what Lori saw there extinguished her anger like a match dropped in water. This woman, her kid sister, who she loved with all possible ferocity, was broken. A toddler's plastic toy, smashed to colorful shards in a dirt driveway. Eyes mournful, the corners of her mouth turned down and the skin under her bottom lip bunched as if she was about to cry. This wasn't just upsetting to Lori, but alarming. One thing that had always been true—and sometimes infuriating—about Sis was how cheerful she remained no matter how grim the circumstance. This pathetic creature, Lori hardly recognized as her sister.

"Hey," she said. She heaved a sigh and stood up. "Listen. Let's get you onto the couch. You can sleep it off here tonight. But tomorrow you're going home to take care of your son. All right?"

Lori thought that encouragement and tenderness might break through where haranguing had failed. But Sis's expression, an eerie combination of despair and vacancy, remained unchanged. It was as if her sister were at the bottom of a well so deep that sound could not reach her, and she'd been down there so long she'd lost any hope of rescue. And now fear pricked the warm amniotic bubble of intoxication that had served so well for so long as Lori's solace. Which meant another drink was in order, just as soon as she got Sis tucked in on the sleeper sofa. Lori could always leave first thing in the morning, after she had a chance to gauge Sis's state in the light of day.

She reached down, meaning to help Sis to her feet—but her hand, instead of grasping flannel and flesh, passed right through Sis's forearm.

A second passed. Two. The moment after that lasted a year. Or perhaps forever. Impossible to know, because time ceased to have meaning, even meaning ceased to have meaning, everything in Lori's head that could properly be called a thought blown away like an old barn in a twister, replaced by one high endless screeching note of horror, horror beyond language and thus beyond comprehension or utterance, the same ancient, adrenal horror experienced by the lobster held over a roiling pot, the elk when the wolf's teeth sink in, the Marine pinned down by automatic fire in a shallow mortar hole, trying to press herself into and somehow through the dirt, screaming in tongues for deliverance. Horror eternal, unchanged by millennia, and if you should ever be lucky enough to feel it yourself you will know, finally and forever, what it is to be truly alive.

Lori dropped to her knees. "Oh God, Sis," she said. "Oh, please, no."

And Sis continued to stare at Lori silently, tears glimmering now in her eyes.

PART TWO

PRÉLUDE

September 11, 2001

B abs had never forgiven being shoved in a closet for three hours in grade school for the crime of talking in French with her first boyfriend, Remy LaCroix. She had never forgiven being forced to write *I will not speak French in class* on the blackboard until the chalk in her fingers eroded to a nub. The intervening decades had done nothing to diminish the sting of the strap against her knuckles and backside. She never stopped speaking her language, and she never stopped being punished for it.

So when it came time for her own children to go to school, K–8 they attended Babs's Elementary, classes for which took place in an oversize shed Rheal had built in the backyard for that purpose.

"The public school serves the public," Babs told them. "Which means it serves a system. And systems need conforming rows of graded minds. Minds that only think about the right things, and fast. *You* will have slow, deep, dangerous-thinking minds."

When Babs had other things to attend to, Lori and Sis were given lesson plans and reading assignments and were expected to complete their work without supervision. On this morning, Lori had been

writing a history paper on the expulsion of the Acadians from northern Maine, and Sis was half-assing sentence diagrams in Quebecois,
when their older brother, Jean, a senior at the high school, threw
open the door to the shed and told them to come inside the house.

Jean offered no explanation for what he was doing home from
school, but as soon as he parked them in front of the television the
explanation became obvious, if unfathomable and terrifying. Now
they all three sat silent, watching smoke so thick it looked like liquid
pour from fiery gashes in the sides of two buildings in New York
City, a place none of them had ever been.

Jean's ears were hypersensitive to sound—normal conversation
sometimes caused him pain, and a low-level background noise, like
a refrigerator running, could make it impossible for him to think. So
he had, as usual, set the volume on the television to almost inaudi-
ble, so that Lori could barely make out Peter Jennings's halting,
stunned narration. She got up and pressed a button on the side of
the set repeatedly, until it was loud enough that someone other than
Jean and Shortstop the dog could hear.

"That's too much," Jean said from the couch.

"Lore, get out of the way," Sis said. "I can't see!"

"Good," Lori said. "You shouldn't be watching this."

"Why should you get to watch but I can't?"

"Because I'm thirteen, and you're nine," Lori said. She came back
to the couch and sat next to Sis.

"That's only four years," Sis said.

"*Ferme la gueule*, both of you," Jean said, his eyes on the screen.
"And she's right, Sis. Go upstairs."

But Sis didn't budge, and Lori and Jean, too preoccupied with
the horror on TV, neglected to make her.

"And so all aircraft currently in the air over the United States have been ordered to land," Peter Jennings told them.

"*Câlice de Crisse*," Jean said. "We have to do something."

"Like what?" Lori asked. "Send a card? Bake a casserole?"

Jean glared at her. "This isn't a joke, Lori," he said. "We're at war."

"I don't see our house burning."

"Don't talk like Ma," Jean said. "I'm American. You're American."

"We're *américaine*. There's a difference."

An impasse, as always, between them. Jean turned back to the TV. Lori stared at him a moment longer, then did the same. Sis had never looked away from the screen, ignoring their quarrels as was her habit.

On the screen helicopters circled, the holes in the towers vomited smoke, and the sun, bright and terrible, bore witness. For a while, nothing else seemed to happen. And then people in the buildings started jumping.

First, two figures, one of indeterminate sex, the other, in slacks and a white oxford, definitely a man. They went together, stepping out into nothing and seeming to hang in the air for an instant, suspended outside the window they'd just vacated. They might have been holding hands, but it was impossible to see for certain. Then they dropped with sudden awful velocity and became separated, tumbling tiny and helpless and alone against the scrolling backdrop of the towers. Sis made a sound like choking as the camera zoomed in and followed the figures' path down, until they disappeared into the cloud of smoke that hung over the streets.

Then, a sudden cascade of bodies—and they were *jumping*, make absolutely no mistake about it, choosing to leap and die rather than burn and die. Anyone could see that, and you would need to have extremely powerful emotional or religious motivation to say otherwise and believe it. These people spilled from the same floor of the tower as the first two like an Airborne platoon in free fall, twisting and tumbling and jackknifing as they hurtled toward the earth, and what Lori would remember about this moment, years later, was the incongruity of the quiet—no screaming, no crying out to God, no slamming impacts. Just bodies loose and yielding against a cobalt sky, drifting through space, making their departure from this world in silence.

And Lori would remember, too, that it was beautiful.

Then Peter Jennings broke the silence. "Dear God," he said.

Jean's face darkened suddenly, and he stood and marched from the room, cursing all creation in French. There was a crash in the kitchen, the sound of glass breaking against tile, and then Lori and Sis heard the front door slam and the roar of Jean's fire-engine-red Fiero coming to life. He was gone, leaving the two of them alone.

They would find out later—along with Babs, whose reaction to the news was strongly negative, to say the very least—that Jean had driven straight to the Marines recruitment center next to the Subway sandwich shop in Elm Plaza, where within an hour he'd signed paperwork and taken the oath regarding enemies foreign and domestic. He would be gone to Basic at Parris Island and assigned to an armored battalion before the fires were extinguished at what would come to be called Ground Zero.

But today, back at the Dionne home, Lori and Sis still sat side by side on the couch, their bodies edging closer without them intending or being consciously aware of it. An urgent internal decision had been made at ABC News to cease showing images of people jumping from the buildings, but there was still plenty of slightly lower-grade horror to broadcast. A seemingly endless loop of the second plane hitting the south tower. A hole like hell's own fiery maw in the Pentagon. A smoking gash carved from the earth somewhere in Pennsylvania farm country. A woman with a shattered leg being carried by firefighters. A man, his white button-down shirt torn at the chest, his face and knuckles bloodied, kneeling in the street like Jesus fallen on the way to Calvary. Masses of people caked in ash, stumbling like zombies up streets and avenues, not knowing where they were or where they were going, seeking only to Get Away.

Lori stood from the couch and moved toward the kitchen, not really knowing why, maybe to get something to drink as her throat had gone so dry she could not swallow, maybe to clean up whatever mess Jean had left in his rage, but before she got to the doorway between the living room and the kitchen she heard Sis cry out.

"Lore, look!"

She turned back, and what she saw on the television did not make sense to her eyes. A horrible cascade, like a volcanic eruption in reverse, like Mount Saint Helens, which she'd also written a paper about a few years earlier, except instead of in verdant green wilderness this volcano was erupting in the middle of a city.

"The whole side has collapsed?" Peter Jennings asked on the TV.

"The whole *building* has collapsed," a reporter told him.

Sis clasped her little hands together and started to cry, and Lori went back to her, her dry throat forgotten, Jean's mess forgotten.

"What happened, Lore?" Sis asked.

Lori took Sis's hands in her own and did not speak. How to answer, after all? They both had seen what happened, knew what happened. Sis was asking her a different question, one she didn't know how to answer, one that perhaps didn't have an answer.

They watched two women taking shelter behind a car as smoke barreled up the avenue toward them. Below this, on the ticker, scores from the previous night's Major League Baseball schedule scrolled by—Seattle 5, Anaheim 1; Oakland 7, Texas 1—as if they still lived in a world where people cared about baseball, or even *played* baseball. But Lori knew, clearly and surely, that that world was gone, as dead as all the people in the south tower. And now she understood that this was how quickly and violently the world could be destroyed and remade. The baseball scores and stock market data would soon and forever be replaced by other numbers. The precise times the planes hit the buildings, for instance. The number of seconds it took, once the collapses began, for the buildings to fall. The number of firefighters, police officers, and EMS workers killed. The number of units of blood donated in the days following the attacks, and the much, much smaller number that turned out to be needed. The number of children orphaned. The number of days that passed between the attacks and when the United States started bombing Afghanistan. The number of U.S. soldiers killed in Operation Enduring Freedom, among whom, eventually, their brother Jean would be counted.

Finally, for lack of anything better or more meaningful to say in response to Sis's question of *what happened*, Lori settled on this: "Someone did a terrible thing," she said.

But that only made Sis cry harder.

"Hey," Lori said, putting an arm around Sis's shoulders and wiping at her cheeks with the other hand. "Hey, look at me."

Sis did, but before Lori could say anything else to comfort her, Sis asked another question: "Are they gonna do terrible things to *us*?"

Lori knew the answer to this question. She wrapped her sister in a hug, one hand cradling Sis's head. "No way," she said. "I won't ever let anyone hurt you, baby girl."

CHAPTER TEN

July 2, 2016

Lori woke on her couch still in the previous night's clothes, soaked with sweat, the day already sweltering at 6 a.m., and for the first three seconds or so of consciousness everything was fine, or as fine as it could be with the Wagnerian discord of a whiskey hangover blaring in her head and the insistent *dope Dope DOPE* of her monkey. But then she remembered like waking into a nightmare: Sis at her table weeping silently, soaked in a red fluid that might or might not have been blood, and this memory sucked all the air out of Lori's lungs. She dry-swallowed two Oxys, threw on her boots, grabbed the Glock and two spare magazines from her go-bag, and was out the door without even going pee.

Four minutes later she screamed into Sis and Bruce's driveway, threw the truck in park, and ran up the front steps. She found the door locked and pounded on it with both fists, calling out to Bruce, and when he didn't answer she stepped back and kicked the door with the sole of her boot, over and over, a racket that brought the eyes of the neighborhood *vieilles dames* drifting to windows up and down the street. Lori knew there was a direct line between those eyes and her mother's ears, but at the moment she didn't much care. She kicked and cursed, and finally the doorframe started to crack, a bit more give with each blow, until finally the frame splintered and the door swung open on the foyer.

She stepped in, looked around, took immediate note of the blood— a trail of drops and splatters that ran from the apex of the stairs all the way down, rounded the corner at the base of the banister, and led like breadcrumbs down the hallway and into the kitchen. The blood was completely dried, brown and crusty, at least twelve hours old.

"Bruce!" Lori called, following the trail into the kitchen. She found further gore streaked in the stainless steel sink. Two empty ice trays on the counter. The refrigerator door hung open, blood smeared on the handle, the interior light on and the motor running gamely against the mounting heat.

Lori ran back to the foyer and climbed the stairs two at a time to the second floor. At the landing she followed the blood trail into the upstairs bathroom, where she found Bruce, sitting on the floor with his back against the toilet. At least she assumed it was Bruce—his face was so swollen and bruised that a positive ID was hard to manage. He had his head down, muttering as he scrubbed over and over at a single spot on the shirt he'd worn the day before, which was, like seemingly everything else in the house, covered in blood. Beside him on the floor sat a bottle of white zinfandel and a bottle of bleach.

"What did you do to my sister?" Lori asked.

But Bruce either didn't hear her or pretended not to, just kept scrubbing away at that one little spot. Trickles of sweat, stained pink with blood, ran down the ruins of his face. "Monday, I'm pretty sure it was Monday," he said to himself, or to his shirt, but definitely not to Lori.

"Bruce," Lori said, taking a step into the room.

"But it *could* have been Tuesday," he said, scrubbing, scrubbing, sure to wear a hole right through the shirt if he kept it up. "The Sox started a series with Toronto on Tuesday, and I *think* they were playing Toronto that night."

Lori crouched in front of him. "Bruce," she said quietly. "Look at me."

He did, just for a moment, then dipped the toothbrush in the bleach and resumed scrubbing, even more vigorously now. "Babs told me to clean this ketchup stain," he said. "Tell her I'm doing what she told me."

"All that blood seems like the bigger issue," Lori said.

"Babs didn't say anything about that. Just the ketchup."

Lori studied Bruce for a moment. Clearly, he was miles away, whether from booze, head injury, heatstroke, or a combination of the three. She wasn't going to learn anything useful by putting the screws to him. She sat cross-legged on the floor and touched the bottle of bleach and the bottle of wine in turn.

"Better not get these mixed up," she said.

"It was Monday," Bruce said. "That feels right."

"What was Monday?"

"Last time I saw Sis."

"More," Lori said. "What happened?"

"I can't remember," Bruce said. "That's the truth of it. I swear."

Lori reached out and took the toothbrush from him. With her other hand she lifted his chin so he had no choice but to look her in the eye.

"Did you do something you can't undo, Bruce?" she asked.

"I want to help," he told her. "I want my wife to come home."

Lori flinched and closed her eyes. "Then help," she said after a moment. "Tell me who she's been running around with."

"You mean men?"

"I mean anyone you can think of." Lori took the shirt from Bruce's hands, stood up, and put the stopper in the sink drain. She ran cold water. "If the two of you had a scrap and she wanted to blow off steam, who would she call?"

"You," Bruce said.

"Not lately." Lori lifted the bleach and poured a healthy dollop into the sink.

"Aubrey, then."

"Aubrey Genest? What happens at her place?"

"They've been at the Adderall, when they can get it," Bruce said.

Lori stuffed Bruce's shirt into the bleach water, which bloomed instantly pink. "What about when they can't?"

He hesitated. "Crank, I think."

"Jesus Christ, Bruce."

"Don't tell Babs!" he said, curling himself into a ball as if his mother-in-law were already in the room, swinging her nightstick back and forth through the air, warming up.

"Where is she getting that shit?" Lori asked.

"I don't know!"

She turned off the tap and crouched down to eye level with him again. "One more time, Bruce," she said. "What did you do to my sister?"

He blinked rapidly, his left eye only opening to half-mast from the bruising. "Do you think I hurt her?" he whimpered.

Lori held his gaze. "Do you?" she asked.

And on his face, plain as the fact that one day everything must die, she saw that Bruce truly didn't know. And then he started to panic.

"We got a crap marriage," he said. "I'm a crap man, bathing in his crap life . . ."

Lori scowled and got to her feet. "Listen to me," she said. "Sober up. Right now. I'll be back later, and your memory better have improved by then."

In contrast to Rita's sturdy, immaculately kept home, Bernette's house across from the basketball court on Grove Street—the same basketball court where, nearly half a century earlier, Babs had been kidnapped—seemed ready to collapse on itself. The roof undulated like a camel's back, and at this time of year, every crack in the driveway—and there were many—featured dandelions so numerous and hearty it seemed they must have been cultivated like peonies. The last paint job, completed sometime in the 1970s, had been stripped away almost entirely by decades of erosive Maine weather, revealing cedar clapboards dark with rot.

Bernette's garage was in even more grievous shape than her house, canted violently to one side and looking like it could collapse at any moment. In a much earlier life it had featured two doors, but now one bay was covered matter-of-factly with a huge sheet of plywood, and the other hadn't been successfully opened since 1986. The only point of access was a side door which, in a small but noteworthy flourish of irony, wouldn't stay closed unless you locked it.

Inside the garage, Bernette and Carmeline stood gazing at a gagged and blindfolded Dr. LaVerdiere. They'd intercepted him that morning in the driveway of his very expensive lakeside home, bonked him over the head with a blackjack, and spirited him away to Bernette's garage, where kidnappings, though rare, always ended up as a matter of Council policy.

"I still don't get it," Bernette said to Carmeline in French.

LaVerdiere sat bound to a chair from Bernette's dining room set.

Carmeline had taken off his shoes and socks and placed his right foot in a bowl of water.

"It's an interrogation technique," Carmeline told her. "Water torture."

"I don't think this is how that's supposed to go," Bernette said. She pointed at LaVerdiere's submerged foot. "*This* is what you do when you want someone to wet the bed in their sleep."

"That's the hand, not the foot, dummy," Carmeline said.

Bernette gave Carmeline a look that made clear there was indeed a dummy in the room. "What do you suppose this is all about?" she asked.

"A goose chase," Carmeline said. "Babs is losing it."

"The information came from Bates, though," Bernette said, lighting a cigarette.

"Canadian gangsters?" Carmeline said. "I mean, whoever heard of such a thing?"

"Well, *we're* gangsters. Of a sort."

"Yeah," Carmeline said. She plucked the cigarette from Bernette's fingers and took a long drag. "But we're not really Canadian."

"Don't tell Babs that."

They passed the smoke back and forth and waited. LaVerdiere, who had struggled against his restraints and generally made a fuss for the first half hour of his captivity, now sat still and silent.

"We need to talk about the Rita thing," Carmeline said.

"I know what you're going to say, and it doesn't matter, so don't bother," Bernette said.

"Babs has gone too far this time," Carmeline said.

"Stop talking," Bernette said.

"You know I'm right. She can't just throw people off the Council."

Bernette stuck her fingers in her ears. "La-la-la-la, I can't hear you!"

"Tell me with a straight face," Carmeline said, "that you disagree. That you think tossing Rita out on her head is A-OK."

"Whether I agree or not doesn't matter," Bernette said. "Babs's word is holy decree."

"Well, maybe not anymore," Carmeline said.

Now Bernette took her fingers out of her ears. "I'm going to pretend," she said, "that I didn't hear *that*."

"Don't do so on my account," Carmeline said. "I'm not afraid of that old bag."

Outside: the sound of Babs's station wagon pulling into the driveway. Bernette gave Carmeline a look: *You going to keep talking shit now?*

The handle on the side door rattled, and Bernette went and opened the dead bolt. Babs stepped inside, wiping sweat from her face and neck with a handkerchief. She took in the scene and said, "Why's his foot in a bowl of water?"

Bernette pointed at Carmeline. "She thinks this is how you do water torture, but I told her—"

Babs held up a hand. "Never mind. Whatever nonsense you're about to try to explain, I don't care. What do I need to know?"

"You should hear it from him," Carmeline told her.

Babs looked at her a moment, then approached LaVerdiere, kicked the bowl to the side, and yanked the gag from his mouth.

"Why did you put my foot in that bowl?!" LaVerdiere asked.

Carmeline elbowed Bernette: *See? Water torture.*

"Listen," Babs said. "You don't know me, but I know you."

"I don't understand what's happening," LaVerdiere said. "I don't understand why I'm here or what you want."

"Sure you do," Babs said. "Yesterday you had a visitor at the clinic. After hours."

"I'm scared," LaVerdiere said.

"You should be," Babs said. "Because unless you tell me every last thing you said to this visitor, I'm going to drop you in the river with a cinder block tied around your neck."

B ates returned to Sunnybrook that morning to check in on Melinda, more to assuage his own anxiety than out of any hope of comforting his wife, who almost certainly would not remember screaming and crying and demanding that he leave the previous evening. This time Bates came in uniform, hoping the sight of his blues would jog whatever part of Melinda's brain, if any, still retained the knowledge that she had a husband who'd been a police officer for the last forty-two years. Bates doffed his cap as he went in through the whoosh of automatic sliding doors and waved to Krystal at the reception desk as he approached.

"Hey Chief," she said, putting the clipboard with the day's visitor log on the counter in front of him. "How's your morning?"

"Too early to tell," Bates said. "Check with me after my second cup of coffee." He turned the clipboard around and grabbed a pen from the jar on his right.

"Your lady friend is popular today," Krystal said.

Bates didn't look up from the log. "How's that?"

"Lots of visitors, bright and early," Krystal said.

Bates froze halfway through printing his name and glanced farther up the page. There were only five entries before his, and only one listed his wife's room, 208.

Name: Danny Holt

Bates felt his breath catch. Holt was Melinda's maiden name, but in thirty-five years of marriage, through untold numbers of holiday meals and family reunions and weddings and funerals, Bates had never heard of, let alone met, anyone named Danny.

Relationship to Resident: Nephew

Bates swallowed hard. "Well, I'll be," he said, resuming his own entry in the log. "Danny's here? That is an unexpected pleasure. Melinda must be surprised."

He slid the clipboard back across the counter, and Krystal looked up at him.

"But then," Bates said with a wink, "Melinda's always surprised these days, isn't she?"

Krystal smiled. Bates smiled back and resumed limping toward room 208 before the false good humor melted from his face. He had no need of more caffeine now, adrenaline having spiked his bloodstream in its place. Everything appeared normal, just another day waiting to die at Sunnybrook: nurses and other staff milling about, residents gathered around a cribbage board or seated at the window watching the bird feeder. Preparations for lunch were well underway as Bates moved past the kitchen, steam billowing from the dishwasher and a timer beeping insistently. In the dayroom Mrs. Sleamaker, a friend of Melinda's (when they both were lucid), sat working on a Sudoku with an assist from Joanne the occupational therapist. Melinda's next-door neighbor, whom Bates thought of as the Tumor Lady because he'd never learned her name and because she had a fleshy tumor the size of a softball in her neck, had parked her wheelchair in the doorway to her room and sat watching as Bates approached.

"Who's *le renard* in Melinda's room?" she asked, a lusty smile rising at one corner of her mouth. Like more than a handful of the female residents of Sunnybrook, the Tumor Lady was a vocal and unabashed horndog, having long ago dropped the demure facade she'd learned as a girl and young woman. These days she'd give the average Bronx construction worker a run for his money, where sexual harassment was concerned.

"*Le renard?*" Bates asked.

"The fox," she said.

Confirmation that someone was indeed with his wife. "Oh. That's her nephew . . . Danny," Bates said. He noted with alarm that Melinda's door was closed.

"Didn't know she had a nephew Danny," the Tumor Lady said. "When he's done in there, have Melinda send him over. I'd like to grind on his face while I watch *Price Is Right*."

"Got it, I'll let him know," Bates said. He moved to open the door to Melinda's room, letting his right hand slide up to rest on the butt of his .45.

"And bring me some ice cream," the Tumor Lady said.

"I've told you before, I don't work here," Bates said. "And you can't have ice cream. You're diabetic."

"If you don't work here," the Tumor Lady said, "then how do you know I'm diabetic?"

The answer was that the Tumor Lady asked everyone who wandered within earshot to bring her ice cream, day after day, and she'd been told at least two dozen times in Bates's presence that she couldn't have it and why. But Bates didn't bother explaining. Instead he used his left hand to press down on the stainless-steel lever that opened Melinda's door. Before he could see anything, he heard Alex Trebek offering an answer: "This 1950 film directed by Elia Kazan features the 'pneumonic plague.'"

And then: quiet, both on the television and in Melinda's room. Was she stumped? Or had someone silenced her?

Bates flipped the thumb break on his holster and gave the door a push with his fingertips. First he saw Melinda, seated in her easy chair by the window, eyes open and on the television: alive, awake, and apparently unharmed. Then, as the door swung wide, he caught sight of The Man, sitting on a metal folding chair within arm's reach of his wife. At the bump of the door hitting the rubberized doorstop, The Man turned and smiled at Bates.

"What is *Panic in the Streets*?" The Man said.

On the TV the question proved a triple-stumper, and after time expired Alex Trebek confirmed that The Man was, indeed, correct. Bates kept his hand on the butt of his pistol, but left it in the holster for the moment.

"Chief Bates," The Man said. "At the risk of seeming impertinent, may I say that your wife is as lovely as she is demented."

Bates's heart slammed against his ribs, but he tried to assume the air of authority befitting his station. "You a new resident here?" he said.

"Are you asking if I'm new to Waterville," The Man said, "or if I've just moved into this facility?"

"I'm asking what you're doing in my wife's room," Bates said, clicking the safety off the .45 for emphasis.

Melinda went on watching *Jeopardy!* as if they weren't there.

The Man got to his feet and crossed the tile floor, extending his hand for a proper shake. "I'm here to talk to you," he said.

Bates let The Man's hand hang in the air. "And yet you won't answer my questions," he said.

The Man smiled. "That's because I'm here for *you* to answer *mine*," he said.

Bates stared, his face impassive but his brain redlining. After a moment The Man dropped his hand and went back to his seat.

"I understand you're reluctant to speak to me," he said, "and I understand why. Until now you've had a lucrative and safe arrangement, and I am very much a fly in the ointment."

"What is *Uncle Tom's Cabin?*" Melinda said.

"Let's not waste time teasing out the fact that you know about my dealings," Bates said. "Just: What do you want?"

"That's fair," The Man said. "I don't like wasting time either. And what I want is simple."

"Terrific," Bates said. "Then it should be easy to ask for."

"What is cauterizing?" Melinda said.

"An introduction," The Man said.

"To who?" Bates asked, as if he didn't already know.

"Whoever is really in charge of this town."

Bates smiled, said nothing.

"What is crustacean?" Melinda said.

The Man waited another moment for Bates to respond, then asked, "May I outline your options as I see them?"

"Knock yourself out. Though no guarantees I'll see it the same way."

A swift darkness descended on The Man's face, like something huge suddenly blotting out the sun. "Oh," he said, "I think you will."

Bates felt himself blanch, the retreat of blood from his face so rapid it was almost painful.

"What is Fleetwood Mac?" Melinda said.

"Let me offer a bit of context, to help you better understand your options as I'm about to explain them," The Man told Bates. "Are you familiar with the concept of the golem?"

"The greasy little guy in *The Lord of the Rings?*" Bates asked.

"No," The Man said. "Not the greasy little guy in *The Lord of the Rings.*"

"You got me, then," Bates said.

"What is not/knot?" Melinda said.

"The golem is a creature from Jewish folklore," The Man said. "The inspiration for a story you no doubt *are* familiar with: Frankenstein's monster."

"Yep, know that one," Bates said.

"Golems are made from inanimate material, such as mud or rocks," The Man said. "Through incantations by a rabbi, they become animate, usually for the purpose of defending a Jewish community from some kind of threat. But in every iteration of the golem story, those who create the creature eventually lose control of it. Or rather, they never had control of it to begin with. Because the golem is not a person, or even a device, but merely a force. A tremendous, indiscriminate force. And the moral is, you may have the ability to create and unleash such a force, but you should never mistake that to mean you can *control* it."

"Okay," Bates said.

"What is Secretary of Defense?" Melinda said.

"Which brings us to the situation you find yourself in," The Man continued. "I am a power far greater than anything you can understand. Yet you summoned me. I am the parts of yourself you try to deny and ignore. I am your ambition and your greed. Your love, too, and all the awful things you think it justifies. What I am *not* is your enemy, Chief. In fact, I'm here to offer you a chance to be whole, for the first time."

"Do you have anything to say that makes sense?" Bates asked.

"You cannot control or mitigate what you've conjured," The Man said. "You'll try, of course, because you are human, which means you're vain and overestimate your capabilities. But in the end, you'll understand that you can either die, or you can choose what you want your future to look like under my authority."

"Not your authority," Bates said. "I know an errand boy when I see one. You mean your *boss's* authority."

"Indirectly, yes. As embodied by me."

"And who is your boss?"

"I think," The Man said, "that by now you have a good idea of who I work for."

"Sorry, no clue. I'm just a bumpkin police chief, after all."

"What is an ash borer?" Melinda said.

"The White Hand," The Man said. "Le Serpent du Nord. The Pale King. The Quiet One. Maujag—Inuit for 'snow one sinks into.' Finally, and most famously: Ogopogo."

Bates said nothing, but his mask of indifference slipped just a bit, for just an instant.

And The Man, noting this, smiled. "No doubt, on a wall somewhere in your police headquarters, you have an FBI composite sketch purporting to resemble him. So now you know who you're dealing with. And you have a choice to make."

Bates narrowed his eyes. "Do you understand what this uniform is?" he asked. "I'm an officer of the law. I am, in point of fact, the *head* officer of the law with regard to the ground you're standing on. You come here, threaten my wife—and now you want to talk this nonsense?"

"If you have the FBI sketch I mentioned," The Man said, "then you know that Ogo is responsible, directly or indirectly, for the deaths of two dozen law enforcement personnel since 1995. Adding one more to that total would, of course, be of little consequence to him."

The Man leaned back in his chair and folded his hands across his waist. "I'm not here to make you do anything, Chief Bates," he said. "If you believe your station is such that it's prudent to ignore my request, that's your choice. It's an article of faith for me that every man is intended by nature to do as he will. By the same token, I believe every man will sooner or later face whatever is set in motion by his decisions. I didn't create these laws of being—I just obey them. As you must."

"What is Nanjing?" Melinda said.

"Option one," The Man said, rising from his chair and moving past Bates toward the door, "is you introduce me to the person I want to meet. With regard to option two, the details will take some time. I'll need to go away for a while, to do some thinking. Maybe it'll be a few days, maybe it'll be long enough that you'll start to believe I didn't mean what I said—or even that I was a figment of your imagination. But three things are true of me, if nothing else, Chief: I am very real. I do not forget. And I am not in the habit of extending second chances."

"What is *The Scream*?" Melinda said.

"I'll call in an hour for your answer," The Man said. He tipped an imaginary cap and went out, and Bates could hear the Tumor Lady shouting after him in the hallway, telling him to get back here and limber up his tongue.

CHAPTER ELEVEN

July 2, 2016

Lori sat in her truck outside Aubrey Genest's house. Across the bench seat on the passenger side: an Afghan girl of five or so, her clothes tattered and scorched and caked in white powder, the skin on her arms and legs burned to a smooth, waxy sheen. The girl wore a pair of pink Crocs that had melted to her feet, and most of the skin and sinew on the left side of her face had burned away, leaving blackened skull and baby teeth. Her left eye had popped and shriveled, but with her good right eye she stared calmly at Lori across the cab.

"مه پربېرده چ مره شي," the girl said.

Lori had, of course, learned many Pashto phrases during her time in Afghanistan. She still knew how to dicker over a price, compliment a meal, and issue all manner of commands: stop, show your hands, get on the ground, hurry the fuck up. But the only Pashto words that ever invaded her sleep were the ones the girl said to her now, again.

"مه پربېرده چ مره شي."

In the hours before she'd heard these words for the first time, Lori had attended a RAMP briefing and, as at every briefing for the previous three weeks, she thought about mentioning that the waadi route designated for emergency infil/exfil had been used too frequently for non-emergent situations. That continuing to use it except when absolutely necessary was basically inviting someone to plant a fifty-five-gallon drum full of ammonium nitrate and wait for the next convoy to roll through. As a staff sergeant, Lori had some pull. If she spoke up, the captain would have at least given her an audience. But as in the previous three weeks of briefings—three weeks during which she'd begun her first acquaintance with heroin, enraptured and paranoid and convinced everyone knew, or would know if they looked in her eyes for even a moment—she said nothing, not even when Sammy piped up and spoke as though reading Lori's mind about the waadi and the captain responded, in essence: *Thanks for your input, Corporal, now shut the fuck up.*

Looking back, it would have been easy for Lori to blame her addiction on psychic pain, like most junkies did sooner or later. The world was too much, all that. But she knew better. She'd done that first shot and every one after not because she was in pain, and not because she was afraid, but in a deliberate effort to alter what she had come to realize, after three tours, was her fate. This fate was evident in her rapid ascent through the enlisted ranks, in the deference shown to her by officers, in the way her Marines looked to her for guidance, reassurance, and the right answer, always. In short, she was destined to become her mother: to do and do and do but never to feel, and Lori's horror at this prospect was why she floated just above the RAMP briefing even as she sat in her chair with the others, why she thought about the waadi but did not speak of it.

Two hours later, frantic chatter on the radio: a local had driven through the waadi and been blown halfway to Mars by an IED. Lori's squad was ordered to respond, and if she'd been allowed she would have whipped her Marines to get them there faster. That IED had been intended for them, of course. For weeks she'd known they shouldn't be using the washout, and she'd said nothing. And now someone else was paying the price.

They followed a column of black smoke to the remains of a small flatbed truck. The crater gouged by the IED reminded Lori of holes she'd seen left by five-hundred-pound MK-82 bombs. The truck's cab was completely destroyed, the top peeled back like a soup can and flames devouring the interior. If you'd looked at it you would have said, 100 percent nothing and no one could be alive in there. Except that, over the rumble of the convoy's engines, they could hear screams coming from inside the fire.

The whole squad stood there, frozen by something between horror and fascination, for several seconds. The screaming went on. Lori had once heard a squirrel, snatched up off a lawn by a bald eagle, make a similar noise. "Jesus Christ, just fucking shoot her!" one Marine said, his voice cracking, and in that moment Lori came back to herself and grabbed a fire extinguisher and the medic and ordered a secure perimeter. Sammy followed them into the washout with a second extinguisher.

Within thirty seconds the fire was out, laying bare what remained: In the driver's seat, an adult-size corpse, its hands still on the wheel, blackened and mummified, the agony of death in mute physical form. And on the passenger side, the source of the screaming: an Afghan girl of five or so, her clothes tattered and scorched and caked in white powder from the extinguishers, the skin on her arms and legs burned to a smooth, waxy sheen. Her good right eye stared at Lori, wild with pain and fear, and the girl begged, over and over, "مه پرېدره چ مره شي! مه پرېدره چ مره شي!"

Four years later, in America, in Maine, in Waterville, in Little

Canada, in Lori's truck, which had not been blown up or set ablaze, Lori turned and looked at the girl. "Please," she said. "Not today."

The girl, whose plea to Lori four years prior had gone unfulfilled, did as she was asked and disappeared.

But this did not put Lori at ease. She flexed her hands on the steering wheel, tightening and loosening her grip. Her breath came fast and shallow. She closed her eyes and leaned her head back. Sobs rose in her chest and she fought them down, her body hitching and trembling. And then, when she couldn't hold back anymore, instead of crying she screamed, over and over, punching the steering wheel and tearing the skin away from her knuckles, reaching up to rip at her own hair and face—

Five minutes later Lori stood on Aubrey's front porch, composed as a corpse. She rang the bell. Nothing. Rang again. She tried the door and found it unlocked, which was not exactly a surprise. She pushed the door open against a pile of mail on the other side. The lights were off, shades drawn, air thick and stagnant, this pitiless heat.

"Hey!" Lori called out. "Anyone home?"

After a moment a response, distant and muffled, as though from someone encased in the wall: "Hello?"

Lori took two steps into the house. "Aubrey? That you?"

"Whoever you are," said the voice, "can you do me a favor and bring some water to the basement?"

A seemingly simple request, but Lori wasn't sure what to make of it.

After a few moments she crossed to the sink and drew a glass from the tap, then unholstered her pistol and went to the basement stairs. The light was on, illuminating crooked wooden steps descending into an old fieldstone foundation.

"I'm coming down," Lori said. "And I've got a Glock loaded with hollow points, so no fucking around."

"Jesus Christ, Lore," said the voice, "I just need a glass of water."

"Aubrey?"

"Who else would it be?"

Lori holstered the Glock and descended the stairs. As she went, Aubrey came into view: seated on a ratty lounge chair, chained by her ankle to the furnace, a plastic bucket and three empty water jugs on the floor next to her. Aubrey's face was a constellation of scabs, telltale evidence of a tweaker's busy hands. She wiggled her fingers at Lori in greeting, offering a yellowed meth smile.

"Jesus Christ. Who chained you up, Aubrey?"

"Water first, *s'il te plaît*."

Lori gave up the glass and Aubrey gunned it, using both hands, spilling all over her face and chin. She handed it back to Lori. "More," she said.

"Tell me what the hell is going on first."

Aubrey smiled again. "I'm trying to kick."

"You chained *yourself* down here?"

Aubrey let loose a laugh that sounded more like crying. "All other efforts to rid myself of the galloping demons have failed, so . . ."

"The what?"

"They always come for me after a speed binge. Couldn't deal with that shit anymore. So I opted for extreme measures."

"And these demons are on horseback?" Lori asked.

"Sometimes," Aubrey said. "Sometimes they just pretend to be on horses. Like the knights in Monty Python. You know, with coconuts to make a sound like hooves."

Lori stared. "Yes," she said. "I know with coconuts to make a sound like hooves."

Aubrey grabbed the chain binding her to the furnace and gave it a celebratory rattle. "But: five days sober, Lore! Can't argue with success!"

"I don't suppose you've seen my sister."

"Seen her? No. Heard from her."

"When?"

Aubrey's eyes searched the cobwebbed floor joists above their heads. "Ah, lessee . . . Monday? Maybe Tuesday."

"Jesus Christ, not you, too."

"She calls all crying and shit, looking for a ride. Says she's stuck out in Vassalboro. And I says to her, 'Look, even if I *wasn't* chained to the boiler I couldn't come get you anyway, because Kenny has the car. Call a taxi,' I says."

"Did you hear from her again after that?"

"Nope. What's she gotten into? You're the second person to ask me about her this week."

"I thought you've been down here for five days."

"I have. Someone else came to my basement rehab, too."

"And who was that?"

"No one we know," Aubrey said. "Handsome guy—older, though. Maybe. It was hard to tell. Nice suit. Good teeth. Creepy, but in that sexy way. He wanted to know where Sis was, too."

"And what did you tell him?"

"Same thing I'm telling you," Aubrey said. "Fucked if I know. You gonna tell me what's going on with her, or what?"

"I wish I could. She's missing."

Aubrey rolled her eyes and clicked her tongue. "That crew she's running around with, I'm not surprised."

Lori squared her gaze on Aubrey. "What crew is that?"

"You don't want to know."

"The hell I don't," Lori said. "You're going to make an introduction. Where are the keys?"

"Kenny has them. He's back Monday morning at ten. I figured a week should do the trick."

Lori crossed the basement to a workbench, searching for something to cut Aubrey free with. The top of the bench was a jumble of random tools and hardware: claw hammer, screwdrivers, boxes of nails, vise grip. A jigsaw, but that was no match for heavy-gauge chain.

"Lore," Aubrey said. "Please don't make me leave. I have to stay here a full week, or the cure won't take."

Lori threw open cabinet doors, finding paint cans, a giant box of cat litter—and finally, bolt cutters. She came back to Aubrey. "That's bullshit and you know it," she said. "If you want to quit, you can quit. You're taking me to this crew."

Aubrey looked up at her, all the tweaker energy gone from her eyes. "You don't want anything to do with those people," she said.

Lori found the weak spot where a chain link had been soldered and lined up the bolt cutter blades. "Sure I do," she said. The steel gave way easily, and she maneuvered a second cut on the other side of the link.

"If I go up there," Aubrey said, "I'll keep ruining my life."

Lori again squeezed the bolt cutter handles together, and the link cleaved and fell to the concrete floor with a cheerful ping.

"You and everyone else," she said to Aubrey.

J ason sat alone in Babs's living room, playing *Rainbow Six* on the Xbox without much interest, when two things happened simultaneously: he was killed by a sniper shot to the head, and the doorbell rang. He paused the game with his avatar in bloody mid-collapse and sat there, listening for any sound from the front porch. He felt caught somehow, like he was in trouble for something he didn't know or understand, but this was not an unusual state of mind for him—he often found himself in trouble for reasons he didn't know about or understand. Still, the situation was charged enough that it presented a sharper texture of anxiety than normal. Mémère had told him repeatedly that morning: *If anyone comes to the door, don't answer it—call me.* She was worried, which Jason had never seen before. And whatever she was worried about, if it scared her then it sure as hell scared him.

The doorbell rang again.

Jason got up slowly and tiptoed into the kitchen on bare feet. The windows to either side of the front door would offer a view of whoever was on the porch, but in seeing, Jason risked being seen. Instead, he went to the door itself and put his ear against it. At first, nothing. Then a cough, harsh and wet, the hack of a heavy smoker. Jason held his breath and pressed his body against the door, almost willing himself to become part of it.

Then he heard his father's voice. "Babs, c'mon," Bruce muttered.

A relief, sure, but that his father waited outside was not without its own complications. Mémère didn't want Bruce around. She'd made that clear. But she wouldn't be home for hours, and Jason didn't like the way his father's voice sounded. He could open up just for a minute, say hi, let his old man see he was okay.

Jason turned the handle on the dead bolt—still sticky, it took about all the torque he could muster before it gave way—and opened the door. He started to say hello, but the words died in his throat when he caught sight of his father. The protrusions of Bruce's face, the way his mouth lay crooked and one of his eyes was swollen nearly shut, made Jason think immediately of *The Elephant Man*, an old movie he'd stumbled on one afternoon that had made him cry like a little kid at the end. He'd been glad no one was around to see him crying, but now his father was here, and Jason definitely didn't want Bruce to see him cry.

"Hey little man," Bruce said. "I didn't expect you to answer the door."

"Mémère's not here," Jason said.

"That's okay," Bruce said. He coughed again, and clutched at his ribs with one hand. "I'm real glad to see you. Any idea when your *mémère* will be back?"

"Not till later."

They were quiet for a moment. Then Bruce said, "How's the eye?"

"It's okay."

"It's never okay, for someone to do that to you, Jay-Jay. Not even me. Especially not me."

"Then why do you do it?"

Bruce gazed at Jason, his good eye shimmering, and then looked away, to the sky over his right shoulder, as if expecting to find the answer there. "I don't know," he said finally.

Jason wasn't sure what he wanted his dad to say or do, but he knew he didn't like seeing Bruce cry, so he changed the subject. "What happened to you?" he asked.

Bruce wiped gingerly at his eye and looked down at Jason again. "I, uh . . . well, it's embarrassing."

"You can tell me."

"I fell down the stairs last night."

"Were you drinking?"

"Yes."

"Is that why you fell?"

Bruce looked away again, thinking. "No, not really," he said. "Do you know what karma is? We ever talk about that?"

"I don't think so."

"Well, karma is the idea that whatever you do, good or bad, comes back to you some way. So like if you do something nice for someone, something nice happens for you further down the line. Get it?"

"I think so."

"It works the other way, too. What I did to you was bad, and that's why I fell down the stairs."

"How do you know?"

Bruce thought about this. "You just know, sometimes. That's part of how karma works. You say to yourself, 'Okay, that sucked, but I guess I had it coming.'"

Jason looked at the mess of his father's face, the way his back bowed with pain. "Maybe I should go home with you," he said.

"You have to stay here for now," Bruce said. "Until your ma gets back."

"When's she coming back?"

"I'm not sure. She went to stay with some friends for a little bit."

"You don't know where she is, do you?"

This tripped Bruce up. "Listen," he said after a second, "I want you to give your *mémère* a message for me. Okay?"

"Okay."

"Tell her Monday is all I know for sure. Got that?"

"Monday," Jason said. "Is all you know for sure."

L ori pulled off 201 and onto a gravel driveway that wound uphill to an old farmhouse with an attached barn. She did a three-point turn so the truck was facing back down the driveway, then put it in park and looked around. The house was mid-1800s vintage, red brick with an arched front doorway the only embellishment breaking up an otherwise seamless Puritan austerity. The buildings were surrounded on three sides by a field of sedge and Canada bluegrass, and beyond that vertiginous stands of white pine trees hemmed the property. No visible neighbors. No utility wires. They were only a quarter mile from the main road, but in terms of escape and/or help if they found themselves in trouble, they might as well have been on the moon.

"Okay, I showed you the place," Aubrey said. "Don't make me go in there."

Lori took out her Glock, checked to see that a round was chambered, then put the gun back in its holster. "What are you so afraid of?" she asked.

"Aside from the fact that I'm going to smoke up the moment I walk in?"

"Aside from that."

Aubrey sighed and opened her door. "You'll see," she said.

They climbed out, Lori leaving the engine running in case they needed to get out of there in a hurry. They walked together to the front door. Lori knocked while Aubrey stood off to the side, chewing a thumbnail.

"It's open!" a man's voice called from inside. *"Entrez vous!"*

Lori glanced at Aubrey, who shrugged.

"Don't look at me," she said. "You're the one wanted to come here."

Lori turned the doorknob and pushed, and the first thing she noticed, as the door swung wide, was that this place seemed awfully tidy for a meth den. The second thing she noticed was the wood-fired hot tub in the middle of the living room. A man in his early thirties sat chest-deep in the water, smiling broadly as they came in.

He had his arms slung over the sides of the tub, and the ends of his long glam-rock hair were dark with wet.

"Aubrey!" the man said. "Haven't seen you for a minute."

Aubrey kept her eyes on the floor. "Nossir," she said.

"Do me a favor," the man said, his gaze wandering to Lori even as he addressed Aubrey. "Before you get into the crank, throw a couple more sticks on the fire down there. Water's gone cold."

"Yessir," Aubrey said, still not making eye contact. She went to an iron rack loaded with split oak and grabbed two pieces.

"Who's your friend?" Rex asked.

"Rex, this is Lori," Aubrey said. "Lori, Rex."

"I want to ask you some questions," Lori said.

"You a cop?" Rex asked.

"She's not a cop, sir." Aubrey flipped the handle on the furnace beneath the tub and jumped back as flames leaped out. No way that water was cold, but Rex wanted more heat, so Aubrey tossed the wood in, sending glowing cinders adrift in the room.

"Then why is she wearing that piece?" Rex asked, nodding toward Lori's underarm holster.

"Never know when I might get the urge to shoot up an elementary school," Lori said.

Rex stared at her a moment, then laughed. "That's good," he said. "I like that."

"May I smoke now, sir?" Aubrey asked.

"After you close that door," Rex told her.

"It's too hot, sir. I can't get close enough."

"Then flee," Rex said, shooing Aubrey with one dripping hand. "You've shown admirable restraint for a minute and a half."

Aubrey needed no further encouragement; she hied away toward the back of the house, leaving Lori and Rex alone.

"So let's recap what I know about you and why you're standing in my living room," Rex said. "You're angry about something, and you want to ask me questions. You're strapped and making no effort to hide it, which means you want me to know you're strapped, which means that you'd rather avoid trouble if you can—peace through superior firepower, and all that. On the other hand, you don't seem to give even half a fuck about anything, least of all your own life. About right, so far?"

"More or less."

"Also, you're a killer," Rex said.

"I've killed," Lori said. "I'm not a killer."

Rex waved this away. "Semantics," he said. "Why don't you join me in the tub and we'll see whether I want to answer your questions."

"Sadly, I neglected to bring a bathing suit."

"Suit's optional," Rex said. "But as you wish. Ask away."

"There's a woman gone missing," Lori said. "Sis Dionne. I'm told she spends time here."

"That's not a question," Rex said.

"Listen, asshole—"

"Do I look like a milk carton to you?" Rex asked.

"I don't follow."

"A milk carton," Rex said again. "They sometimes have information about missing people. You know, printed on the side."

"That still a thing?" Lori asked.

"Search me. I've been lactose intolerant for fifteen years," Rex said. "But let's pretend, for conversation's sake, that it is still a thing. Do I look. Like a milk carton. To you."

He gazed at her for a long beat, his face inscrutable.

"You look like a man who is very relaxed," Lori said. "Or at least wants to appear so."

Now Rex smiled. "I know a few things about missing girls just generally speaking, having had some experience in such matters," he said. "About this particular girl—Sis, did you say her name was?— I'm afraid I'm drawing a blank."

"I don't believe you."

"What do you believe?" Rex asked.

"That *Homo sapiens* is an evolutionary blunder."

Rex laughed. "You know what?" he said. "You're all right. I like you. And because I like you, I'm going to do you the favor of being straight."

"Terrific."

"Your sister did, in fact, spend time here."

"What makes you think she's my sister?"

"I don't think," Rex said. "I know."

"*Did* spend time here? Past tense?"

"She was asked to leave and not return."

"Why?"

"That's my business."

Lori put a hand on the butt of the Glock. "Mine, too," she said. "Like you said, she's my sister."

At that moment Aubrey came back in, spinning like a top, her eyes wild. Rex turned to her, smiled, slapped the surface of the water with his hand. "Now that you've had your medicine, climb on into the River Lethe with your uncle Rexy," he said.

Aubrey did so, still fully dressed. She settled in next to Rex, who draped an arm across her shoulders and smiled with satisfaction. Then he looked up at Lori, and the smile disintegrated. "You should go," he said.

Behind her, Lori heard the unequivocal *chi-chuck!* of a pump-action shotgun being readied for use. She turned her head slowly, careful to keep the rest of her body perfectly still, and saw at the corner of her vision a woman about her age, a scowl, and double barrels.

"You come here again," Rex said, "and you're going to join your sister on the side of a milk carton."

CHAPTER TWELVE

July 2, 2016

B abs and Bates fucked hard in the mechanic's room at Spare Time, Babs with one leg slung up on the side of a pinsetter, Bates behind her with his hands on her hips, sweating and grimacing. This was nothing to do with lust, and even less to do with joy—just business, really. It ended without even a measure of relief, Bates groaning then turning away, and the two of them set about putting themselves back together in silence.

Once Babs had her blouse buttoned back up, she said, "So tell me."

"He's working for someone," Bates said, pushing his wedding band back on. "Someone serious."

"Don't leave me in suspense, here."

"Name Ogopogo mean anything to you?"

"He works for a sea serpent? That *is* serious."

"He wants to talk to you," Bates said. "Tonight. At the mill."

"The mill? Whose idea was that?"

"Mine. I figured you could find your way around that building blindfolded, whereas he won't have any clue where he is."

"Unless he's casing the place now," Babs said.

"My wife, Babs," Bates said. "He was with my wife."

"Let me at least wipe you off my leg before you bring Melinda into it."

"What are we going to do?"

"Jesus Christ, don't be such a baby," Babs said, pulling on her shoes. "Melinda's fine. It's my daughter who's missing."

Bates didn't respond. Babs found her purse and slung it over her shoulder. "I have to go meet Lore," she said.

"What's the play?"

"Simple," Babs said. "I'm going to find out what our new friend wants, then I'm going to tell him to get bent. And if he has anything to do with why I can't find my daughter, I'm going to kill him."

"I would advise strongly against that," Bates said.

"Talk to you later, Daryl," Babs said, and left.

W hen Babs pulled into her driveway fifteen minutes later, Lori's truck sat waiting at the curb. Lori got out and met her mother on the walkway.

"You're late," she said.

"Inside," Babs told her.

They opened the front door to the cartoonish din of video game combat coming from the living room.

"Where's my favorite boy?" Babs called out over the racket.

"In here!" Jason yelled back.

Babs turned to Lori. "You find out anything?"

"Not really," Lori said.

"'Not really' isn't the same as 'no.'"

"Bruce's memory is still Swiss cheese," Lori said. "Had one other lead, may or may not be something."

Babs took out her cigarettes, lit one, and tossed the pack on the counter. "Let me decide that."

"I went to Aubrey Genest's, and she introduced me to someone interesting. You know a meth dealer out in Albion, name of Rex White?" Lori motioned for the cigarette, and Babs gave it to her, filter-first.

"No."

"Me neither." Lori took a long drag and handed the cigarette back. "But apparently Sis did."

"Meth?"

"Don't shoot the messenger, Ma."

Babs banked her anger, smoked. "What's your read on him?"

"Hard to say. He claims he threw her out a while ago. But he's cagey as shit and clearly thinks he's smarter than anyone else in the room."

"My lead seems somewhat more promising."

"Meaning . . ."

"Meaning I have a social call at the mill tonight. With some out-of-towner who's apparently looking for me."

"Let me guess," Lori said. "Nice suit. Good teeth. Looks kind of like a wax figure come to life."

"How'd you know?"

"He went to Aubrey's, too. Looking for Sis."

"When?"

"Yesterday."

"Maudit de câlice de tabarnak."

"We shouldn't jump to conclusions," Lori said.

"No one's jumping to conclusions," Babs said. "If my options are some speed-freak redneck in Albion, or a professional who's gone around asking questions and systematically closing in on me and my family, seems pretty easy to figure out who's the more likely suspect."

Having met Rex, Lori wasn't so sure. But she said nothing.

"What happened to your hands?" Babs asked.

Lori looked down, having forgotten she'd ripped her knuckles open earlier. She couldn't come up with a plausible excuse for the scabs and dried blood, so she tried to deflect. "It's nothing."

"Bullshit, it's nothing. Something's going on. I can see it all over you."

Lori willed herself not to think about what she knew, believing her mother would be able to read that on her face as well. "Been a long couple of days, Ma. That's all."

"So you went three rounds with a wall?" Babs asked.

"Steering wheel, actually," Lori said. "I'll come with you tonight."

"No."

"Who knows what this guy's up to? You need backup."

"I have backup," Babs lied.

"Who?"

"Bates."

"Jesus, Ma," Lori said. "You'd be better off bringing Jay-Jay."

"You're not going. End of discussion."

"Fine then," Lori said, resolved to go anyway.

Babs looked at her a moment longer, then her gaze shifted to the living room doorway. "Jay!" she called out over the rumble of an electronic explosion.

The sound from the video game cut out abruptly. "Yeah?"

"Come in here for a sec," Babs said.

The boy appeared in the doorway, but seemed reluctant to come any closer.

"What's all the racket?" Babs asked.

"Playing *BioShock*," Jay said.

"As if your *mémère* has any idea what that means," Babs said.

"You have to fight mutants to escape from an underwater city," Jay said.

"Sounds like just another Thursday in this town," Babs said. "Listen, did you hear what Aunt Lori and I were just talking about?"

Jay looked from Babs to Lori and back again. "No."

"Then why do you look like the cat that ate the canary?"

Jason just blinked at her.

"What is it, Jay?" Lori asked.

"I have to tell Mémère something, but it might make her mad."

"Nothing you say would ever make me mad at you," Babs said.

"My dad came over today. While you were gone."

"I didn't say I wouldn't get mad at *him*," Babs said.

Lori shot her mother a look. "Did he say why he was here, Jay?"

The boy nodded. "He wanted me to give you a message," he told Babs.

Half an hour later, Lori and Shawn lay together in his room at the Hampton Inn. This time they were both fully clothed and on top of the covers, a good foot and a half of space between them, Shawn drinking whiskey again, solo. The curtains were drawn against the sun, and the air-conditioning rattled ductwork as it struggled to keep the room below eighty degrees.

"All of a sudden I noticed how *disheveled* he looked," Shawn said.

"Not just sick. That's a given. But he looked like a bum. Hadn't shaved in a week. Little tufts of hair poking up out of his scalp."

Lori let him talk.

"I'm standing there thinking, Here's a guy who never left the house, in forty-five years, without a clean shave," Shawn said. "I can't let him leave for the last time without one."

"You think he's that close?" Lori asked.

"No question. Blood in his piss. Skin's all yellow. Kidneys, liver, everything's shutting down."

Lori closed her eyes slowly. Felt the miracle of her breath, in and out, deep and smooth and mournful.

Shawn went on. "So I clipped his hair and gave him a shave," he said. "Simplest, most insignificant thing in the world. But he was so grateful, you'd have thought I came up with the cure for cancer."

"And then what?" Lori asked.

"Then I went into the bathroom and sobbed for ten minutes. Sure you don't want a drink?"

"I have to be clear-headed."

Shawn poured into his own glass. "For what?"

"That's why I came here," Lori said. "To explain why I didn't show up last night. Best I can."

With a mouth full of whiskey, Shawn made a noise in the affirmative, and swallowed. "Yeah, about that," he said, wiping the corner of his mouth. "I thought I'd be waking up in Boston today, not giving my father a haircut. Fool me once, shame on you. Fool me twice . . ."

"No one fooled you, Shawn. Something happened last night."

"Okay."

"I haven't told anyone yet. I don't have anyone to tell. Besides you."

Shawn took in Lori's expression for a moment, then turned to the nightstand and picked up the bottle again, lifting his eyebrows in inquiry. Lori nodded, and he poured the last of the whiskey into the spare glass and handed it over.

Lori sipped, tasted, then gunned it and handed the glass back. "Something's happened to Sis," she said.

"You found her?"

"No."

"I don't understand."

"She came to me last night, Shawn. When I went home to pack."

"Wait. Are you saying . . ."

"I'm saying I tried to touch her," Lori said. "And she wasn't there."

Shawn stared. "Jesus Christ, Lore."

"I keep telling myself I can't be certain," Lori said. "But I know that's just what I want to believe."

"Okay. Jesus. Uh, okay. I don't know what to say."

Lori stared down at her hands. "I have to find her," she said. "And I have to find out what happened. Before Babs knows she's dead."

"What happens if you don't?"

Lori looked at him gravely. "You remember your Old Testament?" she asked.

"The broad strokes."

"My mother loves Sis more than she loves me, my brother, and my father combined," Lori said. "She will burn this town to the ground trying to find out who did this to her. So I have to find them first."

CHAPTER THIRTEEN

July 2, 2016

B eing high summer, it was still twilight just before nine o'clock when Rita startled awake to a knock on her front door. Half-conscious, she picked her head up at the sound, then glanced around blearily to orient herself: she was in her dining room, seated at the table, empty wineglass in front of her, all the lights off and the sky outside the window an apocalyptic red against the darkened canopies of fir and maple trees. Dogs barking somewhere in the neighborhood. The heat like a noose.

That knock, again. And suddenly Rita remembered everything about the last twenty-four hours, all of it hitting her at once like a crash-test car slamming a wall. She was hammered on Carlo Rossi merlot, her mouth sticky with ferment, and in no shape for houseguests. But she was also as deeply, profoundly, and irretrievably alone as she'd been since the day fifty-odd years before when she finally realized her father would sooner or later kill her, and her mother was too far down the bottle to do anything but look away, look anywhere but at her daughter and the pain and fear that lived in her eyes. And so Rita, age eight, had walked barefoot through Little Canada to the only safe place she'd ever known, the only place on earth where she could sleep with her back to a door: the home of her best and truest friend, Babs. And Babs's mother had cleaned Rita up, dabbing her wounds with iodine and blowing on them to ease the sting, while Babs's father, André, sat across the table from them and said, matter-of-factly, Pall Mall pinched between his fingers, that Rita lived here now—and if Rita's father had a problem with that, André would be happy to solve the problem for him.

This was the manner by which, in all but name, Rita had become a Levesque.

Fast-forward five decades and change, and look at the state of things. Rita rose from the dining table and went unsteadily to the door, not knowing who she'd find on the other side and not really caring, she just wanted another consciousness in the room, another circuit of warm blood, needed to know in as basic and unequivocal a way as possible that she was not forgotten on this earth.

She opened the door and saw Carmeline standing there, unsmiling as always, a fresh bottle of Carlo Rossi in her hand.

"I probably don't need any more of that," Rita said.

"Who said any of it's for you?" Carmeline asked, not waiting for a formal invitation to walk in.

Three minutes later they sat at the table together, each with a glass of Carmeline's Chablis.

"I'd ask how you're taking it," Carmeline said. She lit a cigarette, put her pack on the table, and pulled the ashtray toward her.

"But you have eyes," Rita said.

"You been able to see Tim yet?"

"Talked on the phone, but he can't have visitors until after he's arraigned."

"How is he?"

Rita gazed bleary-eyed out the window. "He's looking at eight years," she said. "So, not great."

"At least he won't have to wonder where his next meal's coming from for a while."

"That's not funny."

"It wasn't a joke."

They were quiet a moment, Rita watching a ribbon of smoke rise from Carmeline's cigarette in the ashtray. A car passed on the street outside, which got the neighborhood dogs barking again.

"You've missed a lot since yesterday," Carmeline said.

Rita shrugged, lifted her wineglass. "None of my business anymore."

"Sure it is," Carmeline said. "You still live in this neighborhood. You've still got skin in this game. Babs can't change that with a wave of her hand."

"Babs can do whatever she wants," Rita said. "That's the deal."

"Maybe not anymore."

Rita stared. "You want to be careful how you talk in my house."

"For Christ's sake, Rita," Carmeline said. "I'm on *your side*, here. I'm trying to get you back in. Babs has gone too far."

Rita stared at her. "Maybe you're not hearing me," she said. "Babs can do *whatever she wants.*"

"This isn't a dictatorship."

Rita lit her own cigarette, took a long drag, and gazed out the window again, where the summer twilight lingered. "Well, you're right about that, at least."

Carmeline poured them both more wine. "Then what the hell are we talking about?"

"Do you remember when I moved to New York?" Rita asked.

Carmeline looked at her a moment. "I'm serious about this," she said.

"So am I. Do you remember?"

"Of course I remember," Carmeline said. "It was all anyone talked about when you left."

"Right. Because that's the thing about a town like this— everybody wants to make damn sure you don't get the idea you're meant for bigger things."

"I thought you were brave," Carmeline said.

"You thought I was an idiot," Rita said. "Be honest. You figured I'd be back in six months, tail between my legs."

"That's not true. I gave you a full year."

Rita smiled dimly. "But I lasted five. And did you know that every one of those years, Babs went to my ma's house on Mother's Day and her birthday, to spend time? Took her out to lunch. Flowers and presents. Every year."

"Can't picture it," Carmeline said. She stubbed her cigarette out with a twist of her thumb.

"Babs didn't want my mother to be alone. It didn't sit right with her. She was better to my own mother than I was, Carmeline. And she did it on my behalf."

"She never told me that."

"You think her power comes from pushing people around. But that's not it. Her power is in here." Rita tapped her fingers against her own chest. "She loves everything—her grandson, her daughters, us, this neighborhood—harder than you even know is possible. If you loved like Babs does, it would break you."

The expression on Carmeline's face made clear that she knew Rita was right.

"But it will never break her. Just the opposite. It gives her the strength to make decisions no one else wants to make. And that," Rita said, pointing at Carmeline, "is why she'll always be in charge."

Of the many things in Waterville that Babs loved so hard, the Hollingsworth & Whitney mill did not count among them. Built with Boston Brahmin capital, it was in Babs's mind a brick-and-mortar manifestation of the prevailing order of things: Anglos rich and getting ever richer off the labor of Francos, who in turn got sick from the devil's bargain they made with the mill and its masters. That the mill was built a quarter mile *upriver* from Little Canada was no accident. That the prevailing winds blew northeast to southwest, the same direction as the river, wasn't either. At best Babs's people had suffered five generations of blinding headaches, the frightening clinch of asthma, and just generally feeling shitty twenty-four-seven from whatever billowed out of the smokestack and glopped from the discharge pipes into the Kennebec. At worst, they died early and painfully from all manner of diseases that were supposed to be rare. Emphysema, Hodgkin's lymphoma, leukemia—each had claimed multiple Dionnes and Levesques, including Babs's own father, whose body had withered so completely that Babs, at age nineteen, could lift him from his bed and carry him to the bathroom by herself. What was more, Little Canada had plenty of "slow" children, who these days would be diagnosed with birth defects and/or developmental disorders, but whose struggles to read and understand simple math were attributed, back then, to the inescapable misfortune of being dumb Frenchmen. At one point in the 1980s, a doctor at the Dana-Farber Cancer Institute in Boston started an inquiry into why she was seeing so much pediatric cancer from this tiny town in central Maine. Like every other attempt to determine just what the mill was pumping out and how it affected the health of adults, kids, and even the unborn, her efforts went nowhere.

So no, Babs had no love for the mill, though it had fed her family for eighty years. Now it sat neutered, stripped of its machinery, vandalized and defiled, which was just fine by her. If she thought she could get away with it, she would have used the five hundred pounds of TNT Rheal bought from the Saucier brothers during the strike years ago and spared the private equity vultures the trouble of leveling the place. She'd given this serious thought on at least a couple of occasions, usually after two too many glasses of wine. Just wire the mill up, hit the switch, and laugh as chunks of brick came down like rain. As she stood beside her station wagon in the parking lot, gazing up at the mill's facade and wondering who, exactly, was waiting for her inside, it occurred to her that she might finally make good on the idea, assuming she lived through the night.

The air hung thick and still, seeming to cling to her skin. It had to rain sooner or later, a big thunderstorm to finally break the spine of this heat wave, but so far, for two full weeks, the skies had refused to open up. Tonight, more of the same: just a few puffs of cloud skimming the full moon. Babs took the compact Springfield .45 from its holster on the back of her belt and checked by moonlight to make sure a round was chambered. She crossed the parking lot and let herself in through what had once been a service entrance, a door to which she'd had the key for nearly fifty years, since she'd taken Sacha Marquette's key ring after stabbing his lung and leaving him to drown in his own blood.

Lori had already been staking the mill out for an hour, having climbed through a broken window on the north side of the boiler house and hidden herself on the ground floor underneath a stairwell.

Riding a steady high from three Oxys spaced an hour apart each, she had nearly dozed off when the screech of the service door opening jolted her back to consciousness. Footsteps on the concrete floor, steady and unhurried, moving toward her. She fought the urge to peek around the stairwell—moonlight from the big windows on the opposite wall made it too risky. The footfalls reached the stairs under which Lori hid and began climbing. Ten steps up to the second floor, several whispering strides across the landing, then up again. Third floor. Fourth. There, the footsteps stopped. For a minute or more, silence. Lori strained in the dark to pick up any sound, but there was nothing. And then, the nicotine timbre of her mother's voice, echoing down the exposed brick:

"I'm on the fourth floor, and I'm done climbing stairs! Whoever you are, you can come find me here!"

No response, no other sounds. The moon inched up above the top border of the windows, the light moving down from the wall behind Lori to form a row of silver rectangles on the concrete floor. Upstairs, Babs stayed put and stayed quiet. Lori checked her watch: an hour and a half since her mother had arrived. When she looked back up, she was not surprised to find her father, Rheal, sitting next to her on the floor—after all, the old man had always liked a captive audience.

Rheal appeared to Lori as he had been most of her life, until near the end: broad-shouldered and powerful, cords of muscle standing out in his neck and forearms, a practical joker's gleam in his eyes. "At the risk of sounding like I don't appreciate your company, *ma puce*," he said, "what the fuck are you doing here?"

Lori gave him a sharp look, pressing a finger to her mouth.

"She can't hear me," Rheal said. "You know that."

"She can hear *me*," Lori whispered.

"Nevertheless," Rheal said, "the question remains."

"What am I doing here? I'm watching out for her."

Rheal coughed violently, his lungs crackling like paper being wadded in a fist. "Not here in the mill," he said. "I mean *here* here. Home."

"I'm here," Lori said, "because you died."

"Don't try and lay it at my door. Way I remember it, you only wasted one afternoon seeing me off. And that was eight months ago."

"You know what I mean, Dad."

"Yes, and you know what *I* mean," Rheal said. "Thanks for coming back to pay your respects. I appreciate that. Really. Now get the fuck out of Dodge. *Sors.*"

"I can't."

"Why not?"

Lori stared at him. "I have to find Sis, for starters," she said.

Rheal shook his head. "Celeste doesn't care if she's found or not. Dead is dead."

"Well, I'm alive. And I need to figure out what happened to Sis before Ma knows she's gone."

"Yeah, that's gonna be a shitshow."

"More like a bloodbath."

"Just one more reason for you to beat it."

Lori sat back against the wall and gazed up at the underside of the staircase. "I can't leave her alone with this, Papa."

Rheal was seized by another coughing fit. He leaned into one closed fist, hacking and gasping. When he'd recovered, he looked at his daughter with wet eyes. "I was married to that woman for forty years," he said. "Does she need help? You're goddamn right she does. But will she accept it? Never. Not from you, not from anyone else. When she finds out about Celeste, everything burns. The best you can do is get far enough away you don't catch fire yourself."

Lori didn't respond.

"So get over this bullshit about needing to *be here* for your mother. You made the right move the first time you split town. You should leave again. Now."

Lori stared at him. "No," she said. "I'm the only one left."

Rheal gazed at her, took a deep, shuddering breath, and let it out with a sigh. "I realize it's against the rules these days to say anything bad about women," he said. "But fucked if you aren't the biggest pain in the ass a loving God could ever have conceived of."

And he was gone.

And in the next instant Lori's phone, which she'd neglected to set to silent, chimed cheerfully from her pocket.

Fuck fuck fuck. She yanked out the phone, almost dropped it, got a firm grip, and hit the mute button, all the while marveling at her own stupidity. The empty mill was as quiet and cavernous as a church; no way Babs hadn't heard that racket. Lori could almost picture her mother tensed and ready above, all her senses straining, maybe even sniffing the air like an animal. The one slim saving grace was that Lori never had any use for a cute, customized ringtone. No snippet of Jimmy Buffett or "Flight of the Bumblebee" for her, and thus no way Babs could tell her phone from a thousand others. Thank Christ for small blessings.

Still, her mother now knew *someone* was in the mill with her, if not who. And that was a problem. Because here came Babs's footsteps again, not clomping the way they'd gone up, but softer, stealthy—and coming back down.

Lori's brain told her body to push upright and run, but after three hours folded in various configurations on a hard floor, her legs took their time responding. She managed to get to her feet and hobble-run the length of the boiler room, away from the staircase, back toward the window she'd come in through, her legs loosening up painfully as she went. Maybe she could never hope to be her mother's equal in most ways, but she was still faster than the old hag, by God, and before Babs had made it to the ground floor Lori was already sliding into the cab of her truck, parked in the shadows on the back side of the building.

She glanced around—no other cars, no other people, no nothing. A siren started up in the distance—cop or ambulance it was impossible to know, but either way it wasn't coming for her. Otherwise, the town was still. To her right, the river flowed black and deep, moonlight winking off the eddies. To the left, at the intersection where Water and Bridge Streets met, traffic lights blinked lonely yellow. All clear. Babs wasn't about to crawl out the window, and whatever boogeyman was supposed to have met her here had obviously taken the night off.

Lori looked down at her phone. One missed call—from Aubrey. She started the truck, threw it into gear, and dialed back.

"Lore?"

"Are you all right?" Lori turned left onto Water Street, past the Kentucky Fried Chicken and the Chez Paree and the American Legion, heading back into the heart of Little Canada toward home. No one on the streets.

"Doesn't matter," Aubrey said. Lori could tell she was high as Sputnik, but there was something else in her voice, too, something earthbound and primal cutting through the meth: she was afraid. "Listen, I only have a few seconds."

A pause on the other end. Lori drove straight past her street without realizing it.

"Rex got high," Aubrey said. "Then he got chatty."

Lori stiffened, her hands tight on the wheel. "Tell me."

"He was with Sis two nights ago. The junkyard out on 32, in Vassalboro. Had her boosting car stereos and copper wire, to get back in his good graces."

"I know the place," Lori said. "What else did he say?"

"Nothing, really. Just that he left her there."

"What does that mean?"

"Coming from Rex?" Aubrey said. "Who knows. He seemed real pleased with himself, though."

Lori whipped a right onto Grove Street, speeding up the hill and past the cemetery.

"I could get my tongue pulled out through my throat for telling you this, you know," Aubrey said.

"Where are you?" Lori asked. "I'll pick you up."

"Probably a bad idea, unless you fancy a face full of buckshot," Aubrey said. "I better get back inside before they notice I'm on the phone."

"Aubrey," Lori said, "listen to me. You need to get out of there."

A pause. "I did," Aubrey said. "Then you cut me loose and brought me back. But no hard feelings, Lore. I hope you find her."

B ack at the mill Babs continued to wait, once again camped out on the fourth floor. It was past three in the morning, more than five hours since she'd arrived, and the sky had already lightened a shade in the east with the sun's approach. But Babs would wait however long she had to. She knew when she was being tested. Whoever this interloper was, he hadn't forgotten about her, and he hadn't changed his mind. He was just making sure she understood this all happened on his terms.

Babs had to admire it. And she looked forward to expressing that admiration.

But for now she sat gazing around the former wash room, a space the size of an airplane hangar whose purpose, when the mill was functional, had been to remove the toxic slurry called black liquor from wood pulp. Back in the day, working the wash room was as close to a guaranteed cancer ticket in your Wonka Bar as one could get; whenever somebody in Little Canada was diagnosed with leukemia or lymphoma the first question out of people's mouths was not "Did he smoke?" (everyone did) or "Did he eat right?" (obviously not) but rather, "He work the wash room?" Most often, the answer was yes, and most often, the person in question was dead before he had an opportunity to draw on his pension. Still, wash room jobs were the best-paying in the mill, a fact that for most was at least as important a consideration as how long they could expect to live if they took it.

Babs removed a clementine from her breast pocket and dug into it with her fingernails, dropping hooks of peel to the floor between her feet. Her right hand shook as she worked, and she was reminded of yesterday morning and how she'd lied to Jason, the same way she'd been lying to herself for three months. She knew all too well what caused the tremors in her hand. It was Huntington's, the frenzied dance that had taken her mother, who'd gone from an odd new hitch in her stride to her eternal reward in three years flat. No treatment, no cure, and nothing to be done about it—then or now. She smacked her hand against her thigh several times, then pried a segment from the clementine and popped it into her mouth.

She needed the clementine for sugar. And she needed the sugar to keep her eyes and ears sharp. Someone was coming, finally—she knew it, the same way she'd known spring 1977 would bring the worst flood Waterville had seen in a hundred years, the same way she'd woken up one morning in the late '80s to the certainty that a neighborhood girl named Janet Brochu had been murdered and dumped in the river. Babs couldn't turn this ability on or off, or know when it would hit her. She also didn't consider it paranormal in the least; to her way of thinking she was just occasionally tuned to a frequency most people couldn't pick up. So now, even though she didn't hear any doors open downstairs, and didn't hear any footsteps on either of the stairwells, she knew that whoever sought her had arrived. She put the last of the clementine in her mouth and stood, brushing bits of pith from the front of her shirt.

When the mill was still running, a row of six massive drum washers had churned wood pulp in this room day and night for forty years. The washers were gone now, but their concrete bases remained, thirty feet long and fifteen across, pierced at five-foot intervals by bolts the diameter of a man's wrist, which had held the washers in place. On the opposite side of the room, another doorway opened on the east stairwell. And in this doorway a black figure appeared, seeming to materialize rather than enter, silent as fog.

Babs planted her feet and lit a cigarette; she wasn't about to do this asshole the courtesy of going to him when he finally deigned to show up. Somewhere in the building water dripped steadily, and in the eaves pigeons fussed and cooed. Babs took a long drag, ready to wait until the second coming if she had to.

But whoever this was, he apparently was finished playing games. He moved from the doorway into the wash room and passed the tall windows in a slow strobe, going from dark to light, dark to light. Handsome but also somehow featureless, The Man crossed the distance between them with a stride so upright it bordered on prim, the hard soles of his dress shoes, silent before, now clicking smartly against the wooden floorboards. He came to a stop an arm's length from Babs, and she continued to smoke, silent and impassive.

"Mrs. Dionne," The Man said.

"That's me," Babs said. "And you are?"

"Who I am is not important at all."

A quiet beat passed between them as they appraised one another, a silent calculus that both excelled at. Babs noted The Man betrayed none of the physiological signs of agitation or excitement she would expect to see standing this close. His gaze on her was steady, pupils normal given the lack of light. His mouth was set in a straight, unmoving line across his face. If he was breathing, she could neither hear nor see any evidence of it. He didn't even sweat, despite the heat that persisted even now in the mill's brick interior.

"Okay," Babs said.

Another moment of silence.

"Listen," Babs said finally, "I know you're probably used to this creepy-calm routine scaring the shit out of people, but I'm sort of underwhelmed. Not to mention dog-tired. So maybe just get to the point of what we're doing here."

The Man smiled, his mouth widening and opening and turning up sharply at the corners to reveal uncannily perfect teeth. "My employer is a man named Ogopogo," he said. "Do you know of him?"

"I've heard of the giant snake."

"Different Ogopogo."

"One would assume."

"Biennially," The Man said, "Ogopogo performs an audit of his areas of business, to determine how both his contract employees and his product are performing."

"Do you always talk like this?" Babs asked.

"Like what?"

"Like you sell plumbing supplies and not dope."

Another smile from The Man. He glanced over at the window-sill. "Do you mind if I sit?" he asked. "I've been on my feet for days."

"Be my guest," Babs said.

The Man brushed bits of broken glass from the sill and sat down. "In the latest audit," he said, "it became evident that Waterville and surrounding areas have grossly underperformed for the last two years. This is a period when, on average, sales have increased tenfold."

"What does that have to do with me?" Babs asked.

The Man tilted his head at her. "You said it yourself: Ogopogo sells heroin," he said. "And *you* sell pharmaceutical opioids."

Now it was Babs's turn to smile.

"You can see, then," The Man said, "why I'm here."

"I can," Babs said, taking a last drag of her cigarette and flicking the butt to the floor. "But before we get to that, maybe you'll indulge me for a moment."

"Certainly," The Man said. "I've been waiting long enough to speak with you. There's no need to rush."

"Great. Then let me ask you a question."

"Whatever you like."

"Are you Catholic, or Protestant?"

The first sign that The Man could be knocked off his game, however slight: he paused in answering, a twinge of bemusement in his eyes. "I wouldn't describe myself as particularly religious," he said. "But I was born into a family that observed Lutheran traditions."

"That's what I figured," Babs said.

"May I ask how that's relevant to the issue at hand?"

"It *is* the issue at hand," Babs said.

"I'm afraid I don't follow."

"You're Protestant. I'm Catholic. Being from Canada, I'm sure you understand the significance of those facts."

"Dogmatic differences are not the point of contention here."

"I'm sure you believe that. Because you have no sense of history. Anything happened longer ago than last week, you think it's nothing to do with today."

"It is true," The Man said, "that I see limited utility in spending time thinking about—or arguing over—the past."

"Well, let me give you a bit of history that, like it or not, is right smack in the middle of this discussion," Babs said. "Three generations ago my family came here from Quebec to avoid starving to death. They worked in this mill. For the first couple of years they lived down there in the mud on the riverbank. Got paid next to nothing. By men who observed the same traditions as your family."

"Again, this has nothing to do with what we're here to discuss," The Man said.

"That's what you think," Babs said, taking a step toward The Man. "Because no one torched crosses on your lawn. No one stuck you in ghettos and let diseases burn out of control. No one made you write 'I will not speak French in class' on the chalkboard a thousand times."

A sudden darkness crossed The Man's face, so dramatic a shift it seemed less like an expression and more like his features, such as they were, had morphed somehow. Whether he was reacting to her words or her posture Babs didn't know—but she was getting to him, which was what mattered.

"You know very little about me," The Man said.

"Maybe," Babs said. "But let me tell you something I do know. Every time Francos let English-speaking men run things, our customs disappear, our language disappears, our God disappears. Well,

not this time. Not here. You can have the rest of the wide world—
but you can't have this place."

L ori was neither a detective nor a master criminal, but she knew
better than to drive into the dirt lot of Colbert & Sons Salvage
and leave tire prints all over the place, if this was indeed where she
would find her one and only kid sister. Instead she pulled onto the
shoulder of Route 32, parking the truck in a hollow in the underbrush where it was less likely to be noticed by passing cars. She checked
her weapon, took the flashlight from the glove box, and peered at what
was visible of the junkyard's campus through the foliage. The steady
buzz of nocturnal insects and the way moonlight caressed everything should have seemed peaceful, even comforting. Instead, alone
in the cold light reflected off a distant orbital rock, among bugs that
sought dead things to eat, Lori felt chilled despite the heat. The meek
would inherit the earth, indeed, and good luck taking any comfort
from that fact.

Lori got out of her truck, and before she'd even closed the door
it hit her: The malignant bite of char in the air. This was not the ionized, electric scent of an active blaze, but rather what was left when
the fires went out: ash, soot, sorrow. The fumes stung her eyes and
the back of her throat, and she became suddenly unstuck in time
and space, transported to the waadi outside Kandahar, watching
wisps of smoke unravel off the little girl's shoulders and burned-bald
head as she begged not to die. The world slid sideways and Lori fell
back against her truck, gulping air, waiting until her head cleared
again.

Under the full moon, endless mounds of junk stood out as clearly
as if it were daylight. Still a bit unsteady, Lori walked past the mass

graves of dented washing machines, old outboard motors, and refrigerators with their doors torn off. Hubcaps of every imaginable
design sat lined up like toy soldiers in rows a quarter mile long. Old
tires, of course—thousands of them, ranging in size from tricycle to
tractor-trailer. Three-foot cubes of compacted scrap metal stacked in
a ziggurat twenty feet high. A whole section of loose machine parts,
a bin of lawn mower blades, another of timing chains curled together
like gassed snakes. The great, grimy beast of American commerce—
of which Lori herself was just one more spent part—on full, ignoble
display.

She came around a hill of unsorted scrap that put her in mind of
the detritus left behind when a tsunami recedes: random pieces of
thousands of lives thrown together in an undifferentiated mass. And
on the other side of this monument to loss and grief was where Lori
found the cars—some compacted, some jacked up from accidents,
some just aged beyond repair. Foreign and domestic, coupes, hatchbacks, wagons, vans, SUVs. A sea of them, stretching a hundred
yards to the back of the junkyard, which ended abruptly at a legion
of white pines that seemed to stand sentry over it all.

Lori knew where she would dump a body, if she had to.

And so she started checking cars, walking up and down the rows
between vehicles, shining her flashlight through windshields and
side windows. She found the furry husk of a squirrel on the dash of
a '97 Explorer. A Chevy van wall-to-wall with bundled newspapers
from more than a year earlier. Some aspiring author's sci-fi manu-
script on the passenger seat of a mid-'90s Jetta.

Interspersed among the repos and vehicles that had simply quit
were the twisted, crumpled bodies of wrecks, their interiors a conga
line of gore: Someone's front teeth embedded in a dashboard. A spi-
derwebbed windshield with hair and bits of gray matter stuck to the

inside. Old blood on everything: seat belts, upholstery, center consoles, airbags.

Lori paused and looked up, gazing across the whole of the car area again, despairing at how long it would take to check every last one, and what other horrors she would find in the process. There were ten acres of vehicles. She'd be lucky to get through half of them by daybreak.

But then she thought of the smell of smoke on the air, and she knew, suddenly and with terrible certainty, that the car she was looking for had been burned.

You may be wondering," The Man said to Babs, "why I'm here to talk, instead of just killing you and being done with it."

"No, I figured that out," Babs said.

"And what conclusion did you reach?"

"It's easier for you to convince me to work for your boss, rather than setting up your own infrastructure with your own people."

"Very good," The Man said.

"There's just one problem," Babs said. "I don't work for anyone but myself and my neighborhood."

The Man smiled and rose from the windowsill. "Forgive me," he said, "but you work for your neighborhood how, exactly? By flooding it with OxyContin?"

"You're in the business, so you know as well as I do," Babs said. "Laws don't control drugs. Throwing people in jail doesn't control drugs. The very fact you're here demonstrates that what I do isn't *dealing*. It's regulation. I control which drugs come into my neighborhood. I control how much. And I control who does and does not have access."

"And the profits you reap. Are those incidental? Merely the by-product of this regulation you so nobly take upon yourself?"

Babs shrugged. "Doesn't matter what the work is," she said. "Someone always has to be paid."

The Man continued smiling at her for a moment, then looked out the window he'd been sitting in. "It's a tidy philosophy you have. Unfortunately, it's also irrelevant. I've enjoyed this talk, Mrs. Dionne. Truly. But now it's time to get down to the essence of the matter at hand."

"Which is?"

The Man turned to Babs again, the smile gone from his face. "The fact that this is not a negotiation, as you seem to think," he said. "There is no room for compromise, or discussion of terms. There is simply me telling you what to do, and you doing it."

Babs looked at him, incredulous, a smile spreading on her own face now. The smile widened and opened, revealing teeth, and Babs barked a laugh. Then she laughed some more. She went on laughing long after it would have been comfortable, in most social contexts, to keep doing so. She put a hand to her mouth, her eyes squeezed tight with real mirth. She put her other hand against the wall and leaned forward, struggling to breathe, caught now in that liminal space where laughter and tears mingle and meld. The Man watched, expressionless as granite.

After a few more moments, Babs began to compose herself. She sighed, wiping at her eyes with the back of one hand. "I'm sorry," she said, still chuckling. "I'm not trying to be rude. It's just . . . it's just . . ."

A click, the glint of moonlight on steel—and Babs held the short, wide blade of a push dagger against The Man's throat, to the right of his Adam's apple, where his carotid artery pulsed just beneath the skin.

"It's just you obviously don't have any idea who you're dealing with," Babs said.

"I'm developing a sense," The Man said.

"Don't move," Babs said. "Wouldn't want to ruin that nice suit. Now. Where is my daughter?"

"Which one?"

"Cute," Babs said. "You got information from LaVerdiere about Sis."

"My conversation with Dr. LaVerdiere was private and confidential," The Man said.

"Don't worry, barrister, he told me all about it," Babs said. "As you know, he tends to wilt under questioning. What did you do with the information he gave you?"

"I'm afraid," The Man said, "that my business is just that: my business."

Babs applied pressure to the tip of the dagger, just enough to draw a pinprick of blood. She studied The Man's face as she did this, analyzing, looking for any reaction, but The Man didn't flinch, and his expression remained impenetrable.

"You tell your boss to stay in his lane," Babs said. "And I'll stay in mine."

"That's simply not an acceptable answer," The Man said.

"Why not?" Babs asked. "Will your boss string you up?"

The Man said nothing, but Babs saw something flicker in his eyes.

"Ah," she said, "I get it. Not your boss. Your *lover.*"

Another flicker. She'd hit her mark.

"You aren't afraid of Ogopogo—you want to please him. You want his approval. It's like the sunrise to you."

"Regardless of the reason," The Man said, "the fact is I can't return to him with a no."

"Feel free to stick around, then. I may want to see you again, once I find my daughter. But the answer's not going to change."

"It will," The Man said. "Because it has to."

He pulled back, breaking contact with the blade. He put a fingertip to his neck, examined it. Nodded at Babs. Drifted away.

O nce Lori laid eyes on it, she realized that it would have been impossible to miss the car she was looking for. Not because it had burned to a husk, though it had, and not because it was set slightly apart from the rows of other vehicles and clearly did not belong here among them. The real reason she could not have failed to notice it was, quite simply, because it was still recognizably her sister's car. A 2013 Subaru WRX, hood-mounted air intake to feed the turbo engine, aftermarket whale tail Lori had always thought ridiculous, and, still legible despite scorch and soot, the vanity plate: L8R.

Lori stopped dead twenty feet away. Took in the car's blackened frame, the whale tail melted like candle wax, the license plate. Her legs went weak, then numb; she had to lean against the hood of a nearby Toyota to keep from crumpling to the dirt. Six months earlier Lori'd had a day surgery and Sis had driven her home afterward, and when Lori went to climb out of the WRX her legs, still in thrall to anesthetic, didn't get the message and she wound up face down in the driveway, cackling, wasted, oblivious. This was like that, minus the laughter. The Subaru's windows were shattered, whitewalls flattened, frame black as a barbecue that hadn't been cleaned in two summers. And then the waadi appeared again, transposed over the junkyard like a viewfoil. Lori was here, but she was also there. Both a shiftless junkie, and a staff sergeant in charge of a squad of Marines.

A woman who knew the very notion of saving anyone from anything was vainglorious fantasy, and a woman convinced she could save a little girl who was as good as dead. And neither her present nor her former self could change what had happened, or rescue anyone, or absolve herself for failing to do so. All she could do was carry the burden of bearing witness, *à jamais et jamais, amen.*

And so Lori willed her numb feet forward. Step by staggering step. Tears forming and flowing, her breath coming in ragged gasps. She moved alongside the Subaru, saw what was inside, and collapsed as if she'd been struck dead herself, suddenly still and mute. This was grief far beyond tears, a mind-erasing sadness. Lori lay catatonic on her side, head resting on one arm, her eyes staring blindly. Sis in the back seat above her could have been a nascent sculpture, the barest suggestion of a human form, carved roughly from a block of obsidian. The insects went on chirping. Half an hour passed, then an hour, Lori still absent, a cognitive void. Ursa Major rotated around Polaris like the minute hand on an analog clock; by the time Lori became aware of herself again, it had gone from two o'clock to halfway between three and four. As she slowly came back to this time and place, Lori could think of only one thing. She staggered to her feet and pulled on the rear door handle; despite the state of the car, the door opened with ease. Lori bent down and leaned into the passenger compartment. She reached around where Sis's neck had been, keeping her face turned away, and unclasped the locket Sis had worn every minute of her life since first putting it on more than a decade before.

Then Lori ran. Locket in hand, she ran back through the rows and rows of derelict cars, past the pile of tsunami debris and the scrap metal ziggurat, the machine parts sorted by type, the tires and hubcaps and refrigerators and washing machines, ran all the way back to her truck by the roadside, and she jumped in and reached under the dash where she'd taped a blister pack of Adderall for just such an occasion, namely an occasion when she intended to fuck someone up and didn't want fear or good sense getting in the way. She crushed and snorted the Adderall and turned the ignition and threw the transmission in drive with one hand while with the other she pulled the Glock from its holster and rubbed her thumb raw against the grip and the truck's engine screamed and her headlights chewed up the darkness.

A party of sorts was still in full swing at 5 a.m. when Lori opened the front door to Rex's foyer. The room overflowed with tweakers, gone gone gone, some half or fully undressed, a few wearing animal heads (a male lion, complete with stiff-bristled mane, in the hot tub; an antelope's vigilant countenance atop a woman's nude torso in the far corner), all communicating in some language unknown to Lori, a primitive tongue accessible only to those who had lost their minds. The tweakers immediately recognized the intrusion of someone who did not vibrate on the same frequency, and immediately moved to fall upon her, like a pack of zombies in a horror film. Their mistake was believing they were the scary people in the room, that everyone should and would be afraid of them because they were strange, because they were insane with drugs, because they'd given up hope.

But Lori was also hopeless, and she had two things these amateurs did not: training, and her mother's rage. She could have easily ended the entire thing with a couple of well-placed rounds from the Glock, but she'd come here for a fight, and she meant to have one. So she kept the gun at her side. As the tweakers rushed her she grabbed a narrow, solid stick of ash from the firewood rack and set to work. The man closest to her got the stick in the side of the neck, vagus nerve, lights-out immediately, and he went down in front of the others, keeping them at range for several seconds as they clambered over him and Lori kept swinging. Her vision narrowed, a viewfinder that saw not people but targets: a nose to pulverize, a collarbone to shatter, a larynx to collapse. More tweakers fell, but more kept coming, pressing in on her as she backpedaled. Hands grasped at her hair, her shirt, and Lori hacked at them with the piece of wood, bloodying knuckles and breaking one wrist with an audible pop. Then four or five tweakers rushed her as one, closing the range to inches, the stick pried from her grasp as a dozen hands punched and clawed. Bloodied, Lori began to buckle under the weight of them, and she knew that, just as with dogs, if these people got her on the floor she was finished. So that's when she started shooting.

Three rounds was all it took to clear the room, people running through doorways and leaping out of windows, scrambling across the floor on all fours. Only those unlucky few who found themselves with fresh holes in their bodies remained—along with the lion in the hot tub, who still sat chest-deep in the roiling water, lion face turned toward Lori, impassive, inscrutable. Rex. The King. Still holding court even after the court had been shot to shit.

Lori wiped blood from her nose, crossed to the hot tub, and pressed the Glock's muzzle right up against the lion's. "Take it off," she said, "or I'll kill you."

"You're going to kill me anyway."

Lori grabbed a fistful of the mane and pulled, tossing the lion's head to the floor. The man underneath was not Rex.

"Where is he?" Lori asked.

"Where is who?"

Lori raised the Glock like a hammer, meaning to bash this fucker in the head for her trouble—when she felt steel press against her back. She turned and saw the same woman from before, with the same shotgun.

"Drop it," this woman told Lori.

"Shoot me," Lori said, turning fully and stepping forward into the barrels.

"I'll do it," the woman said.

"Promises, promises," Lori said. She grabbed the end of the shotgun and pulled it into her chest. "Shoot me, you fucking cunt!"

But looking in the woman's eyes, Lori saw that if she wanted deliverance, she was going to have to seek it elsewhere. She yanked the shotgun away and kicked the woman to the floor, straddled her, and put the Glock between her eyes.

"That's the second time you've pointed a gun at me," Lori said. "There will not be a third."

"He's in the shed!" the woman told her.

"Who?"

"Rex. That's who you want, right? He's out back, in the shed."

Lori pulled the Glock back and got to her feet. "If you move," she told the woman, "I'll kill you. You, too, Mufasa," she said to the man in the hot tub on her way out.

Lori stepped off the back porch, sending a few lingering tweakers running for the trees. She assessed the shed as she would any building she meant to breach—for starters, it was more like a cabin, an outbuilding twenty or so feet square, the windows blacked out, slivers of interior light escaping at the edges. From the look of it, a single large room. No way for Lori to know what awaited her inside. But she had to assume Rex was on alert, given the chaos her arrival had caused.

So surprise was out, but misdirection remained an option. Lori found a fist-size stone in the grass and tossed it through one of the shed's side windows, then ran around to the front and lifted one boot to kick the door in—when she heard Rex's voice through the newly broken windowpane.

"Would you get in here and kill me already?" he called out. "You'll want to hurry up, or else your friend Aubrey's likely to bleed out."

She felt a flare of alarm at the mention of Aubrey, and then the flare mellowed, leaving behind the cool glow of reason: a ploy, of course, and not a particularly artful one. Maybe Rex wanted to die, maybe he didn't; either way he surely planned to do his best to reunite Lori with Sis. She stepped back, imagined a line between herself and the broken window, angled to the left, and fired ten of her remaining twelve rounds through the door. A groan, a thump. She turned the doorknob and pushed, jumped back as it swung open and a column of jaundiced light spilled out into the yard. No shots, no movement, nothing.

Lori crouched and stepped through, sweeping the Glock across the room. No threats. Two figures, both prone, one on the floor, one lashed to a bare mattress on a metal bedframe, the only furniture in the room. Aubrey. Flayed and bleeding slow, out cold or dead, hard to say. Lori went to her, pressed fingertips to her throat. A panicked thrumming, blood volume way down but still enough, for now.

Nearby, Rex kicked his feet against the floor. Lori slid across and pinned him with a knee to the chest, searched his pockets, found his phone, dialed 9-1-1 and threw the phone down as it rang. Rex laughed breathlessly, his own blood bubbling from wounds in his shoulder and above his collarbone.

"Nine-one-one, please state your emergency . . ."

"There's a woman here trying to kill me!" Rex cackled.

Lori kicked the phone away. "I'm giving you ten seconds to get right with God," she said to Rex.

"It's going to take longer than that, I'm afraid."

"Then I guess you'll have to settle accounts in person."

"Did you find your sister?" Rex asked.

"Why do you think I'm here, motherfucker?"

"She okay? Where was she?"

Lori put the Glock against Rex's forehead. "Five seconds."

"No no no," Rex said. "Don't be *merciful*. Shoot me in the knees first. Blow off my fingers. Make it *hurt*."

Lori jammed a thumb into the hole above his collarbone, and Rex howled.

"That hurt enough?" Lori asked.

"It's a start."

Lori wiped her thumb on his shirt. "Time's up, Rex. I have to go. But you're going first."

"I knew I had you pegged," Rex said.

"How's that?"

"You're a killer."

"That's right," Lori said. "And I'm going to mount your head on my fucking wall, *pardieu*."

She pressed the Glock against his chest, over his heart. Rex closed his eyes and breathed in slowly. Lori wrapped her finger around the trigger, looked up, and saw the Afghan girl standing in her melted Crocs just a few feet away, gazing at her with the one good eye.

"كلذ لعفت ال," the girl said.

"Go away," Lori told her. She straightened up above Rex and put both hands on the Glock, pressing down against his chest.

"كلذ لعفت ال," the girl said.

"He killed my sister!" Lori said. "You don't understand what this is! Now go away!"

Beneath her, Rex had opened his eyes again, and was smiling. "Christ, you're even crazier than I am," he said.

"كسفنب اذه لعفت نأ كديرأ ال .هب متهأ ال ال انأ," the girl said.

The words made Lori want to weep, but she refused to cry in front of Rex, so she stood up and ran out of the shed and around the main house, got into her truck, and sped out of there, dialing her own phone now.

"Come on," she said, spinning gravel under her tires as she peeled away from the farmhouse and lurched onto the road, headlight beams bouncing. "Pick up, Bates, goddammit."

On the fifth ring he did, his voice low and irritable with sleep.

"Listen to me carefully," Lori told him. "Don't talk, just listen."

"Okay," Bates said.

"My sister is dead."

"Oh Jesus."

"The guy who did it runs a meth operation out of a farmhouse out on 32. Rex White. There's another girl there right now, and she's pretty close to being dead herself. I already called 9-1-1, ambulance and probably sheriff's deputies on their way. But I need you to get out there. Ten minutes ago."

"Why?"

"Because I shot the place up."

"Jesus Christ, Lori," Bates said. She could hear him moving now, probably climbing out of bed. "There's only so much I can do. This is going to end up with the Staties. If I try to cover for you, we could all be exposed."

She hung up. Watched her headlights for a few minutes. Then placed another call, this time to Paul, the friend she rang when nothing but a spike in a vein would do. Despite the hour, Paul answered right away.

"I need you," Lori said. "My house. Whenever you can get there."

And then she sped home, went inside, drew a bath as hot as she could stand it, and got in with her clothes still on. She took Sis's locket and dipped it in the water and wiped at the soot with her thumb. But that accomplished nothing, so she grabbed a nailbrush from the soap shelf and scrubbed until the etching became visible.

SFC. JEAN DIONNE
1984–2006
RAMADI, IRAQ
DIED FOR A LIE

Lori dropped the brush into the water and, with her thumbnail, flipped the locket's tiny clasp open. The picture embedded inside— Jean on his graduation from Basic, blue dress uniform, a sternness that he occupied with utter conviction, single chevron on his shoulder to designate him private second class, which rank he'd been given instead of buck private for having enlisted as an Eagle Scout— had been obliterated by the heat of the fire. All that remained were cracks and bubbles and swirls of scorched color.

Paul appeared in the doorway. Queerer than a three-dollar bill, he'd been friends with Lori since freshman year at Waterville High. Lori raised her pleading eyes.

"Oh my," Paul said at the sight of her. "Let's get you fixed up."

He came into the room and put the toilet seat down. Lori said nothing, just rolled up her sleeve and put her arm on the edge of the tub, the locket still dangling from her fingers. Paul opened the small vinyl carrying case that held his wares. "I've got a few options," he said. "The usual white lady. Fentanyl. I can supplement either. What do you want, honey?"

Lori stared at the wall while Paul tied off a tourniquet around her biceps. "What do I want," she said distantly, as if she didn't understand the question, or even the language it was posed in.

"White lady, then," Paul said. Spoon. Bindle. The asthmatic hiss of a butane lighter, and under that, Paul humming cheerily to himself. Several minutes passed while he cooked over the sink.

Then Lori finally answered the question. "I want to remember," she said. "I want to forget. But mostly I want to die."

Paul clicked his tongue, mock-scolding, as he turned to her with the syringe. "No one's dying tonight, my love. But here: Let's give you some wings."

CHAPTER FOURTEEN

July 3, 2016

B efore daybreak the State Police, summoned by the sheriff as was protocol in a murder case, had already closed off the salvage yard and Rex's property and begun processing both scenes, detectives snapping photographs, uniformed Staties walking the yard in pairs, sweeping the ground with their Maglites and taking notes. A few hours later, just as they began the process of removing Sis's corpse from the back seat of the charred Subaru, Babs sat in an overstuffed leather lounge chair in the well-appointed, tastefully decorated, precisely sound-dampened, marble-floored, mahogany-trimmed waiting area of the office of the president of Waterville's Colby College, Robinson Hegemony. She had no idea yet that only one of her children was still among the living. She was being made to wait, for no reason other than to remind her of her place. She looked up at the brass Patek Philippe wall clock that told time in twenty-four cities and, after a few moments of translating the concentric circles and numbers, determined that, here at least, it was twenty minutes past ten in the morning.

"Ten o'clock, right?" Babs asked.

The receptionist, an infuriatingly cute woman in her mid-twenties, looked up from her computer, eyebrows raised.

"Our appointment was for ten, I thought," Babs said. "Was I wrong about that? Am I early?"

The receptionist favored Babs with a smile that oozed condescension. "He'll be with you shortly," she said.

"Is he actually here?"

The receptionist smiled even more widely. "He'll be with you shortly," she said again.

"Can we maybe give 'shortly' a more concrete definition?"

The smile evaporated. The receptionist stared.

"He'll be with me shortly," Babs said. "Got it."

She passed another five minutes figuring out the time in Caracas, Moscow, Bangkok, Sydney . . . and finally Hegemony's door opened. He stuck his head out, gestured impatiently at Babs as though *he'd* been waiting on *her*, and retreated back into his mahogany hole.

"President Hegemony will see you now," the receptionist said brightly.

Babs moved past her without a word and entered the office.

"Close the door, please," Hegemony said from behind his desk.

Babs did so, then came and sat in one of two chairs, identical to the ones in the waiting area, on the near side of Hegemony's desk.

"Everything set?" he asked.

"Yes," Babs said. "We'll have the presentation at the building site this afternoon. It's been moved to three o'clock on account of the heat. Tomorrow, before the parade, we'll hold a small potluck with French Canadian cuisine, Franco-fiddling, and—"

"You don't need to read me the brochure," Hegemony said. "That's not what we're here to discuss."

Babs took a deep breath. "Okay," she said. "What are we here to discuss?"

"Etiquette."

"I don't follow."

"Behavior," Hegemony said. "Yours. Around the trustees. What we're trying to project."

"And what exactly would you like me to project?" Babs asked.

"Mother Teresa might be a good point of reference," Hegemony said.

"Mother Teresa was a propagandist who used the poor to further the Vatican's ends."

"See, that's exactly what I'm talking about," Hegemony said. "While it may be *true* that Mother Teresa was a parasitic ghoul, decent people don't actually *say* that. Don't you understand how all this works?"

"False piety makes the world go 'round?"

"That's right," Hegemony said, pointing a finger at Babs. "That's it precisely. So: Pretend to have regard for the trustees. Pretend to respect their dumb bourgeois opinions about everything. Pretend you can abide the fact of their existence, and they'll do you the same courtesy. Nod along to the tune they're whistling past the graveyard, that old ditty about how money and good manners can save us from the mess we've made of the only habitable planet in the known universe. And in the end, you'll get your school. Can you do that? Can you hold that tongue of yours for forty-eight hours?"

Babs looked at him squarely. "I can," she said.

"Good. Jesus. I shouldn't have to explain all this to you, Babs. Neither I nor the trustees give a damn about Franco-fiddling, or any other goofy peasant hoedowns. What *we* want is to be convinced you're going to fix things in Little Canada. So the people who send their kids here will stop asking why they spend a hundred thousand dollars a year on a school adjacent to a slum."

Babs imagined grasping Hegemony by what little hair he had left and plunging her push dagger into his larynx. "I see," she said.

"And the best way to convince us is to play the role of devoted citizen, whose only desire in life is to improve her community."

"That's exactly what I am," Babs said.

"Sure, sure. But that's not *all* you are, now is it?"

R ita was nearly finished packing her car to leave town when she got the call from Clement: a summons to the rectory. He made clear this wasn't optional, and he wouldn't say what it was about over the phone. But she had an idea, one that involved precisely what she was running away from.

This life being what it was, her idea was confirmed when Rita arrived and found Clement on the steps of the rectory, smoking a cigarette and looking haggard in jeans and an old paint-spattered T-shirt.

"How are you, Father?" she asked.

"How do I look?"

"Like you did something to piss off your boss."

Clement smiled ruefully. "Haven't we all?"

"Fair enough." Rita sat one step down from Clement and lit a cigarette of her own. "So why am I here?"

"I heard about what's happened between you and Babs," Clement said.

"Of course you did. You're a bigger gossip than any of my so-called friends."

"I'm not a gossip. I keep tabs on my flock."

"You say potato . . ."

"I won't bother beating around the bush, Rita," Clement said. "This day has not gotten nearly as awful as it's going to, and I need to save my energy."

"Okay."

"Celeste is dead."

A pause. Then Rita whispered a prayer. *"Ne laisse pas les âmes que tu as créés être séparés de toi, leur créateur."*

Clement continued. "Lori came to me this morning. She found Sis."

"Oh God. Does Babs know?"

"Not yet. That's when my day gets worse."

Rita stared out across the church parking lot and smoked.

"Babs has never needed you more than she does today," Clement said. "Not after Sacha. Not even when her son was killed. Right now."

"Please don't ask me to do this," Rita said. "I can't."

"I understand why you're angry with her. You've got every reason. But Tim is alive, and Sis has been murdered. You have to walk across the space between you, and put your arms around your sister."

*J**ust like the movies*, was the inane first thing Lori thought when she reached room 324 and found two unsmiling cops, one big, the other gigantic, guarding the door. She gave them her name, and the merely large cop ushered her in: gray walls, tile floor, overhead LED tube flooding the space with light the color of rigor mortis. In the center, squarely under the LED fixture, the room's only furnishings: a metal folding chair, a small rolling tray on which sat a paper coffee cup, and a standard-issue hospital bed, propped up in which was Rex White, his good arm shackled by a pair of handcuffs to the bed's steel frame, his bad one in a sling. Rex smiled up at her as though the prospect of spending the rest of his natural life in prison was as agreeable to him as a sunny summer day.

"*You* again," Rex said. The door closed heavy behind Lori. She looked over her shoulder and saw the guard still standing there, eyes on them through the small square window.

"I'm told you wanted to talk to me," Lori said. She sat down opposite Rex. "That you won't talk to anyone *but* me."

"Against the advice of counsel, I might add," Rex said. "His professional opinion is I should not open my gob to anyone ever again, you included."

Lori nodded toward the guard outside the door. "I half expected Tiny out there was going to arrest me."

"Why would he?" Rex said. "After all, you were nowhere near my place last night."

"I wasn't?"

"Not if I say you weren't."

"So who shot you?" Lori asked.

"Masked men," Rex said. "Maybe a rival crank dealer, maybe just a robbery. Hard to say. In any event, obviously one woman couldn't wreak all that havoc on her own."

"So what's my *quid* for your *quo*?"

"Let's start with a smoke."

"You called me down here to ask for a cigarette?"

"No," Rex said. "But since you're here."

"I think it's been a while since you could light up in hospitals."

"Just crack that window. They're not going to make a fuss," Rex said. "I'm the biggest fish law enforcement in this state has ever seen. This time tomorrow I'll be more famous than Charlie Manson."

Lori opened the window, took out her pack, lit two cigarettes, and handed one to Rex. The chain securing him to the bed was just long enough for him to lift the cigarette to his mouth, and he took a long drag, inhaled, and held it, his eyes closed.

"You know," he said after a few moments, smoke puffing as he talked, "people have forgotten the sublime pleasure of the single cigarette."

Lori ashed in the coffee cup on the tray. "They tend to focus these days on the wasting-away-from-cancer part."

"There you go," Rex said. "Everyone's so determined to live forever. They rarely stop to ask themselves what they want all that time *for*."

"Do me a favor," Lori said. "Tell me why I shouldn't use those handcuffs to choke you out right now and save John Q. Taxpayer a whole bunch of money."

"Simple," Rex said, ashing in the coffee cup. "I didn't kill your sister."

"And why should I believe that?"

"If you recall, I said I like you and will tell you the truth."

"You also had someone put a 10-gauge in my face."

Rex smiled. "Listen," he said, "right now they're getting ready to dig up every square inch of my property. When they do, they're going to find ten bodies. Why would I lie about an eleventh?"

They sat looking at each other. Rex took another drag of his cigarette, his gaze steady.

"I'm a killer, not a liar," Rex said. "You and I understand each other, I think, in that regard. Do you want me to tell you what I know about Sis's last night?" he asked.

"I'm still waiting to hear what it is you want from me, in exchange for not ratting me out to the Staties."

"We're getting to that. You in some kind of hurry?"

"I've got nowhere to be," Lori said. "I'm just trying to avoid my mother until it's time to let her know my sister is dead. Speaking of which, you're lucky you're in here and not out on the street, or else she'd be showing you what your insides look like in a few hours. I'd recommend not posting bail."

"I've got nothing to worry about from your mother."

"I doubt you've ever been so wrong about anything in your life."

Rex winced as he leaned back against the pillows. "The last time I saw Sis, she was alive, if not well, at the salvage yard where her body was found."

"What do you mean, 'if not well'?"

"She was very upset."

"Because . . ."

"I'd had enough of her impudence and told her she was cut off. Forever. And I'd pulled the starter fuse on her car, so it wouldn't run."

"Why?"

"As a kind of exclamation point."

Lori stared at Rex, smoked. "So let me make sure I have this straight," she said. "You are, in fact, a serial killer."

"More prolific than some, less than others."

"And my sister was murdered on a night when you admit you were with her, in the place where her body was found."

"Correct."

"But you want me to believe you left her alive, and it just happened that someone else came along and killed her. For no particular reason."

"See, that's where you're getting off track," Rex said.

"Which part?"

"That whoever killed Sis did it for no reason," Rex said. "Don't make that mistake. There's always a reason, and it always falls into one of two categories: passion, or profit."

"Which is it for you?"

Rex smiled again, grotesquely coy. "Mine is a peculiar *kind* of passion, I suppose."

"Why are you telling me this?"

Rex took a last drag and dropped his cigarette in the coffee cup, where it died with a brief hiss. "I loved Sis," he said. "That's why I cut her off. She was giving me every reason to kill her myself, but I didn't want to. So I want to know who *did*, as much as you do."

"I doubt that."

Rex sat back again, shook the hair out of his face. "Doesn't matter what you believe or don't believe," he said. "All that matters is what *is*. I didn't kill your sister, but they're going to be more than happy to say I did, and bury her under the prison with me. And that's what I want from you, in exchange for my silence: You can't let them do that. Find out who really did this."

Six neighborhood boys stood sweating through their Sunday best: clip-on ties and short-sleeved oxfords and shoes that hadn't seen a shine brush in a very long time, if ever. One of the boys strummed a guitar, and all six of them sang, in passable harmony:

Un Canadien errant
banni de ses foyers
Parcourait en pleurant
des pays étrangers

To the left of the boys stood Babs and Father Clement, listening intently next to an easel covered with a drop cloth. A few paces away, facing the boys, were Robinson Hegemony and a dozen well-heeled

Colby trustees, smiling awkwardly and glancing around as if they expected to be mugged at any moment.

And not without reason. This was bar-none the gnarliest neighborhood any of them had ever spent time in without the doors locked and the windows rolled up. They stood in a dirt lot by the decommissioned Kentucky Fried Chicken, which they'd learned was occupied by squatters when one stuck his head out the front entrance to puke, the erstwhile contents of his stomach—Night Train wine, mostly—splashing on the pavement as though someone had tossed a bucket of mop water. Soon after, a carload of young men had crept past and tossed a string of firecrackers at the trustees; when the car circled back around a few minutes later they were spared a second volley only when the young men saw Babs seeing them and realized that they were now neck-deep in shit. After that things had quieted down, but for the trustees—who, of course, made a habit of paying others to ensure they never had to see or interact with poor people— a rural ghetto like Little Canada remained quite alarming. All of which, Babs believed, only served her purpose. Let them be frightened into opening their wallets.

Clement leaned toward her. "I'm not sure 'Un Canadien errant' is the cheerful message we want to be sending."

"As if they're listening," Babs said. "As if they could understand even if they were."

The boys concluded their song:

Et mon pays, hélas
je ne le verrai plus

Polite applause from all assembled. The boys moved off to the side, wiping sweat from their foreheads and necks, and Babs stepped forward to take their place, turning toward Hegemony and the trustees with a broad smile on her face, suddenly the consummate saleswoman.

"We're standing on the site of Waterville's first Catholic parish, St. John's, built in 1852." Babs pulled the drop cloth off the easel to reveal a daguerreotype print of a wooden building with a modest belfry and spire. "This," she said, "was the beating heart of Little Canada. It's where people came to worship, to celebrate, to mourn, to accompany one another through the best and worst moments of their lives. It's where the bonds of community, language, and culture were forged and sustained. And with your support, it will be that place again."

She pulled a plastic overlay from the back of the easel and, transposed over the old church, they saw a modern institutional building, steel and glass and clean lines, a playground, athletic fields, lush grass, and landscaping.

"St. John's French Immersion School will teach Little Canada's children not just writing and arithmetic, but also who they are and why their community matters. I can tell you from experience that when you're poor, you seek a meaningful identity. Someplace, someone to belong to. It's as basic as breathing, especially when we're young. And we will choose whatever's available to us, good or bad. Take street gangs, of which we have a few around here. Most people believe gang members should all be thrown in prison, but they provide their members with the same basic human needs we all have: camaraderie, love, safety, a place to call our own. In that sense, a gang isn't any more criminal, or indeed immoral, than church or the Elks club. Or, say, the alumni association at a prestigious and absurdly wealthy private college."

The trustees laughed quietly, while Hegemony shot Babs a *watch it* look through his fake good humor.

"Let's be plain," Babs said. "You want wealthy parents and do-nors to stop asking why they're giving millions of dollars to a cam-pus adjacent to a slum. And I want to turn Little Canada back into the place of belonging it always was. We're both after the same thing, viewed from different angles. And St. John's School is the way to make that happen."

Babs stared beatifically at the trustees; they gazed back, sweating and blinking.

"I'd say it's time to let you get out of this sun," Babs told them. "I'll be happy to talk with each of you more informally tonight at dinner. Until then, please enjoy your time here. Have a look around. Those boys with the firecrackers won't be bothering you again, I can promise you that."

I t was late afternoon before Bates got up the nerve to call on Babs. Still ninety-four degrees at 6 p.m. as he pulled slowly to the curb and sat in his cruiser for a few moments, Father Clement on the front passenger seat beside him, dressed in the starched black shirt and pants of official church business. The chief hadn't been back to sleep since Lori's call, fourteen hours with no end in sight, shuttling back and forth between Rex White's homestead, where it turned out cooking meth was nothing compared to what else they had found, and Colbert & Sons Salvage. State Police mobile crime labs had locked down both scenes, taking notes, measuring, dotting the ground with their little numbered table tents to mark evidence. At first Bates had rationalized not going to Babs right away by telling himself they hadn't made a positive ID on Sis, so there was nothing yet to tell her mother except that Sis's car had been found torched with a body in the back. Then he'd put off going to Babs's because the State boys had stumbled on two skeletons, both female, in the crawl space under Rex's floorboards, and were now setting up a much larger operation to look for more bodies, dividing the property into a grid, calling in a couple backhoes. This drew the media like flies to shit, camera crews coming from as far away as Boston, and for the past few hours he'd had to deal with that, too—as if discovering a serial murderer had been plying his trade under Bates's nose for God knew how long wasn't plenty for one day.

When Bates had finally admitted to himself that he could wait no longer, he went home, put on his dress uniform, had a healthy slug of the Macallan in his kitchen cabinet, and called Lori and Clement. And now, with Lori not yet having arrived, it was the priest who got them moving toward an obligation neither of them wanted to fulfill.

"Sitting here wishing things were different won't do any good," Clement said. He climbed out of the cruiser and closed the door softly behind him. With a sigh, Bates put on his cap, squared it in the rearview mirror, and followed.

They were halfway up the walk when the front door opened and Babs stood there looking grim as rain in November, wearing a cocktail dress and full makeup, a cigarette smoldering in one hand. Both Bates and Clement froze at the sight of her. Babs didn't move, didn't say anything, didn't even smoke, just stood there gazing at them, looking, despite the glamorous getup, as though she hadn't slept in a month. Her right hand trembled at her side and she made no effort to hide it. Because she knew. Just from the fact of the two of them coming to her door, she knew. Nothing else would have brought Bates and Clement here together, especially in their finery.

Seconds passed. Finally, Babs spoke, almost too low to hear:

"Come in, if you're coming in." And she turned and went back inside, leaving the front door wide open just as Lori's truck finally pulled up.

The men waited for Lori, and the three of them went in together and found Babs at the head of her kitchen table, a mug in front of her. The rim of the mug was smeared with fresh lipstick stains.

"Coffee's on," Babs said.

Clement and Bates went to the counter in silence and poured themselves cups from the Mr. Coffee. Lori sat at the table with Babs. Neither of them spoke. Lori leaned forward and put her hand over her mother's, stilling the tremors. Babs laced her fingers together with Lori's and squeezed, and Lori hung her head for a moment and closed her eyes.

"Where's Jay-Jay, Ma?" she asked in a whisper.

"He's in the spare bedroom."

Lori stood and released her mother's hand. "I'm going to take him to eat," she said. "So the three of you can talk."

"You can't tell him anything."

"Then who will? And when?"

"I will," Babs said. "In a few days, when I have the time to spend with him."

"What about Bruce?"

"What *about* Bruce? He's lucky I don't go over there and kill him, just to cover my bases."

"He needs to know, Ma."

"Then tell him, if you want."

Lori got up and walked off into the living room, calling for Jason, trying her best to sound normal, whatever that meant anymore.

"The boy's going to wonder what the two of you are doing here," Babs said to Bates and Clement.

Clement lifted his mug. "If we don't let him ask," he said, "we won't have to answer."

Babs nodded. A few moments later, Lori came back through with Jason. He looked at the two men sitting with his grandmother, his eyes lingering on Bates and his uniform.

"I heard," Babs said to him, "that your aunt is taking you out for dinner. Where you heading?"

Jason lit up. "Bonanza!"

"Gross," Babs said, her face twisted in disgust. "Better you than me."

"Whatever, Mémère. Bonanza's awesome."

"I know that you think so," Babs said. "And I love you anyway. Get out of here, but first come give me a hug."

Jason did. Babs opened her arms and pulled him close. Squeezed a little too hard. Held him a little too long.

Lori exchanged glances with Clement. "All right, let's go," she said to Jason. "Before they sell out of the Jell-O cups with the crusty old whipped cream."

She took Jason by the shoulders and guided him out the door.

A beat. Two. Babs looking at Bates, then Clement, then Bates again. She lit another cigarette. Dragged deep, let it out, her gaze still moving between them. Finally: "Now tell me where you found my daughter."

"Colbert & Sons," Bates said. "Out in Vassalboro."

"I know the place," Babs said. "What else do I need to hear?"

"They burned her car with her in it," Bates said. He sipped his coffee, his own hand shaking a bit. "Coroner thinks she was dead before the fire, but confirmation will take some time."

Babs kept her gaze steady on Bates, her eyes dry. "If she was burned," she said, "how do you know for certain it's her?"

"We don't," Bates said. "Checking dental records now. But there's every reason—"

"It's her, Babs," Clement said in French.

Babs turned to him.

"She was wearing her locket," he said. "The one of Jean."

Now Babs closed her eyes, bracing herself against the table with one hand and inhaling sharply. The men waited in silence, watching grief fill her to the skin. Finally, Babs let her breath out and opened her eyes again. They were still dry.

"We have Rex White in custody," Bates said.

"It wasn't him."

"Babs. He did this. We've got God knows how many more girls' bodies out at his property. He was well on his way to killing Aubrey Genest when we showed up."

"She make it?" Babs asked.

"So far," Bates said. "He carved her up pretty good. Doctors put her in a coma."

"What does he have to say about Sis?"

"He doesn't have anything to say about anything. He hasn't talked to anybody but Lori and his lawyer."

Babs looked at him sharply. "And what did he tell Lori?"

"You'll need to ask her."

Babs absorbed this for a moment, then shook her head. "No," she said. "You're wrong. It's not him."

"He's at Kennebec County right now," Bates said quickly, trying to get out ahead of what he knew Babs was thinking. "He'll be arraigned after the holiday, then transferred to Warren. They'll hold him in protective custody until tri—"

"Daryl," Babs said. "You know who did this. And it's not some hillbilly crank dealer."

"This is as open-and-shut as they come, Babs. I don't know what else to tell you. Except we have the man who killed your daughter."

"We'll see," Babs said simply.

Bates stood, unsteady on his walking cast. "I have to get back. Father, you want a ride home?"

"I'll take him home later," Babs said. "We have a dinner to attend."

"Babs," Clement said, "are you sure you—"

"I'm sure."

"Be smart," Bates said to her. "Use your head. That Canadian freak has zero reason to start trouble, and every reason not to. Going after him will only bring the shit down on all of us."

Babs looked at him, an acid smile on her lips. "My daughter is dead," she said. "I'd say the shit has already descended, Chief."

T oo-bright lights, racket from the kitchen, stainless-steel utensils clanging against stainless-steel pans, a medley of warm and humid and unidentifiable odors, buffet tables under steady assault, children crying, children laughing, children silent and staring from inside the poisonous amniotic bubble of poverty and subpar parenting. In the midst of this squalid hubbub a woman and her nephew sat in a molded plastic booth, smiling at each other across the Formica tabletop, identical molded plastic glasses of Coke and molded plastic dessert cups with green Jell-O sitting on their identical molded plastic trays. Each cup of Jell-O had a scabbed-over dollop of whipped cream on top. The aunt's nervous system was howling for dope behind her smile, and the nephew was in the first twenty-four hours of this new life with his mother gone from the Earth, though of course he did not yet know that and was thinking only of getting through the cube steak he'd ordered so he could have dessert. There was hardly a child in Little Canada between the ages of three and thirteen who didn't go psychotic with happiness over a cup of Bonanza Steakhouse lime Jell-O, and the boy knew he would be enjoying not one but two, because no way his aunt was going to touch hers—adults, in the dull ignorance they called maturity, were uniformly turned off by the stuff.

Lori begged off to the bathroom, warning Jason not to ruin his appetite with the Jell-O before their meals came out. She crossed the dining area, sidestepping several young boys chasing each other around the hot buffet table with tongs, and went into the ladies' room. Checked the stalls, entered the last one in the row, took an Oxy from the plastic baggie in her breast pocket, and crushed it on the top of the toilet paper dispenser. Hoovered it up, her nose flush to the plastic. Actually licked the top of the dispenser clean, because who was she kidding. Sat on the toilet seat. Counted to ten. Felt warm relief blossom in her brain stem and filter down through her body. Cried, the tears like poison being expelled.

Lori was of course not surprised to see Jason halfway done with the second Jell-O cup when she emerged a couple minutes later, their steaks still nowhere in sight. She was also not surprised to see Sis seated next to Jason in the booth, dressed for eternity in the same flannel and jeans she'd been wearing at Lori's kitchen table, the flannel and jeans she'd been wearing when Rex, or the Canadian, or someone had doused her Subaru with gasoline and sparked a match. Lori sat down opposite them and smiled at Jason, motioned at her own face to let him know he had some whipped cream on his. Then she looked at Sis. Something about her appearance had been troubling Lori since she'd first seen her that night in Lori's kitchen, some detail Lori couldn't put her finger on that nevertheless wouldn't leave her alone, kept tickling her brain, demanding explication. And then, sitting there in Bonanza with her orphaned nephew, it finally dawned on Lori: the burgundy stains on Sis's shirt, the sticky mess that tangled her hair. Too thin to be blood, but still, what was it? Wine? Sis hated wine, red especially. So that couldn't be it—

"Aunt Lore," Jason said, following her gaze. "What are you looking at?"

Lori came back to this time and place, smiled at her nephew. "Nothing," she said. "I was just thinking." .

"About what?"

"None of your business," Lori said. "And stop trying to avoid the topic at hand: Weren't you told explicitly not to eat your Jell-O before dinner came out? And hey, what the heck happened to *my* Jell-O?"

Jason laughed. "You weren't going to eat it anyway," he said.

"I guess now we'll never know," Lori said.

Jason tucked back into her dessert, and Lori looked at Sis again. Though she couldn't say anything out loud to her, Lori concentrated on one bitter sentiment over and over, repeating the words like a mantra in her mind, willing Sis to hear her through some kind of telepathy: *Sure*, she thought, *now you want to be with your son.*

B ruce had been sober almost two days. His neck and face and skull, every square inch from the shoulders north, throbbed with healing. He still had the shakes, and couldn't concentrate on the Sox game for more than a few pitches before careening off into a black despair that made it hard to breathe. It reminded him of the time in sixth grade when Ernie Bourgoin had led him to the ruins of a colonial-era powder magazine and they'd picked their way down the crumbling granite stairs, deep underground where neither light nor sound could penetrate, and Ernie turned off his flashlight and in an instant Bruce found himself floating alone in a darkness so huge and silent he might have been dead—might, in fact, have never existed at all. Terrified, he called out to Ernie to turn the light back on. But Ernie didn't answer. The blackness pressed in on Bruce like a physical thing. He was blind and deaf and he couldn't breathe. He yelled for Ernie again, but Ernie was gone—Bruce would find out later that he'd planned all along to leave Bruce there, as a practical joke. Before too long Bruce realized with certainty that he would be there forever. That there was no escape from the darkness, because the darkness wasn't a place, couldn't be moved into or out of. It simply was. And now, on his couch, in front of the Sox game, sober and raw, Bruce was not merely in that darkness, the darkness was somehow *in him*, Ernie B. and his flashlight long gone. Yet Bruce did not drink. Every half minute or so he felt a fresh urge to die, but he did not drink.

The bottom of the inning ended and a teaser came on for the local news.

"Tonight at eleven," said a female newscaster, who was young and very pregnant, "with three straight weeks of record heat, farmers all over Maine are watching their crops wilt, and many say they'll need government help to survive the worst growing season in a generation. Also, we'll update you on a murder investigation in Vassalboro, where police say an as-yet-unidentified woman was found burned in a car. See you after the game."

And this was how the darkness in Bruce, which had only seemed absolute when he'd been trapped underground as a child, actually became so.

R obinson Hegemony's dining table accommodated fourteen with room to spare; one couldn't have one's guests bumping elbows, after all. Everything about the dinner was refined and utterly blood-less: the anodyne conversation about globalism and campus politics, the gentle tinkle of flatware and crystal, the 2005 Pinot Noir, the music, the expensive, obvious artwork looming on the dining room walls. The only interesting thing about the evening was the smell: charred salted flesh (*côte de boeuf* being the main course) and money. That, at least, felt honest to Babs.

As a guest of honor, she sat at one end of the table with Clement to her left and a woman named Abigail Kinsey to her right. She was a well-preserved sixty or so, with lustrous black hair and a tasteful amount of cosmetic surgery around her eyes and throat. Abigail had been hitting the Pinot every time it came around ("A *legendary* vin-tage!"), and after her fifth glass, just as the salad course was being served, Abigail admitted that she'd asked to be seated next to Babs.

"You might regret that before the night's out," Father Clement said to her. The two of them shared a laugh, while Babs just stared dully at Abigail. She knew she had to keep up appearances, but she also needed to see her daughter Celeste, no matter what state she was in, and the more Babs drank, the deeper she burrowed into this need, the room and its occupants becoming small and indistinct, as if viewed through the wrong end of a telescope. The best Babs could do was keep her mouth shut. The saleswoman had gone home for the evening.

But Abigail wanted to talk. "In all seriousness, though," she said to Babs, "I wanted to tell you that when the question of funding the St. John's project came up, I read everything I could find about the his-tory of Franco-Americans. What a proud and sturdy people you are!"

"That's us," Babs said. "Regular pack mules." Now she was looking over Abigail's left shoulder, where a set of saloon doors led into
Hegemony's service kitchen. Each time one of the doors swung
open, Babs caught a glimpse of a woman her age scrubbing pots and
pans at the dish station, a lock of gray hair hanging down in her face.

"And yet," Abigail went on, "despite all the advantages you enjoy
because of your whiteness, you're still somehow stuck in generational
poverty."

Clement looked at Babs to gauge her reaction, but she had none,
at least outwardly. She was still looking at the saloon doors, imagining the dishwasher's hands were her own: knuckles swollen and
painful in a way she'd long since learned to ignore, cuticles torn and
bloody, the skin of her palms and fingers perpetually parboiled.

And then, as if on a time delay, Abigail's words reached Babs. With
some effort, she looked back and focused on Abigail's face. "I'm sorry?"

"Please understand," Abigail said, "I'm on *your side* in this. Some
of the trustees took a lot of convincing. It's not a great time to be
announcing funding for an all-white school."

Clement moved a foot under the table, making light contact
with Babs's shin.

"No doubt," Babs said. "I appreciate your advocacy."

"The question that came up repeatedly was how we could justify
so much money for children who already enjoy every advantage of
white privilege. When so many other children have the boot of sys-
temic racism planted squarely on their necks."

Babs polished off her third Old Fashioned. "When you put it
that way," she said, "I can see how it would be difficult for you to
answer. Where are you from, again?"

"New York. Upper West Side."

"Naturally. Go on."

Clement put a hand over his mouth.

"My argument to the trustees," Abigail said, waving her wine-glass around as she spoke, "was that while it might be true your people will never know the pain of discrimination, or have to fear police violence, that hardly means they're not in need of help."

Babs stared at Abigail for a beat. The waiter, as attentive and effortlessly skillful as any Babs had ever seen, appeared at her side as if summoned. "Wine, ma'am?" he asked.

"Whiskey, please," Babs said, holding up her empty glass. "Canadian Club, if you've got it. Neat."

The waiter took the glass with a curt nod and departed. Babs turned back to Abigail.

"Pop quiz," Babs said to her. "Do you know how many Black presidents this country has had?"

Abigail blinked, suddenly wary. "Of course. Just the one, unfortunately."

"Correct. And how many Catholic presidents has this country had?"

This she was less certain of. She lifted her wineglass and looked up at the wall behind Babs, squinting in thought. "I *think*," she said, "just Kennedy?"

"Also correct. You're two for two so far, but stay on your toes, because here's where the questions get tougher."

"Okay," Abigail said.

"Francos have been citizens of this state since it became a state. How many of Maine's governors have been French Canadian?"

"Six?" Abigail asked brightly.

"One. Out of seventy. The current governor, Paul LePage. And he's a moronic windbag who's reinforced every last stereotype about dumb Frenchmen."

"I see."

"If I tell you something," Babs said, "can I ask you to keep it from the other trustees?"

"Babs, you've had a long day," Clement said. "Maybe we should—"

"Would you be able to keep it between us?" Babs asked again.

"Of . . . course." Abigail flushed, both pleased and a little nervous at the prospect of being in Babs's confidence.

"Have you heard about the young woman who was found murdered this morning?" Babs asked.

Now Abigail looked uncertain of herself; whatever she'd been expecting, it wasn't this. "I think maybe I saw something on the television in the hotel lobby . . ."

Babs nodded. "That young woman," she said, "was my daughter."

Abigail looked to Clement, who folded his hands on the tabletop. The waiter arrived with Babs's whiskey, and she thanked him quietly.

"I tell you that to tell you this," Babs said after the waiter departed again. "I was raped by a cop when I was fourteen years old, and for his trouble, I killed him. Both my brother and my son died in combat, and my oldest daughter came home from Afghanistan so fucked-up she can't get through the day sober. When I was a teenager, boys from this very school would come down the hill to have fun with girls like me. Sometimes they didn't ask permission. Sometimes they roughed the girls up. But no one cared, because we were just trash. Quebexicans. Frogs. New England Niggers. So, Abigail— if I may call you Abigail—I am here to tell you that life, as it's actually lived, does not fit into your neat little black-and-white categories. And I ask you, please, to stop being so certain of what I am and am not, what I have and have not endured. If you look at me and see a white woman, that's your mistake. Whatever sins go along with being white, don't pin them on me—I've been running from white people my whole life, like most everyone else on the planet."

Babs took a drink and put the glass down, staring into it as if it had no bottom. "I only found out my daughter is dead a few hours ago," she said. "But I shouldn't have been surprised. Violence has hounded me as long as I can remember. And there will be more presently. I can't do anything about that. I just ask that no matter what happens—no matter what I do, or what they tell you I've done—you will continue to advocate for St. John's School."

CHAPTER FIFTEEN

July 4, 2016

Independence Day dawned hot and still, the sound of sirens echoing faint across the valley as fire trucks from four departments hauled ass to a wildfire just north of town. The previous night a particularly zealous patriot had launched a Roman candle into the hayfield at Gervais Family Farm, and by the time trucks arrived the flames had a five-hour, twenty-acre head start. The Gervais's alfalfa crop had been incinerated overnight, and the fire had spread eagerly to the adjacent woods, tinder-dry with no measurable rainfall for over a month. Flames two stories high were now menacing a gambrel barn that held several dozen dairy cows, and the call for help had gone out to every department in the county.

Clement had seen the smoke, black and thick with pine pitch, on his way to Bruce's house just after 5 a.m. Smoke like that, the priest's first thought had been a garbage fire somewhere—plastic, old tires. But as he sat on the front steps with Bruce, nursing some truly wretched coffee and watching the world awaken around them, he realized the air smelled just like when he and his buddies went around torching trees chucked on the side of the road the week after

Christmas, something like a thousand years ago. The forest was burning, and nearby.

Of course Father Clement had more immediate problems, chief among them disabusing Bruce of the certainty that he'd murdered his wife. Bruce had called at four thirty asking for confession, and though Clement hadn't seen Bruce in church since he was confirmed at thirteen, the man's wife had just been killed, so the old priest dragged his arthritic corpse out of bed after only four hours' sleep, dressed and splashed water on his face, and drove down the hill to Bruce's, watching that smoke drift and billow across the dawn.

Bruce's face was hamburger, right eye demon-red with burst capillaries, the left swollen almost completely shut, the skin of his cheeks stretched tight and shiny over multiple contusions. Clement had known without being told that this was Babs's doing, the tax she'd levied on her son-in-law for hitting Jason. So he didn't ask, didn't even mention it, just filed it against Babs's account in case she ever actually came to confession herself, and greeted Bruce as though it were any old Monday and Bruce didn't at all look like he should be rushed to an ICU. Bruce had proffered two mugs of coffee and muttered through fat lips about it being too hot to sit inside, so they crouched on the top step in the shade of the tenement next door, and that was when Bruce told Father Clement that he'd killed Sis.

Clement knew, or thought he knew, that this was impossible, but Bruce wouldn't be shaken from his conviction.

"Tell me one more time," Clement said to him, "*exactly* what you remember."

"She comes home around suppertime," Bruce said.

"This is last Monday night."

Bruce nodded solemnly. "She comes home all worked up, she was supposebly out shopping but her hair's a rat's nest and her eyes are crazy so I know she ain't been shopping, unless these days you can buy crank at JCPenney and fuck on the display mattresses. Pardon my language."

Clement waved a hand. "And so then . . ."

"*Then*," Bruce said, "she starts in on me as if *I'm* the one out doing drugs and sleeping around. She's mad because I'm drunk and Jay-Jay's upstairs and hasn't had supper yet. Sure I've been drinking but it's not like I've forgotten about the kid. I got hot dogs boiling on the stove. And so I says 'Maybe you should just leave and come back when you're not so freakin' spun out of your mind.' And you'd think I told her to go take a long walk on a short pier. Next thing I know she's up in my face saying 'Yeah maybe I should leave and not come back at all, see how you like that.' Then she says the thing about how maybe if I didn't have whiskey dick for the last year she wouldn't need to go looking for it somewhere else."

"And that's what started it . . ."

"I just snapped. Saw red. Like, really *saw* red, I thought that was just a thing people say but it really happens. And next thing I know my hands are around her neck and I'm squeezing and her eyes are all bugged out."

"And then . . . nothing?" Father Clement asked.

"Not till the next morning."

"So why do you think you killed her?"

"Because the last thing I remember is choking her, and now she's dead and my boy don't have a mother anymore."

Clement was quiet while Bruce wept.

"Bruce," he said when he'd gathered himself a bit, "I can't tell you what I know about the investigation. But there are a lot of reasons to think you aren't the one who did this."

"Sure seems like I did, Father."

"I wouldn't be so certain. You really think you killed Sis, drove her out to Vassalboro, set her car on fire, and somehow managed to get back into town, all while in a blackout? And without Jason noticing anything?"

Bruce was quiet. "All I know," he said after a moment, "is I wanted her dead. In that moment, I really didn't want her to live no more."

"That may be," Clement said. "But that's not the same as actually killing her."

The old priest stood, looked up at the drifting smoke, and sighed. "There are two things I know for certain right now, Bruce," he said. "The first is your son needs you. The second is the coffee at the morning AA meeting in the church basement is a lot better than this shit."

T he ladies were, at that same moment, having coffee difficulties of their own. They had heard about Sis, but Babs had gone silent, so instead of gathering at her place for coffee they met downtown at Jorgenson's Café.

After a long time trying unsuccessfully to sort through the twenty different roast varieties arrayed in self-serve carafes, Stella went to the counter, where a tall, thin young man with a dusting of silken facial hair worked the register. He held a book titled *The Stranger*, and appeared bored with the fact of existence.

"Hi," Stella said.

"Good morning," the young man said.

"We'd like some coffee," Stella told him.

"You just walked right past it," he said, pointing behind her, where Carmeline and Bernette stood expectant, empty cardboard cups in hand.

"No I know, but we don't want Saddam Hussein Aromia or Chiquita Banana Pepe, whatever that is."

The young man set his book face down on the counter. "All the coffee we have," he said, "is on that table. What kind of roast do you like?"

"Coffee roast."

The young man chuckled. "What I mean is—"

"What are you laughing at? Did I say something funny?"

He looked at Stella, noted the sudden flatness of her gaze. "No."

"Tell you what, smart guy. How about you just point me to whichever one of these tastes the most like Maxwell House."

When they had their cups of Cream and Sugar light roast ("Notes of caramel and milk chocolate!") the ladies sat at a window booth and spoke low to each other in French.

"You see that smoke, driving in?" Bernette asked.

"See it?" Stella said. "I smelled it before I even got out of bed. Where's it coming from?"

"This coffee is garbage," Carmeline said, mostly to herself.

"Brush fire just across the line in Fairfield." Bernette took out a pack of Virginia Slims and lit one up, to a muffled sound of distress from a woman two tables away. "Burned all night before anyone noticed. Took out a dairy farm—cows, barn, everything. Now it's into the woods. Sounds like real trouble."

"You're the one going to be in trouble," Stella said, pointing to the register, "if Sleepy over there sees you smoking." She opened a flask and poured whiskey into her coffee, tasted, poured a little more.

"Like I care," Bernette said. "Sis is dead, and now everything's burning. It feels . . . what's the word?"

"*Apocalyptique*," Carmeline said.

"That's the one," Bernette said. She dragged on her cigarette, and the woman who'd taken offense, though too timid to confront Bernette, made a show of her disgust as she stomped out of the café, a half-eaten egg sandwich clutched to her chest in lieu of pearls.

"It's not an apocalypse yet," Carmeline said. "But it's getting there. And I would submit that Babs can't be counted on, under these circumstances, to make smart choices. For herself or anyone else."

"Maybe not," Stella said, "but what are we going to do about it?"

"Twenty-Fifth Amendment," Carmeline said.

"Damn, I left my pocket Constitution at home," Bernette said. "What the hell is the Twenty-Fifth Amendment?"

"Removal of the president when he—or she—is unable to discharge the duties of the office."

"Oh," Bernette said, "if you wanted us to commit suicide, why didn't you just say so?"

"I talked with Bates," Carmeline told her. "We're stuck with two bad choices. Either we let Babs take the whole town down with her, or we stop her somehow."

"Again," Stella said, "it's one thing to say it. But how do we actually do it?"

"We get help," Carmeline said. "We've got to convince Lori, for starters. Bates is already with us. Then we find this Canadian ghoul and tell him it's over—Babs's Pharmacy is going out of business. And he goes back to Canada and lets us all live."

"Not gonna be able to afford five-dollar coffees anymore," Stella said.

"Am I the only one who wants to tell this guy to stick it up his ass?" Bernette asked.

"No," Carmeline said. "But *that* would be suicide."

"How do we know? Let's at least try to kill him before we roll over and play dead."

"If we kill him," Carmeline said, "in forty-eight hours there will be an army here looking to return the favor."

The young man from the register appeared at their table, looking like he'd rather be anywhere else on earth other than where he was. "Uh, ma'am," he said to Bernette, "I'm afraid there's no smoking in here."

Bernette turned her head slowly to look at him. "You sure about that?" she asked.

Stella smirked.

"I'm . . . well . . ."

"Because I'm in here," Bernette said, "and I'm smoking. Which sure makes it seem like there's smoking in here."

"Yes, but . . . can I just get you to—"

"This one must piss sitting down," Bernette said to the others in French.

"Ma'am, I don't want any trouble."

"No one ever does, and yet it finds us anyway," Bernette said. "I'll put this out when I'm finished smoking it, and not a moment sooner. Now leave us alone; we're trying to have a conversation."

The young man went away, and the ladies were quiet for a moment.

"God, Babs must be a wreck," Bernette said finally.

"Exactly," Carmeline said. "There's no time to waste."

"So what's the plan?" Stella asked.

"We find Lore," Carmeline said. "Then Bates will put us in touch with this guy, whoever he is."

B abs would have already been out hunting The Man herself, but she had duties to attend to, trustees to perform for, a fifty-million-dollar investment, two decades in the making, to secure.

Tomorrow, she could fall apart. Tomorrow, she could shed tears and blood. Today, she stood in front of the full-length mirror in her bedroom, clad in jeans and a black T-shirt with the Franco-American flag—white star on a blue background and, inside the star, the fleur-de-lis—printed on the front. But Babs wasn't checking her clothes. She was checking her face.

Over and over she smiled at herself, trying to nail down the mix of beneficence and good cheer that people expected to see at a parade. She smiled with teeth and without, waving and not waving. She smiled straight on and in profile. No matter what she did, every attempt felt Plasticine and grotesque, as though someone were using their hands to push her features into position and approximate happiness. And no matter how she contorted her face the smile refused to touch her eyes. Her right hand shook so violently it made the flesh of her cheeks tremble. Nothing looked right. Nothing felt right. And then it was time to go, and Babs swung her leg back and kicked the mirror like she was punting a football, and the mirror broke and fell to the floor in daggers. Babs walked out of the bedroom, thinking maybe she'd pick it up later, then again maybe she wouldn't. Things would just keep breaking, after all.

In the living room she paused at the long white end table where she kept family photos. There were a bunch, stretching back years—Babs as a girl in black and white, standing in front of this same house with her mother; another with both her parents, three brothers, and four sisters, all standing in the driveway, everyone clustered together except Babs, thirteen or so, standing off to the right by herself. Fast forward: Rheal and Babs on their wedding day. Jean, three days old, swaddled in baptismal white. Shots of Lori and Sis on a beach, a bed, a horse. Jean with the girls, first when Lori was a baby and Sis just a glimmer in her daddy's eye, then with both of them,

Lori four or so, Sis an infant, laughing toothlessly, the full head of hair she'd been born with flyaway crazy. The last picture of the three siblings ever taken: the parade grounds at Parris Island, Iwo Jima monument in the background, six bronze Marines hoisting the stars and stripes over Suribachi, Lori nearly grown and Sis still buck-toothed and all limbs, Jean tall and stern in his uniform, an arm around either sister. Then Jean went to Iraq and disappeared from all photos forever, joining his uncle and namesake in the Saint Francis cemetery.

Closer to the present—Jason as a baby, a toddler, a kindergart-ner. A big gap in his ready smile here, the gap closed again there. Babs and Sis laughing together at Christmas. Finally—but wait, that picture was missing, the frame sitting empty at the right end of the table. The photo had been a minor treasure for Babs, a shot of everyone (except Jean, of course) from two summers ago, Lori home on leave and the entire family gathered for hamburgers and bone-in chicken at Sunset Beach. The Dionnes, but also some remaining members of the Levesques, Babs's uncle Normand and aunt Anne (both since deceased), two of their grown children and several of *their* children, as well as Aunt Anita, a Levesque by marriage to Babs's uncle Georges, who'd died two decades earlier.

Babs stood there, flummoxed by the empty frame, listening to sirens wail in the distance. Then she went to the spare bedroom, found the door closed. She knocked, and Jason opened up.

"You want to tell me," Babs said, "where the picture is that's sup-posed to be on the table in the living room?"

Frightened by her sternness, which he was not at all accustomed to coming from his *mémère*, Jason stood there mute, the bruise around his left eye beginning to fade in spots from black to a sickly yellow.

"Jay," Babs said, "I'm not mad at you. I just want the picture back, sweetheart."

Should have been simple enough—no harm, no foul—but the boy remained reluctant. His eyes pleaded.

"Okay," Babs said, crouching in front of him so they were on a level together. "Let's start over. Do you know what happened to the picture I'm talking about?"

"Yes."

"Good. Did you take it?"

"Yes."

"Why, Jay-Jay?"

"I don't know."

Her brow furrowed. "Of course you know," she said. "You *did* it, so you have to know why."

Jason went silent again. Babs sighed and put a hand on his arm.

"Listen," she said, "why don't you just get the picture for me so I can put it back where it belongs? I don't need to know why you took it. We'll forget this ever happened."

"You won't be able to forget."

"Why not?"

"Because I did something to it."

Babs absorbed this, peering at her grandson. "All right, Jay-Jay," she said. "Go get the picture. Now."

He responded immediately to her not-fucking-around voice, going to the nightstand and removing the 8x10 print from the drawer. He came back to Babs and shoved the picture at her as though it burned his hand, as though by giving it back with such alacrity he could undo the damage he'd inflicted on it, a hole the diameter of a magic marker worn straight through the glossy paper.

She flipped the picture over and saw the happy scene, everyone lined up arm in arm and squinting into the sun with the lake in the background, the people near the middle of the group laughing at a crack someone's made, even Lori hinting at a smile despite how gaunt and exhausted she looks. The hole, it turned out, was where Jason's face used to be. The boy had scratched away his own image, leaving the rest of the photo untouched.

Babs let the picture fall to her side. She looked at Jason, and he looked up at her, his gaze frightened and also, beneath the fear, confused. He'd been telling the truth when she'd asked why he took the picture—he didn't know why he'd taken it, and he didn't know why he'd erased himself from it. He only knew that he'd wanted to, for reasons probably more evident to Babs than to him. And now he stared at her, hoping, perhaps, that she could explain him to himself.

"Are you mad at me?" he asked.

"I am *not* mad at you," Babs said, gasping at the very notion, the horrid and intolerable thought that she could ever be angry with her grandson. And now tears came, for the first time in half a century. Babs had not wept when her parents died, or when her son's flag-draped casket had rolled off the plane at the Bangor airport, or when Rheal had taken his last breath and let it out with a sigh that still lingered in their bedroom at night, but now she wept, and there was no point in trying to control or hide it, so she let it come as she crouched before Jason again. "I will never be mad at you. Ever. I will only love and protect and cherish you, no matter what. Do you understand?"

Jason nodded.

She pulled him to her, felt his heart hammering against her own ribs. "Jason," she said, "the world will try to erase you, every day. That's what life is. You can't let it. You can't believe the lies it tells you about yourself."

"Okay," he said.

"Remember what I said," Babs told him. "Everyone else is weak. But not you. And not me. Don't ever, ever forget."

"I won't."

She held him awhile longer, then pulled herself together and allowed him to step back while she wiped tears from her face.

"Okay," Babs said. "Enough of that. When's your aunt supposed to pick you up for the parade?"

"Eleven."

"Sounds good. Don't go outside until she gets here. And stay inside, with the door locked, after she drops you off again. I'll be home later tonight."

"Why do I have to keep hiding?"

Babs looked at him. "Won't be much longer," she said. "Mémère has a problem to take care of, but once she does, you can go out whenever you like."

As Waterville's Fourth of July parade got underway, what began as a bright summer morning had darkened to an uncanny twilight, streetlamps flickering to life as the valley filled with smoke. The wildfire, fanned by a steady north wind and spreading into deep woods that municipal fire equipment couldn't reach, continued to grow. People still lined both sides of Main Street, waving their little flags on sticks, and parents still brought their kids, but the more cautious among them, in the absence of official guidance on what, if anything, to do, covered their faces with bandannas or held tissues to their mouths and noses. Details about the fire, both accurate and not-so, moved through the crowd like viruses as they waited for the head of the parade to arrive. They'd never seen anything like it, people kept saying as they wiped a mixture of ash and sweat from their faces. It felt a little like the end of the world, was the consensus.

The martial rattle of snare drums drifted to them through the smog, drawing steadily closer, and then the Waterville High marching band itself came into view, high-stepping more or less in unison, feather plumes atop their caps waving to the beat. Children clambered toward the rope lines for a better view, their enthusiasm undiminished by the smoke, but the adults, while they went through the motions of cheering and clapping and pointing out things of interest to their kids, felt themselves laboring under the weight of a shared uneasiness. The heat, in its relentlessness, was starting to feel like a curse, and perhaps a divine one—an Old Testament plague visited upon them for some collective sin they had yet to recognize and amend. Then these horrid murders—girls' bodies planted in the ground like garlic bulbs, for God's sake—and now this fire, which no one seemed capable of doing anything about. One of the rumors drifting through the crowd was that a call had gone out to the Forest Service to send in several crews of smoke jumpers. Which did not seem to augur well at all.

Behind the marching band came a dozen beglittered girls from Maureen's Danceworks (30 YEARS OF DANCE, according to the banner), followed by what remained of Waterville's Korean War vets, four old-timers in loose, threadbare uniforms limping and smiling, one with an aluminum-frame walker bearing the insignia of the Fifth Marines. Bates's patrol car trailed slowly behind the crusty vets, blues slicing the haze that hung in the air, and the Little Canada float, a giant papier-mâché maple leaf in the bed of an F-150 draped in bunting, hung on Bates's back bumper. Babs sat on a lawn chair next to the leaf, which was a little worse for wear from having been used on a rainy Fourth two years prior. She smiled and waved, smiled and waved.

Behind the Little Canada float, a dozen Shriners buzzed about in circles and figure eights, the engines of their miniature Corvettes humming. And while it was true that most of the time you couldn't get three Americans to agree on the color of the sky, one thing most *could* agree on was that Shriner cars were the highlight of any holiday parade. Funnier than clowns, more exciting than a big Snoopy balloon, the Shriners were the ultimate crowd-pleaser. Even the adults cheered and laughed, forgetting for a moment that the Apocalypse seemed quite literally upon them as the old men with their funny hats zoomed back and forth in a surprisingly precise choreography, tossing candy and making goofy faces.

And it got better. As the parade made its way down Main Street and passed the small park at Castonguay Square, a soloist broke away from the rest of the Shriner cars. He sped past the F-150, zipped up alongside Bates, then hit the brakes and yanked the wheel to the left, fishtailing through a complete 180-degree turn as the crowd hooted and clapped. The other Shriners came to a stop, as did Bates and the F-150 with Babs in the back. The rogue Shriner tossed a handful of candy to the kids and gunned the engine again, speeding back in the other direction. He cut the wheel once more, this time without brakes, tracing a sharp screeching parabola until the little Corvette wobbled up onto two wheels, finished the turn, and headed back toward Babs. In its amazement the crowd hushed for a few moments, then began cheering even louder as the car slowed to a stop just behind the F-150, lingered on two wheels for a moment, then crashed down on all four and was still. Even the other Shriners applauded.

The Man, who was driving the miniature Corvette, smiled up at Babs from under his fez, the black tassel fallen off to the right side of his face. He reached down with both hands into the driver's compartment, dug around for a moment, then pulled his hands back out and tossed more candy to either side, keeping his eyes on Babs the whole time.

Last chance, he mouthed to her, still smiling.

Hundreds of people watching, many of them children as young as two or three. Her own grandson somewhere in the crowd, not to mention Hegemony and the trustees and half the police force and reporters from the local paper. Also, of course, the omniscient eye of the smartphone camera, peering at her from every angle. All of them delighted by The Man's performance, unaware that they were about to see another performance, equally spectacular but of an entirely different kind. Babs got to her feet in the bed of the truck and yanked both push daggers from their sheath on her belt. Her vision narrowed, everything at the edges blurry and indistinct, with only the image of The Man, unmoving at the center of her sight, clear and urgent. She tasted metal, like she had a mouth full of loose change, as she hopped down to the pavement, three or four strides away from the miniature Corvette, The Man beckoning her now, waving her in with the fingers of one hand: *Come and see*, he mouthed, and by God Babs would. And though she suspected, distantly, that The Man was not in fact beckoning her with his fingers, nor mouthing that invitation over and over, that that part at least was only in her mind, she didn't care, it didn't matter, none of it mattered, not the fact of an audience, not dying in a cage of Huntington's, not even Jason seeing her gut a man, what mattered was *settling accounts*, once and for all, and after that she could breathe again, after that there was no punishment in God's infinite imagination she could not endure.

One stride toward The Man. Ash falling like radioactive snow around them both. A second step, and suddenly there were hands on her, grasping at her wrists, arms wrapping her up from behind. She flailed with her left hand and felt the blade there meet flesh, and then both arms were twisted painfully behind her and The Man sped off in his ridiculous little car and Babs was face down on the F-150's tailgate, Bates in her ear saying, "Calm down, for Christ's sake, *relax*," and she heard the click and rattle of cuffs underneath the sounds of a wild animal snarling and growling, and she realized after a time that the snarling and growling were coming from her.

CHAPTER SIXTEEN

July 4, 2016

This has to be it, Ma," Lori said.

"Meaning?"

"Meaning no more blood."

Babs sidestepped. "Where's Jay-Jay?"

"At your place."

"You left him there alone??"

"That was the plan, Ma. Because *you* were supposed to be back there after the parade. The parade that never actually made it to where we were standing. Because of some commotion that happened at the very beginning. Was all we heard."

"Go get Jay-Jay and take him to your house."

"I'm going to. But not until you agree to stand down."

"He killed my daughter."

"Goddammit, Ma, you don't know that," Lori said. "Besides, it doesn't matter."

"I'm going to pretend you didn't just say that."

"Don't. Hear it, and let it sink in: *It doesn't matter.* Sis is gone.

But Jason is still here. I'm still here. The neighborhood is still here. Though not for long, if you keep this up."

A pause. In the administrative area on the other side of the locked door, they could hear a couple of uniformed officers bullshitting.

"I can't just let it go, Lore."

"Of course you can. Just choose differently."

"You make it sound so simple."

"It is."

"I can't change now," Babs said. "Not after all this time."

"Promise me, Ma."

"Lore—"

"I'm the only child you have left."

Another pause, silence pulsing through the cell.

"You're going to go get the boy?"

"After you promise me you're done."

Another pause.

"Before I do," Babs said, "let me tell you something I know about laying down your sword."

"Okay."

"When you lay it down," Babs said, "be ready to run."

"No kidding," Lori said. "Now promise me. I want to hear you say it."

O ne might reasonably have hoped that Bruce would keep his two-day sober streak going, but it would have been naive to *expect* that he would do so. His son had been taken from him, after all, and it was confirmed now that his wife was dead, perhaps by his own hand, and every feeling of guilt, shame, inadequacy, and all the other perfectly humdrum psychic agonies that people used as an excuse to get blotto until they died from it had pulled up a comfortable chair in Bruce's head and made themselves at home. He'd sat through that morning's AA meeting with Father Clement beside him, and listened to a guest speaker who had taken up the entire hour with his biography, an epic horror story that began when he—the guest speaker, whose name was Mark—became a full-bore alcoholic by the time he was twelve. This was hardly rare, Mark told them, where he came from, and Bruce thought *No shit Mark, it's not exactly unheard-of around here, either.* But Mark's story, of course, didn't end with prepubescent chemical enslavement. By his mid-twenties, he was addicted to heroin and crack, and he had a routine involving both that he called the Hillbilly Speedball. He would fix up the biggest hit of crack he could fit in the pipe, and cook up the biggest hit of dope he could fit in the gear. Then he'd tie off and ease the needle into a vein and make sure it was ready to go by drawing a bit of blood into the syringe, stopping short of actually injecting the dope. Because the front end of the Hillbilly Speedball was the crack, one massive, stupendous, by all rights lethal hit, and Mark would fire up and hold that hit for as long as he could, like a free diver determined to set a world record or die in the attempt, his ears ringing and his heart fighting to burst out of his chest and a blessed darkness spreading across his vision like spilled ink. He would bring himself right up to the edge of unconsciousness and the no-doubt fatal cardiac event to follow, and then, just as he was about to pass out, he'd hit the plunger on the syringe in his arm—and his vision would come rushing back and he'd slump to the floor and stay there for hours, blissed-out like before he was born. The point wasn't to get high, Mark told them, the point was to see how close one could snuggle up against death without actually dying. And Mark should have been dead a thousand times over, but he wasn't, somehow. He'd never been that lucky. Instead he was stuck here, sober as fuck and doomed to relive for all eternity every last shameful shocking unforgivable thing he'd ever done, for the benefit of an endless succession of addicted assholes like the present company. Like Sisyphus pushing the rock except instead of a rock it was a two-ton boulder of his own smelly shit. Mark's story horrified even hardened, seen-it-all addicts, which was the whole point of his being a twelve-step free agent and going from town to town, from church to bingo hall to American Legion basement. The implication was that if an irredeemable shitstain like Mark could get it together and come back from the brink and be standing there with nothing more heavy-duty than caffeine in his bloodstream, anyone could do it.

Sure, Bruce thought, *that all sounds real good, except as big a fuckup as you are, Mark, you never maybe killed your own wife, did you?*

There was no denying, however, that the coffee at the AA meeting was light-years better than the swill Bruce had at home.

Still, Bruce went straight home from Notre Dame and got drunk. And the whole time, sweating and drinking, he thought about Jay-Jay at his grandmother's house, and wondered if anyone had yet told him that his mother was gone, and realized they probably hadn't, and realized further that it was his responsibility, Bruce's, the boy was still his son after all, not even Babs could do anything to change that fact. And the more he thought about it and the more he drank, the more it made sense to him, and before he knew it he was out of the house and stumbling through the smoke and the heat, headed to Babs's.

N ow Clement sat in the holding room of the Waterville Police Department, on the opposite side of a steel mesh door from Babs. He plucked at the mesh with a finger, smiled wanly.

"Remind you of anything?" he asked.

"Very funny."

"Never too late, Babs. Just you, me, and God here."

"Keep holding your breath."

Clement chuckled. "Do you have any idea how much easier your life would have been, if you'd just asked forgiveness?"

"I didn't do anything that required forgiving."

"In the eyes of man, perhaps," Clement said. "God has somewhat different standards."

"Have you considered the possibility that I was God's punishment for Sacha?"

"Babs, the avenging angel?"

"Have you?"

"Of course. Didn't pass the smell test."

"Why not?"

"'The Lord does not deal with us according to our sins, nor punish us according to our iniquities.'"

"You and I must be reading different translations," Babs said. "I'm a King James girl, myself."

Clement snorted. He pulled a pewter flask from his back pocket, took a sip, and handed it through the bean chute to Babs. She smiled at the inscription—HOLY WATER—and took a long drink.

"How come you never asked how I came to the priesthood?" Clement said.

"What?"

"I know you were curious, when I first got here. The whole town was."

Babs thought for a moment. "I guess," she said, "that when in doubt, I err on the side of minding my own business."

"But what if I've been dying to tell someone? What if, for the last fifty years, I've just been waiting for you to ask?"

"Then you probably should have spoken up."

"Isn't that what I'm doing now?"

Babs looked at him. "*Okay*," she said. "How did you come to the priesthood, Father?"

"Well, at first I just wanted to have sex with little boys. Same as any man of the cloth."

"Naturally."

Clement sat back in the folding chair Bates had provided, lacing his fingers together over his compact little paunch. "First you need to know that all the rumors were true," he said. "I was, in fact, a jazz trumpeter. Like any two-bit white jazz trumpeter, I did, in fact, have a heroin habit. And I was, in fact, married."

"What happened?"

"Well, that's what this is all about, isn't it?" Clement said.

"You've been waiting fifty years. You tell me."

"Her name was Simone. She died of an overdose. While I was asleep next to her."

"So you got her into dope, and when she died your penance was to become a priest."

"Not exactly," Clement said. "For one thing, she got *me* into dope. For another, she was pregnant and, as far as I knew, by mutual agreement, we were not using."

"*Baptême.*"

"*En effet,*" Clement said. "Times like that, you get back to basics. Whether you want to or not. You know what people ask for, more than anything, when they're dying? They want to visit the house where they grew up. Go all the way back to the beginning, finally make whatever sense of it they can, and close that circuit. This is well-known among the priesthood, to the point of being a cliché. My mentor in seminary used the term 'putting a bow on it.' After ministering to hundreds of dying people, I'd say that's just about right."

"I guess I'm ahead of the game, then," Babs said. "Having never moved out of the house I grew up in."

"You were always quite wise," Clement said. Babs looked to see if he was giving her shit, but his face was sincere as sunlight. "Anyway, before Simone died, I hadn't given much thought to God one way or another since I'd convinced my parents to let me leave the seminary after my sophomore year. But when I woke up and found her next to me, and when I put my hand on her belly and felt how still it was, I remembered what I had been promised in school, and thought I could reject: that I would suffer. This is the only promise God makes. Not that we will have love, or riches, or health, or even life everlasting—that's all conditional. The one thing He promises us, without requiring anything *from* us, is suffering. It's our true birthright. When Simone and the baby died, and I saw the form my suffering would take, I made the only choice I could—to not suffer alone."

Clement made a sweeping gesture with both hands, indicating his white collar, black shirt, and black pants.

"And what does all that mean for me?" Babs asked.

"Sadly, the Church is a little retrograde, in that it still won't allow women to be ordained. So that option's out."

"Jesus had a cock, after all."

"It's not mentioned in the literature, but we can safely assume," Clement said. "In any event, I think by now you get my point."

"That I have chosen to suffer alone."

"Again and again," Clement said, "for decades, despite how many times God has offered to share your suffering. And look at you now, Babs. For the love of all things holy, look at you now."

Babs didn't respond. She took another swig from the flask, capped it, and handed it back through the bean chute. "Why are you here, Clement?" she asked.

He blinked several times. "Why am I *here*?" he asked. "It's not because I want to be, I can tell you that. I'll be eighty next May, for Christ's sake. You think I still want to be splashing grumpy babies with holy water? Mumbling through the liturgy because half the time I can't remember the Latin? The bishop has tried three times to get me to retire. Last time he all but forced me."

"Then why don't you?"

"You can't seriously be asking that question."

"I just did."

"Well, that settles it—you're officially the dumbest smart person I know," Clement said. "Fifty years ago, you chose me to be your spiritual caretaker. Just my luck, really. And that work isn't done yet. *That's* why I don't retire, you ninny. I keep trying to get fired, but I can't retire. Because I'm still waiting on your goddamn confession."

A pause. Babs gazed out the barred window, which framed a rectangle of sky clotted with smoke. "I thought it was that you couldn't envision life without my company," she said.

"I envision it every day."

"I'm sorry about Simone. And the baby."

"Me too," Clement said. "They were beautiful."

There didn't seem to be much more to say on the subject. After a few quiet moments Babs stood, went to the window, shook her right hand vigorously, and said, "So where does that leave us?"

"Right where we started," Clement told her. "This is happening, Babs. And not even you can do anything about it."

"And you're with them?" Babs asked.

"I'm not *with* anybody," Clement said. "But insofar as it means you get out of jail, yes, this is the choice I'm advocating. Otherwise you're looking at five years, minimum. The state frowns on stabbing a police officer, even if you didn't mean to. This time."

"If Bates puts me away," Babs said, "I'll put him away."

"He doesn't want to put you away. What he wants is for you to stand down. Spare yourself—and everyone else—trouble that nobody needs."

Babs stared at him through the steel mesh. "That man killed my daughter, Clement."

He looked down at the floor, lacing his fingers together between his knees. "Not according to Bates," he said. "And not according to common sense."

"What does that mean?"

"It means they're still cataloging body parts at Rex White's house," Father Clement said. "He murdered at least ten women. Sis spent time with him, then she turned up dead. Doesn't take Columbo to put it together."

Babs didn't respond.

"Make the deal, Babs," Clement said. "Let the professionals run the dope business. Get out of jail and build your school. And get your ass to confession, finally. For your own sake. And mine."

She considered for a moment. "The idea of retirement does have its appeal," she said.

"Tell me about it." Clement stood, grimacing as he put a hand to his low back. With the other hand, he held the flask out to her once more. "Want another nip before I go?"

Babs waved him off.

"Okay. The plan is to meet at nine o'clock behind the bowling alley. Bates, of course, will escort you. I'll be there with the others. And the Canadian."

"Fine," Babs said. "But do me a favor on your way out."

"What?"

"Tell the chief," she said, "that I want my phone call."

J ason knew his father was drunk again, but that didn't matter. His father had always been drunk, as far back as Jason's memory went before blurring into nothingness. Sis liked to tell about how on the occasion of Jason's birth, his father had spent all sixteen hours of labor at the bar across the street, and was so pie-eyed by the time Jason arrived that he had to be scruffed off his barstool, like an ill-behaved dog, by an extremely irritated Rheal. In fact, Jason was so accustomed to Bruce being drunk that he would have been unnerved to find his father on Babs's porch sober, instead of bleary-eyed and swaying as if the ground were moving under his feet. Drunk Dad was the dad he knew.

Jason knew other things, too. For instance, he knew that his father hadn't fallen down the stairs, that in fact it was Babs who had beaten his head to meat paste. Jason knew now that his mother was dead, and that she'd been murdered. He knew his uncle Tim had been tossed in jail, and that Babs and Lori had put him there. He knew all these things because he knew perfectly well how to speak and understand Quebecois, and he knew how to speak and understand Quebecois because his mother had taught him the language, usually at night after supper and before bed, going back to when Jason had been just four—old enough to understand what a secret was, and how to keep it.

"French is your superpower," Sis reminded him at least once a week. "But only if people don't know you know it."

And because Jason did everything his mother told him and hop to it, he'd always kept the fact that he knew French from everyone, his father included. In this way he'd become, like all his family, expert at pretending, at lying by omission, at preserving the secret of who he actually was from those who loved and should know him. Which meant they all thought they could just speak French when they were talking about something they didn't want him to know. Which in turn meant that he always knew everything but could never speak a word of it, lest his superpower be rendered not super at all but just another dumb ordinary thing he could do, like hit a curveball or rub his belly and tap his head at the same time.

This was how Jason was able, when he opened the front door and Bruce started sputtering about how his mother was dead and he thought he might have killed her, to tell his father otherwise.

"It wasn't you, Dad," he said.

"How do you know?"

"Because Mémère knows who really did it."

Bruce stared. "Where is your *mémère*? She here?"

"No," Jason said. "She never came back from the parade."

"You're by yourself?"

"I'm by myself a lot."

"Well, not anymore. Get your things, you're coming home."

Now it was Jason's turn to stare.

"What are you waiting for?" Bruce asked. "Go get your stuff."

But Jason didn't care about his stuff, and instead of going back inside to find it, he threw himself out the door and wrapped his arms around his father's waist, wanting only to hug and be hugged, to smell the warm formaldehyde scent of metabolized alcohol that had always meant love to him. He stood there, eyes closed, clutching his father, breathing it in.

"Okay, son," Bruce said after a few moments, rubbing Jason's back with one hand, his throat tight with tears. "Let's go home. Then I'm gonna go see if I can find your *mémère*."

A nd so when Lori arrived at Babs's half an hour later and found the front door unlocked, lights on all over the house, Jason's clothes and baseball mitt and *Minecraft* LEGO set still in the guest bedroom, though she was not a woman given to panic, she did have to fight the urge to run into the streets screaming Jason's name, to bolt from house to house pounding on doors and threatening people until she found her nephew. She willed herself to calm down, and when will didn't manage it she crushed and inhaled two Oxys on her mother's kitchen counter, thinking *Think, THINK*, and within thirty seconds the Oxy hit her brain stem and then she could—she could think again, and she forced herself to make decisions based only on what she knew, which was next to nothing, she didn't know where Jason was or whether he'd gone there on his own or was taken but she did know two things: first, that she had to pick up Clement and make the meeting behind Spare Time in six minutes, and second, she couldn't let on that Jason had vanished, or else her mother would kill this Canadian on the spot, and as much as had already been lost and as bad as things were, that would be far, far worse, that would be the end of all, that was something Lori could not allow to happen come whatever else may.

CHAPTER SEVENTEEN

July 4, 2016

Bates and Babs arrived at Spare Time at twenty minutes to nine, Bates pulling in behind the bowling alley slowly, his Town Car cruising through the twilight like a metal shark. When he completed the turn to the back side of the building, his headlights fell on another vehicle—a little Chevy Cruze hatchback, already parked and darkened.

"Now who the hell is that?" Bates asked, putting the Town Car in park but leaving the engine running and the lights blasting the Chevy.

"Rita," Babs said.

"What's she doing here?"

"Search me," Babs said. "But if I had to guess, I'd say she's joined those other turncoats in rolling over for our Canadian friend."

Babs knew this was not, in fact, the case—Rita was there because Babs had asked her to be; her phone call from jail had been to her de facto sister. The death of a daughter had a way of making bygones decidedly bygones, and here was Rita, reliable as death itself, more punctual than even Bates, who'd meant to arrive before any of the other parties involved in tonight's summit.

Bates killed the engine, and the headlights blinked out. He and Babs dismounted the Lincoln, and Rita emerged from her Chevy. The air smelled like what's left after a firepit is doused with water; they could feel the carbon prickling their throats.

"What's the latest on that fire?" Babs asked as they walked toward Rita.

"Twice the size it was this morning," Bates said. "Burned up the Melody Ranch sometime after lunch. There's talk of evacuations. As if I don't have enough to deal with."

They stopped in front of Rita. She neither looked at nor acknowledged Bates, simply stepped forward and put her arms around Babs, who stood there stiff as a mannequin.

"I'm sorry," Rita said into Babs's shoulder. "Celeste. *Mon dieu*, Babs, I'm so sorry."

This would be the only part of their exchange that was sincere—everything that followed was put on for Bates's benefit.

"Thank you," Babs said. She pulled back slowly. "What are you doing here?"

"Carmeline asked me to come."

"So you're with them."

"I'm with whoever is making sure this town doesn't burn to the ground," Rita answered.

"In that case," Babs said, "instead of worrying about the Canadian, maybe you should grab a garden hose and head out to Fairfield. I hear the firefighters have got their hands full."

All heads turned as two more cars—Carmeline's Ford Focus and The Man's bone-white Impala—pulled in at the same time and parked on either side of the Lincoln. They watched as Carmeline, Stella, and Bernette got out of the Focus, and The Man—dressed in a tan double-breasted suit, his white shirt open rakishly at the collar—stepped out of the Impala. They walked, more or less together, toward Bates, Babs, and Rita.

For a moment they all stood in a circle, no one speaking. Nervous eyes flitted to Babs, reading her face, but she appeared the very picture of calm resignation.

Carmeline was the only one bold enough to interrupt the silence. "Babs, I know you're mad enough to chew glass," she said. "But we're doing this for everyone, you included."

"Thank you," Babs said.

More silence. Carmeline and Stella exchanged incredulous looks; whatever they'd been expecting, it sure as hell wasn't to be thanked.

"Shall we get started?" The Man asked, his eyes on Babs.

"We're waiting for two more," Bates told him. "Everyone with a stake has to be here, so you know we're all in agreement."

"The only person whose agreement I don't feel assured of," The Man said, "is already present."

Babs said nothing, refusing to even look at The Man. She stared impassively into the distance beyond the cars, like she was already past whatever would transpire here tonight, like she was searching the darkness for whatever came next.

For a while, no one spoke. Carmeline and Bernette lit cigarettes and dashed glances at Babs. Stella took a big slug from her flask, grimaced, sucked air between her teeth, then had another drink to grow on. The Man produced a knife from his hip pocket—a single piece of stainless steel, narrow cylindrical hilt tapering into a razor-like blade—and went to work on his cuticles and under his nails, casual as you like. Bates's gaze shifted back and forth between The Man's hands and Babs's face. Through the brick walls of Spare Time came the occasional crash of a bowling ball smashing pins, like thunder rolling underground.

Bates's watch read 9:08 when Lori's truck finally came around the back of the bowling alley and parked next to a dumpster.

"'Truly I tell you, one of you will betray me,'" Babs whispered, watching Lori get out with Clement.

The Man put his knife away, and everyone stood up a little straighter as Lori and the priest approached.

"Okay," Bates said. "Let's get this over and done with."

The Man cleared his throat and took a step forward. "First, the terms," he said. "From today on, no one traffics in opioids—prescription or illicit—except those that come from Ogopogo's distribution network. The addendum to that is you *will* sell Ogopogo's products, using the personnel and infrastructure already in place. There is no opting out of this. Put simply, you all work for Ogo now, and you will do so faithfully and without complaint for as long as he decides to keep you in his employ."

The Man glanced around the circle, gauging expressions in the dim orange light of streetlamps. Grim faces all around, except for Babs, who remained vacant, inscrutable.

"You will be allowed to sell Ogo's products at a ten percent markup over wholesale. This markup will represent your income, and it is not to be increased even one one-hundredth of a percentage point. You will keep meticulous financial records according to a coded system used across Ogo's network, which we will teach you. You will not, under any circumstances, modify or dilute the products. What you sell will be exactly what you receive, nothing more or less. I can't emphasize that last point enough."

Bates lifted a hand. "The risks I'm taking," he said, "aren't worth it at ten percent. We're making five times that right now."

"No," The Man told him. "You're making *nothing* right now. Remember—you are not choosing whether to accept Ogo's terms.

276

You are simply choosing whether to survive. I encourage you, Chief Bates—I encourage all of you—to erase the paradigm you're accustomed to from your minds. Treat it as though it never existed. Comparing the way things are with the way things were will only make you unhappy. And unhappy people are prone to mistakes.

"And that's all. Going forward, you will have new contacts, people responsible for distribution, billing and accounting, et cetera. You will not see or hear from me again, unless you fail to obey these very simple rules as I've outlined them. In that case, you *will* see me again, but it will not be a happy reunion, and I will not be coming back here to talk."

The Man paused again, glancing from face to face.

"And now I need a verbal indication, from each of you, that you find these terms agreeable. A simple yes will suffice, and will be considered binding."

For a few moments no one spoke, each imagining somebody else would spare them the indignity of going first.

Finally, Carmeline spat her consent: *"D'accord."*

Now Babs's eyes turned away from the distant dark and focused on these people who represented her entire life and times.

"Yes," said Bates.

"Yes," said Bernette.

"Yes," said Stella and Clement at the same time.

"Yes," said Rita.

Lori took a breath, looked at her mother. "Yes," she said.

All eyes on Babs.

"I don't want to turn this into a debate over semantics," she said. "But since my assent is, as you say, *binding*, before I give it I have an objection to register."

"Ma," Lori said.

The Man smiled. "The floor is yours, Mrs. Dionne."

"My objection," Babs said, turning to square herself with The Man, "is to your use of the word 'agreeable.'"

A pause, tension growing among those assembled. "Go on," The Man said.

"My baby girl is dead," Babs said. "You're taking everything from me—my life's work, my neighborhood, my reason for being. And I'll be goddamned if I'm going to let you go back to your boss and tell him that I find his terms, or what he's done to me and my family, *agreeable.*"

"I understand," The Man said. "Nevertheless, I have to warn that your posture seems threatening. Your pupils are dilated."

"She's not armed," Bates said. "It's okay. I brought her straight from the jail."

"Don't worry, Canadian," Babs said. "I'm not going to hurt you. I made a promise to my daughter that I wouldn't. I just want to make sure—before I never see you again—that we understand each other."

She offered her right hand. The Man looked at it, then back up at her face.

"I think we do," he said. "But let me explain my view of things, to be certain. You will agree to Ogo's terms, but you will smolder with fury while you do so, still convinced that I murdered your daughter. And every minute going forward, you will try like hell to find a way to repay her death and reclaim your sovereignty. You will be sick with it, this need for vengeance. It will torment you day and night. You will have no rest, for the remainder of your years. Everything you care about and take pleasure in will cease to matter, until what you used to call your self is finally, fully consumed. The fierce, intelligent, ruthless woman will cease to be. Not even a trace of her left. You will become a husk. A vessel for the storage of wrath, and nothing more."

"That sounds about right," Babs said.

"Then you've gotten your wish," The Man said, grasping Babs's hand in his own. "We understand each other."

The moment the two shook it seemed the tension was relieved, and those watching let themselves relax a touch. But both Babs and The Man were operating on a higher level of instinct and intuition than the others, every sense acute to the point of being painful, every reflex spring-loaded to a degree usually seen only in wild animals, whose math is the simple arithmetic of eating or being eaten.

There are multiple explanations for how shaking hands came to be such a widely observed custom in the Western world. The most commonly accepted theory is it started in ancient Greece, as a means of demonstrating that neither party held a weapon. Millennia later, when the nuns rapped Babs's knuckles bloody in an effort to force her to write with her right hand, they didn't know it, but their fury was drawn directly from this ancient prejudice against the left-handed, the belief that they were not to be trusted.

The nuns failed, of course, the same way they failed to get Babs to stop speaking French. She remained a southpaw to this very evening, and The Man was right-handed, and this small difference was, in fact, all the difference. Because as they stood there shaking hands and staring at each other, Babs was deciding whether to make use of the stiletto Rita had tucked into her waistband when they'd embraced. If she reached for it she'd be an instant faster than The Man, because she would be using her dominant hand and he would have only his off-hand to protect himself. She kept her eyes flat and neutral, careful not to give any hint of the machinery grinding in her head, of the fact that every instinct she had was screaming at her to jam the blade between his ribs and leave him here like so much trash and let her daughter's ghost rest, come whatever else may.

But there was the fact of her remaining daughter, and the promise Babs had made. No small matter, but in order to keep that promise all she had to do was nothing. Let go of this man's hand and walk away and allow everyone to go on living. Babs was old, her pride in tatters already, the fight, whatever it had been or she'd imagined it to be, long since lost, if she was honest. The world went on erasing and remaking itself. When you stood in front of a locomotive, all you got was squashed.

So, fine. She'd keep her promise, and stand down. Even as she realized this, she marveled that it could be true. The great Babs Dionne, conceding to this WASPy fuck, and in front of her own people no less. Shame rose, though she willed it not to; she could feel it singeing her cheeks. But she let go of The Man's hand and turned away, her capitulation total, the shame well-earned. And then she heard the shot.

Everyone but Babs ducked on reflex, looking around with their hands over their heads, trying to understand what had just happened. Babs turned back toward The Man, and as she did so she registered, distantly, a slash of burning pain across her left shoulder. She looked to The Man, and saw he was clutching his neck with both hands. Blood began to seep between his fingers. Everyone stared and blinked, their minds racing to catch up with what their eyes were showing them, as The Man staggered back a step, hacking as if he could cough up whatever had ripped into his throat but instead just coughing up blood, a great thick clotted glob that burst on his lips like bubble gum. He took another hesitant step back, his toe searching for purchase on the pavement, making sounds like a giant arachnid with hard shiny legs was trying to escape from his larynx. Babs watched

The Man stumble and falter, and she smiled. She reached up with her right hand and pressed her fingers against the pain in her shoulder, where the bullet now lodged in The Man's neck had grazed her. Her fingers came away red. The Man staggered one last time and collapsed, and now everyone turned toward where the shot had come from and saw Bruce standing there looking gutshot himself, pistol down at his side, a wisp of smoke seeping from the bore.

After a moment Babs turned to the group, breathing hard, weary eyes moving from one to the next of them in turn as blood ran down her left arm and dripped from her trembling hand.

"Well," she said, "I guess we're all fucked now, aren't we?"

CHAPTER EIGHTEEN

July 5, 2016

Three figures, side by side by side, occupied a bench on the Dufferin Terrace in Old Québec, the many-spired grandeur of Château Frontenac looming just behind them. Bright sun blared in a cloudless sky, and despite the steady wind swooping up the ramparts from the Saint Lawrence, Quebec was, like everywhere else on the eastern seaboard of North America at the moment, hot as fuck, even when measured in centigrade, and particularly on the Dufferin Terrace, where not a lick of shade was to be had. But despite the heat the boardwalk teemed, hordes of tourists scurrying around like ants that somehow both knew how to take photographs and had a pathological compulsion to do so. Musicians strummed Leonard Cohen tunes for spare change, *crêpe* stands did brisk business with their Grand Marnier and Nutella varieties, and several living statues, each painted head-to-toe in shiny silver paint that just *had* to be monstrously toxic, creeped children out and made adults unwillingly aware of the uncanniness of existence.

With so much to eat and smell and see and take pictures of, no one seemed to pay any attention to the three figures occupying the bench.

Which was just how they wanted it. Well, two of the three, anyway. Carmeline and Bernette, both in sunglasses and golf visors with *Vive le Québec Libre!* stitched in cursive on the front, flanked the third figure, which someone looking at closely would have noticed was somehow *off*, though that someone would likely have been hardpressed to say how, exactly, except for maybe the fact that he was so slumped, a fleshy parenthesis, and also kind of preternaturally still, speaking of creepy uncanny things no one needed. The guy seemed like a goddamn mannequin, if you wanted to know the truth, and this was because he was not technically a guy at all anymore, but rather a corpse, specifically The Man's corpse, which Babs had dispatched Carmeline, Bernette, and Stella to return to Canada in a very public way. After that they were to make themselves scarce, while Babs awaited Ogopogo's response in Waterville.

But despite the fracture created by their attempt to make peace with The Man, leaving Babs to face her fate alone was not sitting well with Bernette, even on this cheerful summer day.

"I mean, I don't know about you, but I feel like I've gotten my fair share of life," Bernette said to Carmeline. "I don't want to be a life pig."

"What the hell is a life pig?"

"You know," Bernette said. "Hogging all the life for yourself."

"I'm going to Niagara Falls," Carmeline said flatly. "I'm almost seventy. It's now or never. Happy to drop you at the bus station on the way, if you want to go home and die so badly."

The Man's body listed against Bernette, and she shouldered him back upright. "I mean, what the hell are we doing, running away from Le Petit Canada? After all this time? Don't you think maybe we're *supposed* to go back?"

"We're supposed to go back and die?"

"No. We're supposed to go back and fight. Like Babs will fight."

"Ah, so we're supposed to *fight* and die."

"Yeah. Maybe. Is that so crazy?"

"In case you haven't noticed," Carmeline said, "there's precious little left to fight for."

"That's what I'm saying. There's no one holding things together except us."

"But we failed!" Carmeline said. "We didn't hold anything together, Bern. We just stood still, while the rest of the world kept spinning. We're going extinct. They just haven't bothered to tell us yet."

Bernette looked around at the swarming crowds, the old-world architecture, the street signs in Québécois. "I don't know," she said. "Things seem pretty alive and well here."

Carmeline scoffed. "This place is a museum," she said. "Or maybe a zoo. Either way, it's a cage that Francos are only allowed to keep for as long as *le roi le veut*."

They were quiet for a moment, watching the world spin while they sat still.

"You ever been?" Carmeline asked.

"Where?"

"Niagara Falls."

"You know I haven't."

"Come with me."

"I'm going home. I can't leave Babs there alone."

"Babs is the one who told us not to come back."

"All the same," Bernette said, a placid finality in her voice.

They were quiet again.

"I did everything I was supposed to," Carmeline said finally, squinting into the sun. "I crapped out eight kids, raised them all in the Church. I prayed the rosary every day. I sewed collars and cuffs for forty-five years, swallowed so much fiber that if I coughed hard enough I'd probably hack up a whole oxford, buttons and all. I stayed with Henri even though he was a cocksucker most of the time. Now everyone's either scattered to the wind or dead in the ground, and *pardieu*, I'm going to Niagara Falls."

"Who you trying to convince?" Bernette asked. "Me, or yourself?"

Silence, once more. Then Carmeline sighed. "I'm never fucking going to Niagara Falls, am I?"

"You might catch a glimpse of it on your way to heaven."

Carmeline laughed, and The Man slumped against Bernette again.

"This guy is really starting to stink," Bernette said, shoving the body upright again. "Where the hell is Stella, anyway?"

"She said she was getting a *crêpe*."

"Yeah, half an hour ago. A hundred loonies says she stopped at a bar and forgot to leave again."

"Well, let's go find her. I could use a drink myself."

Bernette looked at her. "We just leave him here?" she asked.

"We didn't *Weekend at Bernie's* him all the way from the car for nothing," Carmeline said. "Babs told us to put him somewhere he'd be found. We're sending a message."

"What message is that?"

Carmeline hooked a thumb at his shirt. "He's wearing it," she said. "Let's go. Just stand up and walk away."

They did, and without Bernette to prop him up The Man listed to the side again before they were out of sight. He sat there, folded in on himself and baking in the sun, for hours, long after Carmeline and Bernette dragged Stella out of the Pub L'Oncle Antoine and pointed their car back toward the Jackman border crossing into Maine. Passersby saw not a corpse but a drunk, and it was well past seven in the evening, the sun on its final descent behind the clock towers and spires of Old Québec, before a pair of Sûreté du Québec officers walked by and, having noticed The Man twice before, went to the bench to roust him. They shouted for him to wake up. They clapped their hands sharply. When this failed, one of the officers poked The Man with his nightstick, sending The Man toppling backward off the bench, and in this way, the officers became the first to read Babs's message to Ogopogo, airbrushed on the front of The Man's T-shirt, florid black cursive against a cartoonish beach sunset:

Welcome to Maine
Now Please Go Home

L ori stood on the front step of 134 Cherry Hill Terrace, in the fancy part of town where the doctors and lawyers and Colby professors lived and every house had Doric columns out front and an in-ground pool in the back, a considerable luxury in a place where there were maybe a dozen days a year when you really needed a swim. A generation before, Shawn's family had lived in Little Canada like everyone else, but Shawn's father, Wayde, who lay dying on the other side of the door as Lori knocked, had finessed his way from rank-and-file grease monkey to owner of a miniature empire of collision-repair garages, and by the time Lori and Shawn were in second grade the Paradises made the move to the right side of the tracks, only coming back to Little Canada for Mass on Sundays.

But even on the right side of the tracks, the air was heavy with smoke this afternoon. Lori knocked a second time, stepped back, and waited. The house was buttoned up against the heat, the central-air unit buzzing confidently around back. Two squirrels chased one another across the grass to the right of the garage, and Lori could hear, in a distant way that made her feel like weeping, the laughter of children as they splashed around in a pool somewhere up the street.

Finally, the front door opened, and Shawn's mother, Maddie, stood there, dressed in sweats, her hair yanked back into a frizzy topknot. Her eyes went wide. "Lore," she said, breathless with surprise. "Jesus Mary and Joseph, is that you?"

Lori tried to smile. "Ten years and two rehabs older. I'm sorry to be calling at such an awful time . . ."

Maddie stepped aside and waved Lori in. "Nonsense," she said. "Get in here."

Lori did, and Maddie closed the door and wrapped her in a hug. "I heard about Sis," Maddie said. "Lore. There are no words."

"No," Lori said. "But thank you. I'm sorry about Mr. Paradis."

Maddie pulled back, her hands still on Lori's waist. "What can you do?" she asked. "It's all awful, it always has been, and life is about fooling yourself into believing otherwise until you can't keep pretending anymore. How's your mother holding up?"

"Rock of Gibraltar," Lori said. "Is Shawn around?"

Maddie eyed her for a moment, then nodded and let it go. "Sure," she said, stepping toward the kitchen. "He's with his father. Let me get him."

Lori followed and sat at the kitchen table while Maddie went into the study, which had been converted into a bedroom for Wayde several months prior when he could no longer make it up the stairs. Lori listened to a few moments of conversation, Maddie's alto and Shawn's bass in a call-and-answer too muffled for her to make out the words. Then Shawn emerged from the den, Maddie following.

"Hi," Shawn said, standing to the left of the doorway. Maddie moved past him and sat at the table.

"Hi," Lori said.

"Are you okay?"

"No. Are you?"

"Mostly. I guess. My father's dying, and if the wind doesn't let up we're going to have to figure out a way to evacuate him. Other than that, things are tip-top."

Maddie reached into the pocket of her sweatshirt and pulled out a joint rolled as perfectly as a mass-produced cigarette. "Wayde refuses to take his cannabis prescription," she said to Lori. "But I sure could use some medicating. You?"

Lori smiled dimly, nodded.

Maddie sparked a lighter. "Shawn, join us," she said, and he did. They passed the joint around the table, and when it reached Shawn he pinched it awkwardly between his fingers, took a tentative drag, inhaled, and hacked like a car backfiring.

"I can see you're very experienced with drug use," Lori said, taking the joint again.

"I'm experienced with having a job," Shawn said. "Being an adult."

"Getting your nails done," Lori said. She turned to Maddie. "Do you know about that?"

"Hey, to each his own," Maddie said. "Let's be honest: My boy, much as I adore him, was never tough enough to be with you. Speaking of which, how was Afghanistan?"

"Beautiful," Lori said.

Maddie offered her a wry, rueful smile, seeming to understand everything Lori meant with that one word. "Well," she said, "no doubt you two have something to talk about that doesn't involve me. I'll go sit with Wayde and leave you to it."

When Maddie was gone, Shawn went to the liquor cabinet and returned with two rocks glasses and a bottle of Jameson. He poured for them both.

"Shit, I forgot to ask if you want ice," he said.

"I'm good with just the brown liquor."

"Right."

They clinked glasses and drank.

"I realize this is possibly the worst time for me to ask a favor," Lori said. "But I need to ask a favor."

"Let me make something clear, and then I don't want to discuss it again," Shawn said. "There is never a bad time for you to ask me for anything."

Grief and gratitude surged in Lori's throat, and she took another drink to beat them back down. "Okay," she said. "Does the offer of a place to stay in Boston still stand?"

"So long as I have a place in Boston, so do you."

"This is going to sound completely fucked, mostly because it is," Lori said. "But here's the deal: You can't ask anything of me, least of all that I kick. You and I are not together. I have no idea what I'm doing, or on what time frame. Right now I just need to get out of town. And that's it. I'm basically using you, and I'm way too fucked-up and sad to pretend otherwise."

"You drive a hard bargain, Dionne," Shawn said.

"Yes. Well."

"But you've got a deal. *Mi casa es su casa*. For as long as you need it."

"Are you sure?"

"As sure as I've ever been of anything." Shawn lifted his glass, seemed to consider something for a moment, then drank the rest of his whiskey.

"Don't you have any self-regard?" Lori asked, not unkindly.

Shawn lifted the bottle of Jameson and looked at her, bemused. "Don't you know what it means when someone says they love you?"

Lori had no good response to this.

"Anything else?" Shawn asked.

"No. Just thank you."

"Okay, then. Are you leaving tonight?" Shawn got up, searched the pockets of his jacket hanging by the doorway, and came out with a set of keys. He returned to the table and handed them over.

"I'm leaving as soon as I can," Lori told him. "I just have to settle one thing."

"And what's that?"

"I have to figure out who killed my sister."

Shawn raised his eyebrows. "I thought they arrested the guy."

"They arrested *a* guy. But he said he didn't do it."

"And you believe him. The gentleman with, what, seven other bodies on his property?"

"Ten. And yes, I do."

"Okay," Shawn said.

"Can you do me one more favor?"

"Name it."

"Don't wait for the evacuation order," Lori said. "The shit's going to hit the fan, and you don't want to get any on you. Figure out a way to get your parents out of here, and go. At least for a few days."

"This have anything to do with your mother?" Shawn asked.

"She is, in fact, the fan."

"Want to tell me about it?"

Lori stood and went to the door. "She's got even less time than your old man," she said, and then she was gone.

Babs sat in a long line of standstill traffic on Silver Street, a few hundred yards from the turn to Notre Dame du Perpetual Secours. Since when were there traffic jams in this town, she wondered, before noticing all the vehicles in front of and behind her had cargo containers on top and bikes hanging off the back and were stuffed to bursting with kids and dogs and suitcases, as if everyone had suddenly decided to go on vacation at the same time. And Babs realized that, in a way, they had—these people were not waiting for the mayor or the governor or whoever to tell them to flee. They'd all seen the curtains of birds flying south in a panic, and they'd felt the hair on their arms stand up as, driven by the fire's approach, the winds began to rise and swirl and moan like hell's own chorus. And they were out of here, thank you very much. Or they would be, just as soon as they were able to inch their way onto I-95.

Fifteen minutes later, Babs finally parked her station wagon in the otherwise-empty church parking lot and got out without rolling up the windows. One would have normally found the church buttoned up on a Tuesday afternoon, but on this day, Babs knew, the doors would be unlocked.

She stepped out of the heat and smoke into the bracing cool of the nave. When her eyes adjusted she saw Clement kneeling in the first pew, praying to the same bloodied Christ that had hung in eternal agony behind the altar since before Babs had been conceived. She slid in next to Clement and waited, silent, until he was finished.

"You should be packing your things," she said. "You should already be gone."

"What am I running from? The fire, or the wrath of Ogopogo?"

"Take your pick," Babs said. "Either way, praying won't do a lick of good."

Clement rose with a groan and sat back on the bench. "Oh ye of little faith," he said.

Babs smiled. "Let me explain it in terms you can understand. You remember De Niro in *The Untouchables*?"

"Let's see. 'I want him dead! I want his family dead! I want his house burned to the ground! I want to go there in the middle of the night and piss on his ashes!'"

"You must be terrific at bar trivia," Babs said.

Clement shrugged. "Celibacy has its upside."

"This is real, Clement. They're coming here to make a point, and they're going to be damn sure no one misses it. They aren't above killing a priest."

"They're going to have to get in line, these days," Clement said. "And if you're so concerned about my welfare, maybe you shouldn't have had your son-in-law shoot that man."

"I didn't," Babs said. "He did that all on his own."

Clement stood and squeezed past Babs and took the three carpeted stairs to the altar one at a time. From the cabinet underneath the altar he pulled out the tabernacle—a box inscribed with Latin in silver script, with a relief, on its side, of a lamb lying beneath a cross. Clement opened the tabernacle and removed a large crystal cruet filled with wine. He yanked the stopper, took a healthy slug, and returned to Babs, holding the cruet out to her.

Babs's eyes moved between the wine and Clement's face.

"You won't burst into flames," he reassured her. "Hasn't been consecrated yet. Still just cheap Chianti."

"All the same, I'll pass."

"More for me," Clement said, and sat beside her again.

"You are the strangest priest I've ever known."

"*Oui, bien.* I told you I've been trying to get fired for years. This might actually do it." He took another drink. "What brings you to God's house on this fine, fiery afternoon?"

"I already said. You need to get out of town."

Clement snorted. "Not even you are marble-headed enough to think that's why you came here today."

"Are you saying I don't know my own mind?"

"No. I'm saying *I* know your heart, and I know you think about how life might have been if you hadn't killed Sacha. I know you long to let God lift that burden, and all the burdens that followed. Plenty of others have wanted salvation far less and still taken it. And it's not too late. All you have to do is ask."

"I won't be blackmailed into saying what I did was wrong."

Clement looked at her. "No one's asking you to say it was wrong," he said. "You just have to say you're *sorry*."

"But I'm not."

"Sure you are," Clement said. "You're sorry you had to be the hardest case on two legs since General Patton. You're sorry your parents had to work so much and get so little in return. You're sorry you passed their hurt to your own kids like a piece of heirloom jewelry. Should I go on?"

A pause, and then: "Please."

Clement nodded, took another drink. "You're sorry love is imperfect and people are helpless to stop hurting one another. You're sorry about whatever fucked Sacha up so badly that he raped a little girl. You're sorry life is full of suffering. And you know what? So is God. He's been waiting a long time to commiserate with you on that point. So just say you're sorry. And then I can pack my shit and go, so you don't have one more thing to be sorry about."

Clement sighed and pressed his thumb and forefinger into his eyes. "My entire life in the priesthood has been about one thing: learning to accept that which cannot be changed. I can't bring Simone back, I can't make our baby live—and I can't convince you to live, either. But I *will* get you into that confessional, Barbara, and I *will* see to the salvation of your eternal soul. Or else I'll be damned myself."

With that, Clement was done. He stood and moved past Babs again into the aisle, crossing over to the confessional with the cruet of wine. He opened the clergy entrance and looked back at Babs. "See you on the other side," he said, slipping in and closing the door behind him.

Babs let out a breath, felt the new emptiness of the nave envelop her. She looked around, remembering that long-ago day when she was skinny and coltish and covered in blood like she'd just been born, and Clement, with his ginger crew cut and freckles, had saved her. Now look at them: Babs shaped less like a Thoroughbred and more like a pear, just around the corner from completely used up, and Clement's freckles traded in for liver spots and melanoma.

She had to smile. Clearly, someone with clout must have found all this pretty amusing, because otherwise it would be a much different world, and hers a much different life.

She looked up at Jesus, the prime suspect. "You're a real cocksucker, you know that?" she said.

Jesus continued to stare sadly and bleed.

"Fine, fine," she said, getting to her feet, following Clement to the confessional, letting herself in through the penitent's entrance. She closed the door and knelt in front of the partition screen and before she could think better of it, before she could think at all, she began to speak.

"Bless me, Father, for I have sinned," she said. "It's been . . . forty-eight years since my last confession."

A pause. Silence between them.

"When you put it that way," Father Clement said finally from the other side of the screen, "I'm not sure I have that kind of time."

And they both busted out laughing.

U nlike Father Clement, Bates was packed and ready to go by the time Lori arrived unannounced and uninvited, and as she came up his driveway he cursed that he hadn't been thirty seconds faster getting out of there.

"It's over, Lori," he said, getting into the Lincoln and starting it up. "I'm going to get my wife and I'm leaving. If you're smart you'll make yourself scarce, too."

Lori put her hands on the frame of the driver's-side window and leaned in. "Did you check the phone records?"

Bates looked at her. "What are you talking about?"

"Sis's phone. Aubrey said Sis called her looking for a ride that night, and Aubrey told her to call a cab. Did you pull her phone records?"

"Of course."

"And?"

"And there was nothing there."

"She didn't call a cab?"

Bates put the car in reverse, pointedly. "Lori, look—"

"It's a simple question." She held fast to the window frame, and Bates put the Lincoln back in park.

"Yes, she called PT Taxi. And obviously no one came to pick her up. You know how I know that, Lori? Because *we found her dead body in the same place she made the call from.* She never left that junk-yard. Jesus Christ, how thick can you be?"

"So you got her cell location records, too, then, to confirm she never left the junkyard."

Bates glared at her. "GPS data is a whole other kettle of fish. Fourth Amendment hoops to jump through. And we didn't need it."

"Fine," Lori said. "I'll head over to PT Taxi and do your job for you. Good luck with the rest of your life."

She let go of the window frame and made to walk back down the driveway.

"Lori!" Bates called after her.

She kept walking.

"I'm going to give you some hard-earned wisdom from forty years of investigative work," he said.

Now Lori stopped and turned back. "This ought to be good," she said.

"Occam's razor, young lady. The simplest answer is the most likely answer."

"That's not what Occam's razor means," Lori said. "At all."

"Oh, who gives a shit," Bates said. "The point is, you ignore the truth that's right in front of your nose, you end up finding out things you don't want to know. And life's hard enough already."

B ruce insisted he was finished with drinking, felt it with a cer-tainty he'd never before experienced. As surely as he knew his own name, he knew this was his last hangover. He was now a man who had killed, and he was now a man who would never touch al-cohol again as long as he lived.

Babs was less convinced.

"You've got, what, twelve hours of sobriety under your belt?" she said. "Let's not get ahead of ourselves."

And her scorn was withering, as always. "I'm pretty sure, Babs, really," was all he could manage, a rebuttal so limp that Babs almost didn't bother to respond.

"'Pretty sure' isn't sure enough," she said. "You're not even supposed to have a houseplant for the first year you're sober. I can have Jason taken care of until you're ready."

"By who?"

"Lori."

"Lori?" Bruce asked. "She's so messed up on dope she can't even take care of herself. How's that any better?"

It was a fair question, but one Babs had no intention of answering.

"Bruce," she said, "you should worry less about where Jason's going to end up, and worry more about getting yourself out of here. You won't be any good to him dead."

"I don't understand," Bruce said. "You said they'd think you did it."

"They will," Babs told him. "But this is going to be scorched-earth. They'll kill anyone I ever had a cup of coffee with, just to be thorough."

Bruce took a moment to absorb this, touching the fingers of one hand to the protrusions around his right eye, as he'd been doing compulsively since Babs arrived. "I did right, Babs, didn't I?" he asked. "For once, I did right."

Far, far too late, was Babs's first thought, but she would be gone soon and needed the father of her only grandchild to believe in himself. "You did, Bruce," she said. "And I'm proud of you. But now I need to see Jay-Jay."

"I . . . I can't let you take him."

Babs looked at Bruce. "Let me talk to the boy," she said. "He can decide."

"Okay."

"But, Bruce," she said.

"What?"

"While Jay and I are talking," she said, "you need to pack."

CHAPTER NINETEEN

July 5–6, 2016

In her time as a Canadian Border Services officer, fifty-plus hours a week for fifteen years, no vacation or sick leave, utter dedication to the job both to support and avoid her family, a total of 1,625 man-days spent receiving, questioning, and searching people crossing the border between Quebec and Maine, only three interesting things had ever happened to Kay Whiteduck. A measly three stories worth telling over drinks at McVeigh's, where she repaired most evenings (again, to avoid the aforementioned family, who she loved but also experienced mostly as a weight around her neck) when her shift ended at six. Only three anecdotes worth mentioning to sum up the entirety of her professional life, which was her whole life, really, when you got right down to it. And now one of those stories was being snatched from her, usurped under mysterious and more than slightly shady circumstances. Kay was being told—not in so many words, mind you, but in effect—to look the other way, to not ask questions, to pretend that the three old American ladies with blood, and lots of it, in the trunk of their rental car trying to get back into

Maine had never come through the border crossing from Saint-Théophile to Jackman.

Kay Whiteduck was a lot of things—a habitual and heavy drinker, a woman tormented by her inability to stop sleeping with men other than her husband, a nearly full-blooded Mi'kmaq, a loving but distant mother—but she was not a liar. Pretending, with a smile, that the facts were something other than what they obviously were? Pissing on someone's leg and telling them it was raining? That was white-people shit. And now, sure enough, here were these two white people, smiling at Kay and making clear they expected her to play their game, and for their purposes. And expecting, further, that she wouldn't trouble her little brown head about what those purposes were.

One of the white people in question was Kay's supervisor, Hunter. Did it get any whiter than that? Fucking *Hunter*. And yes, she'd slept with him, too. But that meant nothing. It didn't obligate her to lie, or break the law. It didn't mean she had to jeopardize both her job and her freedom to go along with whatever game he was playing. What was happening here? Why was she not at McVeigh's, three Negronis deep on this blazing-hot night, instead of sitting in Hunter's office long after her shift ended, with the distinct sense that she had been caught up by some massive, malign force, a consciousness with power just short of divine that expected her to play ball, or else?

"Sometimes," Hunter was saying to her, "not often, but on rare occasions, circumstances come up that require . . . discretion. *Suppleness*. The ability to make decisions that don't appear to match the letter of the law, but one hundred percent adhere to its *spirit*. Do you follow, Kay?"

The condescending bastard. As if she hadn't spent the last decade and a half working this job. As if during that time she had operated as some kind of automaton, no need for human judgment or interpretation. As if she hadn't been taught, both as a cadet and in countless refresher trainings, that in border work there was no such thing as a situation that could be papered over, swept under the rug, pick your cliché.

Kay wondered: How much was Hunter being paid?

None of it made any sense. Because look at this other person in the office, the person who represented the malign force Kay felt flowing around them like spring runoff: aging soccer-mom type, beatific smile persisting moment to moment like it was painted on. This woman said her name was Amy, but Kay had significant doubts about that. Allegedly Amy was the kind of person you'd trust your kids with five minutes after meeting her. She looked like she'd been manufactured at a facility dedicated to churning out women in their early fifties who had, perhaps with some relief, given up on being objects of sexual desire: ill-fitting Breton top with horizontal blue and white stripes (horizontal!), off-white linen drawstring shorts, thick thighs, comfy white sneakers. Normal, anodyne, above all *harmless.* And yet, everything about her made Kay's spidey sense tingle in the worst way. And that had been *before* it became clear that Allegedly Amy intended to take the three old ladies from Maine and do God knew what with them, and further that Allegedly Amy somehow had the clout and wealth and power of threat to convince Hunter to let her do so, no questions asked.

"No," Kay said to Hunter. "I don't follow."

"Doesn't matter," Hunter said, his gaze darting over to Allegedly Amy, who kept smiling that freaky clown smile, and back to Kay. "Basically I just really, really need you to understand that neither one of us has a choice here, and the less you know, actually, the better."

Allegedly Amy spoke up, her voice every bit as peppy as that smile. "I can answer any questions," she said. "I'll tell you whatever you want to know, honey."

Hunter put a hand over his eyes and rubbed at his temples, muttering indecipherably.

Kay looked at Allegedly Amy for a long moment. "Where did the blood come from?" she asked.

"What did the women tell you?" Allegedly Amy asked back.

"That the car's a rental, so if we want to know we should call Hertz."

"Sadly, they killed a colleague of mine." Still smiling.

"A colleague?"

"He was found this very afternoon in Quebec City. These women are returning from having dumped him there, poor thing."

"So you're some kind of government spook. Intelligence."

"No."

"RCMP?"

"Nope."

Allegedly Amy continued to smile at Kay, eyes wide and bright.

"Are you starting to get the goddamn picture, Kay?" Hunter asked.

Kay was. And though she knew she'd already heard too much, she wanted to know more. "What are you going to do to them?" she asked.

"Honey," Allegedly Amy said, "do you mind terribly if I answer your question with a question?"

"I guess not," Kay said.

"Have you ever been *really* thirsty before? Like, you know, one of those super-hot days like . . . well, every day in recent memory, I guess!"

"I'm pretty thirsty right now," Kay said.

"Yeah, but I mean so thirsty you can feel it all over your body, you know? Like every cell is just crying out for water. You ever been that thirsty?"

"I'm not sure," Kay said.

"Then I can tell you that you have not been. Because when you *are* that thirsty, there's nothing you've been more certain of in your life. Now I can't say for sure what's going to happen to those ladies— that's up to my boss—but what I can say is there's no worse way to go that *I* know of than from thirst."

"No?" Kay asked.

"Uh-uh. I mean, give me a .45 hollow point under the chin every day and twice on Sundays, thank you very much. Makes a mess, sure, but at least it's fast! You know what I mean?"

"I'm . . . ," Kay said.

"Boom, done. As opposed to the dying-of-thirst thing. You're tied up in some windowless room, and they've got the heat lamps on you. No way to tell how much time is passing because there's no day or night and whenever you nod off they wake you right back up again. Sometimes they press a moist sponge against your lips, even let you suck on it a little bit, but that just makes it worse, as you might guess. Maybe, if they're really mad at you, they'll give you an IV with just enough saline to keep you alive. You can live for weeks that way, but what's weird is it doesn't do a thing for how darn thirsty you are. Eventually, before you die, you lose your mind completely, of course."

"I can imagine," Kay said.

Allegedly Amy's smile grew even brighter. "Can you? That's perfect, honey. That's exactly what I want. For you to be able to imagine just how awful that would be. Because now I'm going to leave, and

I'm taking those women with me, and if in years to come you ever fancy talking to anyone about what we've discussed, before you open your mouth I want you to think again about what it would be like to die of thirst. Weigh how much you want to tell someone what happened here today against how much you'd rather not suffer that fate."

With that, Allegedly Amy stood up, lifted an oversize leather shoulder bag that Kay just *knew* had a forgotten half roll of Life Savers fossilizing in the bottom, and left Hunter's office, not bothering to close the door behind her.

Half an hour later Kay was already into her second Negroni, and though surrounded by a quartet of girlfriends, she barely spoke, even when prompted, even when given repeated *what the hell's wrong with you* nudges. She drank until she no longer knew where she was, and her friends drove her home and hauled her up the front steps and opened the door with Kay's keys and left them in the lock and deposited her in a snoring heap on the sofa in the living room. All that booze failed to keep the nightmares away, though, and when Kay woke up screaming several hours later she could not remember her mouth ever having been drier.

W hen Babs stepped into the doorway to Jason's room she found him lying on his back on the bare mattress, tossing a racquetball into the air above him and catching it, over and over.

"Hello, my favorite boy," Babs said.

"Hey." Jason didn't look at her. He tossed the ball straight up, and it landed back in his palm with a hollow *plock*.

"Did you hear what your father and I were talking about?" Babs asked.

"I hear everything," Jason said. "And I understand everything. I always have."

"What do you mean?"

"*Je parle français, Mémère*," Jason said. "*Je sais tout ce que tu pensais être un secret.*"

And in that moment Babs felt Jason floating away from her, the same way Jean had, and Lori, and now Sis, beyond her ability to influence or keep safe. "Well, then, you know what I'm here to ask you."

"Where are you going?" Toss, *plock*.

Somehow Babs hadn't anticipated this question, and she was caught without a ready answer. "I'm not going anywhere," she said. "You have to go away for a while, though."

"Why do you get to decide that?"

Now Babs really had no idea what to say. She didn't recognize this version of her grandson, so direct and self-possessed. This boy whose mother had been murdered was very different from the boy she'd always known, and the sense of him as a stranger, and a hostile one at that, had Babs scrambling. "It's not my decision, Jay," she told him finally.

"Then why are you the one telling me?" Toss, *plock*. "You know what I think, Mémère? I think you decide everything. I think you always have."

"Well, now it's your turn," Babs said. "You have to go away for a while. That part's nonnegotiable. But do you want to go with your father, or your aunt Lori?"

"I don't want either of those things," Jason said. "I want my ma to come home, and I want Aunt Lori to be okay, and I want to stay here in my house, where I belong."

"Mémère can't make any of that happen, sweetheart."

"Sure you can. You're the decider. Everyone does what you say."

"Jay-Jay, I—"

"You're the reason my ma is dead," Jason said. "You're the reason Aunt Lori is so messed up. You're the reason my dad would even think about letting me go somewhere without him. It's you. So just undo it all."

Babs stood there stricken, trying and failing to come up with a response.

Toss, *plock.* Toss, *plock.*

After a moment, Babs sat heavily on the bed near Jason's feet. He didn't look at her, just kept tossing and catching his ball.

"Jay-Jay," she said, "you seem like you've grown up pretty much overnight. So I'm going to level with you, one adult to another."

"Okay."

"This is the last time we're going to see each other."

The racquetball landed again in his palm, and this time he held it. "Why?"

"I can't change, and the world can't change, and I can't undo anything. And that's it."

"So someone's going to hurt you now?"

"Oh, I've done it to myself, Jay-Jay. Just like I did it to all of you. Just like you said."

Jason sat up. "But I don't want anyone to hurt you."

Babs waved a hand. "Whatever's coming, your *mémère* can take it," she told him. "But one thing I can't take is going away without telling you I'm sorry. And I am, baby boy. So very sorry. I wish I could have seen another way. Tell your father that for me, too. And your aunt Lori, when you see her. Tell anyone who will listen, for the rest of your life, that I was sorry. Can you do that for your old *mémère*?"

Jason nodded. His gaze was different: empty and cold, whatever was joyful and candid within him now locked away behind his eyes. Babs recognized the look from many years before, late summer of 1968, when instead of preparing for her freshman year of high school she found herself with the Sisters of St. Joseph in Rutland, Vermont. Her own eyes, that first morning at the nunnery, staring back at her from the medicine cabinet mirror of the bathroom she shared with five other novitiates. She'd gazed at her image for most of the morning, struggling to recognize herself, as she struggled to recognize Jason now. And her eyes had stayed that way, until they no longer looked unfamiliar, until she could barely remember a time when they'd been anything other than empty and cold.

Babs leaned over and put her arms around her grandson, but it was like hugging a statue. After a few moments she let him go and stood quickly and left the room. She found Bruce downstairs with two ratty old suitcases open on the sofa.

"Take your son and get out of town," Babs told him, and then she went out into the wind and the heat, the sky glowing red to the south, the end on its way, one way or another.

f this was the guy they were all supposed to be so terrified of, Carmeline was pretty sure they'd been duped.

"He's been crying," she said in French to Stella and Bernette, pointing at the man who had been introduced to them as Ogopogo. "Look at his eyes! They're all red."

"Could just be allergies," Stella said. "Grass pollen's through the roof right now."

"Ladies," Allegedly Amy said.

"Like a baby, this one," Carmeline said.

"Either of you ever seen pictures of El Chapo?" Bernette said.

"El who?" Stella said.

"Ladies, can I get you to hush up a sec?" Allegedly Amy said.

"The little Mexican fella," Bernette said. "Looks like an avocado farmer. But he's killed more people than heart attacks and cancer put together."

"Ladies, Ogopogo would like to speak," Allegedly Amy said.

"Innocent people, too," Bernette said. "Kids. Maybe this guy is like El Chapo."

"I bet El Chapo doesn't cry like a little girl," Carmeline said.

"It's true, I have been crying," Ogopogo said. "I'm not ashamed to admit that."

"Oh shit, he knows French," Stella said.

The ladies were seated on an armless Nordic love seat upholstered in linen, the kind of piece you'd see outside the dressing room in an extremely high-end clothing store. The room they sat in was massive and in-the-round, marble floors polished to a lethal shine and a domed granite ceiling high overhead. The overall impression was of the rotunda in a state capitol building. But it was just a room in Ogopogo's home—one of many, presumably.

Ogopogo himself—white, balding, medium build, brown eyes, brown hair flecked with gray, thin wrists, glasses, dressed in chinos and a red-and-blue Montreal Canadiens polo, the kind of man you'd passed in your life thousands and thousands of times without noticing—sat opposite them in a similarly upholstered easy chair. Allegedly Amy stood off to his side.

"I've been crying," Ogopogo said, "because I'm still getting used to the idea that the one man I've ever loved is gone. And not just gone, but murdered—shot in the throat and left to rot on a park bench like so much garbage."

"You know what they say," Carmeline said. "Garbage in, garbage out."

"Uh, Carmy," Bernette said.

"What? Fuck him. He's going to kill us anyway."

"I was saying," Ogopogo said, "that I'm not familiar with grief, and so I want to apologize for my appearance."

"Grief, please," Carmeline said. "You were fucking some guy, and he went and got himself killed. You want grief? Spend fifty years with someone. You have to learn to hate them before you can really grieve them."

"That's a dim view of life," Ogopogo said.

"I earned it," Carmeline said simply.

Ogopogo smiled a smile so slight that they might have imagined it. "In any event, you're wrong when you say I'm going to kill you."

"Really?" Bernette said, hopeful.

"I'd prefer to avoid it, if possible," Ogopogo said. "Your friend Mrs. Dionne, she has to die. But I'm not a thug, or a sadist. I want to make money, and I want to not worry. So if you choose to, you can survive by giving me one less thing to worry about."

"And what does that mean?" Carmeline asked.

"Simple," Ogopogo said. "When Mrs. Dionne is gone, as she will be in a few hours, you'll return home and run things. For me."

"Fuck that," Carmeline said.

"You don't want a minute to consider? Talk among yourselves?"

"I kind of wouldn't mind talking it over," Bernette said.

Carmeline turned to her. "Fifty years of friendship," she said. "Of *sisterhood*. And you're going to trade it away for what? Getting old enough to start shitting your pants again?"

"What about Niagara Falls?" Stella said.

"Overrated, they say," Carmeline said. "You go, you get wet, you buy something in the souvenir shop. The End."

"Twelve hours ago you were ready to cut off an ear to finally see the place," Stella said. "Now all of a sudden it's overrated?"

"Ladies," Ogopogo said.

"And what's with this sisterhood business?" Bernette asked.

"Principle," Carmeline told her.

"Principle? Where was this unshakable principle of yours when you were scheming to undermine Babs and give Waterville over to that ghoul?"

"Ladies, please," Ogopogo said.

"We all agreed that Babs had to be overruled," Carmeline said. "For the good of everyone."

"Well, for the good of everyone *currently present*," Bernette said, "I think we should consider the arrangement being proposed by . . . Octopago here."

"Ogopogo," Stella said.

"Whatever," Bernette said.

"Never mind," Ogopogo said. He rose from his chair and walked out of the room without another word. The ladies and Allegedly Amy watched him disappear around a corner, listened to the sound of a heavy door opening and latching shut again.

"Now what?" Bernette asked.

"Now," Allegedly Amy said, "well, now, bad news, ladies, I'm afraid. I'm going to get on out of here, because the real Ogopogo will be along in a jiffy, and I'm not allowed to see him."

"The *real* Ogopogo?" Stella asked.

"Yes," Allegedly Amy said. "The only way you get to see his face is if you're going to die. And since I'm not ready to be pushing up daisies quite yet, I'm gonna go ahead and skeedaddle."

Allegedly Amy said no more. She walked out of the room swiftly, the soles of her sneakers slapping the marble, leaving the three of them alone, but not for long.

W e read about a factory explosion in Kansas. Drought some-where in Africa. A minor-league pogrom in one of the -stan countries we could maybe point to the general location of on a map. We glimpse, in passing, at an airport or a doctor's office, footage of tsunamis depositing whole seaside towns ten miles inland. What a pity, we think—and then the gate attendant calls our flight number, the nurse calls our name. Maybe later, after the plane touches down, after the small procedure, we remember to donate. But either way, life, as they say, goes on, at least for those who remain alive.

Except that given a long enough time line, the Thing we've seen happen to so many others eventually, inevitably comes for us. And now It was gathering for Babs, at a former industrial storage facility outside Toronto that served as a base of operations for one of the more unpleasant aspects of Ogopogo's vast business. This Thing was comprised of men, numbering around the size of a standard army squad, all of whom came from Special Forces and/or wet work back-grounds, had made their way from instruments of government pol-icy to mercenary jobs, and finally were handpicked into Ogo's employ, which was, by design, interesting and lucrative enough to retain their services for the balance of their useful careers. These men who comprised the Thing were not subtle, and were not paid to be. They knew but did not often use the tactics of covert warfare. The situations that called for their skills were usually of the kind Babs presented—situations in which Ogopogo wished to send a clear and unmistakable message that was best conveyed by the U.S.

Navy SEALs policy of overwhelming firepower: Killing what required killing, quickly, loudly, and without mercy. Making an impression, in blood.

Like top-flight security details and asymmetric warfare teams the world over, the Thing used large black SUVs for transport. Its particular two SUVs were late-model Chevy Suburbans with the usual custom features for this kind of work: ballistic steel armor, anti-mine skid plates, run-flat tires, window glass that could pancake an AK-47 round, and grotesquely powerful engines to haul all that weight at 140 miles per hour. One of the Suburbans also carried electronic countermeasures for thwarting IEDs, rocket-propelled grenades, and guided anti-tank missiles.

Decades of training and killing had effectively stamped out every last remnant of what one would call humanity in the men who comprised the Thing. They only needed to know what to kill, never why. They were weapons-delivery systems, and gave no more thought to the blood they spilled than would a tank, or a fighter jet. And now they piled into their SUVs and headed around Lake Ontario's western shore, then due east into New York on Interstate 390. The GPS told them they had nine hours' driving ahead before they reached Waterville, plenty of time to get familiar with the list of targets they'd been provided.

T he fat guy in the sweat-soaked RETURN OF THE JEDI T-shirt running dispatch at PT Taxi apparently moonlighted as an attorney, because his concern over PT's legal obligations not to disclose information about customers was both pronounced and, to hear him tell it, firmly anchored in case law.

"*Bushell v. Lenny's Liquorland*, 1973," the dispatcher said, eyeing

Lori steadily. "In a majority opinion written by Chief Justice Burger, the Supreme Court held that no identifying or otherwise sensitive information can legally be released without a warrant that names a specific customer as its object. *You* don't happen to have a warrant, I'm guessing."

"All I need to know is whether you got a call from someone out at Colbert & Sons in Vassalboro a few nights ago," Lori said. "You don't even need to tell me who made the call."

On the desk in front of the dispatcher sat two old rotary phones. They began to ring shrilly, one after the other, but instead of answering, the dispatcher took a bite of a ham Italian and talked and chewed at the same time. "But if you already know identifying information about the caller, and I confirm it by telling you someone did indeed request a car to Colbert & Sons on—what night did you say it was?"

"Last Friday."

"If I confirm your supposition about the identity of a caller from last Friday night, legally that's the same as giving you the identifying information myself."

The phones kept ringing, and the dispatcher lifted a fountain soda and sucked on the straw, still staring at Lori.

"Besides," he continued, putting the soda back down, "we don't know or record anything about who calls. All we know is where we pick them up, and where we drop them off."

"Which is perfect, because that's all *I* need to know."

Ring ring ring. The dispatcher gazed at Lori impassively, eyebrows raised, and said nothing in response.

Lori closed her eyes, steadying herself. "I want you to understand, before I say what I'm about to say, that I'm not threatening you," she told the dispatcher. "I'm appealing to your decency. I'm asking you to show me that it still exists somewhere in the world, in whatever small amount."

One phone went silent, then the other. The dispatcher looked uncomfortable, and not just from the heat; this wasn't the turn he'd expected the conversation to take.

"I'm not sure *I* have any decency left," Lori said, "but for some reason it feels like if you show me you do, there's a chance I do, too."

"Okay," the dispatcher said.

"There are half a dozen ways I could force you to give me the information I want," Lori said. "I've got a pistol, for starters. That usually works. I'm good at all kinds of joint locks. It wouldn't take much for me to make it very difficult for you to breathe, and that almost always gets people's attention. But really what makes it possible for me to force you to do or say pretty much anything I want is that it doesn't bother me to hurt someone. Most people, it bothers them a lot. They may think they could do whatever they'd need to in the right situation, but until you're causing someone pain—*real* pain—and they're looking in your eyes and begging you to stop, you don't know how hard it is. Most people just can't bear it. But if I want something and I need to hurt you to get it, I can. But I'm not going to do that."

The dispatcher's evident discomfort grew.

"I've lost everyone," Lori told him. "My sister is dead. My brother has been dead so long I can't hear his voice in my mind anymore. My dad died eight months ago. In the next day or two, my mother will be dead. Way of the world, you might say. And you'd be right. I knew toddlers in Afghanistan who'd lost their entire families. So what? All life is suffering. Still, I'd like to suffer a little less. And you can help. Maybe."

"And if I still say no?"

"Then I'll walk out of here."

The dispatcher stared up at Lori a moment longer, then moved his sandwich to one side and brushed bits of lettuce off the desk with the edge of his hand. He centered a spiral notebook in front of him, flipped back several pages, then turned the notebook around so it faced Lori.

"Friday, July first," he said. "Entries are in order of time received. I'm going to hit the head, and you should be gone when I get back. And don't touch my dinner."

He left the room without another word, and Lori leaned over the notebook, putting a finger to the column on the far left side, which listed call times. These were all a.m. She turned forward a page, then another, her heart beginning to thump, and as she got closer to the deep overnight of the first the thought intruded that maybe Bates had been right, sleeping dogs and all that, what was she about to find and did she actually want to, or should she just flip the notebook closed and walk right now, get in the truck, get Jason, get the fuck out, live the rest of her life without knowing any more than she already did. She *could* live that way. After all, Sis was dead. That was the only truth that mattered.

But then her eyes fell on this entry, and the decision was made for her, once and forever: *11:28 p.m., Colbert Salvage → 11 King Street.*

Lori's breath caught in her throat. This was, in point of fact, impossible. Obviously Bates *had* been right, Sis had made the call but never taken the ride, because if she'd actually gotten into the cab and gone to the address listed she would still be alive. So somehow, for one reason or another, the cabdriver never found her. That had to be the truth. Except that the last column, all the way to the right of the page, bore the header *Completed*, and beneath this header, on the line of Sis's call, was an unmistakable, unequivocal *Y.*

A memory came rushing at Lori like the grille of an 18-wheeler: last Friday night, with Babs and Jason playing Xbox, Babs telling Lori if she was so worried about Rita she could feel free to go check on her, and Lori deciding against it. And now that she'd seen this entry in the dispatcher's logbook, Lori would spend the rest of her life running those few moments back like a scene in a movie, willing the actress portraying her to somehow make a different choice this time, to immediately jump up and run out the door and sprint the few hundred yards to her aunt's house, cutting across lawns and hurdling fences just like they did when they were kids, scratches on her arms and legs from thorn vines and the jagged broken top of a picket, getting to Rita's a couple hours before the cab dropped Sis off and thereby saving her, and Babs, and Rita herself.

CHAPTER TWENTY

June 27–July 1, 2016

Maybe the most quotidian and demoralizing way to look at Sis's murder is to consider that it was no more or less than a case of shitty timing.

Babs's timing in deciding she'd had enough of Tim. Tim's timing in deciding to knock off a string of pharmacies. Bates's timing in deciding to take a hard line with this particular item of neighborhood business. Sis's timing in deciding that the evening of July 1 was when she needed to unburden herself to the one person she imagined would understand and sympathize.

On the Monday of the last week of her life, Sis came home after a three-day absence knowing damn well that she shouldn't go anywhere near her house, let alone her son. She hadn't slept or eaten the entire time she'd been MIA. There was no way to disguise that she was half-crazed with meth; this fact filled up a room the moment she entered it, making the air vibrate with a dangerous energy, like a smoldering fire waiting for a breath of oxygen to flash over. And yet, she went home, because Aubrey had bailed and Sis was desperate and couldn't think of anything else, because something formerly irrepressible inside her had shifted or broken, because for the first time she was scared that she'd maybe strayed too far to ever really come back.

She entered through the back door and found no one in the kitchen, which was a relief even though she'd come here seeking her family. On the stovetop a small saucepan billowed steam, filling the air with the fatty, salty smell of waterlogged Tasty Bites. A bag of hot dog buns rested on the counter, the end hanging open and limp, little white plastic fastener still clinging to the bag. Dishes lay jumbled in the sink like a puzzle. The Mickey Mouse clock, an American classic and a favorite of hers since she was a little girl, hung on the wall over the table, Mickey's arms, lacking a fresh battery, locked on a time from weeks ago.

Sis took a shuddering breath and put a hand to her mouth. Her kitchen. Her home. Hers for the asking. If she could just.

Bruce would be in the living room, watching the Sox game. Sis went there and found him. She was overwhelmed with love and relief at the sight of her husband, his little belly and his silly bald head. All the accumulated rot forgotten. She tried to confess everything, but didn't get very far. Because Bruce suddenly put his hands around her throat and squeezed. She couldn't breathe and she didn't understand. How could an apology make him so angry? Had the words she'd thought and the words she'd spoken been the same? The crank sometimes scrambled things. Oh Jesus. Had she said horrible words, instead of loving, repentant ones? She could feel her eyes bulging, feel blood bursting capillaries in her cheeks. Bruce's gaze, burning and vacant. The world faded into twilight, and all the fear and love faded with it. Sis knew she was dying and that was okay. And then Bruce let go.

Sis fell to the floor, gasping, and Jay-Jay had draped himself protectively over her, glaring up at his father and yelling "What's the matter with you, leave her alone, don't you hurt my ma!" Bruce had come back to himself, Sis could see—his eyes were now tenanted, swimming with confusion and his steadiest companion, shame. He turned and rushed through the doorway to the front hall, and Sis could hear his feet climbing the stairs, and now Jay-Jay was crying and hugging her awkwardly as they both lay on the floor, and suddenly she knew she had to go, had to get away from this poor boy, and she was up on her feet and out the back door and on the run again.

The truth stung, burned like acid, the truth could make you crazy if you weren't already, and crazier if you were, and like it or not the truth remained that Rex was the only person who understood exactly what Sis was going through—never mind that he was the person responsible for putting her through it. So she burned rubber all the way out to the farmhouse, and when Rex invited her into the hot tub she stripped down and clambered in, and Rex psycho-soothed her, examined the bruises on her neck with care, lit the pipe for her like a gentleman, waving the flame beneath the bowl with a steady hand. "There, that's better, isn't it," he asked sweetly, and it was, it was horribly, undeniably better, no one took care of Sis like her uncle Rexy, he was so good to her, in fact, that she didn't even mind that he'd only asked her into the tub to rinse three days' tweaker sweat off her body so when the men showed up an hour later Sis wouldn't stink like death, but by then she was miles and miles away, in fact the whole *point* of getting this high was to separate herself from her body and its incessant petty demands, hunger, pain, all the aching feelings it produced and insisted were real and important, the meth made clear that they were neither and as long as she was high she was safe, her eternal soul drifting free, and while aloft whatever painful demeaning thing was being done to her body was none of her business. After they were done, Rex told her she needed to get some rest, and he gave her a shot that brought her soul crashing back down into her body, and she slept.

The next morning she woke into despair and checked her phone and saw she had messages from Babs, Bruce, and Lore, but at first she didn't respond to any of them, couldn't, because what would she tell them? The truth? Babs would kill her, Lori's disappointment was more than she was willing to deal with, and Bruce, well, Bruce already knew, didn't he? The other option was to lie and obfuscate to her mother and sister, paint a pretty picture that no one was asking for and no one would really believe, and what was the point of that?

So she responded once, strictly business, to her mother, saying she was on the ball with the day's cash dealings—picking up from the small network of opiate distributors, processing and cataloging the earnings, and depositing them in random totals into four separate accounts. Business Sis had been conducting for years, business she could do standing on her head. She dragged herself upright, hit the pipe, and got moving.

She spent hours crisscrossing central Maine, driving out to Babs's dealers in Oakland and Fairfield, Benton and China. Though she'd smoked up she couldn't get high enough to cleave herself from her body and still reliably take care of her duty to Babs, and so the dark despair she felt at turning tricks for Rex—he wouldn't take money for meth anymore, just her body—weighed on her with the heft of original sin. The work helped distract Sis a bit, but not much; a bass note of shame thrummed in her belly for hours, and all she could think about, by the end of the day, was that she would do anything Rex asked her to, to make that feeling go away. She hurried, in fact, to find out what he wanted, though she already knew. This was the cycle, then: she whored for release from the despair caused by whoring. And around and around it went. It was not a complicated scheme Rex had locked her into, just an effective one.

The shot, the crash, the waking bleary and sore and wondering how much longer this could go on. Maybe she should go to church? Clement could help? The thought fled as quickly as it surfaced. Up, smoke, out the door. Only one stop for Babs today: cash drop to LaVerdiere. But Sis couldn't do it. For some irresistible reason without a name. Instead, she smoked again, browned out, lost several hours of the midday, and came to wandering the aisles at Target, trying to ignore the ache that persisted in her lower belly, touching objects she had no need to buy as if encountering them for the first time: a blender, a child's bicycle helmet, a linen wall hanging imploring her to *See the Good*. Eventually—how long, who knew—a security guard, little more than a kid in an ill-fitting fake-cop outfit, black polyester slacks two inches too long puddled over the tops of his shoes: "Miss? Are you okay?" Maybe, with all the moony fondling of merchandise, he thought Sis was shoplifting. Maybe she was; impossible to say. She left.

Four days and change since she'd last eaten. Food—that was the thing. No matter how little she actually wanted to eat. She sat alone in a booth at Burger King, a Whopper Jr. with nothing on it but ketchup, to avoid any potential offense to her palate that would put her off the attempt to eat. She managed three bites of the burger, half a dozen fries, which actually tasted pretty good—all that salt cutting through the haze. But it was difficult to swallow. The food kept sticking in her throat, felt like it wanted to go down the wrong pipe. Sis stared at the quarter-eaten meal, trying to convince herself to have one more bite, then looked up and around the dining room, saw a woman about her age overrun with three young kids, a pair of blue-haired widows chatting over coffee, and a man in a remarkably nice suit, handsome but with skin freaky smooth and shiny like something out of Madame Tussauds. He looked up. Noticed her noticing him. Held her eyes. Smiled, maybe. She'd never seen him before but the way he gazed at her it was as if he somehow knew *exactly* who she was, what she did, what she would have to answer to before God when her ticket got punched. Sis looked back down at the smeared mess in front of her. Shot up and hustled out the door, leaving her tray on the table. Glanced over her shoulder double-timing to the car; no one followed. She tripped over her own feet, nearly went down, somehow righted herself, and got in the Subaru. Another glance in the side mirror—no sign of the man. She peeled out of there.

High, then higher still, so very high that she didn't just leave her body but disappeared almost entirely, became a bare abstraction, a rumor she'd heard, a sad story without basis in fact about a woman who once loved people and had been loved in return. Not true, and she didn't believe a word of it, even though the story came from inside her. Then the sting of Rex's needle once more, and next thing she knew she was in the hot tub next to him.

A party, people coming and going, nauseating swirls of music and light and voices. Animal faces that had to be hallucinations. Sis slipped beneath the water and Rex had to fish her out and prop her up. She was not awake but she also would not sleep. Another shot, risky, but it did the trick. Rex moved her to the guest room and she woke the next afternoon in a rage, found a knife and caught Rex in bed and threatened to cut his balls off, she was done turning tricks for him or anyone else, she actually had his balls clenched in one fist and the blade, very sharp, pressed to the bunched wrinkly skin of his scrotum, wouldn't take much and he'd be a gelding, he'd belong to

Sis forevermore, and even Rex wasn't so cool that he didn't sweat this just a little bit. He talked in soothing tones, made wild promises, told Sis he loved her, and she broke down and dropped the knife and expected he would beat her but he didn't. Up, smoke, out the door, together this time, Rex in his Mustang and Sis following in the Subaru.

Her phone bristled with messages from Babs and Lori. She scrolled through dully as she drove, dismissing most without half a thought and certainly without responding. But then, this from Lori:

1:32 PM: *Do you need help?*

And Sis did, of course, she very much did, she could not break free of Rex and if anyone could deal with him it was Lori, tough, reliable Lori, who only needed to hear the word and she would take a baseball bat to Rex's skull. But Lori couldn't know why Sis was in such desperate straits. Getting hooked on crank was one thing, but turning tricks? Sis might prefer a baseball bat herself to the disappointment that would bring to Lori's face.

So she did not respond and instead followed Rex to Colbert & Sons Salvage. As always, Rex drove in like he owned the place. But this night, instead of parking behind the shop just past the entrance, Rex cruised deep into the junkyard, winding slowly through the canyons of broken appliances and scrap steel until they emerged onto the great plain of wrecked and defunct automobiles, where finally they parked. They got out, and Rex told Sis he was sending her on a solo excursion. A scavenger hunt, of sorts. A chance for Sis to redeem herself for the very serious and very not-okay threat she'd made to castrate him. She would have two hours to find and return to him a set of fuzzy dice. Here were the stakes: If she succeeded, all would be restored, and she'd never again have to hook for Rex or even pay him a dime to smoke up. Free meth for life, however much she wanted whenever she wanted, and congratulations on winning the tweaker lottery. If she failed, however . . . well, he supposed now was as good a time as any to tell her that he'd strangled a woman named Rhonda when he was twenty and had just bought the farmhouse at a tax auction with money he'd made moving a wholesale load of pot across the Texas border. Rhonda had been a transient junkie and as such no one had missed her, except maybe in Orlando, where she'd grown up. Her death was, if not wholly an accident, also not 100 percent intentional, but in its wake Rex realized he had a taste for it, got off on seeing the light go out of Rhonda's eyes, and over the next decade and a half he murdered nine others and hid their bodies in various spots on his property. Sis grew increasingly frightened as Rex talked, of course, but at the same time did not entirely trust her eyes and ears; this could be—and Jesus hoped was— just another fun-house illusion her addled brain was making up. But Rex had more surprises. He confessed his love to her, and asked if she believed, as he did, that love was an awful, excruciating thing, maybe the worst torment a divine entity could inflict, and further wasn't consciousness itself, as the prerequisite for love and all other suffering, an indefensible thing to do to a soul that had otherwise spent eons drifting happily through nothingness? And wouldn't she, like the other women Rex had known, ultimately wish to be released back into that nothingness? Like a return to the womb? Rex told Sis he was asking her this question because if she failed to bring him a set of fuzzy dice by 10:21 and not a minute later, she would join those other women. He would release her, as he had released them. Sis stared at him in terrified silence, and after a few moments Rex told her she should probably get to it, the clock was running, chop-chop.

And in benumbed disbelief Sis got to it, moving on foot through the maze of vehicles, finding all kinds of random or horrible things but no fuzzy dice, the whole endeavor hopeless from the very beginning, and as the moon slid across the black sky and time wound down she thought to run—it would be easy to slip off into the woods—but then Rex's words about consciousness being an affliction came back to her with the power of absolute truth. So she returned to him empty-handed just as her watch indicated 10:21. Ready, more or less, to be released back into nothingness.

But then Rex wouldn't do it. He tried to save face, pretend this had been his plan all along, that he'd meant for her to believe he would end her suffering but in fact her real punishment was to be excommunicated, cut off from him and his supply forever. But Sis knew with sudden clarity, watching Rex and seeing the confusion behind his eyes, the real reason he wouldn't kill her: Now that the time had arrived, he couldn't bring himself to do it. He cared about her too much. And he had no idea how to deal with that.

So he yanked something small from underneath the steering wheel in her car, bade her have a nice life, and peeled out of there. The Subaru, of course, wouldn't start. Didn't do a damn thing, in fact, when she turned the key in the ignition. Whatever Rex had removed, no matter how small, the car obviously would not function without it. So Sis sat there. Coming down, hard, and beginning to panic.

She unlocked her phone and called Aubrey, who took twelve rings to answer. No help there. Aubrey just laughed and told Sis to use her noggin, she had a phone she was talking on right now and could just as easily call a cab as call her. Then Aubrey hung up. Sis was alone again, and still terribly alive beneath the moon.

She cursed Rex, cursed herself. Leaned her forehead against the steering wheel and wept. But when the tears were used up, a strange and wonderful thing: Suddenly, she saw exactly why all this was happening. Without Rex in the picture, this was her opportunity to clean up. To be a mom again. To sort out her marriage, one way or the other. To stop being everyone's adorable little fuckup. It was so clear. She just needed a place to lie low.

But where? Rehab was not an option; nothing made you want to get high like the eggshell walls and benign condescension of a detox ward. She couldn't go home, not for a few days, at least. This was going to get worse before it got better, and the next time she saw Bruce she had to be sure the words she was thinking matched the words she spoke. Her mother's place was out, as was Lori's. And Sis had zero friends whose households would be at all conducive to new-found sobriety.

But then: Aunt Rita. Who blew on skinned knees when Babs would have told Sis to walk it off. Who'd taken her to Poore Simon's and bought her first nice bras. Who'd covered for any number of Sis's early indiscretions (drinking at bars with grown men, shooting out the car windows of a high school rival, stabbing her cousin Tim with a fork when he tried to pick food off her plate one Thanksgiving), and who always counseled Sis afterward, sternly but lovingly and in private. Aunt Rita who, together with Babs, just about made one complete mom.

Sis called PT Taxi, and even though she was out in the sticks it only took five minutes for the car to show up. She got in and gave the driver Rita's address: 11 King Street in Little Canada. He glanced at her in the rearview mirror while the interior light was on and asked, You okay? and Sis sat back and rested her head against the seat and looked up at the dirty smoke-stained upholstery on the roof of the cab and said, Once you take me where I'm going, I will be.

Twenty-three minutes later the cab pulled from the curb in front of Rita's house as Sis made her way up the perfectly level brick walk. She was relieved to see lights still on inside, given the hour. She took the stairs, took a breath. She pressed the doorbell and waited. She thought this was the start of something new, and in a way it was, because she had about two minutes left to live and then something entirely new would indeed begin.

The door swung wide, and Rita stood there with a glass of wine in her right hand.

Aunt Rita, Sis said. I need your help.

CHAPTER TWENTY-ONE

July 6, 2016

The door swung wide, and Rita stood there with a glass of wine in her right hand.

"Aunt Rita," Lori said. "You have a minute?"

"Of course."

Lori held out the page from the PT Taxi logbook, and after a moment, Rita's face collapsed into understanding. Her whole body went slack, though from relief or weariness it was hard to know. "Oh, *petite* Lori," she said.

Lori let go of the page, and it fluttered to the floor between them.

"Are you here to settle accounts?" Rita asked.

"I don't know yet," Lori said. "Right now I just want to know what happened."

"I'm not sure you do, sweetie."

"Fair enough," Lori said. "But you're going to tell me anyway."

Rita nodded, turning back to the interior of the house. Lori closed the front door and followed her aunt into the dining room.

"You knew I'd come sooner or later, right?" Lori asked.

"You or your mother," Rita said. She resumed her seat at the far end of the table. "Want some Cabernet?"

"I can't stay long. And I have to drive."

"Skipping town?"

"The moment I leave here."

Rita nodded. "Babs know about this plan?"

"She insisted," Lori said. "I guess she decided two dead kids was enough."

"Won't be long now," Rita said. "If the Canadian's men don't get us, seems like this fire sure will."

They were quiet for a moment.

"Maybe start with why," Lori said.

Rita closed her eyes. "You know better than to think there's a why, something like this."

"Something like what?"

"You want me to just say it plainly?"

"No," Lori said. "But I need you to."

"There's no way to explain—"

"*Reasons*, Rita. Tell me. Fucking free-associate, if you have to."

"I was angry about Tim."

"Angry?"

"Furious. Sad beyond words."

"Of course. What else?"

"I'd just been tossed out. By my own sister."

"Keep going."

"I was drunk."

"Don't you dare."

"What?" Rita said bitterly. "Do you think if I *hadn't* been drinking I would have done it?"

Lori stared at her. "Done what?" she asked.

R ita looked down on Sis from a great wavering height. It was only half a step up from the porch to where Rita stood in the front doorway, but it seemed as though Sis were talking to her from the bottom of a ravine. Still, Rita was able, by and by, to make out what was being said.

I just came from the junkyard out in Vassalboro. My car's dead. I need a place to stay for a little while.

Of course she did. On the same day Rita's son was hauled off to County and Rita herself had been tossed out on her ear by Babs, here was Sis asking for—no, *expecting*—Rita's help. The utter magnitude of the offense was incomprehensible. Like trying to imagine whether a trillion tennis balls would fill the Grand Canyon, or seeking to understand the mind of God. The brain simply refused to do the math.

I fucked up. Went in too heavy with meth. I can't trust my own mind anymore.

This couldn't really be happening. Was it just another turn of the knife, courtesy of Babs? Had she put Sis up to this, told her to come over and prove once more who in this family was valued and who wasn't? If so, Sis deserved an Oscar nomination. And the red badge of courage. And she kept laying it on:

Ma can't know. I need you to keep this a secret.

And Sis fully believed that Rita's home and confidence would be provided—happily, lovingly, with no questions asked. Because being Sis meant always knowing someone else would be there to pick up your mess—unlike other members of the family, who at that moment were being made to actually answer for their mistakes. Rita had seen men in her family go into prison for long stretches, and she'd seen what they were like when they came out. Now she was about to watch the same thing happen to her son. And here was Sis, crying about problems very much of her own making, asking Aunt Rita to kiss it and make it better. The injustice, the utter *absurdity*, made her tremble with rage.

You have to help me.

Did she? As she stood there listening to Sis's sob story, Rita felt a peculiar and alarming pressure building in her belly, rising into her chest, squeezing all her organs, pushing the blood from her heart, the air from her lungs, all reason from her mind.

Aunt Rita? Are you going to invite me in?

It was a simple and harmless enough act, almost genteel, really. A civilized, dignified way to express anger or outrage, the kind of thing one did *precisely* because it caused harm to clothing and pride and nothing else. Unthinking, point-blank, Rita launched the glass of Chianti into her niece's face, and Sis shrieked and threw her hands up and when she took a step back in retreat her foot missed the edge of the porch and drifted into the space above the top step, and that was that. She went backward, and Rita reached for her and she reached for Rita, but even though she fell with a tortured slowness, neither could do anything to stop her fall. And then Sis was airborne, her scream cut short when she came down across the bottom step and her head snapped back sharply and smashed into a paving stone on Rita's perfectly level walkway, and Sis was silent and still, wine and blood mingling under the limp mat of her hair.

Instantly sober, Rita fell back against the doorframe, the wineglass slipping from her grasp and hitting the foyer floor, smashing into hooks and shards. Grief enveloped her like a black shroud. All she could think was *Oh no Oh no Oh no*, as if she'd merely witnessed Sis's death instead of causing it. But she was a tough woman, almost as tough and coldly pragmatic as Babs herself, so even as her mind continued to screech and spin she recognized, somewhere in her brain stem, that this couldn't be undone or wished away, and so:

She lifted Sis by the arms and dragged her inside and closed the door.

She sat on the floor in the foyer with Sis's ruined head cradled in her lap, weeping, checking over and over for a pulse.

She pulled herself together and left Sis with a throw pillow under her head and made a pot of coffee and drank three cups, quickly, scalding her throat.

She went to the bathroom and stared at herself in the mirror and slapped her face several times, willing herself to wake up out of this nightmare.

She pulled her car into the garage.

She wrapped Sis in a blue tarp and secured it with duct tape and dragged her out to the garage and laid her carefully across the back seat.

She went back and cleaned the porch and walkway and mopped the foyer floor three times. She put her clothes in a trash bag and showered and dressed again and went out.

She grabbed two ancient cans of turpentine from the cabinet under the garage workbench and started the car and pulled slowly away from her house.

She drove carefully but not too carefully, five miles per hour over the speed limit no matter whether it was fifteen or fifty-five. She pulled into Colbert & Sons and cut the lights and drove in circles for an hour before she finally found Sis's car.

She dragged Sis out and unwrapped the tarp and propped her in the back seat and kissed her cheek. She put the tarp on the floor of Sis's car and upended both cans of turpentine all over the interior.

She said *le Notre Père* and lit a match.

She went home and held it all in.

When Babs called for her help, she answered.

B y the time Rita finished telling her story, both she and Lori were in tears. But they each cried alone, isolated by what Rita had just confessed. They sat on opposite sides of the dining room table, angled away from each other, separated by three feet and a bottomless gulf, into which everything Lori had ever felt for her aunt had been dragged, ripped apart, atomized.

Lori looked around the room. "This was my favorite place when I was a kid," she said. "It was for all of us, even Jean. Aunt Rita's was like the safe zone in red rover."

"You kids needed a place like that," Rita said.

"Sis still did."

"I know. I'm sorry."

"Why were you so good to us?" Lori asked.

Rita thought for a moment. "Your mother never knew what it's like to be afraid of your parents," she said. "Your grandfather treated his kids like baby birds, and your grandmother was a saint. But I knew how it felt to be afraid of the people who are supposed to make you feel safe."

"It's all ruined now," Lori said, hanging her head. "Everything. There's nothing left."

Rita didn't respond.

"Bates warned me," Lori said. "He told me not to go looking for things I didn't want to know."

"I wish you had listened to him."

"Yes, well. I guess we've all made mistakes, haven't we?"

"I know you've got your gun, Lore. Do your aunt a favor."

Lori looked up. "No," she said. "Way too easy. You owe us more than that."

"What, then?"

Lori listened to sirens outside, and the blare of a man's voice amplified through a megaphone. The fire was almost here, the man said. Everyone had to leave, and now.

"You can't undo what you did to Sis," Lori said to Rita finally. "But you *can* do right by my mother one last time. You're going to go to her. You're going to stand beside her. And you're going to let her leave this life believing there was at least one person in the world she could always count on."

Ten minutes later Lori sat outside Babs's house, her go-bag behind her in the truck's bed, watching through the windshield as hot embers drifted down out of the dark, skittering and swirling along the pavement. She knew this would be the last time she saw her mother, and all she wanted was to go inside and throw her arms around Babs and hold her without saying a word. To Lori's knowledge no one had ever loved Babs that way, insistently, without fear or expectation. Certainly not Rheal, who'd always made an Olympic-pool-size space for Babs to be Babs without challenge or comment, in a way he probably had thought of as considerate, maybe even progressive, but which, in the end, had also been cowardly. Not the ladies, whose fealty to Babs was, until recent events, ironclad—they would peel someone's fingernails off on her say-so, no questions asked, no explanation necessary. Babs reigned supreme, and in her supremacy had always been alone as Christ on the cross. And like Christ, she had chosen that fate.

Lori imagined what it would be like—just walking in and wrapping her mother in the kind of hug that could last someone the rest of their natural life—and she thrilled at the fantasy. But fantasy it was. Vain imaginings, a literal impossibility. Lori had done and lived through things that supposedly required courage, but she did not have the courage to love her mother the way her mother needed to be loved.

Besides, Babs could be at the kitchen table with her pump-action shotgun, waiting for Ogopogo's judgment, ready to put a load of buckshot through the front door the moment a hand turned the knob. Lori knew, if that were the case, that her mother had already chambered a round. She would not hear the sound of the slide being racked—Babs had never been one to issue warnings.

The Afghan girl sat on the passenger side of the truck's bench seat. With her one good eye she gazed, along with Lori, at Babs's house. All the shades were drawn, and only a couple of windows, in the kitchen and the guest bedroom, had a glow of light around their edges. In the street, smoke danced like mist through the cones of light cast by streetlamps, and the embers continued to fall, thicker now, like a snowstorm picking up speed. Everything was wrong, everything was coming apart. Cells in Lori's body were degrading and dying; her truck rusted slowly underneath her as she sat there; and soon, she would be the last of Waterville's Dionnes still drawing breath.

The Afghan girl turned toward Lori and asked, "اد ساتسو کرد دی؟"

Lori looked down at the girl's ruined face. "Oh, sweetheart," Lori said, "I don't really have a home anymore. But yes, that's the house I grew up in."

"My great-grandmother was born in the house where I grew up," the girl told her. "That makes it my home, forever."

Lori smiled, felt an urge to stroke the girl's upper arm but knew, of course, that her hand would touch only air. "Well, if that's the standard," she said, "then yes. This is my home."

The girl smiled and nodded, satisfied. She looked back at Babs's. "It's very nice. And big."

"Plenty of places for hide-and-seek," Lori agreed. "Hey, can I ask you something I always wanted to know?"

"I guess so."

"Can you tell me what your name is?"

"I don't have a name anymore," the girl said. "But it used to be Shazmina."

"The one who loves too much?"

"Yes."

And this set Lori to weeping again.

When she was finished, the girl said, "It's okay that you didn't save me. You tried."

"But I'm still sorry. Even though no one can save anybody."

The girl turned to face her again. "If you really believe that," she said, "then what are you doing here?"

A minute later Lori took the steps to the front porch and, accepting that it could get her killed, treated Babs's house as her own and let herself in without knocking. Babs sat dozing in a wing chair she'd dragged into the kitchen and set facing the door, and as Lori entered she jumped up and leveled the shotgun and recognized her daughter just in time to stay her trigger finger. Lori didn't flinch or pause. She crossed the kitchen toward Babs without a word and pushed the barrel of the shotgun aside and put her arms around her mother. She placed one hand on the back of Babs's head and pulled it toward her shoulder, and after a moment Babs accepted the invitation, relaxed into her daughter's embrace.

"Jay-Jay hates me," Babs said after a minute.

"What does he know?"

"Everything. More than we ever imagined."

"What?"

"He's understood every word we've said for the last five years."

Lori paused, uncomprehending. "How?" she asked finally.

"Your sister," Babs said. "She must have taught him French on the sly."

Of course. Furtive, clever, mischievous Sis. Lori laughed, but it came out choked and mournful.

"Before you go," Babs said. "Check in the laundry room under the dryer. There's cash taped to the underside. A quarter million. Take it."

"Ma, come with me," Lori said. "I'm going to Boston. We can lay low for a while, then get set up. They won't find us."

"Sure they will," Babs told her. "The only way you and Jay-Jay and the ladies get to live even one day without looking over your shoulder is if I stay here and take what's coming."

Lori knew her mother was right, but she didn't want to admit it. Instead she kept quiet, kept holding her.

"Besides," Babs said, "it's kind of nice, knowing when your ticket's going to get punched. Most people aren't that lucky. They have to worry and wonder every day of their lives. Me, all I have to do is sit here and wait."

"Oh Ma," Lori said. "It's too much. I can't do it anymore. I can't."

"Sure you can," Babs said.

"Because I don't have a choice?"

"No. Because you're *my* daughter. And rest assured, your ma has something special waiting for these *putains*. I may be going, but I'm taking them with me."

"Who would doubt it?"

"Now get out of here. While you still can. Go."

"Okay." Lori took a deep, gulping breath, swiped at her eyes. "Okay."

In the laundry room she felt under the dryer, found the brick of bills, ripped it free, and returned on the hustle, wrapping her mother in one last hug.

"Do me a favor, Lore," Babs said. "Jay-Jay. When some time has gone by . . . when he's old enough to understand. Try to explain it to him."

Lori pulled back and looked into Babs's face. "How can I do that," she asked, "when I don't understand it myself?"

CHAPTER TWENTY-TWO

July 7, 2016

V isiting," or *rendre visite* in French: This was the colloquialism used to refer to the regular casual gatherings of women in Little Canadas all over New England, always in the kitchen, with coffee hot and plentiful and *tarte au sucre* or *pets de sœurs* on the countertop. Visiting required no invitation, or, rather, was an open one: come whenever, for whatever reason or none at all, and there would be friendship and counsel and good humor and honesty, all served straight up, no bullshit and no words minced. These were the kinds of community-fortifying gab sessions that Babs had long ago turned into purposeful meetings. For centuries, women across the North American French diaspora had used Visiting as a way to organize, decide neighborhood business, and leverage collective will to solve problems—Babs had simply codified these aspects of it.

And now Babs and Rita, the only ladies who remained, sat Visiting one last time. The fire had made its way to Little Canada's southern edge, near the sewage treatment plant, and the old tenements by the playground were starting to burn, blanketing the neighborhood with the heavy stench of structure fire. The main fire was close enough now that they could hear the moan and hiss of the massive updraft, hungry for oxygen, as it pulled huge amounts of air into its core. It remained to be seen what would get them first—the fire, or Ogopogo—but being as it was two in the morning and they were about to die one way or the other, Babs and Rita had gotten into the caribou, a cocktail of red wine and Canadian Club that Babs's father, André, had favored. Story was that in bygone times caribou consisted of whiskey and caribou blood, drunk by loggers to fortify them against the cold of the north woods. The drink had a reputation for making already short-tempered Francos downright mean, but it only made André sing dirty songs to Babs's mother until she swatted him in embarrassment and laughed so hard and so long she sometimes had to sit down to catch her breath.

And the caribou had Babs and Rita laughing now, recalling an afternoon when they were eight or nine and shared a room on the second floor of this very house with Babs's youngest sister, Dominique. She was three at the time, and though André would and did claim he loved his children all equally, the worst-kept secret around the Levesque household was that Dominique was his favorite. This seemed a tremendous injustice to Babs—she was the oldest of the five girls, the first, and as such, in her estimation, should have been and remained the apple of her father's eye. Babs being Babs, she wanted to find a creative and unequivocal way to express her displeasure. It turned out to be one of the first times she and Rita realized their talent for acting as coconspirators—they understood each other intuitively, and had the perfect plan hatched between them in a matter of minutes, the simple, brilliant core of which had been Rita's idea.

They waited until André came home from first shift at Hollingsworth & Whitney, had lunch, and sat in his easy chair with that morning's edition of the Central Maine *Morning Sentinel* and a glass of beer, as was his custom. The girls were charged with entertaining Dominique—and keeping her out of trouble—for the several hours between when André got home midafternoon and Babs's mother returned from sewing shirts at the Hathaway factory early evening. Because Dominique was so young, and couldn't keep up with the older girls outside, they usually passed this time in their room, the window of which sat directly above the living room window downstairs, which André's chair faced. This was the central factor in Rita's idea: that whatever happened outside that window would be directly in his line of sight.

The girls gave him time to settle in, drink half the beer, go through his routine of reading the local section front to back, the baseball box scores in their entirety, and whatever national and international news was of interest in the front section. He'd set the paper aside and sat slouched and content, eyes at half-mast, seconds from drifting off—when he heard a cry from the second floor, Babs's voice ricocheting down the staircase and making his eyes flap open again like spring-loaded blinds on a window: "Rita, the baby!"

Half a second later, before André even had a chance to get up from his chair, something decidedly toddler-like pinwheeled past the living room window and landed with a muffled thump on the gravel drive. Then: massive, pulsing silence. André leaped up and crossed the living room and kitchen in three strides, threw open the door, sprinted outside—and found Dominique's Patti Playpal doll lying stiffly on the ground, the white bib of her dress smeared with mud from a rainstorm the previous night.

And then André heard something overhead, and he looked up and saw Babs and Rita hanging out the bedroom window, clutching one another and laughing, as they did now, half a century later at Babs's table.

"My God, the poor man," Babs said. "I've never heard so many *tabarnak*s strung together at once."

"And then! And then!" Rita said. "He looks right at me and says, 'I just adopted you, you little piece of *merde*! Is this how you say thanks?'"

They shook with fresh laughter, which, like memory itself, eventually trailed off into a melancholy warmth. The two women pulled themselves together, wiping at their eyes and muttering happily, and Babs took a cigarette from the pack on the table, her hand trembling so violently it took several tries to light up.

"What's that about?" Rita asked.

Babs took a drag and tossed her lighter back on the table. "You remember how my mother went?"

"Of course."

"That's what it's about."

Rita watched Babs's hand for a few moments. "I suppose," she said finally, "that this would be really bad news, except we're both going to be dead soon anyway."

Babs smiled wanly. "Praise God for small blessings," she said.

Rita looked out the window at the darkness, then noticed something and inclined her head.

"I see fire," she said.

"Where?"

"Three blocks over. Near my place. Paris Street, I think."

"There goes the neighborhood."

"You know," Rita said, "we're going to look pretty stupid if these people don't show and we end up burning to a crisp."

"They'll show," Babs said. "They aren't going to let a little fire keep them away. Speaking of which, want to see something?"

"Depends."

Babs lifted her shotgun and flipped it over, revealing a small switch, much like a doorbell, taped to the gun's pistol grip.

"What is it?" Rita said.

"You remember in '84, during the strike, when Rheal talked about just putting five hundred pounds of TNT in a box truck and blowing the mill to kingdom come?"

"Vaguely. Rheal had a lot of crazy ideas."

"True," Babs said. "But he actually bought a shitload of TNT from the Saucier boys, enough to make even those crazy bastards nervous. He never used it, obviously."

"What changed his mind?"

"I informed him I was pregnant with Jean, and it'd probably be best if the boy's father wasn't in prison when he was born. It's been sitting in the basement ever since."

Rita absorbed this for a moment. Then she pointed at the shotgun in inquiry.

"Dead-man's switch," Babs told her. "Bluetooth. Once I press down, it's armed. If I let go—because I choose to, or because someone's shot me—kaboom."

"Then why are we bothering with the guns, if we're just going to blow the place?"

"Gotta draw them in," Babs said. "Make sure we get all of them."

Rita took a drink of caribou, swallowed hard, lit a cigarette, looked at Babs, looked away, back at Babs. "Listen," she said, "I have to tell you something."

"No," Babs said. "Whatever it is, I don't want to hear it."

"Babs, just let me—"

"The thing I hate most about people dying," Babs said, "is how skeletons always come tap-dancing out of every closet. As if death isn't bad enough, suddenly everybody has to unburden themselves, too. If you need to confess, go see Clement. Though you might have a hard time finding him."

"Well, I hear you, but—"

"Rita, *stop*," Babs said, her voice gentle, almost a whisper. "Just stop, and let me say something instead."

"Still giving orders, right up to the end."

"I'm trying to tell you I'm sorry," Babs said. "If you'd shut up for two seconds."

Rita met this with stunned silence, as if she'd been slapped, or told she'd won the lottery.

"You've probably never heard me say exactly those words in exactly that order before," Babs said.

"I . . . no, I definitely have not."

"Well, I am. I'm sorry about Timmy. I'm sorry about putting you through what I've put you through these last few days. I'm sorry about always being such a goddamn cast-iron bitch. For what it's worth, I imagined I was doing the best I could by everyone. And maybe that was the real sin. Thinking I always knew what was best."

"Might be onto something, there."

"Better late than never, I suppose."

"Well," Rita said, "thank you for that. And now if I can speak?"

Babs laughed quietly. "The floor is yours."

"I wasn't going to confess anything," Rita said. "I was trying to apologize, too."

"What on earth do you have to apologize for?"

"For not stopping Sacha."

Babs stared. "You were just a girl, Rita. There wasn't anything you could do."

"Sure there was," Rita said. "If I'd been more like you. If I'd carried a knife. If I'd been a cast-iron bitch."

"Well, you weren't. And that's a good thing."

"I've spent a lot of time trying to imagine what it must have been like, out there in the woods. Like if I could feel what you felt, somehow I could share the burden."

"That's maybe the dumbest thing I've ever heard."

"Is it?" Rita asked. "I haven't slept through the night in fifty years. I think if I'd been able to stop him somehow, I could have spared a whole lot of people a whole lot of suffering. You most of all."

Babs smiled sadly at her. "Maybe on the next go-round."

"Yeah, maybe," Rita said.

"Listen," Babs said. "You couldn't save me from Sacha, but you've done something way more important than that, for years. You made sure there was never a single day, in any of my children's lives, when they wondered if they were loved. I couldn't do that. I had harder things to teach them. But you always gave them the one thing kids can't live without."

Rita didn't want Babs to see her cry, so she looked out the window again. Embers, driven on the wind, hit the pane in a steady rhythm, breaking apart into tiny fireworks. For a while they were both quiet, and then Rita spotted something outside, sat up straight and alert.

"What is it?" Babs asked, reaching for the shotgun.

"I can't tell. There's so much smoke."

Babs came around the table, shotgun in hand, to stand beside Rita at the window.

"There," Rita said. "To the right of your car. See it?"

Babs did, just barely. A small figure on the pavement beside her station wagon.

"It looks like a dog," she said.

"But why is it just sitting there?" Rita asked.

At that moment a sudden gust cleared the driveway of smoke, and they saw the thing was not a dog, but a fox.

They stared at the fox, and the fox stared at them, and Babs felt something inside her that she hadn't felt since she was a little girl, since before Sacha, before her brother Jean came home with his head blown apart: Peace. A warm assurance that everything, no matter how horrible or trying, had always been exactly as it should be. The relief of understanding that she had never, not once, been in control. Of the world, of the neighborhood, of those she loved, of herself.

"Why isn't she running?" Rita asked.

"Because," Babs said. "She's not afraid."

And then the fox disappeared once more in curtains of smoke.

"Hey, enough with all this," Babs said. "Let's play some cribbage, huh?"

Rita got out the board, Babs shuffled the deck, and it might have been any of a thousand nights that had come before, two old friends drinking too much, love in every gesture and joke. House rules were cutthroat, as always—stealing points and talking shit not just allowed, but expected. Half an hour went by, more caribou went down the hatch, and Rita was well on the way to skunking her sister when they heard something in the basement. If either of them had been alone they might have thought they imagined it. But they both heard the same thing at the same time: a faint whump, as though someone had dropped or bumped something in the dark, the fucking amateurs. Babs and Rita froze, looked at each other with eyebrows raised, put their cards down, and reached for their guns. There were four breach points in the room: Babs covered the window over the kitchen sink and, crucially now, the basement door; Rita had the front door and the porch windows.

"Hey," Babs whispered.

"What?"

"I love you."

"I love you, too, Babs."

"Now take a breath, and shoot straight," Babs told her sister. "Saint Peter won't let you into heaven unless you kill at least one Protestant before you get there."

ÉPILOGUE

And now, two years later, you are born: Evangeline Barbara Paradis, daughter of Lori and Shawn, granddaughter of Babs and Rheal and great-granddaughter of Rose and André. Your parents love each other deeply, but by the time you are yanked out of nothingness and into this thresher, they have already admitted, silently, to themselves, that they will not last. Four years later, when they admit this out loud, to each other, you and your mother move to a first-floor apartment on East Seventh in Southie, two blocks from Carson Beach. The windows are drafty and the people on the second floor never seem to take their shoes off, but you're happy, mostly. Your mother takes you to the animal shelter and you pick out an orange polydactyl tomcat who shares your bed every night. You stay with your father on alternating weekends, and his house is much nicer and cleaner but you miss the cat and there is no beach nearby, only the muddy, shiftless Charles. You prefer the beach, prefer it in your bones and your belly. Something about how the water stretches out and out into nothing. Something about how it seems not merely vast, but unending, like time itself. In the winter when the sea spray freezes to a glaze on the sand, you can get lost staring into the distant unbroken space where blue meets blue, and your mother lets your mind wander out there as long as it needs to, no matter how cold. She speaks only French to you, has from the beginning, *Frère*

Jacques, Frère Jacques, dormez-vous, dormez-vous, and so it is your first language, but when you go to kindergarten no one understands you and you understand no one and before too long your English overtakes your French. This is how it begins: the first rift between mother and daughter, who you came from and who you are and who you will be. Your mother tries to keep up, but no matter how much French you speak and hear in the house, you always speak and hear more English outside of it, and eventually you start to protest against having to speak to her in a language no one but the two of you uses or understands. You don't see the point, and she doesn't deign to tell you what the point might be, if any. The hint of a Boston accent creeps into your diction, long open-ended syllables and dropped *r*'s. Soon, the two of you are locked into a *contretemps* wherein she speaks French and you respond in English and neither will be moved. You've never been inside a church, never had a slice of *tourtière*, wouldn't know a *fleur-de-lis* from a flagellum. Then one day you hop down the steps of the bus and sprint the several blocks home to find everything in the apartment boxed up. Your mother says you're moving. And so you do.

The three-hour drive, for a second grader, is interminable as purgatory. Neither of you talks much. You're confused and hurt and your mother has decided to let you sit with that in silence awhile; one has to learn how to hurt just as surely as how to tie one's shoes, after all. You cross a big green bridge spanning a river and then you're in Maine, THE WAY LIFE SHOULD BE according to the sign announcing your arrival, and you've never seen so much nothing. An endless scroll of evergreen on either side of the highway, punctuated by the occasional EXIT sign and off-ramp, until finally the off-ramp is yours and the U-Haul's blinker tick-tock-ticks and you glide down into the easternmost reaches of a place called Waterville. You drive past the fast food joints and big box stores and strip malls and car washes. You drive past a big round church and a cemetery, down a steep hill, past an outdoor basketball court, broken-down tenements, a VFW post, a convenience store. Something about this part of the town is off, is unlike anything you've ever seen, but subtly. Every third lot is empty and, unlike in the other parts of town you've seen so far, all the trees are small and new, barely taller than you are. Your mother pulls the U-Haul to the curb and gets out. She doesn't say anything, just walks away from the truck and onto the overgrown lawn of a lot that used to have a house on it but now just has a big hole in the ground where a house used to be, fieldstone foundation crumbling and scorched black in spots. Your mother stops at the edge of the foundation and stands there, hands in her pockets and her back to you, gazing around. Eventually you climb out of the truck and join her, no idea why you're here or what you're looking at, and that's when your mother finally speaks up and says this was the house where she lived as a girl. The house, in fact, where your grandmother was born and raised, and her mother before her. This is the first you're hearing of a grandmother, or of family on your mother's side at all; before now it was as if she had sprung directly from Zeus's forehead. You ask what happened to the house, and she says there was a fire and leaves it at that. You think to ask what happened to your grandmother, but you're afraid maybe she died in the fire and you don't want to hear about that and you're pretty sure your mother wouldn't want to talk about it. Neither of you says anything for a minute or two, and you can feel that your mother is waiting for something. Waiting, and hoping. Finally, you ask who or what she's expecting, and at first she doesn't answer, but then she says, I was thinking I might find your grandmother here. And you're not sure why your mother would expect that when it seems pretty certain the whole reason you're here, the whole reason you packed up every last thing and drove it all to Waterville, is because your grandmother is dead. But you don't say anything in response because you can feel there's something at work that you don't understand or even know how to name. After a few more minutes of standing there and looking around, your mother says, I've got something else to show you, and the two of you walk back to the truck and get in and roll down the street, take a right, roll to the end of another street, take a left. This street meanders in tandem with the river, and you follow it for a mile or so and then your mother pulls to the curb and parks again. The two of you get out and stand on the sidewalk. In front of you, on the other side of a sturdy metal fence painted a bright cheerful blue, is the nicest playground you personally have ever laid eyes on. It's well past school hours but plenty of kids are still hanging around, playing four square and swinging from monkey bars and chasing one another aimlessly, the girls in plaid skirts, the boys in black pants and white oxfords. Behind these children is a beautiful glass-and-steel building that captures and releases the afternoon sun spectacularly, like a prism. Compared to everything else you've seen so far in this alien place, the building is so nice it seems it must have been built here by mistake. And as you listen to the children chatter and yell you begin to realize, gradually, that they are speaking French, a language that until now you've only ever heard from your mother's mouth.

And your mother speaks now, in French: I will never force you to do anything else ever again, she says. But you will go to school here, and you, Evangeline, will know exactly who you are.

ACKNOWLEDGMENTS

Thank you to my agent, Simon Lipskar—twenty years, thick and thin.

Thank you to my editor, Daphne Durham, who rescued me—and Babs—in the nick of time, saw what I was doing, and helped me do it better. Big thanks, also, to Team Babs at Penguin/Putnam: Aranya Jain, Nicole Biton, Brennin Cummings, Andy Dudley, Alexis Welby, Lindsay Sagnette, and other friends both new and old, who have believed so much in/worked so hard for Babs.

Thank you to Josh Mohr, an A⁺ writing partner and a better friend, whose only active addiction is to alliteration, which is bad enough all on its own. Also to Rick Russo, for his wisdom, generosity, and friendship.

Thank you to Jack Kerouac, for telling the world about our world. St. Gerard lives on.

Thank you to my wife, Lisa, for riding the wave and, when necessary, bailing the boat.

Special thanks to Heath Trefethen, who educated me on both the science and the psychology of hairstyling.

Thank you, finally, to all the ghosts, for letting me tell their story.